Penguin Books
A Singular Man

Penguin Books Ltd, Harmondsworth,
Middlesex, England
Penguin Books Australia Ltd, Ringwood,
Victoria, Australia

First published in the U.S.A. 1963
Published in Great Britain by The Bodley Head 1964
Published in Penguin Books 1966
Reprinted 1967, 1968, 1970
Copyright © J. P. Donleavy, 1963

Made and printed in Great Britain by
Hazell Watson & Viney Ltd,
Aylesbury, Bucks
Set in Linotype Georgian

J. P. Donleavy

A Singular Man

Penguin Books

1

My name is George Smith. I get up on the right side of the bed every morning because I pushed the left to the wall. I'm in business. I sleep naked between the sheets. And these days always alone unless for accidental encounters.

Barefoot in the bathroom. Standing on the warm tiles where I had the management hire an artist to make a mosaic of a turkey cock with its feathers out. Trampling this in the early morning has always made me feel unsneaky. I shave and shower and dress. Use talc on my private particulars, not wanting to get it into my lungs. Where it gives a funny taste to the first morning smoke.

Matilda brings breakfast. Waddling in bubbling with her hefty good natured muscle. I hired her on the street when I dropped a paper bag with two bulbs of garlic. She came after me with it, refused reward and I asked her would she take a job. She ladles out the scrambled egg.

Looking the mail over. Shivering somewhat. This month of sleet with icicles hanging from the window sills. Take the skewer to the envelope and nip the silver point under the flap, dig through the fold and slice.

Box 0006
The Building
December 13th
You well know which year.

George Smith Esq.
Flat 14
Merry Mansions
2 Eagle Street

Dear Sir,
    Only for the moment are we saying nothing.

Yours etc.
Present Associates

Lingering over coffee to think. Ha ha. Detach this first tremor of amusing fear. Only shot through rapierlike the alimentary tube, merely lurking where Smith hopes things come out all right in the end. Do not relish being accosted with knowing the year. Nine fifteen this Friday morning on the east side of town.

2

George Smith's slouched figure appeared out from under the orange canopy of number Two Eagle Street. Hugo the doorman nodded. Sun out. The morning crisp with hardy sparrows chirping on this eleventh day till Christmas.

Stocky tugs dragging dark barges hoot hoot on the river. Bows aflood with yellow water dripping from the twine. In the park hard grey branches on winter trees. And kiddies with such young mommies, playing in the sand.

Smith darkly dressed and stately walking down the avenue talking to himself without moving the lips. Saying things like, show people you're in command of the situation by not saying much, don't let them get in close, keep everyone at arm's length, stop smiling kindly.

Last night at Two Eagle Street there'd been a party. Figures waltzing in as Hugo white gloved and grey uniformed ceremoniously bowed them in the glass doors. Smith had nipped up the carpeted blue stairs to the Goldminers' flat above. In the glow of a roaring fire between wilting plants George stood briefly with other guests in the subtropical apartment. A member of the party approaching in her late forties wearing a tight black dress, pearls between breasts, hair swept up in a sheen round her head and she said ten feet away pointing to Smith, I'll bet he knows a lot. Offering George her outstretched smooth hand, bracelets all up the vintage brown arm, there was a quick shake. Smith was flattered being only in the early thirties but looking older since running his own business and signing contracts. It would have been nice to ask her down to bed fifteen feet away through the ceiling.

Two miles south of Eagle Street along the river and highway past the high white walls of a hospital for humans. Further under a vast dark bridge and the Animal Medical Center, George Smith turned off the avenue of lurking doormen and down a commercial street. Left into an entrance and one flight up to a wide window overlooking the steady strange click of people and wide beetle cars bubbling by. On the corner lolly pop traffic lights tasted all day from red to green with lemon in between.

Here at number Thirty Three Golf Street George Smith rose in rage and subsided in depression. Sometimes merely tearing down the curtain as he did one afternoon having read a letter of innuendo. The person in the cigar store across the street laughing outright as he caught sight of the momentary rampant chaos. While Miss Tomson streaked in to see what the matter was. She was so new then. And Smith said, by jove a winter rascal fly of the blue bottle variety, I got it Miss Tomson, I think. As Miss Tomson nips her head in now.

'Are you all right for chewing gum, Mr Smith.'

'Yes, Miss Tomson. Are you free this evening.'

'That's a Jew question Mr Smith.'

'I beg your pardon Miss Tomson.'

'You should ask if I can work overtime. Or are you asking me to a nightclub.'

George Smith taking his desultory fountain pen lately bought of a vending machine. Miss Tomson lifting eye brows and lids.

'I hurt your feelings, Smith.'

'Not at all.'

'Yes I did. God Smith. You're so vulnerable.'

'Miss Tomson I'll let you know when I need the care of an institution.'

'You do that.'

'Can you come to my apartment with paper and pencils tonight.'

'Sure.'

The tall blondeness of Miss Tomson's smiles. Her calves strong and long, often turning so airily this way and that, a

8

blue neat vein trembling at the ankle bone. She would make a housewife in whose hands the dishes might melt. Face framed in the kitchen window looking out over the sink across the lawns, every exquisite strand of hair gold and priceless.

'What time, Mr Smith.'

'Seven. I'm leaving at four for an early workout at the club.'

'How's the condition. Learn to fight yet.'

'I can handle myself Miss Tomson. Would you put this letter in the file.'

'Hey, this is good. They're not saying anything. Yet. Pretty good approach.'

Smith watching this tall creature go out beyond the frosted glass. No muscles in her arms at all. Holding the letter and triggering off her index finger rapping it three times, she said it was a test for the quality of the paper. Her underlying nature changed daily. The first time I saw her strut into the office a little chilled and blue at the neck in a collarless black slim coat, dressed for spring. She carried a newspaper and with that finger stood in front of my desk pointing it out to me.

'Are you Mr Smith put this ad in.'

'Yes.'

'I want the job.'

'Won't you sit down.'

'Sure.'

'Well Miss —'

'Tomson. Sally Tomson.'

'Miss Tomson I suppose you do all the usual things.'

'I can type. And I can work. Hard, too. Even though I come from the South. I've got a brother who's a socialite. His picture gets in the paper if that's a help. I can do what you want me to do. With reservations, of course.'

'Of course.'

'This pay isn't bad. I'd only do this work for this pay.'

'I see.'

'Do you want me.'

'You're the first applicant I've seen.'

'Do you want me.'

'Can I have some time to think it over.'

'Sure, I'll go outside for a minute.'

'Look Miss Tomson, before you do, would you mind just answering me one question.'

'Sure, shoot.'

'If I were to hire you, is the behaviour I'm seeing now the natural, everyday behaviour I can expect to get from you here in the office.'

'It'll vary. But I'll be an office girl. Whatever you hire me for.'

'All right, no need to go outside for a minute. You're hired. I think you're a sympathetic person.'

'Don't get me wrong, I'm easy come easy go. But.'

And that morning Smith regathering the voice which had been swallowed down following the guilty quiver, bringing it back up the dry throat with a clearing noise.

'Start Monday. Ten to five. I don't like to rush the day. Hour for lunch. Your desk is the one outside the door. And I'll introduce you to Miss Martin. Don't mind my asking do you, are those fingernails real.'

'Yesh. I grew them that way. And by the way I better tell you now I say y e s, yesh. Said it that way right from the time I began saying it. Some people get the idea I'm trying to be coy.'

'O.K. Miss Tomson, it's all right with me. Look forward seeing you Monday.'

'Yesh.'

So when Monday came. Miss Tomson came. But with an elk hound which she tied to the desk. I came in. Saw the animal. A man killer for sure. Miss Tomson said good morning in true secretary fashion and I simply did not have the words ready to deal with the situation. Especially the inhuman growl and lurchment of Miss Tomson's desk in my direction to which the vast creature lay tethered. I nipped back behind the frosted glass of my office for a moment's refreshment, picked up a letter which lay waiting and which put my bowels in a further state and my hand through what I thought would be soon thinning hair. Gingerly out again to say something like a foolish remark. Does it bark and what does it eat Miss Tomson. Whoosh. Clack. Those were the teeth. This animal again tried to get me. As the pleasantry failed and I made it back again behind the vulnerable glass. From where I ventured voice only.

'Miss Tomson, the dog.'

'Yesh.'

'Will we be seeing it every morning.'

'Do you want to. Got a cute name. Goliath. Goli for short. He's like a lion. Sorry he tried to get you. But he doesn't know you yet. Goliath say good morning to Mr Smith, that shadow behind the glass, go on, Goli, Mr Smith isn't going to bite you.'

That Monday George Smith stood aloof and aghast. Humming. Whispering up to Jesus Christ is there no justice. As Miss Tomson sensed the sorrow of the sheepish shadow.

'Mr Smith, you didn't think I was going to bring Goli to work with me every morning, did you.'

'Miss Tomson, I have a vivid imagination, likely to believe anything.'

'Well, why didn't you say so Mr Smith. Goli is just on his way to the boarding kennel. Didn't have room this morning. Raw steak is his dish. Rump. Thought you wouldn't mind. It's going to be your first time away from me, Goli, and you mustn't eat Mr Smith. Our new boss.'

Again aghast that Monday. Mostly because Miss Tomson's tender reference caught me in the breast. Tuesday Goliath was chained in the boarding kennel one hoped with his dish of rump. Wednesday he had his checkup at the Animal Medical Center and as I passed that place in the morning I fancied I could hear his growl as he chewed up other little doggies. And confess I chuckled at this tasty vision. Growling hysterically myself further on as I stepped straight into dogshit. A half hour on the park bench digging it out of the corrugated soles I wear for nonskid agility.

That midweek morning Miss Tomson had been quick to notice the lurking stink. She sniffed, and fanned herself with a sheet of typing paper, and cleared her throat. When Saturday afternoon arrived I sat lonely collapsed and futureless, staff gone home, cigar store across the street barred and dark. I went and looked on Miss Tomson's desk. The bleak expanse. Picked up her pencils and memorized the brand over and over. I repaired the electric plug of her lamp, battening the wires good-o with a screwdriver thinking of the juice that would go through these very copper threads to give her light. God forbid the passing risque thought as I slipped in the male plug for the electrical connexion.

And a later Monday after a little shopping at the haberdasher round the corner on the previous Saturday. I came in wearing a narrow brimmed hat.

'That's better.'

'What do you mean, Miss Tomson.'

'That hat. It's a slight improvement. Don't ever wear that other thing again, Mr Smith, it just doesn't suit you or anything you're trying to be.'

'O.'

'And if you don't mind, just let me give you a tip. Don't take this wrong. But don't wear that green tie with that green shirt, but that's not bad what you're wearing, not bad.'

'Thanks.'

'Sure.'

Uncontrollably I rushed into my office. Stood there behind the door. Taking a deep breath. Unable to catch it. Then sitting at my desk with the hat on as the first letters and papers come in.

'Hey Mr Smith that hat, is it for real, really. Or on approval.'

'We could discuss that later Miss Tomson.'

'O sure.'

I locked the door after her. Being bullied by good taste is not exactly my dish. When we get to know each other better, let's see the underwear, Smith. The hat was only to take off in a situation where there was nothing else to do. Chap in the shop said this is what they're wearing. Who are they. Awkward to say I am not them. But the burning words, anything you're trying to be. I took my paper shears and dumbfounded by my own dexterity, reduced the hat to pieces and parts. Packaged it neatly. Addressing it elsewhere. And had to let Miss Tomson back in to mail it.

'Mr Smith just one more thing, if you don't mind. I've got an interest in you, I want to see you make it. Don't get the idea I'm trying to meddle in your affairs but the shoes. The colour is definitely too light.'

But as well in those initial weeks of Miss Tomson's employ she was reassuring over some of the letters which shook George Smith's timbers with intimidation. Miss Tomson would take one look at them and say they're kidding.

'Besides, Mr Smith, they couldn't do this to you even though they tried. You've got to know when people are bluffing, don't get the idea that because you tell the truth so are they. By the way, you got a licence for a gun.'

And late one afternoon at Thirty Three Golf Street when the cigar shop man was bringing in the statue of his redskin chained outside his store, and the lights were flicking off high up, and Smith with a warm feeling like the sad taste of goodbye, looked up as Miss Tomson was leaving his office.

'Miss Tomson.'

'Yesh.'

'Miss Tomson, don't mind my asking you a question.'

'No.'

'It's about you.'

'Sure, what about me.'

'Why were you out looking for a job when you came to me.'

'I got jilted.'

'I don't want to pry into anything as personal as that.'

'Sure pry if you want.'

'Well, if I might perhaps ask were you terribly hurt by this.'

'Let's say I was amazed by it.'

'O.'

'I was the cheapest thrill he was ever likely to get in his life.'

'Please don't feel you have to tell me more. I'm surprised you were jilted.'

'Well I wasn't really. Some guy started writing me poems and I thought they were kind a cute. So the guy I'm giving the cheapest thrill he was ever likely to get which was costing him a fortune I admit, hears of this and said get rid of this poetic curiosity and I said no. And then he asked for the gold key back.'

'I take it, Miss Tomson, this gold key was to a nest somewhere.'

'Nice way to put it Mr Smith but it didn't have a cosy quality.'

'Pardon me for using your jiltor's reference, but what happened to the poetic curiosity.'

'He left. I used to feed him and drive him around in the car the jiltor gave me as a present. When I gave the jiltor the car back, the poetic curiosity took off south where he said it was warmer.'

'Although I don't want to suggest this if you think otherwise, the poetic curiosity was really the jiltor.'

'Yesh, put it that way. But he used to give me laughs.'

'I see.'

'Do crazy things like taking an orange and tying it to the cat's tail. He was full of deals too to make lots of money until he said he didn't have time to think if I wasn't able to support him. He was like you in some ways, had no taste at all.'

And hatless George Smith would go home. Out of the dark shadows of Golf Street to the lighted highway streaming with cars. A little pedestrian bridge to stand over watching them zoom by underneath.

3

At four this Friday George Smith walked along Golf Street and west across town on the cold evening pavements. The tall buildings alight, long dangling jewels. Threading through the hurrying shopping throng and river of cars. Under the dingy trellis of the elevated train, down a street of dusty book shops. And out upon a splashing fountain and the great dark oasis of winter trees in the park.

The marble lobby of The Game Club was full of hearty handshakes and members' backslaps. Lights twinkling with Christmas, the gift counter piled with white teddy bears and boxes of beribboned candies. Miss Tomson said she loved to hug soft things and taste the sweet. And as I left Thirty Three I said see you my apartment at seven.

Smith after a few quick sparring rounds with the instructor followed by a beginner's lesson in wrestling, retired to the smoke room where he quaffed a tall beer overlooking the darkened park. Flagging a taxi back to Merry Mansions. The doorman with a brisk salute. Handing across an envelope.

'For you sir.'

'Thank you, Hugo.'

Safely inside Merry Mansions. Don't like the look of this envelope. Relax. Miss Tomson will be here soon. Have another little rosner.

'Matilda.'

'Good evening Mr Smith.'

'Get me a whisky. And two omelettes. Miss Tomson will be here shortly to eat with me.'

'Leave the garlic out, Mr Smith.'

'Leave it in.'

'If that's the way you want it.'

'Just get me the drink, please.'

Soon as Miss Tomson is mentioned Matilda's good natured fat frizzles. When she first saw Miss Tomson there was a half hour's heavy breathing coming from the kitchen, as I attempted to be an attentive host. Lifting the fur from Miss Tomson's shoulder. Tying up Goliath to a leg of the marble table in the hall. Then a crash from the kitchen. Matilda trampling the delf in rage. Miss Tomson looking all about saying, not bad, not bad, not bad at all, strictly not what I expected Mr Smith. And at this cosy interval the hall table crashed with my Tang pot. Miss Tomson put her hand to her mouth. I was up and just got to the hall in time to see. Matilda was pulling a lamb chop back into the kitchen on a string. Miss Tomson said, Matilda just needs her legs opened.

'Here you are Mr Smith, a big whisky.'

'Thanks a lot.'

'You're welcome.'

Nice exchange. With the right amount of formality. Take a gulp of this corn stuff. And open up this envelope.

Dear Sir,

I am aware of the nature of your business. And perhaps it has come to your attention that you are infringing upon my own area of operations.

I should like to take this opportunity of warning you of any further encroachments. I am sure you will be guided by expedience in this matter.

I have witnessed the delivery of this letter to you by your doorman.

Naturally you know who I am.

Yours faithfully,
J.J.J.

Get up and go over to the window. Witnessed delivery by your doorman. That denotes a certain sheepish vulgarity. A man over there selling roasted chestnuts. Or is this rogue renting yonder cold water flat outfitted with instruments of spying with the brass telescope on the automatic ball bearing swivel. To watch my eye whites going brown. Gives that distinct stab of pain between the shoulder and up the keester too. Miss Tomson please come quickly. Ah, the doorman's buzzer.

'Sir, a young lady, Miss Tomson.'

'Have her come up immediately.'

My Christmas gift to Hugo, was snuff, which some idle jokester sent me last year. Of the menthol variety. I treat him as an equal. Not using that handy maxim a man is what he makes his dough at and alas how much. Sometimes it is a gentle gesture to remind people of their big time possibilities. Makes them like you.

'Miss Tomson, good to see you.'

'What's the matter Mr Smith you look as if you've seen a ghost.'

'You're cold, Miss Tomson, do come by the fire.'

'Gee what nice big logs. But aren't they scared you'll burn down the building.'

'That's it, get comfy. The people upstairs have one too. Prevailed on the management. They finally allowed it, for a consideration of course.'

'You could barbecue in front of that with all that nice blazing ember. Would you take me for a campfire girl, Mr Smith.'

'Ha ha, Miss Tomson. What would you like to drink.'

'I could really get stupid tonight. The girl living below my apartment is just driving me nuts. Always waiting to jump me with her troubles. I'll have what you're having Mr Smith. What troubles that girl's got. She goes out into the back garden and starts making faces at me through the window. She hired a detective to watch her husband and catch him with the huzzy. But the detective catches him with a guy. How do you like that, Mr Smith.'

'Irregular certainly.'

'Crazy. Say what's got you so nervous.'

'A letter, Miss Tomson.'

'Not again.'

'I'm afraid so.'

'May I see it Mr Smith.'

'Of course.'

Smith reaching for his back pocket. Too near the keester for comfort. Put things there which are upsetting and sit on them. Handing it over to her long comforting fingers. With a flick of a talon across the paper. One blonde lock falls forward as she reads.

'This is a new one, Mr Smith.'

'I thought so too.'

'You see anybody, Mr Smith.'

'A chestnut vendor on the corner. I suppose someone could be on a rooftop.'

'Be no chestnut vendor. This guy prides himself. Sees himself as a big important operator. Coming on with the dignity. Get this encroach crap. Big bark no bite.'

'I'm not particularly anxious to be barked or growled at.'

'Old Goli put the wind up you didn't he, Mr Smith, ha ha. But got to admit though this guy's approach is nicely sneaking in from the side.'

'Precisely why I'm not underestimating him.'

'But Mr Smith if you want to know the truth you over-estimate these things. And take it personally as well. Here now, don't you get up, let me pour you a drink. You really look white.'

'Thanks Miss Tomson, I suppose it has got under my skin.'

'Mr Smith, don't let it.'

'You're right, Miss Tomson. I shouldn't let it. But it does.'

'Ignore it Mr Smith and see what develops. Soon as you show you're worried that's when they've got you.'

'I do feel it's an imposition of the worst kind to involve you like this in matters which quite frankly are extremely distasteful.'

'You're kidding.'

'I'm not.'

'It's life, Mr Smith. I mean millions are trampling and struggling towards the top, I'd quit if I didn't like it. Anyway, you're not bad to work for. I thought working was going to kill me. Besides it's not me they're after. It's you.'

'Alas.'

'But whatever you do, don't let them shove you around.'

'Matilda's making us omelettes, that all right, Miss Tomson.'

'Are they going to reek.'

'Dear me, I hope not. I instructed her to leave out particularly strong ingredients.'

'Just so I don't leave here smelling like a dago. How did the sport go.'

'O sparred a few rounds. Let the instructor have a few on the button.'

'You must be tough.'

'I can handle my dukes. Also took a beginner's lesson in the rudiments of wrestling, never know these days. Some terrifying physical specimens around that wrestling room.'

'Gee tell me about them Mr Smith. I love hearing about these big tarzans, that's the way my brother's built, the one who gets his picture on the social page, he goes right out under the arms, you'd swear he had no stomach at all. Shape of a V. At home in our kitchen he'd come in without a stitch on and open up the ice box, take out the milk and drink a whole quart in one gulp. His body is really magnificent. Our parents brought us up letting us look at each other. I think that's the way it ought to be. He lifts weights. You should see him. And throws that thing they have at races, that round ball. But Mr Smith aren't you afraid of being killed by one of these guys.'

'I can take care of myself.'

'Cut the kidding Mr Smith one of these guys could break you in half, I'd be careful if I were you. You're just not built.'

'Miss Tomson, this is a club for sportsmen and gentlemen.'

'I don't know, Mr Smith, you just seem too frondlike for that kind of thing. I just don't see it, you grappling with one of these tarzans, not one like my brother anyway, he's really beautiful. Even big as he is, he moves like he was a panther.'

'I'm sure he does, Miss Tomson.'

'Hey come on Mr Smith, I hurt your feelings didn't I. Come on now, I did.'

'O no no.'

'I have, I know when I have. But you're just not one of these big apes. I mean you're no weakie Mr Smith, you've got things they haven't got.'

'What Miss Tomson.'

'Well. Maybe you're not mentally weak, maybe that's what I'm saying. Like you're gentle. Got nice hands. You show consideration. Those things are something, Mr Smith. I just could never, but never, you know see you stark at the ice box under a bottle of milk, that would be just, it would be just –'

'I think dinner's served, Miss Tomson.'

'See there I go, can't control my mouth. How did we get on this anyway.'

'I believe you asked me how the sport went.'

'O yesh.'

Miss Tomson in black. She wore green this afternoon. And she's wearing flat shoes for my sake. Makes me half an inch taller. She stands up straight and walks swinging her hips. Those two handy melons wandering around under the backside of her skirt. As she flashes her head back and catches my globes glued.

'You think I'm walking like I was compromised, Mr Smith.'

'I don't quite get you, Miss Tomson.'

'You know, Mr Smith.'

'I don't Miss Tomson, why are you shaking your head.'

'Because Mr Smith you're one of the most innocent guys. Ha ha, I think. Can't you see I'm walking as if I'm looking for it.'

'For what.'

'For it. Don't force me to say it because I will.'

'Please, Miss Tomson. I don't mind myself but there's Matilda.'

'Don't think she's not looking for it either.'

'Miss Tomson, do you like asparagus.'

Miss Tomson tall, sat at the other end of the maple, Smith's favourite tree. George reaching out to push aside the thriving ferns which Matilda had placed squarely between the diners so they couldn't see each other. The asparagus comes in. Laid out cooked and dead on the moss green plates. Naturally I reached for my napkin and let it fall over my thigh. Miss Tomson spreading hers across her lap. She's looking and waiting. For the asparagus. Can't possibly take it lankly with the fingers until she does. Surely she'll use the knife on them. Not make a move till I see. She's going for the fork. Isn't there some rule don't use a fork when a knife will do. Goodness, she's after butter.

'Matilda, the butter, please.'

'Sure. If that's what you want.'

A simple thing like the butter. Deal with it with careless nonchalance. Pretend I'm waiting for butter too. If I pick up this piece of asparagi and she cuts hers with a fork. Just wait and see. Adjust napkin. And reach for the bread. No. Offer some.

'Miss Tomson, let me cut you bread. White or brown.'

'That brown looks good Mr Smith.'

'Of course, brown. Ah, here's the butter. Thank you Matilda.'

Good appetite has Miss Tomson. And a forceful chewer.

'Mr Smith, you don't mind my gobbling this,'

'Of course not, Miss Tomson, I intend to gobble myself. Much healthier that way.'

'Say Mr Smith, you really go in for this health.'

'Taken an interest in a certain robustness, Miss Tomson.'

'Sure, but why kill yourself.'

'I'm not killing myself. A little exercise to keep my figure.'

'After thirty you can't go back. What's a little pot. Real cute. I like it. No kidding. Why don't you try a corset.'

'Miss Tomson, will you have your omelette runny in the middle.'

'Yesh, please.'

'Matilda, both soft in the middle please.'

'If that's the way you want it. You better get that wine while I'm cooking. I got my hands here full. Never enough time for nothing.'

Miss Tomson leaning across the table. She cocks her head towards the kitchen whispering.

'Mr Smith, she distinctly dislikes me. Why don't you some evening come to my apartment. I've got a typewriter there.'

'That's kind, Miss Tomson, but I wouldn't think of such an imposition. You've got your own personal life to lead. I'm already imposing myself too much on your free time.'

'What free time. I go home now, mess around, listen to music, make some clothes. I do nothing.'

'Some nice young man will be around.'

'That's a laugh. My brother he likes to come around, crowds the apartment out with celebrities. Bunch of stuffy stuck up deads. I told him to stop bringing them around, that I just wasn't interested. They all have to do the talking. I used to be crazy for that kind of crowd. And one day living in the nest, everybody showing up for tennis. You know, seeing them standing in the hall, a really healthy bunch of looking people. You know and just like that, I took a look at this crowd. Just stood and listened, you know, Mr Smith, I was hearing them for the first time. And same day I'm standing on the court with my racket, resting when I get this poke in the back through the fence. It's a guy passing on the street. I turn around, I'm going to say who the fuck, sorry about that, but who the, and he hands me a piece of paper. It's my first sight of the poetic curiosity. There's a poem on the paper and his address on the back. Hey, am I talking like mad. Must be the wine.'

'Miss Tomson I'm most interested to hear you talking.'

'You're not kidding.'

'Certainly not.'

'I was crazy then, you know. Going up with that gold key

to the nest, the elevator crammed with presents I'm buying with this guy's money. Off the roof garden socking tennis balls mad laughing, bounce them on the underprivileged, help keep them down. I said everybody get a load of this, some guy's handed me a note with a poem. I started to read it. I stopped right in the middle. I thought Christ, this guy might have meant this and the words are nice and they were about me too, that's why I stopped I guess. I went all moody. Threw a few real crazy tantrums. Turned on all the water in the nest till it was pouring right down the elevator shaft. I was thinking what's this kind of life, what good is it. It was pretty good. But I was selling myself for peanuts. Funny isn't it, there I got all interested in the real things, you know deep things and the poetic curiosity all the while is interested in the free meal ticket and big time living up in the nest. Boy.'

There was a tear in Miss Tomson's eye.

'Miss Tomson, please don't say any more. Have a little sip of wine. Good mouthful of omelette too.'

'You know Mr Smith, I do you injustice you don't deserve. You're a nice guy.'

'Fresh pineapple. Or apricots.'

'Sure. Love some.'

'Matilda, the apricots.'

Smith reaching to light the candles, scented and rumoured to be aphrodiziac. Out the window in the sky over the rooftops was a twilight of twinkling turned to a blaze of black and gold.

'Mr Smith, you know what.'

'What Miss Tomson.'

'You're a strange guy. Why some debutante didn't nab you I don't know. Weren't they swarming over you.'

'I regret to say, Miss Tomson, they weren't.'

Matilda brought on the raw pineapple all sugar soaked, and a glass bowl full of delightful apricots. Miss Tomson and Mr Smith eating from a knee in front of the fire. Cosier that way. Miss Tomson undoing a gigantic buckle to let it out a notch. Patting the tiny rotundity.

'I'm getting a pot too. I need more padding on me. I could use more right here.'

'You're all right there, Miss Tomson.'

'How do you know these are real.'

'Come come, Miss Tomson.'

'Ha ha, almost caught you guessing though, didn't I Mr Smith, come on admit it.'

'For a moment perhaps.'

'Mr Smith, you give me laughs. Your face the day I brought Goliath to the office. Were you white.'

'Brandy, Miss Tomson.'

'This stuff made of apricots, Mr Smith.'

'Fermented.'

'I could get stinko.'

'Shall we have some strong coffee.'

'I keep forgetting I'm here to do some work. Come on, let's work. Get the letter out. I'm really all set. Let's spread them all out next to each other. I got choice replies to all of them. Dear Buster, they're holding a big sale somewhere down town, full of kite bargains. You are invited. How's that Mr Smith. You don't go for that one. Now this guy J.J.J. how could he be aware of the nature of your business when I don't even know. Takes an opportunity to give a warning, why not Dear Jack, beat it or we'll give you a hot poker up the roosel. Sorry Mr Smith, but I mean why doesn't he just come out with it. Ha ha, he might really give you a scare.'

'Have more brandy, Miss Tomson.'

'Sure. Funny in your house like this I feel relaxed. Mr Smith I don't want to pry but why hasn't a guy like you got a wife and kids. It's none of my business, forget I asked.'

Faintly from the street scraggly children's voices singing a yule song. Miss Tomson going to the window.

'Hey come here Mr Smith look at this, isn't that sweet, group of urchins, they're singing. How do you get this window open.'

'I'm afraid it's sealed.'

'I'd throw the kids some money. Poor things singing out there all alone in the cold. Nobody I guess even listening.

Can't we do something for them. Maybe I could run down there with a platter of stuff. Let's do that.'

'Miss Tomson, I'd rather you didn't.'

'Hey why.'

'You'll get chilled.'

'Not me. I'm as healthy as they make them. I go walking barefoot right out the lobby of my building.'

'I still rather you didn't.'

'What's got into you Mr Smith. You mean you don't want me to give those poor kids sustenance. Is that what you're telling me.'

'Miss Tomson, please, you're misunderstanding me.'

'I wonder if I am. Then why shouldn't I. Look how cold and hungry they look down there. If I were a kid I'd wish someone would come out of a rich place like this and give me something, even though it was only food.'

'I've got my reasons.'

'I guess you have, Mr Smith. But they're a mystery to me. If I had some kids and they were out singing I'd like to know someone was going to react. I've got my pad if you want to dictate.'

'Miss Tomson, O.K., Matilda will give you some cold chicken from the kitchen. Take it down to them.'

'No, it's all right.'

'Now please do.'

'No, no, it doesn't matter.'

'Miss Tomson, it does matter. It matters to me now.'

'It was nothing.'

'Matilda will put it all out on a big platter. There's a silver one in the alcove.'

'It doesn't matter what it's on.'

'She'll give you a tray.'

'It doesn't matter now.'

Miss Tomson sitting, bending her head forward. Her book opened with the pages curled back, scribbling with her pencil. World of woe. Couldn't tell her. And I can't tell her now. She's hurt. Now I'll be blamed for hating children. I don't like them but I don't hate them. Miss Tomson, remember what you said, it's you they're after. I don't expect you to examine every little thing for signs of hostility. But how do I know this bastard watching me get the letter from the doorman didn't send these kids as a decoy. If I told you this you'd ridicule me for imagining things. For getting scared out of all proportion to the threat. Take the damn platter, rip open the cupboards, load it all on. Get Hugo up here to help. We'll all march down.

'You'd like to go home now, wouldn't you Miss Tomson.'

'I've got my pad ready and pencil poised.'

'You're upset.'

'I'm just waiting for the dictation.'

'Well I'm so upset I can't dictate.'

'Well maybe we better leave it till another day then, Mr Smith.'

'Miss Tomson, I apologize for not letting you go out to those children with a platter of chicken.'

'Let's forget it.'

'And see you sitting there miserable. Miss Tomson I'm not in the habit of asking people their feelings about me but because of this, do you think I hate singing.'

'Mr Smith, you're making a mountain out a mole hill, just a whim. Just a plain ordinary whim.'

'O.K.'

Smith turning abruptly crossing into that space the management likes to call the dining foyer. Sound of Matilda moving out of the kitchen. Smith pulling a cape over the shoulders. Opening the mechanically assisted door. Matilda's voice in the sitting room, talking to Miss Tomson.

'You upset Mr Smith, what about.'

'None of your business.'

'Don't talk to me like that.'

'Look Gertrude.'

'Don't call me Gertrude, don't call me Matilda either.'

'Get off my ear.'

'Don't you talk to me like that. I'll pull that blonde mop right out of your head.'

'You come near me you black bitch. Just dare.'

George nimbly stepping outside the door. Let that situation simmer. Pausing for the elevator. Flashing down the stairs instead. Whoosh. By Hugo out the front glass doors.

'Anything the trouble Mr Smith.'

'Just fetching somebody.'

'Can I help.'

'No thanks. Just up the street. Only a second.'

George moving forward, elbows well in, ankles supple, chin up, fingers flapping and well relaxed. Loping past tenement stoops and garbage pails on the other side of the street. Lungs gasping as Smith cleverly switched to mental power to give the muscles a rest. Stopping to ask a slow moving pedestrian.

'Pardon me, see any little kids up this direction.'

'You want a fight bud.'

'No thank you.'

George hurried on. Overt good fellowship everywhere. Peering into the beer saloon on the corner. I've got to get them. If they climb onto a bus I'm whipped. Hold on heart, I hear the voices of urchins. Thin little sounds. Coming up out of warm young hearts in the distance.

Further on the avenue between the remains of two derelict buildings, the urchins standing together on a pile of rubble. Embers of a fire glowing from the wreckers. George stepping from brick to brick and up on an unwieldy plank. One two three four five six of them. Two sizeable girls and a small one. Three rather tough looking boys.

'Excuse me kids, weren't you just singing around the corner.'

'Who says so.'

'I heard you. What are you singing here for, there's no one to hear you.'

'We don't want to be heard.'

'Look I've got a proposition. You, are you the oldest.'

'Yeah I'm the oldest.'

'Look will you come back to my apartment and sing for me.'

'Hey what do you want mister. You a pervert, mister.'

'I've got my girl friend there.'

'We read in a book that don't mean nothing.'

'I see. Well she thinks you're all a bunch of swell singers. She'd just like to hear you close up. And there's cold chicken and lemonade.'

'We want dough.'

'O.K. I'll give you money as well as cold chicken and lemonade.'

'You live in that swank apartment round the corner.'

'Yes.'

'Hey you must be rich. We want a whole lot of dough from you. You sure you're not kidding us.'

'Come and see.'

'O.K. Come on. I give the order follow this guy.'

Smith leading this youthful rank and file. Past the beer saloon where inmates jerked their thumbs out at the parade. To this apartment which may be given over to mayhem. Miss Tomson and Matilda, what a match. The dark solid heft against the light tall sylph. Be a certain amount of head banging on the parquet, an entrance hall alive with tufts of hair, and torn foundation garments. No whalebone on Miss Tomson but perhaps a lot on Matilda.

Smith moving with military bearing, calling left flank in under the orange canopy of Merry Mansion.

'Hey mister you taking us really right into your house.'

'Yes.'

'Hey we're going in.'

Hugo steps forward. Head a little askance. Mouth tight.

'Mr Smith I don't know about this.'

'What do you mean, Hugo.'

'Well. I think maybe you better use the service entrance.'

'These young people are my guests.'

'I had to kick them out of here just a quarter of an hour ago.'

'At the moment they're my guests.'

'I'm sorry but if you bring these little bums in here I'm going to report it to the management.

'Come on kids, follow me.'

'I'm telling you Mr Smith.'

'You've told me, onward kids.'

'It's not permitted on the premises. It's a rule of the management.'

The platoon making its way across the blue lobby. Two kids pausing for perusement in the big mirror. Smith instantly ordering these stragglers to take up the rear. As the spokesman warned Smith to watch the dirty language, his little brother was with them.

Platoon halt. At the top of the landing the military commander facing the white chilly faces outside the thick steel door of Flat 14.

'You, what's your name son.'

'Snake.'

'I see. Well look, here's some money, divide it up later.'

'Hey wow, this is a lot.'

'Well you're good singers.'

'Well give us more then.'

'Wait a minute kids. I'm not made of money. Here, now this is all I've got. Now when I open the door you're to assemble in the hall in two rows and sing.'

'What do you want us to sing, mister.'

'What you were singing in the street.'

'If you give us some more money we'll sing you a dirty song.'

'Not tonight, boys and girls.'

'You mean we come back sometime and sing real dirty ones.'

'Thanks kids, but just go in the door now. And sing a carol or two. I'd prefer for the sake of my girl friend if you kept it clean. More of a friend than a girl friend, you know what I mean.'

'We know mister.'

George inserting his key. Gently making way through for these good little kids. Snake practising the scales. Rather froglike. Girls blinking and taking deep breaths. Kids I beg of you to keep it clean.

Miss Tomson standing with her coat on to go. Sound of

Matilda crashing delf. The expense of keeping happiness. I can't possibly get down on my knees in front of all these kids and beg her to stay. And the racket in the kitchen.

'Kids, sing.'

All lined up. Not a bad bunch of little boys and girls. Could get them some publicity and send them touring somewhere. The singing paupers. Matilda just bust something big then.

> Silent night
> Holy night.

'Please Miss Tomson, don't go. Please stay and listen, the children will be disappointed.'

'I'm too mad. You ought to get somebody civilized to work for you.'

'Miss Tomson aren't you going to watch them eat the chicken.'

The slam of the door sent a neat crack zigzagging to the ceiling. Together with the Goldminer's parties upstairs and Miss Tomson, this little nest I've outfitted here at considerable expense is not going to last long. The management's representative Mr Stone will no doubt bring this up in due course. I've got to stop her.

'Hey kids, keep singing.'

'Sure, mister.'

Smith taking a quick look at the crack above the door to the ceiling. Moving headlong down the stairs in shirt sleeves. Catching a side view of his ignoble appearance as he made it to the curb to see Miss Tomson disappearing in a taxi around the corner beer saloon.

George Smith in front of Merry Mansions. Hugo humbugging inside the door. Cold night wind blowing dust and torn newspaper floating by. Miss Tomson took umbrage. Go ahead, go for good. Plenty of good secretaries around. You think you're something special. Social and smart.

George walking towards the river. Shivering in the chill. Black with glitterings of green and yellow and red on the water. Miss Tomson did not want me to catch her. She could have hesitated. She could have loitered just those few seconds in the lobby. Long enough to effect a reconciliation. Could mean I'll never see her again. No one to inspire pride in my appearance. Or make a laughing stock of me either. O my God what an arse she has.

The park all shut up, locked. Save where there are some little steps to a terrace over the river. Hands in pockets, shoulders hunched. Pneumonia brewing. Planned that little eating occasion to bring us closer together. Looking into each other's eyes, both our elbows on the maple. Knew she'd love asparagus. And the apricots with the neat follow up of mellow distilled fermentate of same.

Tug boats, barges. Car lights streaming across the bridge. Ships have always cheered me up. And the warm light of cabins making a way to sea. Someday I'll take a ship.

And on this terrace, George leaning on the iron rail, growling as both elbows sank in sea gull shit. A woman leading three wretched little dogs of some variety minute and snuffling. Pink hat, bundle of fur coat and pair of furry boots. As George freezed his balls and looked destitute standing there with the white crap stained elbows.

Woman looking George right in the eye. He had only enough fortitude left to sustain a stare for an instant. How do madam. You looking for a piece of ass. I beg your pardon, you stranger. She'd scream. And the arm of the law would extend its fat cowardly hand to clutch me by the garment. If they could spare time away from taking graft.

George was out of that park rapidly having a mind for nightly behaviour in those shrubbery places. To get back to his own cosy fireside. And the urchins. Whom, my goodness, I've left them singing.

Speed was now essential. Smith taking the relaxo stride down the pavement to Merry. Up the steps, three at a leap. No time for elevators. These days. Inside the vault door of Flat Fourteen there was sheepishness. Each urchin trying to stand behind the other and one trying to squeeze out the door as I came in. With no sign of Matilda. And this kid Snake slithering away.

'Hey you Snake, where are you going out that door.'

'Free country.'

'What have you got behind your back.'

'Just my ass.'

'Ungracious brat.'

'Hey mister don't touch him. We'll tell the cops you brought us up here to sing dirty songs and take off our clothes.'

'Little blackmailers. Give me back that bottle and get the hell out of here.'

George Smith lunged. Exodus ensued. The rush for the stairs. Give one of these kids a boot in the hole to remember me by. Boy they can travel. They're going up instead of down. The noise is terrible. Just get round this landing. Whoa. Goldminer's door is open. They'll see me. See me chasing six urchins. This will slander me just nicely. First time I've seen Mr Goldminer look serious in his life.

'Say George, what are you doing.'

Smith pausing quietly in his shirt sleeves, rolled to obscure the sea gull dropping. Resting one calm hand on the glass bannister. And with a generous show of front teeth.

'O nothing. Just a youth club. It's exercise night. Giving the kids a chase up the stairs.'

'O.'

'Toodle oo, got a rush. Put them through a few contortions on the roof. Got to build good sound bodies these days. Stops delinquency.'

'O.'

Mr Goldminer frowning in his doorway didn't laugh at that last remark. Usually laughs at everything. Uncontrollably. And then slaps his wife's bare back and gives her a little nudge under the tit. Distasteful habit.

Deep down below the voice of Hugo shouting up the stairwell. George travelling four steps a leap, attaching a left hooked hand and flying round each landing. Up above a door slamming. Little buggers have reached roof already. If I make the top alive and out of breath they might turn on me all at once and I'll scarcely be able to handle six. Onward. Never show cowardice in the face of children.

The roof. Out the door into the darkness. Over the skylights and round the chimneys. Away in the distance, shaft of searchlight flashing. Could use that here in the dark. Where are they. There. Running across the pebbles. Climbing over to the next roof, which I know for a fact is down twenty feet. With a parachute could leap too and have them trapped, crippled with their broken ankles and begging for mercy.

Smith making it across to the boundary wall of Merry Mansions as the last and biggest urchin, Snake, took a flying leap. With a crunching result darkly below. If there is plaster on anyone's ceiling. Alas it will be there no longer. Retreat out of this. With a shout to send them on their way.

'I'll get you yet. You wretched urchins.'

'Hey mister, what cheap whisky you drink.'

George silent spectre, right hand placed under the shirt to quieten a throbbing heart. This little group of the younger generation shouting their way down the interior of Number Four Eagle Street. Night rife with disrespect. Not to mention outright insolence. Left standing on a rooftop, with probably no maid, no secretary, minus my reputation, a bottle of whisky and god knows what else. Trust Goldminer to be at the door. When mostly they're naked and drunk on the floor, in nude carry on with the indiscriminate display of bare flesh among the tropical flowers they grow in that mad house.

George Smith crossing the pebble roof. Hands in pockets shoulders hunched. Looking down over the edge into Eagle Street. From a doorway two canopies away, shot the urchins. Snake holding a bottle high. Knifing wind blowing. Sky massive with light and faint with stars. Wisps of smoke from the river. Running lights red and green, tug hooting. Up here alone I can think of the time of year it is. Gifts. And of gold in some tropic. My own kids growing up without daddy. Me being just myself walking along the pavement hoping someone will look at me, stop, come back, see into my eyes and say I love you.

>   Without later
>   Turning
>   Utterly
>   Treacherous.

4

That was some Friday night. At Thirty Three Golf Street Monday morning there was no Sally Tomson pecking away at her machine. Nor Tuesday nor Wednesday. And Matilda locked in her room now for five days. Smith acquiring a contraption to make breakfast which woke a person with soft music and leaked out a cup of coffee. Once doing so the middle of the night upon Smith's arm while he lay defenceless asleep in a disturbingly objectionable dream.

Chaos gathering at Merry Mansions. Whorls of dust and cracked pieces of delf. Smith slipping notes in under the bedroom door to the silent Matilda. Who on Monday grunted once. And to the shout on Tuesday are you alive, growled. Smith making his way as usual along the river desperate to hop into one of medical institutions for a mental check up.

Three days of Miss Tomson's empty desk. And Miss Martin came in and said Mr Smith shall I parcel up Miss Tomson's things and send them to her. George shouting no one's to touch that desk, leave it just as it is. And the rest of the day was one of obtuse politeness with Miss Martin coming back with a letter handing it to Smith, saying, Mr Smith I'm afraid you've made an error.

'Miss Martin, I'm terribly busy, can't you correct it yourself, where is it, what's the matter with you, what are you paid for.'

And Miss Martin took her silent white finger and with a fat pink fingernail touched the bottom of the page where George has signed the name Sally Tomson instead of his own.

When the lights start to flicker on during the rapidly dark

afternoons were the worst moments at Thirty Three Golf Street. George nipping out for a walk. And late Monday at an excavation peering down into the floodlit morass of winches, cement mixers and ladles of concrete swinging through the air. All din, dust and unsad. A man near George on the platform recognizing him from prepsterhood, followed Smith as he retreated the short distance to the corner. And saying behind him, why hi, George. And Smith running outright. Hailing a taxi. Taking it to The Game Club where sitting in the library in the deep stillness and chime of a grandfather clock, examining one's behaviour which was getting too weird for words. What harm to say, hello, hi, good to see you, gosh you look great, remember the great things we did as kids and prepsters, the snakes we put in neighbours' kitchens through the window. And I ran. Can't now face the things which happened years ago, both believing in the same God, putting hands up the same dresses.

Thursday the sixth day of Matilda's incarceration. Morning dawning. George reaching to punch the coffee contraption into life which lacked the loving hand, the juice of living. And with one bleary eye awake the flash thought that Matilda was dead. Maid servant starves to death in Merry Mansions. Police and public crucifixion on the front pages. Why did you do it Mr Smith, murder her in this ruthless slow way. Instead of shrivelment why not the knife or gun, you're licensed to carry a pistol. Why didn't you blast her. Members of the jury this murderer is not only a murderer but a twisted and callous person.

And Thursday Smith swept up his nudity in the polka dot dressing gown, plunged tootsies into slippers to pound once again on Matilda's door. Milkbottle silent. And in the polished mahogany, George's eyes culled up a scene of other mahogany. The witness stand. Goldminers giving evidence, sure he's violent didn't I see him with my own peepers chasing those poor kids up on the roof and he goosed my wife last Christmas. Violently. Just a forceful nudge of the knee.

'Matilda are you in there.'

As Smith looking down his dressing gowned person to the bare skin of the legs. Hair ending at the ankles. Yes your honour, his usual was an attack on Matilda Friday nights, sure he was tight, sure we knocked on his two inch thick steel door, yeah I got one too but only an inch, we could really hear him and this poor dark creature, as he took advantage of her colour.

And finally Thursday noon after the constant visits to pound, Smith shivering at his bedroom phone. Reaching for the instrument. A few dials of the finger and buster, the street outside will be full of clanging bells and sirens careering in off the avenue, anything to keep people nervous. The blue uniforms, respirators, acetylene torches and usual safe cracking equipment to get to Matilda's cadaver behind the mahogany disguised half inch steel door. And as George put the dark plastic to his ear and a finger into the chromium dial, his arms rose in rigidity as an icy clutch of water crashed upon his back. A loud shout and laugh from Matilda as she said surprise and Smith said Jesus Christ so it could be heard in the padded cells on the island in the river.

'Matilda, god damn you. What the hell's the idea. The absolute and preposterous cheek after I'm half scared to death.'

'You can't talk to me like that Mr Smith.'

'I'm talking to you like that. Get me a towel. You're behaving in an absolutely stupid manner.'

'That white trash, that blonde bitch.'

'She's my secretary. What the hell are you making out of my life. Don't I pay you enough.'

'Yeah, sure bring up money. Sure bring up the money, Mr Smith. It's the only thing you understand is that old green stuff. Buy everybody off don't you.'

'Matilda you're talking out of turn. I'm soaked.'

'I know my turn to talk, you don't have to tell me when to talk. I'll talk and I'll talk and I'll talk. Slurping up asparagus.'

'We're going to settle this Matilda. Get me a towel.'

'Sure you can settle, can't you. Get it yourself. Everybody in their place, settle up. Fire me. Get rid of those you can get rid of. I don't mind walking the streets. Plenty of jobs.'

'Well you're not working in that room.'

'You want to fire me.'

'No one said anything about firing.'

'Fire me.'

'No.'

'Well you can if you want, just so you understand that.'

'Stop explaining my rights to me and get some clothes on. And get me a towel.'

'O it's business now. You don't mind a little bare tit on Fridays. You want it white now.'

'I've got to be at the office.'

'Sure, everything's black and white in the day time.'

'I just hope that by tonight you're behaving in a civilized manner.'

'Or what are you going to do.'

'Stop pressurizing me. Just telling you to be out of that room. And have something to eat ready for a change.'

George rose sadly in the direction of the bathroom. Reflecting upon the turkey cock unable to flap its wings in the floor. Life's getting like a merrygoround with people getting on and off and no one paying for the ride. I'll try to track Miss Tomson down. No I won't. If she can get more money and better conditions somewhere else, let her. That goes for Matilda too. I've never bought anyone in my life. Cheaply. Is treating people with warmth and concern buying them. And then being doused from behind. Answer me that. Hear her, standing on the verge of stark nudity having an argument with me.

Smith putting on a blue shirt and a black tie dotted with three legged golden stars. No Miss Tomson to reach out and give it a flick and say that's for the birds. Guess you might say I'm going to have a little freedom of expression around my office for a change. And take up the phone with my new adaptor that fades out my voice when the talking gets ticklish and sends the line dead at signs of disaster. Wear white shoes with red dots if urge denotes that attire. I lie. What an empty god forsaken place the office has become. When people are going home, sidewalks crowded. And I'm head in hands. Too sad to look up, out, forward. And late tonight I take the train.

'Matilda, I catch the train at eight and I want sandwiches.'

'Sure if that's the way you want it.'

'Shit.'

'Ooo you said a nasty word, Mr Smith.'

'Are you locked in that room again.'

'I'm delicately attired.'

Smith clenching fists. He raised them slowly. Dropped them and spread out his fingers and looked at the nails. Not much moon showing. I'll just take so much from her and no more. O there'll be changes, no more of this if it's all right with you Matilda. Thinks she owns me. That I live to keep her.

Businesslike George Smith went to the kitchen. Taking four large elliptical white plates. At Matilda's door he raised them above his head and crashed them to the floor. A little white chip bounced right up on the hall table. Amazing.

Smith passing out of Merry Mansions. Dog trotting to Golf Street. To any new meantime of horror. Nearly stopping to ask a female pedestrian were she ever a feeding mother to give some human milk of kindness.

And Miss Martin with worried lines across her brow, stood at the top of the stairs of number Thirty Three, holding one hand in another.

'Good morning, Miss Martin.'

'Mr Smith I was so worried. I was going to ring.'

'Just a little something, Miss Martin, held me up. Sudden conference. Top level, private, all that sort of thing.'

'Shall I get you some apples.'

'Please.'

'Mail is on your desk. There were a few phone calls, you know when no one speaks on the other end. The breathing is awful. I switched the music in with the adaptor.'

'The bag pipes record.'

'Yes Mr Smith. They hung up right away.'

'Good.'

Smith smiled and entered his office behind the frosted glass. Past the top of that desk which is like a desert. Lost on it without water. Letters, there they are, arranged right in a row. I'm just not up to it. Examine the stamps. Always a nice distraction. Whoa, one or two countries I've not yet heard of. What could they be after. I'm putting my soul under lock and key. And by Jesus these three go in the safe, unopened. Miss Tomson come back. I must not weaken. Open this harmless one. With one neat slit. Goodness, hand-made paper inside. No. Not one of these.

Dear Sir,

Quite obviously you intend overlooking the particular seriousness of this matter.

Perhaps you will have to be made to dance a different tune. And we take this opportunity of reminding you that it shall be to our music.

We know you have read this.

Yours faithfully,
J.J.J. & Others.

George Smith putting feeble hand to the buzzer. Still able to press down. Three shopping days till Christmas. Cigar store man has a big sign, Give Smoke For Yule. Soon as good will towards men comes round in the calendar they try to get in a sneaky boot to one's oxsters.

'Miss Martin, come in please.'

'Yes, Mr Smith.'

'Would you get me a glass of water.'

'Certainly. Will a paper cup do.'

'Goatskin, anything.'

'I wasn't trying to be funny, Mr Smith.'

'I know you weren't Miss Martin, forgive me. Put all this correspondence in the safe and lock it. Burn it, eat it –'

'I don't understand Mr Smith.'

'Forgive me Miss Martin forgive me, in my moment of mood.'

'I'll get the water right away.'

'And ice.'

'Yes Mr Smith, right away.'

'Hold it Miss Martin. Stop right where you are. Come here a minute. Right over to the desk. Don't be scared. I just want you to tell me something. In my eyes. See. Just tell me what colour they are.'

'I think they're green, Mr Smith.'

'I mean the whites, what are they.'

'White. Mr Smith.'

'How white.'

'Just white, Mr Smith.'

'You don't think they're going grey.'

'No, Mr Smith.'

'Or brown.'

'No.'

'Miss Martin thank you very much. Really thanks. Stop all calls. I'll be away from tonight over Christmas. And just one more thing before you go. Make an account of Miss Tomson's wages, till the end of this week.'

'Shall I mail them to her sir.'

'Don't be distant Miss Martin.'

'Sorry Mr Smith.'

'No, don't mail them to her. Leave it on my desk. That's some buckle you have on that belt.'

'Like it Mr Smith. Out of an antique shop. I was looking at a brass pig. And just behind it was this buckle.'

'Where is this brass pig.'

'Two blocks over and right across from a building has big sign in front which says Religious Fittings.'

'Thanks Miss Martin.'

Two thirty that unurgent time of afternoon with wandering minstrels toting signs on portable radios, it is possible I may cough again with a transplant throat. Madam I cannot speak but can feel. And past a window full of wines.

And around this corner. There, Religious Fittings. With additional remarks. Crosses our speciality, everyone welcome to come in and look around. Get tacked up. Measurements free.

Smith viewing the large stuffed ape. Under which stood the little brass pig. Overshadowed by the anthropoid's private parts. Miss Martin says she was looking at the brass pig at the time. Mustn't betray eagerness in the shop. Just look as if I'm after a cane or an instrument for some neat little ulterior appetite. I like having satisfied alone. And which I keep tucked away in my personality. Don't like the look of this proprietor.

'Good day, are you the proprietor.'

'What do you want.'

'As a matter of fact I want canes.'

'You want canes, mister.'

'I want canes. Every one in the shop.'

'Mister wait a minute.'

'No.'

'Well wait a minute.'

'No.'

'You mean you want all the canes.'

'Yes.'

'I got two hundred canes.'

'Wrap them up.'

'Hold it. Do you know what you're saying.'

'Wrap them up.'

'I ain't got that much wrapping paper. You don't know what you're saying.'

'Are you questioning my sanity.'

'Yeah.'

'Let me repeat. You own this shop.'

'What do you mean, repeat. You haven't said it once yet.'

'I repeat. You own this shop.'

'Look mister I understand English.'

'And let me repeat. I want to buy every cane in your shop.'

'This is a store. But if you repeat I'm going to repeat. I've had a lot of people come in here in my time. And what is happening at this moment is original. They come in about the ape.'

'A most obscene exhibition too.'

'That's God's problem mister. But you come in about some problem you got, I think.'

'The canes please.'

'I said I got two hundred, what do I know what they cost together.'

'Write a round figure on a piece of paper.'

'How do I know how much two hundred canes are worth.'

'I'm not suggesting you rob yourself. A round figure.'

'What are you trying to do to me.'

'Write a satisfactory figure on a piece of paper. I will fetch a car and you get your bank to phone my bank.'

'Certainly not. You can't make me write anything on a piece of paper what do you think this is.'

'Dear me. You are amusing. Goodness. I can't believe it. Completely irresponsible. Utterly pig headed. Round figure. I repeat.'

'Stop saying that.'

'A simple thing like canes.'

'Mister, before I ask you where you come from, why don't you just buy that jug, look, an antique thermometer, with one of these things tells you the weather. Never have to go outside, and you know it's raining. No insult, but it might suit you good.'

'The instrument looks broken and rather battered to me.'

'What do you expect. Antique.'

'Canes.'

'Can't you get off that subject. Look, here's a table that's got real foreign worm holes. That carving. Right up the leg, a craftsman did it.'

'I'm particularly fascinated by carved canes.'

'Do me a favour mister. Here's a doll, real hair. You could buy a carriage, push it around. I think it would make you feel better because. Look why this chair. Say I got it, here this brass pig. A round figure. Ha ha. That's a good one. How about this.'

'Wrap it up.'

'No kidding.'

'No kidding.'

'Mister thanks, thanks a lot. You sure had me worried. And for you I take ten per cent off. And let for a change me repeat, thanks a lot and merry Christmas.'

George attired in the double breasted suit of the cunning connoisseur, on top of which he wore a great coat with a bear fur collar. Leaving the hairy garment swinging open as he did business. Every little percent helps. And tucking up this brass omnivorous hoofed mammal, reminder of swine everywhere. Smith picked up polish and made it safely to Merry Mansions and past Hugo who pretended to read the early evening paper. Dolt.

Inside Flat Fourteen. Music from the sitting room. White scraps of dishes over the hall. To the left, master's quarters, to the right servant's. One hesitates wondering which way. Well, how do you like this.

'Matilda, I hate interrupting the music.'

'Hey I didn't hear you come in Mr Smith.'

'I'd prefer Matilda, if you'd wear your uniform.'

'What's the matter with what I'm wearing.'

'It's what you're not wearing Matilda.'

'O say that's cute, that's a little pig. Where did you get it. Gee Mr Smith let me feel it.'

'Stand back.'

'What's a matter Mr Smith I just want to feel it. A real cute thing. Mr Smith, you've been worrying again. I know you have. Yes, I see it. You don't fool me. You been to the antique shop to soothe your nerves, I know it. You sit right down there. Here have this pillow. Take your coat. Won't touch that pig. Been thinking Mr Smith, I've got no right to interfere with your business life. No. I've got no right. That's not my place. My place is out there in that kitchen. And in here if necessary to make you comfortable. I just wanted to keep you calm. It's people who upset people. But I think, well, my place is the kitchen.'

'I'm not disputing this little testimony, Matilda. But I come in and find you stretched out on the couch. Appreciate your selection of music. But just making clear you seem to have a place on the couch as well as a place in the kitchen.'

'Mr Smith the resounding crash of those plates in my ears this morning brought it home to me as I was nearly jumping out of my skin in which I was standing at the time, that me and you Mr Smith shouldn't fall out like that, just like the dishes it cracks you up. I just know it does. Loving words that are kind and true, loving deeds and blessings too.'

'I see.'

'My job's to you. Building up the years of faithful service. To go on my record. That's something to be proud of. When they lay me down with the roses all around, lilies, that crazy wisteria, on top, right on that coffin, Mr Smith, so's everyone can see it. That testimonial of the faithful years of service. At those gates, dig that testimonial big God. Note the sacrifice. What's that look, Mr Smith. You sick.'

'I want a bottle of sparkling white wine.'

'Just let me touch this little pig once, Mr Smith.'

'Get back.'

'Gee you're mean. I only want to touch it. Gosh.'

'In due course.'

'In due course my ass.'

'Watch the language.'

'Slave cooking over a hot stove. Sure, you want olives. You go buy a barrel. I got to stand smelling all day. You don't think of that. Hot chocolate drink at night. You find someone to do that. Let me touch your pig. I'm not going to kill it. Here you just feel me. Here come on. That's another thing. You think I'm fat, just feel here, solid I'm telling you.'

'Get some ice in this bucket.'

'Feel me, Mr Smith.'

'Back.'

'It'll astound you. This thigh, Mr Smith.'

'Matilda.'

'Feel, Mr Smith.'

'Our behaviour may be watched.'

'What's a feel, Mr Smith. Before you catch that train.'

'A feel at this moment is foolish.'

'Press here, Mr Smith.'

'Stop getting close.'

'Show you it's not fat, Mr Smith. Feel.'

'My my.'

'Told you Mr Smith. Aren't you surprised.'

'No one would ever know, how solid you are.'

'That Miss Tomson's a bag of bones. Not a nice mattress like me. She tried to knee me, Mr Smith. Right there. And you see her claws.'

Out the window across the street a happy family having ham and cabbage. A mother, father, eight little kiddies. One kiddie getting a wallop across the mouth disappearing from view. He must wonder, that father, what it's like to be free of those burdens. Well mister, in the first place, its marvellous and in the second, again marvellous. See, put lips to the rim of this hand blown glass. Let the white grape have its timorous say on one's chops. My God he's looking at me in a resentful fashion.

'Matilda, draw the drapes.'

George sat chewing the cud over matters. Unhappy memories. The vague muscle in Miss Tomson's arm and the last bang she gave the door and the black mounds of her rear. Is it wrong my mouth waters. Chime of a church steeple tolls seven. How the sound can get through the roar of traffic. Tomorrow morning awake early for a walk in the sun over the snow.

Goodbye to Matilda. Smith on his way out of Merry Mansions. Crossing the lobby just catching that reassuring polished look of himself in the mirror, when confronted by a gentleman just taking off his hat and taking a hanky to wipe cold steam from his spectacles.

46

'I may have introduced myself before, I'm Mr Stone, and of course you're Mr Smith.'

'Hello, Mr Stone and good-bye, I'm catching a train. Compliments of the season, of course.'

'Mind if we tarry a moment.'

'Afraid I do.'

'In that case might I quickly advise you of certain facts.'

'No time for facts.'

'In that case, I may have to insist. A crack is progressing up through the Goldminers' apartment. They are most disturbed by the appearance of this gulch in their wall since it undermines their confidence in the structure of the building which as you know my management has taken great care to keep sound and durable. I'm sorry to have to say such a thing to you, Mr Smith, but the management likes to also give the impression of high tone. We feel the tone was kind of lowered by the noisy chase made up through the building.'

'Merely, Mr Stone, a rather boisterous end to a youth rally. Surely not objected to by any reasonable tenant. A good deal of my time is spent with the underprivileged.'

'Mr Smith it is my sad duty to inform you that while two tenants of the next building lay innocent in their bed and so far as we can judge by the information available, nearly asleep, they were stunned awake to find themselves covered in plaster.'

'Lucky it was not –'

'Please don't say it Mr Smith. I am human too and out for a laugh. But two innocent people of the next building were in their bed asleep and were stunned awake to find themselves covered in, please, plaster. Hugo was on duty. We have evidence members of your youth rally, which again, there's been some question about, that they leaped off the wall nearly going through to these people's bedroom. Luckily the general structure withtook the shock and only the ceiling collapsed.'

'I gather there is a question of money.'

'We shouldn't like to give that exact impression. But of course there is a certain question of satisfaction.'

'My train. Bye bye.'

'Mr Smith.'

'Mr Stone, bye bye, do I make myself clear.'

'Mr Smith you can't. My management has always been impressed by the respectful and high tone of your personal life. Remember the mosaics. The extra thickness of your door. Remember things like that.'

'Bye bye, Stone.'

'Please, Mr Smith, I must be instructed. What about this crack sent up the wall from your apartment. I don't know whether you care but the Goldminers are listening through it.'

'What's that, Mr Stone.'

'I see no way out for you, Mr Smith. The feelings of the Goldminers have been troubled. I don't know if it's what they're hearing or what. But the rapid appearance of the crack was disconcerting for Mrs Goldminer especially. She tried covering it with a creeper but they said the racial atmosphere coming through the opening is killing it.'

'I gather there is again a question of money, if not semantics.'

'Of course again there is the matter of satisfaction, Mr Smith, if not, ha ha, semantics.'

'Be grateful Mr Stone if you would send all further matters and misunderstandings to my business address, where I will take them up without prejudice.'

'As you wish, Mr Smith. I think you have acquitted yourself just as the management would have expected you would.'

'I'm pleased you said that, Mr Stone.'

'We need tarry no longer, Mr Smith.'

'Then this is good-bye Mr Stone.'

'Yes, Mr Smith.'

'Then good-bye.'

'Good-bye Mr Smith. Merry Christmas.'

'And a yingle yule to you Mr Stone.'

Hugo sheepish at the door. How intolerable can this entrance get. Rumour has it he had doings with the aristocracy. Even rode a horse. Hightailing it round a palace on speaking terms with crowned heads. Titillated with his past tone as a present footboy. Merry Mansions had a certain Hilda before the elevator became automatic. With whom, I have it on good authority, Hugo was not past the odd knee trembler.

'Good evening, Hugo.'

This is quite interesting. No answer. Seems he is looking up in the sky at the threatening snowflakes which are beginning to fall. It would seem this could be a struggle of wills.

'I say there, Hugo, taxi.'

This is enthralling. If I had the time one might try a triple hot foot. He heard me speaking to Mr Stone. It would seem in life when all is said and done that it is unwise to speak to anyone if it can be avoided. I don't suppose it has ever passed through his head that I am a shareholder in the management and could lop his ears off.

'I say there, my good man. You there. I say. Bung ho. Over the top. Charge.'

This is quite beyond comprehension. Must have his ear plugs in. Like myself he has had experience with the military. Naturally one tries comraderie when possible. When leading men it is essential not to be scared. Taking the season into account I will not utter some taboo word. I will try volume.

'Taxi.'

Hugo stiffened. Boy how he would like to spin around and snarl. However there was need to shout. Normally I would crawl out into the snow on the fours rather than be unkind. But you see Hugo I must have a taxi to take me to the station.

Snowflakes coming thick round the orange canopy, George climbing in on the leather seat. Pulling bag behind. Door slammed resoundingly. Taxi man saying to Hugo,

'Easy on the vehicle bud.'

'Drive Grand Central please. Want to make an eight o'clock train.'

'Not in this snow, mister.'

'I quite understand.'

'You do.'

'Yes.'

'In that case you'll be there at a quarter to eight or my name's not Silvershit.'

'I beg your pardon.'

'It's terrible. That's my handle. How do you like that for a handicap. Always I know if a guy's laughing in the back of the cab he's checking with my credentials.'

Smith viewing this unfortunate name on the back of the seat beneath the victim's picture. Outside the snowflakes were big and blanketing the streets softly. Exhaust billowing whitely out behind the cars.

Taxi plunging under the gloom of the river bridge. Dark shelter from the snow. Black figure slumped against the stone. George drawing elbows in close around the ribs. Past Golf Street. Ghost of Miss Tomson. Will flit up and down there for years.

'How's that mister, got sixteen minutes to spare.'

'Most impressive. This is for you. Merry Christmas.'

'I can't take this. It would ruin the whole gesture. I know materialism is important but every once in a while I like to fight against it, that way I can really go in for a big kill without feeling guilty.'

The station tonight, straggling late travellers maybe each looking for a companion. But crossing this huge marble hall with just my lonesome self. With the snowy night and nip outside. The pushed down hats and collars up. Groups of girls in furs. Standing at the clock. With bags at feet. Magazines under the arms. All the trains waiting down on the tracks. I go in the entrance over there with a list of wistful destinations. Stop.

Up beyond in the distance on the balcony, the head moving tall and collected above the rail. It isn't. It is. Couldn't be. All the way here I saw her coming out of lavish doorways. Now coming down the steps. She looks like it was all made for her. And it is. I'm overcome to run. With a heart so hurt. God gave me this chance again. If I walk with my head down I could walk right into you. You might just say oaf.

Smith bought a paper. Folding it up under his arm. Nearly put it up in front of the face. Thought my courage was rock solid. Could walk simply up. Miss Tomson, it's me. You look dazzling, unemployed. Knew all you needed was to get away from me. I'll go on your train anywhere you're going. Oaf, I am going on a gold train with silver wheels. Reserved.

Can't face it. Turn away. Collar up. Hunch over and proceed to the entrance where the machine will take me away. A child no longer and must not squirt emotion all over the place. If you have behaved in a dastardly manner reconciliation is abomination. If it has been interpreted that I am low down I shall not give my person to further trampling and general wiping like a mat. To the ramp. And down to the trains.

Slide in on the wicker seat. Executed the swinging of the bag up nicely. I'm sure other passengers noticed how neatly it was done. Double dirty windows looking out in the dark. O.K. conductor, driver, I'm ready to go. But she could have seen my sad back as I went in the entrance. I bent specially over and then with neat linen blew my nose. Had to stop to do this. Then she could have seen the figure I was. Alone, not in the best of taste, a cuff of a trouser eaten away by a moth, and a rubber sole just beginning to peel back from the toe of my shoe. But I picked up the bag again and descended to track thirteen. Hoping desperately for a tap on the shoulder.

The paper says there will be crisp cold. That north of cities and towns there may be flurries of snow, a powdery kind swirling in the wind. And ice will form. Should have brought my skates. But this would have encouraged jeers over the cocktails, Smith behaving younger than his age. Have a good mind to descend to the lake and skate by moonlight. Who was that figure zigzagging like lightning across the ice last night. Ah ha, you cocktailers. Ah ha.

And we move. Train lights dim. Through the pillars across this tunnel I see other trains. All late night travellers so sad and I suspect flatulent. Lamps lit on the tables. Wonder why we all bother coming and going. It's the money gentlemen. I travel for love. I go because I feel while perhaps passing in some strange hall, using some strange toilet I may find a moment of reverie. Or a touch or feel I've not had before. I am fond of stripping the bark from a branch and handling the sappy wood. And out under wild skies when spring is there I take down the dog wood flower and hold it.

Train comes up out of the dark. Swaying swiftly on the tracks past the windows of the underprivileged. Bunch of little thieving carol singers. Where was Miss Tomson going. Seeing someone she can fall in love with. Maybe a socialite she met through her brother. And they'll all be busy with hi, good-bye, hello, so long. She'll go slapping backs. Or go on her own where no one can slap hers. I have no right to object to an employee's private life but I know she would never do these things when she worked for me. Exposed now to the incredible vulgarity of these flashy rich.

Train tonight quite packed. With gentlemen, coats hung up and hats spotted with melting snow. Salary earners. That chap there is smug in his newspaper with pride in his firm. Until his services are no longer required. I have had profit never having had salary. Stacking the former away. Except when pressed to buy some contraption like the happy awaking machine. Leaking on me in a sinking dream. Give it to Matilda. Who sometimes I wonder if she is all right upstairs. What's this idea feel me. Just as I'm sitting in Merry Manse trying to get the whisky down to take the pressure off. She says feel me, go ahead. I expected her to say George any second. No doubt right now she's got the candles burning and my music on. I don't mean it's mine really. She can listen if she wants. Just makes me feel she couldn't possibly be keeping the place clean seduced with some of the tunes I've got which drive Matilda mad. One particular memory gives me shudders. Matilda on her back in the middle of the floor kicking her legs in the air. I said Good God, she's gripped by some malady. I thought give her something but I could see it was no use. I could never get close enough to her mouth. And I did a terrible thing because I was thinking treat shock with shock. And rushed to the closet and ripping it off the wall. I turned the extinguisher on her. She lay wiggling under the great creamy bubbling blanket and said man I just love that. Naturally I called a doctor. And we consulted there in silence ankle deep in foam. Seemingly there was some question as to who was the patient. As God help me, I happened to be in bathing costume.

In the station tonight nearly ten miles back I did not have the courage to go up and just say, Sally hello. And come let's tear a claw off some lobster. I know from experience that no woman refuses to eat seafood. And Miss Tomson with that tall frame to keep trim cannot lightly turn down the protein. There through the train window, a cemetery high on a hill, great white mausoleums, chilled shadowy crazy trees. In there too I have problems which tonight I shall not go into but get up and go to the bar. Down to the end of the train. All the boozers float back here. To sit quietly letting the mind run away.

Smith in the cocktail bar. All blue and smoke where he sat in a club chair as they would seem to have it. Tinkle, the ice rocking in the glasses. People sparkling. Lampposts go by outside. Under which streams the snow. I wear my long red underwear. Calmly under the trouser leg. Waiter in light blue. Only white thing in sight is his towel.

'Waiter, a cocktail.'

'Of what variety or nature sir.'

This is a new sympathetic behaviour I have not noticed before on trains. I think, place the tennis ball back in his court.

'I'd appreciate your suggestion in the matter.'

'Sir, you might try a derobe, popular with our evening travellers.'

'I beg your pardon, waiter.'

'Sir, derobe –'

'I most certainly will not.'

'Sir, it happens to be the name of the drink if you don't mind.'

'In that case make it double strength.'

Must close eyes. Relax. Fold the hands. Wearing red underwear the mere suggestion of undress is frightening. I can't even cross my legs with abandon for fear the garter gives and the red shank shows. For a late train of travellers there seems to be a note of merriment. Can't see down to the end but the laughter could almost be described as obvious. Even sounds like somewhat pushy laughter I've heard before. For once I feel I'm not being watched. Train moving too fast for a telescope to focus. And from the shadows looks like a rather sympathetic bunch of people. Tall with mouthfuls of even teeth with which they smash ice cubes at will. Ah, waiter. I see a cherry goes with the derobe. And a mint leaf. Hopeless to shield one's privates. However looks good floating in this tea tinted speciality.

'Pardon me waiter, how did this rather fascinating name come about.'

'Simple. Woman comes in one evening. Says she wants something really new that no one has ever had before so Franz concocts this. She sits down drinks it, and next we're looking at her stark naked, we almost had to stop the train. So derobe.'

'How refreshing.'

'Took five attendants from the loony to hold her down. Lucky we were near the State Hospital at the time.'

'You don't say.'

'And mister, yours is double. But I think she was crazy before she drank it.'

'Comforting. Thanks for the folklore.'

'Anytime.'

George put his lips to the edge of the glass. Sweet but soft.

Just touch the cherry with the tongue. Nice little cherry. Can never remember no matter how long I mix in circles whether to take the mixer out of the cocktail. Don't like dripping on the table or poking out my eye. What's this standing in front of me.

'Hey don't leave your mixer in the glass.'

'Sally, I mean Miss Tomson.'

'Sally, why not.'

'Sit down, Miss Tomson.'

'I only just got up to go to the ladies. The rocking of the train makes me want to go. See you on the way back. What are you doing on this train. You don't have to answer that, see you on the way back.'

Wham in just a flash she has me intimidated. What a time for her to pee. God let us get off at the same stop together. No God, let me rephrase that. Just let us continue on this train before reaching any stops. I want time. Must be some surreptitious way I could sneak on the brakes. Or even a slight derailment in open country where Miss Tomson and I must trudge through underbrush looking for a farmhouse. But there is none and we've got to make the best of my coat for both of us, trying our level best to conserve body heat by proximity. Passing a river now. My God, there's the cemetery. Thought we had passed it already must have been dreaming. Great white houses of the dead, lonely in there at night. How's my plot. Engineers say some difficulty with the foundations and a reappraisal of costing is necessary. Whoosh. Up goes the price to box me. Never let Miss Tomson see those letters. Get the impression I was deeming demise. Suppose it's foolish of me, but I sometimes feel things are too complicated for me to die.

'Hey anyway, Mr Smith –'

'Miss Tomson will you join me for a drink.'

'Can't. I'm with people.'

'Just one, Miss Tomson.'

'Can't get over it, isn't it rich, you right in here all the time and I didn't see you. No I really can't.'

'You didn't collect your last pay check.'

'Forget it, Mr Smith. Hey you're derobing.'

'Won't you join me ha ha, Miss Tomson.'

'Ha ha, Smithy, since you put it like that, sure. Always willing to take off my clothes. But I can't stay. See down there. No you can't see. But see what you can see, the big blue shadow, that's my brother.'

'Amazing shadow.'

'Yesh.'

'Waiter. Two derobers here.'

'You catch on fast mister.'

George had never been good at the fast remark. Miss Tomson brings that out. Must put up some sort of show. She's been amused down there with her brother and his socialites. She could easily slip back into that life. I'm so nervous. Just not made for making smart remarks. The waiter in his kind anticipation of a tip could see I was new at it. Let me get away without crushing me altogether. I have warm inner feelings which explode resoundingly at boiling point.

'Miss Tomson, I'm glad.'

'What for Mr Smith.'

'I'm just glad.'

'Mr Smith what are you doing on this train.'

'Just glad I took it.'

'You can't be on a train because you're glad.'

'What stop, Miss Tomson, are you for.'

'The last. What's yours.'

'The Junction. I take a branch line.'

'All by yourself, Mr Smith, on this train like this. I can't get over it. Guess you're seeing friends.'

'Not exactly.'

'You're a mystery.'

'What do you mean Miss Tomson.'

'Why don't you find yourself some nice girl.'

'Are you suggesting Miss Tomson I just find some nice girl just like that.'

'Sure just like that. Crazy for a man living alone not getting any.'

'Miss Tomson –'

'And you could get plenty if you got rid of that Matilda. While she's in the house you won't get a smell. I don't mean to sort of go into your personal life or anything, you know what I mean Smithy. It's unnatural.'

'What's natural, Miss Tomson.'

'This is for your own good, Smithy, and you ought to know. That Matilda will suck you dry. Before you know it you'll be one of these guys running around to museums collecting brass monkeys and that kind of thing.'

Miss Tomson had her mixer out. Waiter gave her a tray with hers. Must be the brilliant pile of blonde on her head and the legs. And in this dim blue her hands look longer than anything I've ever seen before. Her fingernails around the glass. A black sweater and pearls.

'You looking at these, Mr Smith.'

'Yes.'

'Pearls.'

'Nice.'

'Real ones. Ought to be hanging right between here but I don't feel like being half naked on a night like this. I just can't get over seeing you all by yourself on this train. Guess that's all right. But Jesus you're taking the branch line as well. Come and meet my brother and his friends why don't you. Maybe you want to be alone. And I'm barging in.'

'Miss Tomson, no.'

'But you don't want to meet anybody do you.'

'Are you coming back.'

'You mean the office. I don't know, Mr Smith, I just honestly don't know. I've been laying in bed late just thinking of it. And I bought a machine that wakes you up with music and pours out hot coffee. Boy you ought to get one. You know that's what you need, Smith. Lacking a loving hand when you wake up.'

'I suppose so. Miss Tomson does your machine spit and grumble.'

'It's magic.'

'Where did you buy your machine, Miss Tomson.'

'It really was a present.'

'O.'

'I couldn't refuse it. On the floor outside my door in the dark. I tripped over it and broke the glass on the clock. And couldn't give it back. Now I don't want to give it back. The guy I gave the cheapest thrill he ever got to. That's who. You know all the while I'm working for you he had me watched. How do you like that. The nerve. My apartment's like a funeral parlour with all the flowers. I say to the boy, take them and give them to your mother sonny or your girl friend. You know what one little upstart says to me, I laughed, he said I like men. Smithy, can't get over this, running into you like this.'

Miss Tomson's hand came down and for a second touched Smith's knee. The train slowing through a station. A strain of Christmas carol. Look out now in the night. Community singers with a Santa Claus ringing a bell. Soon see the lights of the dam and we'll be reaching the fountains all lit up and then it won't be long. Her eyes are even bigger than they seemed before. And lashes longer. Daren't ask where she got the great bracelet. Looks too much like something I might give her and I feel too much like the guy she gave the cheapest thrill he ever got to. The touch of the hand on the knee electrified me. The dam. Great granite face. And the gem like lake below. Lit up. People on the ice.

'Miss Tomson, they're skating down there.'

'Isn't it beautiful. Love to be on that.'

'You skate.'

'On my ass mostly. Maybe you'll give me a lesson sometime. Say where you going on the branch line.'

'Last stop.'

'Just like us on the main line. But that ain't too far, last stop of the branch, from the last stop on the main. Ha ha, sounds like a song. Why don't you drive over.'

'No car, Miss Tomson.'

'Well, why don't we drive over to you.'

If I told Miss Tomson the whole truth I suppose she'd

understand. But I don't even know myself what the truth is. She's got such a good nature. If I let this chance go, it may be gone forever. It is gone forever. Miss Tomson's brother I see somehow on top of me in the snow, take this buster and it wouldn't be a straightforward manly type of defeat like I could feel some pride being prostrated by a fist, but I get the impression from his blue shadow that there would be snow rubbing in the face and my collar opened to stuff snow down my back. And of course the red underwear would excite him to visit even greater ignominy upon me. He may even carry a whip.

'What's the matter, Smithy, you've gone silent. You don't want us to drive over.'

'Forgive me Miss Tomson, just suddenly lately my mind goes vague. I suppose it's a few problems I've got on it recently.'

'We could go skating together. Unless of course you're all tied up.'

'O no, I'm not tied up.'

Roped with cables I guess would be more like it. But how can I explain. What do you do. Can't say let's take this train ride all over again some other time and just plan to meet by accident. With all the night air frosty and hand in hand walking the ice hard ground. Looking for some chalet in the woods. Find it by its curling smoke. A log cabin made for us to have our hot chocolate drink. Or lemon and honey. When I could just lean over and eat her breath.

'What's the matter Smithy. It's O.K., you don't have to say anything. Just a wild suggestion. I used to love these weekends, mad and crazy. But they don't thrill me any more. Just if you didn't have anything better to do, you might enjoy a skate, that's all.'

'Miss Tomson, I'm not really such good company.'

'You're swell company.'

Station name flies by. Another cemetery. Not much time left. Why do they need a junction. Tearing two people apart. Where the tracks divide. She's never said that before, swell company. Bring marshmallows to the side of the pond. Could support her under the armpit to the ice. Permit me, Miss Tomson, to show you how. Could start off with a flashy backwards figure eight, last year did it twice in a row without thundering on my ass. Need only do it once. So many excuses for grabbing her. And of course both of us could thunder down together. Doesn't bear thinking about. Save she'll bring her brother who seems terribly the type who sweeps around the ice so fast you don't know he's there till he's laid you out unconscious with a collision.

Conductor entering the blue haze. All tickets please. Passing with his little punch. Stuffing pockets. Peeling off bills. A little roving business all by itself. Has false teeth. Says, Pleasantville Junction, next. Euphemisms everywhere.

'Smithy. This is a house party. You know, just sort of drop over. You don't go for them.'

'Never seem to fit.'

'They'd go crazy over the bashful conservative way you are. I just wish myself I could be a wall flower like you. Come on Smithy, you got a girl up here.'

'I beg your pardon, Miss Tomson.'

'Don't hand me that I beg your pardon, Miss Tomson stuff. You got some nice rural nest tucked in the woods somewhere. Is she beautiful. A hick, maybe a farmer's daughter.'

'Really, Miss Tomson.'

How do I tell her with only minutes left that there is nothing of the sort. That I want her to come over the country hills. Meet me where I wait at some junction under the frozen winter trees with a gleaming pair of skates slung over my shoulder.

'Smith like all quiet guys, boy. Maybe I'm thinking you're a real operator. Anyway I got to go.'

'Please stay.'

'Your stop's next. Anyway I better get over to my brother, see the way he's rocking back and forth, means he's bragging. Don't fall through the ice with this little dish you're seeing. Thanks for the derobe. And Smithy, really have a good time, I mean it, so long.'

'Good bye, Miss Tomson.'

'Try Sally.'

'Ha ha, Miss Tomson.'

'Ha ha, see you.'

Smith watching her dark figure float away down the blue train. I care so much. Inside me. And wonder why in this world you've got to look you're going someplace. To trains, planes or meetings, otherwise you get ignored. George George George. No sad now. Life is a big bowl of cherries. Provided you get most of them. Just grab. And you'll get Miss Tomson. Sure you will. Have her dark sweatered bosoms. Kissing those mounds like mad. Goodness. And hands gripping each thin shoulder. Four freckles under the right eye. Something awkward happening in my trousers. Which could block the aisle of the train, God and his apostles forbid. Conductors and commuters trying to get past. Watch the pushing, please. O watch the shoves. As George Smith in bare skin. Spiritual. Steps down from the high frosty train on to the snow of Pleasantville Junction platform. Light shines yellow under a green glass shade in the station office. Conductor with lamp and whistle. Swinging and blowing. Train gliding away on the track turning into the winter trees and snowy woodlands.

Smith a solitary figure with his little bag. Save for an old lady and a dog. As the great grey cars click down the rails, window by window, moving away. Give anything to be able to stand in a crowd. She'll be looking out the club car showing me to her brother as they pass. Stand here. Show utter indifference to big country house parties everywhere. Here come the windows. All her friends will be looking too. Ready now, the pose just right. These first windows. No. The second. Must be at the observation glass at the end. Look more indifferent. Gee. Not a soul. To look at me.

> Or get
> The message
> I'm self
> Contained.

5

White clapboard country hotel. The Goose Goes Inn.
Often reminding George regrettably of Mrs Goldminer.
Last night the snow flurries turned into a blizzard. Whiteness now lays heaped high through the morning woods and
pink on the sunny hills.

Smith arrived at the hotel in the dark. And in his room
pulled the curtains over and sat in the big flowered chair
with legs crossed sipping a drink. Said snow you can't get
me all cozy and warm in here. Standing in front of the
mirror, red from neck to ankles. Rotating the throat and
outstretched arms. A little ritual for the good night's sleep.
It's freezing outside. And with that cold thought tuck the
head into the white crisp pillow to sail away on the magic
carpet. First checking the zip on the red underwear. Never
know who might trip to the wrong door in the night. It is
a matter of basic good manners to be properly zipped up.
And then when they say O I beg your pardon, one can smile
and pass for a glowing ember.

Few taps on the phone. Gay voice.

'Good morning, Mr Smith.'

'I think two eggs, toast, honey and coffee.'

'The juice of some fruit, Mr Smith.'

'Not this morning, thank you. Think there'll be ice today.'

'Hard to say Mr Smith, going to be a white Christmas,
sure was a lot a snow last night.'

'Skiing, how's that.'

'Plenty.'

And breakfast on the big maple tray. As Smith snaked up
from behind the blankets when the maid was gone. Toast
hot in the napkin. Pop on the butter and honey. Live and

62

let live. Pour out the steaming dish of coffee. And the train just pulled out of the junction and Miss Tomson never took a peek or gave a wave. Didn't even want her pay. Just disappeared off to her house party and fun with the flashy makers of her life's laughter. Why do the odious manage so well in this world. And people with principles get trampled and kicked and crushed to the bottom of the pile.

And Smith in galoshes, a parcel tucked under each arm, set off down the road from The Goose Goes Inn, walking in a tyre track. By a closed up shack for selling summer vegetables. And another two miles by white fields, to a fork in the road. Where a narrow lane climbed a little hill lined neatly with young trees. And beyond a stone wall the white gabled roof of a house. In the first month I bought it I planted a rare row of saplings along the drive. Carried away by the thought of summer evening strolls under a canopy of leaves. The kids got at them with hatchets. What's left looks all silver now.

Smith gingerly making tracks through the snow, drifts up to the knees. Stone wall with a tall rustic figure and light and sign. Mrs George Smith. I don't suppose she'll be looking out the window or God forbid, down the sights of a gun. Always had a horror of living near roads. Now when I come out here I wish I could hear the odd car go by. Catch my breath. They don't see me coming. She's in there combing out her hair. Which is brown. She used to say when I first met her, hey George grab handfuls of it and pull me down on your knee. I obeyed in a stiff mechanical manner because it was all so overt. Yet once she gave me a whole bowl of cherries and they were side by side on the kitchen table and I thought this will be the test, she's always withholding and depriving and I counted the cherries in each bowl and I was stricken when mine had two more than hers. Found all the good things about her in some secret moment.

Up the little path press the bell and the chimes are ringing. No carefree children's foot prints out in the snow. Maybe they're not up I hear a clatter, and a voice inside.

'It's daddy.'

'O.K., it is. Open up the door and let me in.'

'Hey daddy, you a snowman out there.'

'Please open the door, it's rude to leave someone standing on a doorstep.'

'What's the snow, hard or soft.'

'Please open the door.'

'No.'

If you don't live with kids they grow to hate you. If you live with them they hate you more. Not a shred of respect. Left standing on what technically is my own doorstep. Just one careless night, getting carried away, George pull me by the hair down on your knee. Then end up standing stiff with cold and they won't let you in.

'I'm asking you, quite civilly and calmly if it's you Roger, to open up this door.'

'No. This isn't Roger.'

'Whoever it is, open it.'

'No.'

'Why won't you open it.'

'Because I don't like you.'

'Who's speaking in there, is that you, Wilbur.'

'Stop calling me boys' names.'

'Clarissa.'

'Smart. How did you guess.'

'What's happened to your voice.'

'None of your business.'

'I'm asking you for the last time, Clarissa to open up this door. I'm frozen.'

'It's not your house.'

'It is my house.'

'We live in it and that means we own it and that means I can keep this door shut and you out of here if I want. I guess you understand English don't you.'

'Call your mother.'

'You call her.'

'Where have you learned to be so revolting.'

'Out of a book.'

'Sassy little bitch.'

'And you're a revolting degraded human being.'

Smith chose silence. Toes hardening to ice. Can't see through the steamed up glass. If this goes on any further I'm going to turn on my heel and walk straight back to the hotel, pack and if necessary hitch hike back to town. After a couple of miles ramble through the snow overstraining my heart I have to stand here and take this offence. Can see what open country, summer green fields and shady woods with crystal lakes do for kids. Makes them into savages. Ah, a sound of authority.

'Just a moment George, it's bolted with half a dozen locks. Now get, Clarissa.'

'Thanks. I'm frozen.'

'Come in, you're early. Just lost my slipper coming down the stairs. Forgive the chaos. Roger and Wilbur were building a jail on the stairs last night.'

'For me I suppose.'

'Don't be so sensitive.'

'Naturally one wants to feel welcome.'

'Well, all right, you're welcome, George. Give me the galoshes. Take a seat and I'll get you a drink. What would you like.'

'I had a derobe on the train last night.'

'Is that you being objectionable or a drink.'

'Just a drink.'

'I'll make you one. How do you make it.'

'I don't know. I don't know anything.'

'Don't bleed all over the furniture now.'

'It's two miles walk here.'

'I know.'

'Well what do you mean don't bleed over the furniture. I've come in an absolutely friendly mood. Ha ha, he he. Just bubbling with good nature.'

'So am I, ha ha.'

'And get locked out on my own doorstep.'

'O.K. George, I know you own the house.'

'Just an ordinary decent reception is all I'm asking for. And I get abuse.'

'Do you have to take a young child seriously.'

'A revolting, degrading human being. No father wants to hear that.'

'Well you heard it.'

'That's what I'm saying.'

'And George, I'm saying don't sit bleeding over it.'

'Welcome. Come in George. Sit down George. Attempt a pleasantry.'

'A gruesome pun.'

'Even so, you ask me if I'm trying to be objectionable.'

George leaning back. Stare out at the family unit. Her handfuls of brown hair. I have never asked my kids to treat me like God. Or for that matter even like some saint. O I've been guilty. Shouted when I should have shut up. Shut up when I should have shouted. I admit those things. Lashed out when the child was only trying to give me a friendly punch in the kidneys. Even got down on my knees with the toys and they tell me get away, you're ruining our game. I said O.K. kids I don't mind, youth wants to play together. Youth is exuberant. All I was trying to do was push one of the little trucks up the ramp and they push me away. Why should I mind. Haven't I been honest with you kids. What's the matter, don't you get enough to eat and the best of everything. I never had toys like this as a kid. They look up at me and say coldly, don't blame us, we weren't your father. And when feelings are hurt. O.K. that's that. But make no mistake, I've got feelings.

'Georgie, boo. Georgie. Boo. Here's a nice little cocktail for Georgie. Made it all my ittle self.'

'Look Shirl, it's a long way in the snow out here, if you don't want me, say so right now.'

'You say that every time you come, George. You're dressing differently George.'

'I'm sorry.'

'Don't be ashamed, George, it's an improvement. How's fat.'

'I'm not answering that.'

'George she's fat. O.K. how's Matilda.'

'She's all right.'

'Make nice yummy meals as usual.'

'Matilda's quite adequate as a cook.'

'Well guess so long as that's all you use her for that's swell.'

'For your information I don't fornicate with my servants.'

'No one has ever suggested such a thing. Excuse me while I get dressed, the kids are locked in the cellar, you're safe.'

'Very thoughtful.'

'Knew you'd see it that way.'

Smith saw cross the sitting room. Wide maple floors. Great brick oven fireplace and glass doors to the garden shutting out the winter. Nearly ten years ago. My God I was young. And today take a frosty journey to suffer a stream of smart remarks. The way I met her first by paying for her ticket on a train and I've been paying for her ever since. When people are fidgeting through a handbag with a conductor hanging over you, naturally you want to be of assistance. And so for my few pennies of kindness I purchased a nice background of fast back chat, the big pile of brown hair, George get your hands in this, shoe bills, George you know how I need a change since everybody looks at my legs. Then once in the courtship she said she wanted to say something serious, something she knew I would understand and she wouldn't be misunderstood. She said promise you won't mind. I said of course. She said George, I know you speak very educated and I know there are awful things like those who live on one side of the tracks and those who live on the other side of the tracks. Well, this is my problem, you know what side of the tracks I'm from and it's not my fault that it's the best side, but what side of the tracks are you from, George. Don't answer if you don't want, George. You're hurt now George, aren't you, that there's a track running between us. It's only sometimes, George, that your grammar and I know you may be only using this sort of usage to be funny, but even your selection of ties and shirts, now please, we both know that there are two sides to every track and matters not a damn really except that there are two sides. George what side of the track are you from. And we had that little talk on a train. Which while we were talking was putting people on their side of the tracks. I was confused and must admit terribly flustered. I had no warning except having a remark of mine remade by her and she'd add, sounds better that way. I never told her what side of the tracks I was from. And I suppose she assumed it went right through my house. Wow was I deeply shocked by her question and woo hoo, surprised she ever felt it needed an answer. And a big dark hand came out and pushed the sun out of our togetherness. Still I took a fistful of the brown hair. With no mention of tracks when I was taking it.

'Penny for your thoughts, George.'

'O I was just thinking.'

'About money.'

'No.'

'Do you like these things you just slip on. Do you think it suits me, don't you think it has that Saturday lunch about it.'

Shirl stopping abruptly to shift a hip in front of George, throwing out the cloth just so. This Friday lunch feeling, the snow outside, kids in the cellar, the presence of the kid's father, a half mile of open country in every direction two feet deep in whiteness.

'Hey George stay for dinner and I'll show you something else I got, gorgeous things for feet in gold thread. Hey. Your mind's so far away, George. You take being a father so seriously. Trudge through the snow with your little presents. Get left on the stoop of your own house. Do we cost too much.'

'Enough.'

'We cost too much.'

'You're saying it, not me.'

'How's business, George.'

'Depressingly full of insult.'

'O you poor ruthless thing, let me get something cold to put on your head.'

68

'I think I'll be going. There's no point having you irresponsibly get at me. As regards cost, I'm indifferent.'

'So funny how you changed. You must have been the tightest guy I ever met. Remember the time –'

'Now shut up.'

'Gee.'

The time was a dance. Not long after I met her on the train. I was leaning out with my hand to touch her on the eight o'clock summer evening like to take a handful of that brown thatch. She said don't touch me. She saw what this remark did to my face. She said O touch me, but later tonight when the dance is over, I don't want to look mussed. Touch me then, then I'll love being touched. She said people will have to see me tonight, I want to look well groomed, just that I hate being touched, well like a meal on the table before everyone is ready to eat, you don't want me to feel all tampered with, don't you want to save it all for later. I took my hand away, and wore it in my pocket. I went standing around the dance, along the edges when the couples glided by and she smiled over the shoulders. The music stopped, she ran right across the floor, grabbed me, hands on the lapel and said we're all going road housing and wild and ending up at the country club, it'll all be crazy hitting the golf balls in the lake, and crazy when we get really crazy. I put my other hand in my pocket and was wearing them both there, she said what's the matter, I said I didn't know, she said you do, I said it's expensive a night like this. She just said there's Claude. And Claude never wilted at expense, just went into his thin folder and took out a single note of massive denomination. I should have turned then for home. But I couldn't because she would have gone with them and what if the night were crazy and she could say when she was a meal ready to eat, grab me by my brown thatch. I went in another car, she was a plaything for the crowd. At the top of a table suggesting all the songs. Dripping candle wax on Claude's hair and he worshipped her for it and it just made him look like the victim of some crime following after of course the crime his father and mother committed getting him. She made him open his mouth and she dripped it down his throat. I thought she was carrying my being a cheapskate too far. I got up, walked across the maple, stepped through, and on the flag stones looked out at the shadows of the hills and down over the trees to the long lake. Hands flat out on the wall and she came out and saw me and thought I was vomiting. I said I ought to be. She said you have no rights on me, I'm not your possession, these are my friends, I've known them most of my life, if anything they have more claim on me than you have, but if you'd stopped your little act of silence and sulking and joined in the fun or if you just said you had no money, that you couldn't afford, or said something like that, why wouldn't I understand, I know some poor people too, but they don't mind spending money. She stepped back, put her hand under my chin and lifted it up. She said look at me, I want you to look at me, I'm commanding you to look at me, now smile, smile, bigger, O.K. you can take a handful of my brown thatch.

And today ten years later and three days before silent night holy night when business volume is at a peak and downstairs a loud bellowing noise in the cellar with four kids pounding on the pipes. And Shirl swirling with her new cocktail dress. And I told her to shut up, and wham she goes all silent. My how things have changed. There was reason for my being the way I was. When I was young. When Shirl one weekend fell for some big blond brute who she said lifted her up and kissed her against a wall with her feet dangling. But we had got too close then and she went away a weekend begging she had to, would I let her go because she needed to stay in circulation just so she could still stay exciting to me. She said let's play with each other's emotions. Torture each other with jealousy, let's George betray the faith we have in each other and build it all up again after. And just this one weekend with the blond brute, so she could walk in the gates of the college and the blond brute could brag about how she was his date. She came back to me with not much to say except when she talked about it she got shifty eyed and started breathing heavily. Then she said I hate the way you are, you never tried to stop me.

'George, I got an engagement tonight after dinner, so you don't mind we can call a car maybe to take you back.'

'I see.'

Shirl when she says things picks something up off a table. Puts it back. Then she goes towards the kitchen and talks over her shoulder. Wags her behind. A neat compact soft thing in the days when I was in a position to feel it. I suppose if I just went up to her now and touched it. But I have no right to presume in our separated state that I could lay hand on this part of her. There's little more than I can take of this kind of thing, because I ought to take her and the dress off and give her a boot out in the snow. No one around here to complain, Mr Smith seen driving the stitchless Mrs Smith into the elements. I own this land.

'George, you're wearing your sense of ownership on your face.'

'It's my face. You've got your own face.'

'Gee thanks George.'

'Anytime. What's your engagement.'

'Interested. You want to come. These people are dying to meet you. Because you've got such a weird reputation. The way you swam at the island picnic last year. Everyone was impressed the way you dove into the cold water and stroked superbly out to the float, the masterful smoothness of your movements, I personally know for a fact all ladies were desperate to wiggle out of bathing garments and dive after you.'

'Are you finished.'

'George if you saw yourself. If you hadn't been so flamboyant no one would have minded.'

'I almost drowned. That's not amusing. I took a very discreet dive. I have never tried to show off swimming.'

'Sometimes I wonder where all the big strong men in this world have gone. If there ever were any.'

'I was drowning. Big strong men can drown as well as people like myself. I mean I'm not all that weak.'

'Boxing and wrestling lessons at The Game Club.'

'Who told that.'

'Never mind. Got your face beat in, too, I heard.'

'Balls. Who told you that. I want to know where you got that information.'

'Ittle George.'

'Shut up, Shirl.'

'I guess this is just like all our weekends. O you're just one big great long bluff.'

'I reject that.'

'George what's that. Hey what's that red thing. You're not wearing long red underwear.'

'I'll wear whatever I feel like and stop torturing me.'

'George, you're made for it. Look at what I had to do to make you masterful. And soon as I made you masterful and you made money –'

'Do not mention money, Shirl.'

'So anyway I made you masterful.'

'I'm masterful myself.'

'The only time traffic will stop for you, George, is when you're dead.'

'Get me my galoshes.'

Dust sifting through the sunlight. When the silence gets terrible and Shirl sees an ash white face on a once gentle Smith. Like a sudden thoughtful finger up to her lips.

'George. I'm sorry I said that.'

'It's all right, get me my galoshes.'

'I really am sorry I said it. I wish I didn't say it. Strike me for saying it, George. Strike me anywhere you want.'

'I'll get the galoshes myself.'

'George I beg of you to strike me for saying it. I say the wrong things. That come into my head and I wish you wouldn't listen.'

Shirl silent at the door. Leaving it open with the chill wind rushing into the house as George walked out. The lane along the orchard, in summer such a sweet place of tall grass and black snakes. And now they must be sleeping under the rocks. And it seemed on the air that a voice shouted something more but it got cold and hushed. Snow plough moving down the road, leaving a wide track and high drifts. Driver wearing orange ear muffs. Only thing I noticed. And going all the way back I hardly knew I was going. Could have relented, tucked down the dinner and took a car back. I'm like that. Withdraw utterly from the ultimate insult. And left the kids in the cellar. Not that they like me anyway. Take my money, and then look me in the eye and say who asked you to be our father. That's the kind of remark those kids make. They were watching out a cellar window, heard their mother screaming she didn't mean it, that she'd take it all back. Be a new one for the kids. Gee, dad was like a clam, walked right away in the snow and he never turned around.

The Goose Goes Inn with several cars collected and some guests throwing snowballs one of which caught Smith between the shoulder blades making a round white blot on his coat as he climbed the hollow wooden steps. His dispirited nature and oblivion drew some comments about the fellowship this time of year of some people wasn't worth mentioning. Inside, the Christmas tree, tinsel and strains of music of the modern yule variety from the cocktail lounge. Crossing the lobby for the key.

'Sir there have been three phone calls.'

'I'm not in to anybody.'

'Not to anybody. They said it was urgent and tell you soon as you got in.'

'I'm going for a nap.'

Worried looking receptionist. Don't worry, it's just Shirl who thinks I may be wiring instructions to my bank where they've got all my legal tender neatly stacked from which they take and send a handful often to Shirl. She's afraid she might have to sell her horse and the kids' ponies, cut down the guest list, summer itineraries. While I sit in that box with my secretary's ex boyfriends spying from buildings across Golf Street. Opening letters of obnoxious intimidators. Sure, go ahead, buy that fabric with the lunch look, get a dinner, breakfast, any look you want.

Sadly Smith derobed. Plunging into a steaming shower to unfreeze the muscles and bones. And put a face to the showering water and breathe it up the nose. Feel it cascade off the privates so lonely these days. Only thing bright about climbing into this afternoon bed is the red underwear. To sleep, lay with a hand outstretched on the pillow, open, palm upwards, will someone's head lie back in it, tighten a fist up in the brown thatch. Can you ever go back to bodies where you've been, once you've left. Count the cherries in the bowl and see if I've got the most. Join hands while music plays. See summer lanterns burn the fireflies. Or walk by an autumn river, stand against a tree just seeing each other in the ordinary afternoon. You make a baby. Then you can't sleep at night. Go to a park bench for two years to catch up. Another baby comes. Finally one day you can breathe. And these former babies tell you stop breathing.

Smith rolled over, pulling up the crisp sheets. Digging toes down. Self employed slave. Shirl never made me masterful. If anything she's contributed to my cringing. Dazzling crowds in train stations the tanned beauty in white linen suits while I was just walking along behind looking like her employee. Telling me to do the right thing so people will be impressed. No one could take their eyes off her eyes, her legs, hair and I started grabbing on all sides. Goodnight now. And hello. I see a woman walking along a road wearing nothing but a cardboard sign which she's showing me and it says be my valentine. And jumping into a fast car, making for the highest hill, I erected another sign which you can see for miles around and it said, in no uncertain words, you bet.

The phone by George's bed was ringing and ringing. It's dark. Must be late. Grab this ringing thing. Just pushed my glass of water over. I can't face turning on the light. O.K., what is it, phone, what are you going to tell me out of that black hole.

'Mr Smith.'

'Yes.'

'Sorry to disturb you but there seems that there is a Mrs Smith –'

'No calls from Mrs Smith, please.'

'But she's not calling, Mr Smith.'

'What is she doing.'

'She's smoking and having a drink.'

'You've just woken me out of a sound sleep to be flippant.'

'She's in the lobby. Said she'd stay till I got you.'

'Tell her to go away.'

'Mr Smith I'm afraid you'll have to do that yourself.'

'Tell her to come up.'

'Yes.'

God here I am in the red underwear inviting disaster and laughs. Better to face this situation stark naked. She'll wonder what I'm doing in bed at eight thirty in the evening, my life, my body, I'll put it in bed whenever I want. Second thoughts which I'm making first again, I'll leave on the red underwear. What am I, unclothe myself just to suit her. Come to show me the gold slippers. Just tell her simply, the cheques are still going to come, O I'll keep pouring the money in, keep those little kids healthy so they can tell me to my face that I am a big unwholesome cad. This is new, a discreet knock.

'Come in.'

'George, may I.'

'You may.'

'No light.'

'I know.'

'Where are you George.'

'In bed.'

'Can't we have some light.'

'No.'

'Well can I come in.'

'Come in.'

'Should I close the door.'

'Close it.'

'Is it all right with you if I sit down.'

'By all means. There's a chair three paces to your right.'

'Thank you George.'

'Any time.'

'I've got it.'

'Good.

'Can I talk, George.'

'Sure.'

'You know what I want to say, George.'

'Beep beep.'

'What's that funny noise you're making.'

'You mean, beep beep.'

'Yes, beep beep.'

'O that's just beep beep.'

'Sounds strange coming out of the dark.'

'Beep beep.'

'George.'

'Yes Shirl.'

'George.'

'I'm listening Shirl.'

'I sound so loud in the dark.'

'Beep beep.'

'Don't do that George. Please.'

'Beep beep.'

'I know I deserve it George.'

'Deserve what.'

'Beep beep.'

'Beep beep.'

'George are we cars.'

'You said it.'

'I wanted you to see my gold slippers George.'

'Too dark.'

'Yeah. But do you want to feel my gold slippers.'

'Stand back.'

'I know I deserve it George. Do whatever you want to me.'

'Pretty risky talk.'

'I want to be risky.'

'What are you doing Shirl.'

'I'm undoing.'

'Beep beep. I'm a car.'

'This is the way we used to be, George.'

'I've just stopped for traffic lights.'

'Are you sitting up George.'

'I'm waiting for the lights to change.'

'And we should have been like this more often. Don't you think, George.'

'Beep beep, I'm going again.'

'Should we have a crash.'

'Are you suggesting I'm not a careful driver.'

'No George.'

'Well watch it, beep beep.'

'I can see you George. I can.'

'He he. I can you too, Shirl.'

'We've wasted so much time, George, haven't we.'

'Don't drive your car too close.'

'I want you to crash into me.'

'Safety first.'

'George.'

'What are these Shirl.'

'Feel them.'

'Wow.'

'Feel this.'

'What is this Shirl.'

'This is what I want you to feel.'

'I'd be a fool to feel it.'

'Be a fool and feel it.'

'What a foolish feeling.'

'Just because you're feeling foolish.'

Reach out a hand to help. It's only polite. And she puts up her wrist and a hand softer than I ever thought it could be. This holiday in the country in the red underwear. O I raged. Of course I was insulted. How did she get over to the bed, in just the gold slippers. Climb right up on top and sit on it like a flagpole. I was thinking of just going into the village to buy a soda. Miss Tomson please don't go loose and lax at the holiday house party, all yule and yessy. Or engage with the empty balled vice presidents. What right have I to persist, I daren't even call you Sally in my dreams. Just press my face into Shirl's headlamp. Most comforting thing you can do. I hate cars. But amazing the lies you get up to in order to bring upon complete delusion. She's just come here like this to use me. Not for my personality but my organ.

'You like it, George.'

What can you say to that. No. I don't like it. I suppose I could have a machine under the bed answering back in firm tones, yet giving way slightly to the emotional excitement of the time. Gee, Shirl. And Miss Tomson you touched my knee however briefly or lightly you touched it. I'm glad you didn't lean forward and grab. It was a movement of the arm. That light tap on the knee. Wanted so much to see your face and your wave goodbye. I was too full of seeing myself watched by the whole train as passengers wiped the sweat from the windows, all faces pressed on glass and they all began to sing together, up out of their seats, train's leaving, rush to the end of the car and all wave, can't see the faces for the hands, or Miss Tomson's because they're all so sad I'm gone, in there struggling to say goodbye to me. The train just clicked down the track away. And I was left.

'George I like my bread and butter.'

Only that it's dark someone would be watching us from a far hillside with field glasses. I can't match Shirl's lightning conversation. Am I her bread and butter. Does she spread me. Like now. This could not have happened with the lights on when we would have behaved like adults. She's stitchless save slippers just like her bravado in early marriage when I told her I would never have her scramble my eggs without her clothes on. No nude cooking. Garments must be worn in the kitchen. When we early loved she said she liked to hold it, talk to it, tell it stories as it stood and rub it softly on her eyes, good for the sight. Now grabs my belly in handfuls. Just to bring out my inferiority. For her age not bad, still built. Women flower annually and maybe

I'm catching her in bud or she's in bud and I'm her bee. And if I gave orders for the parade. Shirl shows up with cigarette holder. Of course the first four will carry drums. Naturally, why wouldn't they carry drums. It is agreed among us that the rear shall be brought up by a steam organ. A musical one.

'Fat belly George, what are you mumbling.'

She butts in just as I was going to give the signal for the parade. Let us again recast the scene. Four drummers first. The balloon carriers each with a hand on the hot steam organ will naturally bring up the rear. Shirl, will you get back, out of the way, I happen to be the director of this parade. Yeah, I'm the director. Not be intimidated by your breasts which drove me into wedlock, sagged and stared at me ever since. I had the steam organ specially brought from a country where it was the last one. You've always wanted to steal the stage from me. Until naturally I got up this here parade to bring back my self respect. Now get back in line with the rest. You heard me. Get back. Now I want four people to come forward and volunteer to carry the community chest. In which of course is the brass pig. All employees of George Smith please step forward and take your places in the central position. Gosh, only Miss Martin. Get back Shirl. You just spend my money, you don't help me make it. Put away that cigarette holder and wipe that smile off your face. O.K. all of you to whom I have given scrolls of merit, hold them up. Gee, I hope you deserve them.

'George don't slip out it's a year since you were in.'

I'm just ready to give the signal to march but I can't with these constant interruptions. The steam organ is losing valuable steam. Almost forgot the friends I had in childhood. Slip them between people who live in Merry Mansions who have just rushed out because the Goldminers set it on fire. Members of The Game Club take up the rear, each carrying an acorn as an item reminding us that any one of us can get bigger than we appear on the surface. Shirl get back in line. Nobody wants to keep in line these days. All out for special attention. Do it once more Shirl and you're out of the parade for good. And cut out the immoral gestures, no one's stopping this parade for turpitude. My God, Miss Tomson. Just going to start without you. You could lead it. I've just jumped out of an alley and wrote your name with a bucket of paint over a giant wall. Didn't have the crass to put Sally. People said it was physically impossible to do it while being director of the parade but I did it. Till those dirty little urchins came along and ruined my heartfelt statement with another one. O.K. ready everybody. My goodness, just looked down in time, my fly's open. An order under these circumstances would sound ridiculous. If not downright impertinent. Hold it, folks. Must tidy myself up a bit. Get back in there and don't come out again till I tell you. Naughty. All right now. Ready.

'George.'

Don't shout my name in vain. You've done every sly thing to ruin the parade. With the tables set in the park. Where we were going to march to eat with banners, streamers red white and blue. And the organizers would have given out prizes. While the directors watched from the stage. I know what you would have done Shirl, gone up to the microphone and sung a song into it. Embarrassed me as director. Because you wanted to appear before the public. Hear your voice floating over the crowd. So they would clap and cheer and say you're great. And I was only an acquaintance. From the other side of the tracks. You've interrupted my parade for the last time. Boom boom boom. Just got it going again. Thank you drummers.

'George what parade, shut up, it's up and enter me again.'

'Shirl watch the underwear.'

'What made you wear red.'

'A predilection.'

'Take it off, it rubs me.'

'You're holding my head down by the ears and stop tearing the garment, Shirl.'

'Kiss my bazumma.'

'Shirl, you're tearing the garment.'

'I'm pulling the zipper.'

'It's tearing the garment Shirl and is caught in the hairs of my belly.'

'It rubs me.'

'I didn't ask you to come in here.'

'George you wouldn't turn on the light. Shut up and take a handful of hair. You were so nice when you were a car. Drive you bastard.'

'Beep beep.'

'Kiss my bazumma.'

'Stop telling me what to do Shirl. I've got my own mind.'

'I'm the hottest handful you've had for months.'

'Don't be too sure.'

'So you've been into Matilda.'

'That remark is false.'

'Was she a good fuck, I don't mind.'

'I repeat that remark is false and your use of language regrettable.'

'Ha ha George.'

'Ha ha Shirl it's not funny.'

'Once more, fast George.'

In this rural retreat of The Goose Goes Inn, the Friday before the Tuesday of Christmas. I wake to find my person used for a motive of which I had no notion. Torn out of the red underwear. Bereft of that red safety. Shirl a master at that tempting tickle, cupping up pearls blowing a warm air saying it was bigger than she remembered and she had memories. Till the energy I was conserving to get back to town, all gone. She'll take this as a renewal of hatred. A right to snoop round Eagle or Golf Street. Once getting hands on her, can't get them off. Deepest darkest kisser. And what can you do when it's upright. As she says wow. When it's downright rude to do nothing.

'Faster George, my friends are waiting.'

Snowy owl hoots. Hear him out there in the night. When all the other animals are snug or more likely tearing each other and feathers apart. And in here I am agog and speechless at this last remark. I am no machine. I am no piece of old rope. I'll pretend the physical excitement has made you utter statements without meaning.

'Hurry George.'

Between the parted curtain shines the white so white romantic moon. Right across the carpet, half way up the wardrobe and on the sleeve of my shirt. You're just getting carried away Shirl. Since you haven't as I hope you haven't, had any for a while. Ha ha, friends are waiting. I suppose if I had any mine would be waiting too. We've come together panting mechanically which is what disturbs me. I should have said no.

'Faster George, harder. Now you know why I ride horses.'

The village church bell rings, quarter mile down the road. We're in here like this with flowers on the bedroom curtains and on the chair. Shake your brown thatch all out over your shoulders, be the last time I'll grab. I will not go faster.

'My friends are waiting, George.'

In summer on this road they sell the stacked up pumpkins, purple aubergine and zeplin watermelons. And fresh farm eggs. Not for nude cooking I said. And Shirl this is a joke no longer.

'Shirl what do you mean your friends.'

'They're waiting down stairs.'

'They're what, Shirl.'

'Waiting.'

'Get out of this bed.'

'Hey we're not finished.'

'I will not give myself to being used while your friends wait for you. Get out.'

'I'm not dressed.'

'Get out.'

'You're not pushing me naked into a hotel hall, George, you're not doing that. That's one thing you're not doing.'

'I am doing. Out. Into the hall.'

'No.'

'Go to your friends. Waiting for you. Bunch of ambitious

little commuters. O Shirl's just upstairs having a throw with some guy. Don't make me a laughing stock.'

'You are already. Everybody knows how you make your money. And they laugh, boy do they laugh. They laugh because they know.'

'You take it from me and spend it.'

'I wish I didn't because it's horrible money.'

'I reject that.'

'And they know what happens with that nigger in that apartment. Don't try to fool me.'

'Simply get out of this room before I lose my temper.'

'Always knew you were from the wrong side of the tracks.'

'A little vulgar fantasy of yours.'

'It isn't. You sneaked into society.'

'I see. I'm in society now.'

'They saw you sneaking, don't worry. My friends know. Your phoney little cultivated habits.'

'I reject that.'

'Mosaics all over your stupid house. How they let you in The Game Club I don't know. And trying to make some baronial hall sowing trees up our drive. My friends were wise to that, don't you worry. Can't find my things. I want the light on.'

'You came in in the dark you go out with all lights off.'

'You rat. I'm glad I can't see your face. It's the only way I could bear you fucking me.'

'I think perhaps you've said enough.'

'Tell me to get out. And I'm going.'

'Splendid. Bring your little playmates downstairs with you.'

'You bet I will. You'll hear from my legal counsel.'

'Can't wait.'

'My friends are better than you are and I'd like to know where all that other money goes. And I'll find out. You can't kid my lawyer, he's smart.'

'Since I pay for him I'm glad to hear that.'

'I ought to have half of what you possess.'

'Ha ha.'

'Go ahead and laugh. Where's my purse. You'll be laughing. Boy you'll be laughing. I'll make you laugh. You'll laugh all right. Boy you'll be laughing.'

'Ha ha.'

'Laugh all you want. Go ahead. But I'll squeeze you dry.'

Across the room somewhere in the dark there was the momentary silence. Four hoots of that snowy owl. And summer comes back and the tangled worms squirming in the white silk nets they weave in wild cherry trees.

'George, George, what terrible things am I saying.'

'You were saying, boy, you'll be laughing. And I'll squeeze you dry.'

'George, I'm scared and shivering. What's making me shiver. Turn on the lights. I'm scared the things I'm saying.'

'Can't you find your purse.'

'No George and I'm scared. Don't throw me out. I didn't mean that about legal counsel.'

'Forget it.'

'George, I can't. What about the kids. God legal counsel. Don't make me go to court George.'

'I'm not making you go to court.'

'They'll scream down at me. I know they'll scream down at me. A judge with white hair. He'll eat up my soul George.'

'Don't be silly.'

'Never make me go before a judge, George. As you lie there now promise me that. I'm scared. Let me sit. I'd be accused. The judge would accuse me and it would be horrible.'

Can see the shadow of her hair. See the shoulders she covers with her shirt. And I know she's breaking right in two. Tears pouring down her cheeks. Wait and the sniff and sob will come. Shirl all women cry. The lousy life. But outlive men. I mean you no harm. Let no judge get you. Even on judgement day. When all the country yokels are clustering in the trees and I step down the steps of my tomb. To cheers. Remember under the snow lies summer. Done that for a lot of years. Can sit then sucking a straw of grass and it hardly matters nearly that one is in society. Or that I went out in the world ruthlessly. Maybe sneaking across the tracks. Shirl you're crying. I could cry too. I went so far in the snow today. Walked back along the tracks in the road where it was hard. Thinking so much about the silence you hold like a child's hand and it was all up over the hills. I came last night when it was snowing. A rich man. The papers said it would be crisp and cold. At the junction it began to snow. I was hurt when the train left. I hate anything to leave. Stay. Stay longer. I only told you to get out because it was a fiasco. Paper hats and jumping bodies in the lobby. Tell me nice things and I'll believe them forever. Shirl don't cry. What harm really for a fast one and for you to run down and meet your friends and go out speeding over the snowy roads and even sit on a stranger's knee. Why should I mind. Except that I suppose I have no friends. Save one old one standing staring at me at some excavation site when I ran. So Shirl little girl. Dry up your eyes. I've got your purse here under my pillow. And now I'll give it back. Made of mesh like your slipper. And you can go away then. Out to friends. I think you're right, the only time traffic will ever stop for me.

> Is when
> I'm dead.

6

Christmas Eve. And this Monday morning George Smith dressed in black passed out the lobby of Merry Manse. Hugo some yards up the street in conversation with another doorman. But the chauffeur was there with door open of this long low wide black gleaming car. A tinted green glass between Smith and driver. Who said his name was Herbert.

And last Saturday I sent Shirl dogwood blossoms. Wax this time of year. And sat near the phone in my room in The Goose Goes Inn before I left on Sunday. It never rang. And I could not cheer her up. She left the room bent and sad. And perhaps never played with her friends. In the village I had a pineapple soda midst a lot of larking kids. Then trudged in the little cemetery knee deep in snow, reading names and poems.

Sunday I rested my bag on a cart and sat beside it in the railway station. Feeling sad for all little children. The cold evening. Lights blinking on. In the tavern just beyond the war memorial a jukebox played. Heard the train engine roaring, its light shining down the white tracks, almost empty, streaked and stained. Got off at the junction and had a cup of hot chocolate. Kept me warm looking out at the winter evening the rest of the way to the terminus.

Merry Mansions Sunday night, with loud parties in the distance. Matilda said she was going to have a good time at some heaven. And George Smith sat alone staring across the room. And out the window for a bit, at a roistering gathering of folk across the street. A city full of fathers with gathered arms of presents to give and get, this complicated time of year.

And now Monday morning, day before the great birth, in

this car crossing town in the jammed traffic. George Smith sitting one leg folded upon another, ankles in black silk, cane and briefcase. Slipping off his dark capeskin gloves. A lap full of mail. The season's summonses. Without glad red berried holly leaves. Deep long lasting and sincere. Heartfelt wishes this time of year.

Car speeding up the ramp to the highway, tyre chains gripping and humming on the hard snow. Past parked ocean liners, tall ships, steaming funnels and rust stained anchors hauled up against the bows. Ice flows in the river. And across it, a bleak winter skeleton of an amusement park stands on top of the hard straight cliffs.

Smith opening up the mail. To each a quick glance. One school chum, alas from an institution. A risque one from Matilda. A big santa claus holding a bottle of whisky from the kids. Nothing from Shirl. Others blaring good business and prosperity. Make a million throughout the coming year. And happy new year too. And what's this, amid this. Within this. Poor quality envelope, a little letter from far away. Hold it on my dark knee. Makes me blink.

Post Office
Cool Village
December 19th

Dear Mr Smith,

I am sorry to have to acquaint you with bad news. On December 14th your mother died peacefully and your father passed away in the same manner yesterday, Tuesday the 18th, your mother having gone the Friday before. They both told me while they lived that they did not want to bother you as they knew you were a very busy man. Your father said I was not to give you any bad news that might worry you. But since he has now passed away too, I am writing. I hope to the right address which I found in your father's papers, and that this reaches you. As your whereabouts has been unknown.

The details are that the clergy found a definite sum of money of which they will tell you soon, which they found useful for expenses regarding the undertaking and costs of other arrangements. They knew you would wish a suitable stone and they selected their grave under the yew tree in the old cemetery near the big rock. I know you may know this burial ground has been out of use but it is now believed here by anyone of the modern out-look that the rumoured vampire has been driven out, having been dealt with by the Clergy with a good sprinkle of the holy juice.

And I would like to add a personal note myself that the dear old couple minding their own business may rest in peace. I know it is such a blow to you I will not add further news. Except that the passing away is much mourned here in the village. It seems there are enough twisters and chisellers loose on the roads these days trampling graves of honest respectable people that I don't mind telling you the old folk are a loss. And condolences. The Clergy say they will be in touch with you later with the details.

Mary Needles (Miss)
Of The Post Office
With deepest sorrow.

Out the window the highway dips down under a stone bridge and up on hills stand lavish houses surrounded in grey brown thickets of trees. George Smith's tear fell plop on the paper. Out of a weak left eye. They never had a chance. None of us have. For what. A private telephone like the one in this car. Didn't want to worry me. When Shirl's father died she spat on me. Out of the blue. Right across a table in a drug store. Had I known her better, I would have punched her. She was having a chocolate soda. Had her father and mother died at once I would need an umbrella. News comes like this, and something is saying I knew all the time. I knew. Just as I went then back to our apartment with Shirl after the spitting and lay on her in the afternoon till she went fast asleep crying and crying. Waking when a warbling bird came pecking at a pot on the window sill. She said hear that sound. I had a hand on her young breast. I said it was a bird dipping in a dish. She said it's my father tapping on a tomb. I listened again. She said it's dark, birds don't come out at nights. I said bats do. And rearing up naked and thin in my arms she said O George it isn't a bat, please tell me it isn't a bat, bats come out for blood and get in your hair and God I don't want that, no. I held her down close beneath me. Just as we'd lain night and nights together clutched. And suddenly she bit me and I screamed. She said I hate you.

Chauffeur turning and with a white gloved hand pointing to a sign. George picking up his microphone. Clearing his throat because nothing came out at first.

'Next turning driver. Cross between the fences of the golf course. And straight at the next traffic lights.'

A little touch of the peaked cap. Had this driver before. Not servile but civil. Keeps an ever ready eye on the road. Minds his own business. For mine is properly sad. And when I married Shirl my parents sent her beads on which to say prayers and later my mother's pearls. Shirl stood over them in the brown wrapping paper, wondering if they were real. I had hoped she would have the good breeding to take it as a gesture on the part of my mother and father. And not as she did one day at her jewel box whisper loudly, I wouldn't be caught dead in this junk. On the part of my parents it had been a sacrifice. And now one after the other they've been carried along the sea road and up the ancient lane in their coffins. And if Shirl stood in the cow pasture nearby, in her shimmering green and oriental amethysts watching them go, I can hear what her lips are saying, his god damn peasant parents without a pot to piss in. Shirl this one's jade which I send to you now. Use in their memory.

Two trolley tracks in a cobbled road. Smith's car crossing them to tall iron gates laid open. Man in a grey uniform kicking his black booted feet together and clapping his hands in the cold. Looks and makes a gesture of pushing the gate wider which weighs three tons at least. But I appreciate that. Nod. He nods. Salutes. Never knowing I suppose if it's proper to smile as well. And one more letter here to peruse before further business.

> 1 Electricity Street
> December 22nd.
> The year is irrelevant.

Dear Sir,
  Obviously you intend ignoring my communications.
  I do not think you quite understand who I am.

> Yours faithfully,
> J.J.J. & Associates

I dispute that this man is the result of what his mother and father did. Joyless as it must have been. If you get slammed with one thing. Another, don't worry, is on the way. Where once there was no hope there is horror now. And if you are sad and remembering, wham, not long till they wake you. One brief reply for Miss Martin to send off when she comes in on Wednesday. And ask the obvious question with perhaps something as a post script. Make jocularity his lot. For the moment.

Main Gate
Renown Memorial Cemetery
December 24th
Do choose a year.

J.J.J. & Associates
1 Electricity Street

Dear Sir,
  Who are you?
  Are you possibly a live wire?

Yours sincerely,
G. Smith

P.S. What are your connexions?

George Smith's car pulling up in front of a grey stone building. Entwined with winter shrunken ivy vines and in summer full of buzzing bees. Tiny windows sunk in the thick walls. A gable roof, so like the little country cottage one keeps in a dream. Chauffeur popping up the steps. Nearly skidding on his arse on the porch. Whoops, neatly regaining balance. Pity. Gone by the board. Nice little action for damages. Liability for one shattered pelvis. And while I build my monstrous mausoleum my mother and father go to their small graves.

Cemetery looks whitely sleeping. Big tombs. One round, with pillars as high as five men standing on each other's heads. Something to be said for these blue spruce trees. For their silence. And cold perfume. My mother and father lived laced in by roses. And walked once a week along the train tracks by the sea to buy pressed beef, four miles away. A spring at the bottom of their garden. Grey cat called

Snooky who was a good ratter even with his balls cut off. Nature's full of foolishness. They had me late in life. Nothing else to do in the country on the edge of a bog with the sea getting nearer every year until it would take it all. Just like the village post office fifty years ago, now three miles out under the waves.

Chauffeur carefully back down the steps. Smiles, looks over his shoulder, one glove on and his bare hand carrying a long white cylinder. His friendly face. What more can one ask for in these obtuse times. And handing the scroll through the window to George Smith, the car moved off down the crackling curving road. Sandalwood Drive. Marble, granite mausoleums bleak, cold. Up to a steep hill. Along an avenue of leafless trees. Past a pink squat edifice, and a sharp turn into a narrow lane of spruce. Buttercup Drive. An open space of land, dark mud turned up on the snow. Tripod derrick and winch standing over the white stack of chiselled blocks of stone.

A man with a soft smile round the edges of his mouth walks out to Smith's car. The door opening. He climbs in with George. The plan withdrawn from the cylinder is pulled open across their laps. Click, the map light. On.

'Well Mr Smith, mighty cold.'

'Yes. Cold.'

'That way this time of year.'

'Yes indeed.'

'Well I think I know what you want here, Mr Smith. Given it a lot of thought. Kind of gate house you have in mind. The fireplace has in fact been passed by the committee.'

'Good.'

'But the wall surrounding the plot the committee has decided must not exceed eye level.'

'Whose eye level, Mr Browning.'

'Ha ha, Mr Smith, that's what I said. And they want to be liberal. Been objections raised by several neighbouring plot owners but as they are some way off we feel they won't object to a height of six three. And of course upon that will be your boxwood hedge which ought to give you another foot or two in five years.'

'Mr Browning are you a happy man.'

'Ha, Mr Smith you always ask me that question.'

'Are you.'

'No.'

'Good. You always give me that answer. There's a blue jay.'

'Savage mean bird Mr Smith. A grabber. Steals.'

'Seems I've blundered on to rather awkward ground here Mr Browning.'

'Are you satisfied with how the work is going. As you can see we're at about sixteen feet now. Might make completion date with a month to spare. With luck and a good summer. And we don't run out of stone.'

'Know a gentleman by that name.'

'Use him Mr Smith when we run out.'

'Ha ha Mr Browning. Certainly you achieved my general vision. One gem of rustic simplicity. With several small inconsequential motifs of sadness. Ivy leaves unevenly hanging over the entrance. But discreet.'

'Discreet, Mr Smith. As we discussed.'

'As we discussed. Glad about the wall. And a most merry Christmas to you Mr Browning. And would you divide this among the men with my compliments.'

'They'll appreciate this Mr Smith. Thanks. And a most merry Christmas to you Mr Smith.'

'Thank you Mr Browning.'

'Just one thing before you go Mr Smith. Nothing at all. But thought I'd just mention it. It's just had me wondering. But you know the great black slab over there, the big financier who died mysteriously. Well for about the last couple of months or so, maybe twice, three times a week a woman comes. Spends an hour or more. Sitting on the bench there. In black, thick veil over her face. I'd say she was fairly young, really beautiful legs is her distinction. For a while we took no notice and just thought she's visiting the guy's grave but the funny thing is, I don't think she's coming to that grave at all but is watching this mausoleum go up. Just strange. Thought I'd tell you. Brought opera glasses last few times.'

'That is interesting Mr Browning. But sounds like just someone interested, perhaps in the design, which as we know is a departure.'

'To say the least, Mr Smith. I mean, you know, pioneering so to speak.'

'Well merry Christmas, do take care of yourself, Mr Browning.'

'You too, Mr Smith.'

'Bye bye.'

'Bye.'

Waves of the hand. Car moves off quickly across the hard snowy road. Past the black slab all white now. Brings opera glasses. Beautiful legs. Mr Browning says it's nothing at all but why say it isn't anything if it isn't. At all. Legs. Black veil. Pity I have not employed the latter myself. Everyone tries to pry. And after prying they want to jeer. Good legs is her distinction. And my mother and father are dead. In a watery cottage with creepers growing out of the wall. But had they lived, to take them away from that, ripping them up, bringing them to a world of impersonal luxury. Snuff their lives out in no time. Crashes on you this Christmas eve. Lonely. Out the window, death everywhere. Stacked up. Sealed up. Paid up, a few celebrated, some famous, the rest rich. Things God gave them. And when I beat up my children's mother, they ran clutching round our battling knees and those who could reach higher did so, they screamed leave our mommie alone, leave her, leave her, tears streaming down their faces. Each of those four little bodies came on four distinct afternoons when take me George, take me, from behind, in front anywhere you fancy because golly. Never remember what side I took Shirl. Four little freckled faces with constant throats and beating little fists drive it out of your mind.

George Smith directed the chauffeur to drive round the lake once before leaving Renown Memorial Cemetery. Near the frozen waterfall car halting. Smith viewing nature through the glass. Ice broken, two ducks swimming. One multicoloured male, one drab female. Things are different in the spider kingdom. And over there, a monument sticking in the sky. Stiff stone garments in the cold grey air. Statue of a wife. One hand reaching out, one upturned. Come hither.

Forty minutes past twelve. And the car sweeps out of the high black gates. Grey guard, saluting. Back across the trolley tracks. Down through the woods again. By a little hill. Children in bright red and blue caps sleigh riding. Ice crystals in the trees. Smith swallowing curious tears from the top of his lip. Christmas has always been so sad. At night when young with newly combed hair, tie and shirt all clean, all full of promise for this eve. I was sad.

Black limousine whistling down the highway, passing across a bridge where far down flowed the little river into a big river. No one to talk to, to meet, to laugh. When no one knows I'm alive at all.

Black car sweeping by above the piers and ships, under the shadows of stations, by the shut up markets, empty freight yards. Tell the driver to stop by a grey building. The fireboat station. Two tugs tied up. Now walk across the cold windy park. Staring at two statues. A cannon. Out on to the ferry slip. A cruise for the price of a small coin. Until seven o'clock in the dark evening. Passing back and forth across the grey cold waters. Staring up at the towers as they receded and rose. Somehow at the tip. Down here. One can always jump. Somewhere. Or take a ferry.

And up between the canyon buildings. Walking and wandering the streets looking in the windows. By bars. Peer through a grating. See down into a room. A girl lying back on a dim couch under bedclothes. Sad little fire flickering. Against fire regulations. Flames melting on her face. Wan and dying.

A taxi back to Merry Mansions. Manse of rich mischief. More parties in progress. No sign of Hugo. Up the steps into Flat Fourteen. And the dark empty rooms. Light on in the foyer. And then to the sitting room. Where something moves. Shudder of fear. Goodly flash up the keester. And hair up on the back of the neck. Flick on some light. Sitting in black, a cowl over the head. For one second it looks like death. And the next with the veil back Shirl.

'Hello George. I was waiting for you didn't think you'd come. Hugo let me in. Don't get angry, not his key, got it right here, he got it from a Mr Stone. Here it is.'

'Thank you.'

'I'm here George because I'm pleading for my children and myself. O.K. I said things. You said things. But still there are four children. Each with a future.'

'Do have a drink, what would you like.'

'No. I'm not staying. I just want to say what I've got to say and I'm catching the nine fifteen train. It's Christmas eve.'

'I know it's Christmas eve.'

'I don't want to fight.'

'Well what do you want to do.'

'I'm here because it is Christmas and I'm asking you to stop.'

'Stop what.'

'You know what, George.'

'I haven't the faintest idea what you're talking about.'

'Your mausoleum.'

'I beg your pardon.'

'Let's not beat around the bush George. Please. Not tonight. I'm just asking you not to go on with it. You can't go on with it.'

'Why wear that get up to tell me this. Black veil.'

'And why are you wearing the get up you've got on.'

'That's my business.'

'And I know why, because that's what you wear when you go to that infernal cemetery.'

'You better have a drink Shirl because that's all you're going to get from me. I have nothing further to say.'

'You've been there, haven't you, in that ridiculous car with the radio telephone. As if you were playing cops and robbers.'

'And you've been hanging around.'

'There. I knew it. It's yours isn't it. Admit it now.'

'Shirl if you don't mind, you're going to miss your train. In short I live here.'

'You don't have to tell me that. On your bathroom floor is Matilda. Absolutely unconscious drunk. And practically nude.'

'How refreshing.'

'Don't be so smug. I call it enticement, not that she probably has to.'

'I prefer not to discuss my servants.'

'You're such a God damn phoney.'

'Now look Shirl I'll clout you across the face if you continue. I've had enough bad news today.'

'Why, run out of marble. O God.'

'My mother and father are dead.'

'Ha ha ha.'

'Are you laughing.'

'Yes. I'm laughing.'

Smith standing stiffly, silently. Shirl leaning deeply back, drawing in a deep breath. Black feather crossing down upon her cheek. Brown eyes. Raising one brow. As the staring contest is engaged. When her mouth moves she's weakening. With both her mouths such soft things. And kissed them honeyed blossoms both so many times. She can draw love out of stone. Even now. Four children later. Ripe under linen in summer, soft wool in winter. And clings and black silk now. Eats an apple while she pops a baby out like a pip. They grow as little kings and queens.

'Aren't you going to hit me George.'

'I'm tired.'

'What a rotten little trick, mother and father. You try everything. And what's that now.'

'None of your business.'

'Don't tell me you're taking snuff. God.'

From the tiny turquoise casket Smith pressed a pinch at each nose hole. Shirl crossing legs. Beautiful legs that is her distinction. Means she's got something more to say. And beyond Shirl's head, across the street, out of this dimly lit room, a slattern mother. And her grey husband holds his head in hands. Over his eight mistakes.

'Your train Shirl. This weekend's been enough already.'

'I can stop you building that edifice.'

'I still don't know what you're talking about.'

'I'm talking about one acre, foundations thirty feet deep, imported marble, and the biggest mausoleum built in Renown Cemetery. Doctor Fear.'

'What are you talking about.'

'That's who you are. Doctor Fear, who's building, whose name is connected with it. None other than George Smith.'

'You've been reading too many comic strips, Shirl.'

'My legal counsel is going to take steps. Are you pretending I can't stop you squandering what my children and I have a right to.'

'You're amply supplied with money.'

'And what happens to the rest of that money.'

'What money.'

'Why haven't you got accountants. Answer me that.'

'What do you really want, Shirl.'

'I want more. Because you've got more. You're rotten with it. You tried to buy two thousand canes from an antique dealer.'

'Two hundred.'

'And then walked out with a bronze pig worth a fortune.'

'Brass.'

'You admit it. And the poor man is hysterical.'

'The whole world is hysterical.'

'You robbed him.'

'I did nothing of the kind. Brass. Recent.'

'Bronze and ancient. My detective said so.'

'I see. Some detective.'

'Yes as a matter of fact he is. And happens to be a college graduate, something you're not.'

'This is a problem of yours Shirl. Take it on the train with you.'

'And that ghoulish monument is going to be stopped.'

'And I'm going to tell you perhaps for the last time, you're being fed, clothed and housed.'

'Don't use that even voice with me. Save your precision for Matilda, you'll need it getting in there.'

'This way please.'

'O you big shit. You shit. Phoney. We'll get an injunction.'

'My advice Shirl is to stay away from the law. It can grind both ways.'

'You're not scaring me.'

'And I assure you I'm not paying to have it grind me.'

'We'll see.'

'We may. Meanwhile you've enough money to hire some college kids if you need a quick one.'

Shirl lunging forward, slapping Smith across the face. Moving a knee up to pound him in the privates. Smith neatly blocking with a deft thigh. She runs. Clicking across the floor of the foyer. Having caught the side of George's face with one lash of her claw. And a vase with one blossom of the wax dogwood flower. Held above Shirl's head and thrown. And a bark. Matilda. On all fours. Naked. One could charge admission to this zoo. Door slamming. Wince. One more crack sent through Merry Mansions. Smith shouting.

'Get out. Get out of here. Just get out. All of you get out. Stay out. And leave me alone.'

Smith in his dark suit. Giving Matilda traffic directions back to her room. Didn't last long at her heaven. Once more step over shattered pieces of delf. And go and sit with a bottle of whisky. Lever off the silvery cap. Put it to the lips. Pour it down the throat. This time of year gives everyone a chance to pass out insult, and if possible, injury. The things that come out on Christmas eve. I beg your pardon. When so many things seem to happen. And you want to cry O God. Sent to a new world. With a father and mother dead in the old. Where all will grow over in white flowered bramble. Sink slowly in bog and be covered by the waves. Tinker people lined the roads. With fires at night. My father kept a hay fork leaning near the door to give them a pike in the ass if they got fresh near evening because that countryside was terrifying after dark. By day once when I was passing on my horse. A blonde woman with gleaming eyes beckoned. Nodded towards the bushes and raised her brows. I was a child king who owned all the land. Get down and do something with her. A little awkward with the garb I was geared in. To mix my blood with road louts. But she was young. A woman. And dirty. But hair golden. She said come lay, hush now, with me. Fluttered her dress, held it wide with pretty dots and bows. Covered too, in horseshit. How can I risk my thin fingers with her strong bones. Tangling in the briars. In the yellow hair. And she turned away, aloof. Head high and haughty. And I got down because I thought I was no prince and this woman would do something strange. Something I had never heard of and young as I was I had sifted out a lot of information. She ran. Ducked under a wire in the hedge. And down the field and into the tall standing hay. I thought, Christ the farmer will kill us trampling this. She played with her pink blouse. And blue buttons. Laughed and pushed me back as I got close. Till I tried to grab. Like falling into my own grave. My God how are her teeth. From here you could see the sea. She sang close to my ear. All the fright and fear blew away. Christ if someone sees us. Got to do it, to begin life. She put her lips there and tasted me. Slowly gently just like the sailing vessel I could see beating its way up the shore this summer time and her voice so low and friendly.

I gave
Her
The Young
Horn

She said.

As the
Grazing
Was
Green.

7

On a day when winter was ending. On a promontory near
a dead end of street pushing out into the river by the fish
market. Dark sheds. Barges bumping derelict. I walked out
here on the first day I moved office and have come lunch
times ever since. To watch the ferries, the pigeons scared
into the air by hoots. And to conjure up a future for my
past.

The new office is two interconnecting rooms where I sit
in the back one watching out on the endless white tiled
wall of a warehouse. Brought Miss Martin with me. Had a
a going away party too. Sportsmen from The Game
Club. A buffet. With beer, wine and tidbits. It was disas-
trous. Matilda trooped in to Thirty Three Golf Street
drunk with several celestial friends and danced with my
topper and hardly anything else. Dispersing the less hardy
guests.

I got letters. Delivered by post, by hand, by elephant, by
God. I objected to some of the innuendo.

1 Electricity Street.
We are firm in our wish
that the year is immaterial.

George Smith
Room 604
Dynamo House
Owl Street

Dear Sir,

Do not pretend not to know who we are.

Yours faithfully,
J.J.J. & The Associates

P.S. We assume you were attending a funeral.

And to answer these this month of March I sat chilly and

wagging my feet on a capstan on a wharf the end of Owl Street. Feeling easier out under the open sky.

Room 604
Dynamo House
Owl Street

1 Electricity Street
Dear Sir,

I require details to establish identification. How many eyes have you all got.

Yours sincerely,
G. Smith

P.S. Also be glad if your next letter were accompanied by a brief medical history.

On Wednesday, some days later a note was slipped under the front office door.

1 Electricity Street
Our former comments in
this heading will suffice.

Room 604
Dear Sir,

We can do without your crass attempt at jocularity. We inform you that our appointees have been instructed to institute moves. In the light of the seriousness of the situation and in case you are under any illusion we inform you that we are in the possession of two eyes each.

Yours faithfully,
J.J.J. & The Associates (Global)

P.S. There is no need to go into our medical history.

Grey Thursday afternoon to spell out a reply to J.J.J. from room 604, Dynamo House.

J.J.J. & Associates (Global)   Turdsday
1 Electricity Street
Dear Sir,

Watch out.

Yours sincerely,
G. Smith (Local)

P.S. I am also blessed with two headlamps, which I should be glad to focus on your medical history.

And on this day. At her plywood desk with a slender vase

of chrysanthemums. Miss Martin's shoulders slumped forward and she burst into tears over her typewriter. George Smith went to her. Her hair brown and full round her head. Placing a hand across her back, the little acorns of her spine.

'Mr Smith, I'm sorry.'

'It's all right, Miss Martin. Don't worry. You cry.'

'Mr Smith, I don't want to ever let you down. But I'm scared.'

'Is it the office here.'

'I suppose I'm just getting used to the long anonymous halls and staircases. It's not like Golf Street. I shouldn't cry like this. But Mr Smith I feel the whole world is horrible and mean. And the letters.'

'Miss Martin, don't you fret. That's not your worry. Here try my hanky.'

'Thanks.'

'Give a good blow. That's it.'

'I'll wash and iron it.'

'Nonsense, you keep it now.'

'I read in the paper that poor boy was shot to death. Just because he recognized someone on the subway train.'

'Miss Martin, you mustn't take things so seriously. Now wipe these away. Feel better.'

'Such a nice smell your hanky.'

'Lemon.'

'I like it. I feel better now and Mr Smith this letter just came registered special delivery.'

Mount Ararat
March 17th

My dear George,

I write to you alas for some material aid. At the moment I am completely banjaxed. I am trying desperately to escape from this God forsaken place to make a fresh start in the new world. I hope you will be able to assist me in this. We hear that you are now very successful and a happy family man and I am glad. Can you wire as much money as you can reasonably afford to 'Departing Passenger' Volta Steamship Lines – to their office here or there will get me, and mark it 'hold for collection'. You will never know how much you will have saved my life. And may God protect you as He has not yours truly.

See you soon,
BONNIFACE

Smith folding the letter carefully, putting it back in its envelope. Miss Martin with liquid wide whites around her eyes. In this room where one is waiting for something awful to happen. Cedric, the awful Bonniface, Clementine. College classmate. Amateur historian of his own recent history. No fear Miss Martin. A friend. It's my turn for tears.

Miss Martin coming each morning to room 604, Dynamo House at nine. She put on a little burner for coffee. She rode two hours on the train. Said it went over bridges and bridges and the salt water was covered all along the shore in ice. She told me how the workmen put boards on the train and it stopped at the middle of the bridge way out over the water and they climbed out in the wind, boards on their shoulders. And her house. Her little tiny bedroom. Wind whistled round it all the night. Heat came up in the morning with pipes creaking. And when very sad she would go down the street in the early morning along the row of empty boarding houses, grey and shuttered up and look out across the flat sea. To watch a sun red and cold coming up. Her ears would sting. Then get on the train, sit on the slippery seats, see the people get in. Same ones sometimes. Until it would get like sardines. Then climbing up out with a crowd, crossing the park by the ferry terminus and through the shadowy streets to the little world of room 604. And the grand dad clock would chime. And nine canes in the cane rack.

Now Miss Martin sits all forlorn. Her voice tired. The vein trembling across her wrist. Shaves the hair off her legs. Grey wool dress with short sleeves. She is twenty six years old. From there step down into years of waiting. For marriage. Light hair on her light skin. Her face up close, new born, all fuzz and peachy. Her lids and lashes lay down over her eyes as she thinks. Want sometimes to gather her up in my arms. Say, little girl you're safe while I hold you. And instead I ask her let's go out. Take a walk in the park.

George Smith leading Miss Martin across the lobby of Dynamo House. Past the great glass covering all the little names of firms right through the alphabet. And at S. There is George Smith, room number 604. Third Floor. And down the wide steps. Across the busy street. Passing the little cemetery by the church. Needle spire like a toothpick. Might have had a little plot in there had I been in time a hundred years ago.

Into the park by the barge office. Drizzling rain. Sky dark and heavy. Ferries squeezing along the greased pilings and clanging against the little metal bridge of shore. Cars start engines and off they come. Others go taking the people home to the lights across the water. And a monstrous ship passing down the river. Little circle of people on the fan tail. Two figures pointing and waving at the park. Hear the vessel's engines. Feel them on the soles of the feet, shaking the ground. Passengers' streamers fall away and land on the water. Gay tidings in the mist.

'Miss Martin, a majestic sight.'

'I'd love to go on a ship.'

'Yes.'

'Mr Smith, it's letting off steam.'

'Hooting bye bye. Takes you away from a lot of things.'

'Mr Smith, you say that so sadly.'

'Come, Miss Martin and we'll get something to eat.'

Two figures crossing the windy park. Miss Martin taking Smith's arm over the street. And inside where wieners were being turned on a hot skillet behind the steamed glass. Always wanted to have the constitution to eat these fearlessly, perhaps with a glass of orange. I know it will warm up Miss Martin. Her ears, just showing out of her hair, tinged with red.

Mr Smith and Miss Martin taking a table in this eatery. A cross section of humanity. One belching secretly over his decoy coffee. Two secretaries with side plates of buns they peruse. A waitress with black hair and large searchlights.

Going round the restaurant straightening her hair, training her huge beams on the goggle eyed. The other waitress slipping out among the customers with a broom flashing among the legs. To scare up dust for hay fever and sprinkle debris on the cups of coffee. The chef roasting, slipping coins into an oversized trouser cuff.

And as George Smith stood at the counter to get his cups of coffee and plates of wieners in a roll, there was a hissing sound. Growing louder and louder in the coffee machine. Chromium steaming tank. Now starting to scream. Customers looking up. Counter boy deftly moving away as the sides of the tank were bulging. The quietest customer of all, huddled over a decoy cup of coffee was up like a flash and out the door. Two secretaries screamed and held their ears. Miss Martin ducked over. George Smith cowering. The chef trembling behind a display of doughnuts. As Smith could see the decoy coffee drinker now safely on the other side of the street, with his hands up round his eyes like binoculars to witness the thunderclap.

All tense. Waiting. Crouched. Come in here to renew. To give Miss Martin fuel for her tummy. And find a little team of barefaced shirkers. Bent upon feathering their own nests at the expense of the absent proprietor. If you don't shut your eyes to some things, the cheating and chiselling that goes on would drive you out of your wits. Now we're to be blasted to kingdom come. And I've not made a will.

The unmerry group frozen at positions of hopeful safety. Beep. A tiny pop from the coffee machine, a whistle and wheeze. A final whimpering into silence. The all clear. Customers slowly stand again. Smile. Old friends now. The decoy coffee drinker returning from across the street. He takes a look through the glass in at the now silent cylinder. Pushes open the door. Nods to these embattled wiener patrons. Sits down on a stool and emits a nervous laugh. Ha ha. Girl with mountains gives the peaks a twitch. Whoosh. An avalanche. Endangering anyone making the way up the slopes.

Miss Martin finishing her wiener licks her lips. Wipes

away a little crumb of meat. Her nose red round the nostrils. And shiny just at its tip with a flat spot like streamlining. Tiny ship sails round her mind. Stopping at ports where perhaps I am some naughty foreigner. And just four days ago I was passing outside a great department store. Suddenly stopped. Recognized a face on all the manikins in the battery of windows. Wearing spring evening gowns, swim suits and negligees. Miss Tomson. Figure and face. Same slight puzzled look around the eyes, same blue, same blonde and careless flinging out of limbs. Find her standing there. All night in plaster looked at by the empty street. And Miss Martin here is not a Miss Tomson nor a Shirl. And were one to enter a kiss in her ear. Make her thrash her legs in the air, cause mayhem. Pant as Shirl did on the carpet, the neighbours hearing her out in their gardens, while tending cabbage. Or their own ears. Of corn.

George Smith and Miss Martin walked back towards Owl Street. Passing in front of the great grey darkness of the custom house. The little round park of green in the middle of the road. Miss Martin feeling better for her wieners and coffee. Smith silent and protective. No boyfriend to take her out at night. Said she curled up with a magazine while her mother cooked the supper.

Turning the corner of Owl Street, Smith stopped and bought a bag of roasted peanuts. Threw one high in the air, caught it neatly in the mouth. Miss Martin chuckling, wide eyed, stopping in the noisy thick traffic of the street. Sad the world made such a din. One whole afternoon sitting in Dynamo House, hot water bottles hanging over each ear. Go to the mausoleum while still alive and live in it. Withstanding the regulations that say you must be dead. A pity. Be quiet there, on the marble, satin pillow under head. And through the tall iron fence round the cemetery, Shirl would point, level the finger, hire attorneys, fat necked to recite off laws and say I can't do what I'm doing.

'Miss Martin, I like your eyes.'

Smith viewing the way ahead. Then stealing a glance at Miss Martin who was all eyes cast down. Whispering in

Smith's heart were little words, nearer my God to thee, and please, never force me to wear shoes of grasshopper skin. For leaping high out of all the terrible traps set everywhere these days.

The lights on in the blocks of windows. Time of afternoon sadness. Sky all threatening and dark. Wind picking up the torn newspaper in the gutter. Outside these merchant banks, houses of exchange. Sugar, cotton and fish. And approaching the wide steps of Dynamo House set back from the street and overshadowed by two tall buildings on either side. Miss Martin and George Smith slowly climbed the steps.

Half way up. Great blobs of rain fall. Rumble of thunder. Lightning streaking blue on the buildings. Miss Martin stopped and caught George Smith by the arm. Two figures stepping from behind a pillar in front of Dynamo House. Smith raising an arm across his face. Blinding camera flash bulbs. Smith and Miss Martin running into the entrance. Across the lobby and to the stairs. Pounding feet behind them. And more flashes of cameras. And shouts.

'That's him.'

Smith had Miss Martin's hand. Speeding up one two three flights. Making one abrupt detour on the fourth. Where Smith pulled open a door just off the landing.

'Into this mop closet, Miss Martin, fast.'

'God.'

'That's it.'

'Will we fit, Mr Smith.'

'Got to.'

'But they'll find us.'

'No they won't. I've got the key. Lock us in.'

'God.'

'Miss Martin I'm not making you too uncomfortable. My foot's in this pail. Quiet now. I hear them.'

Feet outside the mop closet. Two of them stopping to tug on the door. Locked. Moving onward. Silence. Heavy breathing. Had they put an ear to the key hole.

'Am I stifling you Miss Martin. I'm terribly sorry about this.'

'I'm all right, Mr Smith.'

'Just get my foot out of this pail. Hold it. I hear feet again. They're coming back this way.'

'Mr Smith why do they want our picture.'

'Hush now.'

Smith raising hand to signal silence. In the near blackness. So close to Miss Martin. Closest I've ever been. Her breath smells sweetly. And hear her heart pounding. Nearly taste her. And feel her too. Twin precious things pressing against my arm. A tugging at the door knob of this mop cupboard once more. Strange, so many times I passed this closet, and said there's a little harbour in a storm.

Feet moving off again. Sounds like four pairs. Or five. Some of the rags in here are odiferous. Touched Miss Martin's lips with my finger. Face to face in the black. Feet on the landing. Voices. Confused. The pounding they make down the steps is too loud to be trusted. No hoof hoodwinks me. Somehow all I could see of them as they jumped out were their ears. And they had noses too. Of newshounds.

'Are they going Mr Smith.'

'May be a ruse. Are you all right. Like to move your arm over. Wretched pail. My foot's deeper in it than ever. Never get it off. And be caught for sure.'

'I'll push back further.'

'No don't Miss Martin. If I can just get my foot loose. Be all right. Then we can get out of here.'

'I don't mind.'

'Soon we'll need air.'

'I still don't mind.'

Smith's ears twitching. At that last remark. A tingle and glow rears up at the bifurcation of the legs. With the little room in here, hardly any space for expansion. It will stand up and she'll ask what it is. Many mops, Miss Martin and handles too. My hand feels her hair. What's this. Not again.

'Miss Martin. Tears. I feel tears.'

'Yes.'

'Why.'

'I don't know.'

'Are you scared in here with me.'

'No.'

'Were you frightened by those men.'

'No.'

'Is it something I've done or said.'

'No.'

'Why do you cry.'

'I just don't know, Mr Smith. I have to.'

Smith reaching a knuckle under the eye. Picking up a tear. Feel her lips. Opening. Taking in George Smith's finger between her teeth. Whole knuckle of the hand. Biting and nibbling. And her voice all choked. With fingers in her mouth. And whispering.

'Mr Smith I dreamt about you last night.'

'You did.'

'Yes. You were standing on a hill. And I was at the bottom of the street. And they were trying to capture you. And they held you. And at the bottom of the hill old women held me and I started to cry.'

'Why.'

'I can't tell you.'

'Tell me.'

'A great white river flowed down the hill from you. Right by me on the street. And I wanted to drink and the old women wouldn't let me. And held me. And I was crying. And just cried. And the white stream flowed by.'

Outside the thunder clapping. Must be monumental drops of rain. Even in Miss Martin's dreams, it would appear they try to get me for something. She sleeps in her little room and has books she likes. Her shade pulled down and it flaps and thumps when the wind blows. And the wind was nearly always blowing. The air thickens in this closet. No wind. Nor my God, lay waste one. Till love begins, when you can listen with a smile. Backfiring after wieners is no laughing matter.

George Smith put out a hand. Just in under Miss Martin's open coat. Felt a little tide of flesh nipping up over her underdraws. It was spare. Personal part of her. Give it a little pat. Women are desperate for love. And when they give theirs, they get short shrift. Wash my socks. Get me juice.

'It may be safe now to go Miss Martin. Before we suffocate.'

Smith turning the key slowly. Opening the door to the light. And somewhat fragrant air. Blinking. Peering both ways in the hall. A forward movement and crash. Smith flat on face both feet in pails.

'Are you hurt.'

'Pull those God damn things off me, Miss Martin. Please. Woke the dead.'

'You poor sweet.'

Miss Martin pulling off the pails. Smith to his knees. Hobbling on these a yard or two. Just trying them out in case one loses the rest. Just make it one flight down on tip toe. Someone wants to discredit me. Get my picture. Plaster it. And say there's that skunk.

Empty hall outside room 604. Save coming round the corner. A cleaning woman with a waxing machine. Madam thanks for your closet. Smith opening, closing 604 tightly and locking the door. Miss Martin standing defenceless in her coat. Here, allow me Miss Martin. To divest you of this. Hang it up. Sad girl. Just light your lamp over your desk. See the nice glow. Quite an afternoon. Of near explosions. Riots. Peanut catching in the mouth. And a mobbing by reporters. Finally Miss Martin you said you poor sweet.

Smith in his back room. Fiddling in his papers. Stacked this way and that. Out the window. The globs of rain. Popping down the narrow air shaft grey and fat against the white tiles.

'Mr Smith, this came while we were out. It's a nice pink envelope.'

Smith picking it up. Opening it bravely. Perhaps a request to donate my body to medical science. Great shortage. Ask you to incorporate it in your will, which will be read when the time is nigh, and at their expense and within a reasonable distance, they will come and fetch you. Donate a part if you cannot donate the whole. Help train tomorrow's scientists.

The Management
Merry Mansions
Eagle Street
Saturday

Dear Mr Smith,

A preliminary report has now come to hand concerning the crack sent right up your wall into Mr & Mrs Goldminer's apartment.

Although our engineers are baffled to know how this was done especially having regard for the quality of the structure, they are satisfied it was the result of a violent slamming of your door. As you are aware this door was made to your own specifications of a surgical steel. Our engineers are of the opinion that such a door, having regard for its great weight should open and close by mechanical means if further damage to the building is to be avoided.

We, of course, await respectfully your reply in this matter and any suggestions you may care to put forth.

Regarding the plummeting plaster on sleeping inhabitants of the next building caused by members of your youth rally, we hope to have further news soon.

I, personally, of course, accord you my friendly greetings.

Yours most sincerely,
S. Stone

P.S. Pink stationery is an indulgence of mine which I feel is a happier colour than white.

S.S.

P.P.S. We note your change of address.

S.S.

George Smith raising the paper to the light. Good watermark and cotton content. Miss Martin stands by the cream door jamb, one hand held in another. And when I say take a letter she will go back to her pool of light, poised before her machine rapping those little lettered keys. Gloomy, raining, so chilly and cold. Her wool dress clings so. Trim and sad. Pink stationery. Pink buds on Miss Martin. To remember these little items when the whole grey vista is so vast.

'Miss Martin, take a letter, please. Dear Mr Stone. Thank you for your letter concerning the crack in Merry Mansions and the news that I shall be hearing soon of the plummeting plaster. New paragraph. I am presently engaged in deep research concerning the market price of human judgement as applied to profit making in my new egg breaking plant. As soon as conclusions have been reached about such cracking I will deal with the one in Merry. New paragraph. I would only mention that I do hope the incident of the plummeting plaster can be settled amicably. I sense that the repentant and aggrieved members of the rally who were responsible would like me to extend to you and the victims of the plaster their most sincere apologies, and regret they have brought the rally and other members into disrepute. Yours sincerely. Got that Miss Martin.'

'Yes, Mr Smith.'

'And just add, enamoured of your pink stationery.'

'Shall I send this registered Mr Smith.'

'Yes, do, Miss Martin.'

Seems so long ago now since the mop closet. Only one letter since. Having slept in 604 last night, I applied a reputable deodorant for masculine freshness. Some women make you suffer a smell to love them. And you bury fingers under a pillow. Like the river water the end of the street, so sweet till you taste. Shirl was a clear mountain spring, her mouth, teeth gleaming, white heavenly doors. In the shadows of her lips. Light pink colour of her tongue. Which she will lay out between lips while her lawyers draft appeals regarding this testator's unsoundness of mind. I sit here now with elbows pressed on desk, waiting for Miss Martin to type the ultimate draft of my final wishes.

Smith drawing down the white shades on the two back windows of 604. Which one was tempted to call a suite. Live honestly but briefly. Now Miss Martin, you sit so stiffly having made a rough of my pencilled final instructions. You think me strange and peculiar. And afraid to look me in the eye in case maybe my own are spinning like ball bearings. I am easy of heart. Delighted to be rich. And when called to higher service let there be this document which I peruse now between my living fingers.

I, George Smith, hereby make known my last will and testicle. First off I should like to rear up and haunt all those who tried to screw me up while living. Special attention to be given those fuck pigs who have communicated with me by letter attempting thereby to get funds from my unrelenting clutches.

All my chattel possessions whatsoever remaining gripped in my lunch hooks at the time of stepping into darkness which I do not care to have herein mentioned as the eternal shid, there having been a sufficiency of same throughout my casual meander through life, are to be held to public auction. The entire sum of money proceeding from such auction is then to be converted to bank notes of small denomination and placed in a steel receptacle six feet high and one foot in diameter and so placed and constructed as to withstand the rigours of a hoard. The receptacle shall be positioned at a spot chosen to be the most public and central with comfort stations available. A day shall be announced, described as next Turdsday, upon which day, all streets leading to the area will be cordoned off and cleared of any human or vehicular traffic. At twenty minutes to midnight the area is to be floodlit. Cameras will then be set up in several strategic positions and be protected to ensure their free and easy operation. At twelve midnight on this aforesaid Turdsday, a sound of an adult human breaking wind shall be made which shall act as a signal which sound shall be so magnified on suitable sound equipment to sound like a volcano. Referees shall be appointed and take proper measures to prevent the carrying of any lethal weapon by the surging mob. However, persons availed of sports equipment, fishing rods and the like, are to be allowed. For this purpose, croquet mallets of regulation weight shall not be considered as lethal. But citizens appearing out of the blue in skin diving equipment are to be looked upon askance. Upon the signal aforementioned the camera operators shall proceed to record the scene as the various citizens approach the cash and continue to do so until the money can be reasonably thought to be gone. At the discretion of the trustees a director may be appointed to film any further incident thought interesting following upon the disappearance of the money from the said receptacle. The film will be duly edited in a sequence that shall be thought tastiest. Without background music. Close ups of the scene will take precedence over long shots except in such long shots catching the mood of the mob. The film will then be made available free of any charge save that of carriage, to any institution engaged in any recognized research programme of any reasonable description and to all other charitable institutions, communities, clubs or organizations which can be thought of as reasonably being in the interests of any section of the community or the community as a whole, these to include gatherings for good fellowship, singsongs, chats or birth control.

A corpse which shall well and truly have been determined to be me and such determination being absolutely beyond any shadow of doubt or mistake, such corpse shall be further untouched and placed immediately in a sycamore coffin, and such coffin put in a subdued manner and fashion in the tomb erected for this purpose for which adequate provisions have already been made. My name, George Smith, shall be carved deeply in the sycamore and followed by the inscription hereinafter set forth.

> The innocent
> Were cowering
> As the guilty
> Closed in on them
> Murderously.

8

Something about the hoot of the vessel entering the river, made George Smith shiver. Two weeks of rain storm and hurricane. For three days Miss Martin could not get to work because of flooding in the subway. And suddenly it stopped. Sun up, clear sky, air fresh, all vernal on the first day of May. And arrival of a telegram.

S.S. CINATIT

MAY 1

DOCK THIS MORNING BROKE DESPERATE

BONNIFACE

Miss Martin arrived whistling. Could hear her swing her little basket up on her desk. And her jaunty step to the water cooler installed during the raging hurricane. Nipping her head in the door and smiling.

'Mr Smith, it's wonderful out.'

'Good.'

'Everybody's so cheerful. I walked across the park. Just as a ship was coming in. I feel marvellous this morning. I want to sing. What's the matter, Mr Smith.'

'Any letters.'

'Just one. Got my nail file. I'll open it. Here.'

Rear Room   1 Electricity Street
604
Dear Sir,

To hand your letter of 'Turdsday' so unseemly spelled, in which you threaten us with the words 'Watch out' and the postscript that you are blessed with two headlamps to focus on our medical history.

We now require by telegram that you send us something to salve the outrage caused by these recent remarks to this office.

Yours faithfully,
J.J.J. Jr.

'Miss Martin, did the ship this morning look cheerful.'

'Funny thing you should ask that Mr Smith. You know I thought it looked very strange. I don't know why but it seemed crippled in some way. And a phrase just came into my mind. Ship of shame. I had the feeling no one would want to meet that ship.'

'You said a mouthful.'

'What Mr Smith.'

'Nothing Miss Martin. I'll just scribble this reply to our friend, J.J.J. Jr. Just mail it.'

May 1st
Owl Street

J.J.J.
Dear Junior,

Under separate cover and under appropriate wraps I am sending you a piece of ass.

Yours truly,
G. Smith

'On second thoughts Miss Martin. Send this letter by telegram.'

'Yes Mr Smith.'

Smith taking a few moments to peruse in the mirror. View the eye balls. Father of four children. None of whom one would dare call Junior. A lonely life. Miss having a few youngsters around. Driving the breath out of me. Miss Martin in there on the phone will you ever have kinder. Some little baby all your own.

'My God, Mr Smith.'

'What is it, Miss Martin.'

'O Mr Smith.'

'For Jesus sake, what is it.'

Smith running in. Not far to go. Must be wary of gathering too much speed, else land in Owl Street having torpedoed the partition and another suite across the hall, the Institute Of Higher Graduation.

'Have you seen the newspaper. It's got your picture. Right on the front page.'

'Great scot.'

'Says full story page sixteen. Your arm is raised up. You can just see my shoulder and a bit of hair.'

'I want you to call a car Miss Martin. To be here right away. Pack up my papers on my desk. Put in an eraser. Have you sent off that wire.'

'Yes. I just want to say something Mr Smith.'

'What Miss Martin.'

'Whatever else happens I just want you to know that your self control in the mop closet was wonderful. I wanted to say that to you before.'

'Then I can ask you something, Miss Martin. And I hope you'll understand.'

'Of course Mr Smith.'

'Would you like to come with me to the country for a few days. Let me make it absolutely clear this is entirely up to you. And needless to say you would have your own bedroom.'

'You mean at a hotel Mr Smith. Well I'd have to tell my mother.'

'Phone her. But you know how mothers are Miss Martin. It might only be politic to say you're house partying fully chaperoned, with other young people.'

'All right, Mr Smith. But how long.'

'Two, three days.'

Smith returning nervously into the rear of 604, opening up the newspaper across his desk.

WATCHFUL WAITING IN OWL STREET

There was renewed buoyancy without bouncing in the financial district of this city where the spotlight has narrowed on one or two personalities today when the market appeared decidedly bullish.

It was against a background of corrective pause, which observers found no longer refreshing, when it was thought certain members of this city were taking profits home and most stocks were marked down as a result of heavy selling. Sentiment however, was strong that this selling would be short lived. Many members wanting to avoid being caught napping or short lived, lurked throughout the afternoon to get a glimpse of Mr George Smith who was briefly seen to leave Dynamo House, Owl Street, early this afternoon.

It is not definitely known what part, if any, Mr Smith has played in the recent holocaust although it is thought by some members that Mr Smith might give an inkling of the future and they have been closely watching the situation.

Mr Smith's return to Dynamo House was witnessed by a large crowd, who had gathered on the pavements from early afternoon. He was seen to enter the building wearing a red carnation followed by his secretary and he hastily attempted the steps to avoid photographers. Reporters putting questions to Mr Smith were greeted by a rude noise, and an airy quip by Mr Smith 'Report that to the sanitation department.'

Mr Smith, a military strategist in the last conflict, has consistently refused to give interviews, however, it is known that he occupies two back rooms at Dynamo House having recently removed from an office midtown, but the true nature of his business remains unknown. It had been previously said in some quarters that Mr Smith was of no fixed address. It is now established he keeps an apartment in Merry Mansions where many of the city's celebrities reside. It is further rumoured that Mr Smith has been long engaged in the construction of a tomb to house his remains, reputed to be one of the most elaborate ever erected, entirely air conditioned with special foundations to protect the structure from floods and earthquake. The Renown Cemetery authorities refuse to comment on this, said to be the most costly construction to date in the Cemetery and which till now had been associated with the name of a Doctor Fear.

Smith emerging from the back room. Level lipped and grim. Phone ringing. Rapping on the door. All at once. Everything.

'I'll get the door, Miss Martin. You get the phone.'

Smith opening the door. A little boy in uniform. A letter.

'Special messenger delivery.'

'Thank you.'

Smith slowly closing the door in which it seemed a small foot was put.

'I beg your pardon, little boy. Your foot's in the door.'

'Yeah.'

'Won't you take it out.'

'Hey some people, I guess you don't get any appreciation.'

'What are you talking about sonny.'

'A tip.'

'What do you mean a tip.'

'Ain't you this guy with his picture in the paper this morning. Well you should give me a tip for bringing a message.'

'Just hold it sonny, I'll read it.'

604 Dynamo	1 Electricity Street
Owl Street	

Dear Sir,

How dare you attempt to mail me such a thing. Do not refer to me as Junior.

J.J.J.

P.S. You will hoot before long.

'Now sonny, if I ever see your face again, I'll put it through the floor. Bye bye.'

One finds that the pressures in the world build up and that one unfriendly act begets another. Zoom. Suddenly all dignity is gone. People go in using blows with the shod foot. On the prone figure. Sometimes, even when interpreted as weakness, it's as well to try a certain amount of easy latitude which can lend a bit of nervous laughter to a situation. Therefore I will scribble one last response showing a vestige of faith in his sense of humour.

Dynamo House
Owl Street

Dear Fellow and Junior,

I thought the incredibility of mailing you an unsolicited piece of ass might amuse you. Toodle oo.

George Smith

P.S. I see well in the dark.

'Miss Martin just send off this last letter before packing up.'

'Mr Smith, it's the News Of The Truth asking for comments, what shall I say, about an air conditioned grave.'

'Say they've got the wrong number.'

'You've got the wrong number, sorry. No. Yes. Mr Smith. Yes. Mr Smith, they say they know it's not the wrong number.'

'Tell them it will be soon.'

'Mr Smith says it will be soon.'

'Now hang up, Miss Martin. Let's get cracking. Find out when passengers debark from the S.S. Cinatit. Check on the car, see it's on the way. Pack up my papers, the green files marked go and lock up the yellow files marked caution and the red marked stop. Don't forget the eraser.'

'Please Mr Smith. I'm already up to my teeth.'

'What's that.'

'I'm trying to do everything.'

'Miss Martin we've got to scram.'

'Give me a chance. One thing at a time. Mr Smith.'

'Don't be disloyal at a time like this Miss Martin.'

'For God's sake Mr Smith I'm not being disloyal. I'm going crazy. There. The phone again.'

'Just say Beetroot Department.'

Miss Martin closing her eyes as she picks up the phone. These are troubled times.

'Hello, Beetroot Department. Who. No. Not here, wrong number. Mr Smith's it's a message, from J.J.J.'

'What is it. Out with it.'

'They're reading it.'

'What, for God's sake.'

'They say, all of us here have been acquainted with your kind before. And as married men with children we will not stand for this latest sauciness.'

'Tell them wrong number, beet barge disposal unit for dumping in the bay.'

Poor Miss Martin, delivering the message, putting down phone. Pulling out drawers. Collecting papers. Phone ringing again. Marvellous the rapidity of communication. And she says yes mom, I told you mom, chaperoned, yes, just a bunch of young kids, going to the country, games, swimming, tennis, very rich important people mom, I'll never have another chance like this one, she's going to loan me all the clothes I need, mom, please, don't worry, yes, I'll ring you, you worry about nothing, you have to trust somebody, do you want me to die without any fun mom, all right, O.K. I'll phone, goodbye mom, I will, I promise, goodbye.

'Mr Smith, guess you heard that was my mother.'

'Yes, Miss Martin.'

Smith retreating to rear room, lifting the white shade a mite to peer out at the glistening tiles. For way up at the end of the shaft the sun is shining and just a ray or two is getting reflected down. I want peace. Candlelight, wine and olives. So many people feel resentment and jealousy. A whiff of spice then, in the window. Out of the warehouse a few buildings away. Cinnamon. Cloves. Bonniface at this second is flatfooting it down the pier stopping momentarily to don roller skates the quicker to nail me at Dynamo House. Ask me if he can stay in my tomb. I say, George, sport, just let me rest up in there.

'Miss Martin the car.'

'Mr Smith I told him the newspaper kiosk at the corner in five minutes.'

'You genius Miss Martin. You're ready. Good gracious we've had quite a little morning of it. Don't answer that phone. Somehow I know who it is. Out now. Lock the door. Got the files.'

'Yes, Mr Smith.'

'You're sure now you don't feel awkward coming with me.'

'No, Mr Smith.'

'Your mother's at ease.'

'No.'

'That's the way with mothers, Miss Martin. They can never cut the apron strings, always afraid someone will take advantage.'

'I know Mr Smith, it's terrible. I always have to lie.'

Sun pouring through the glass doors of Dynamo House. Pigeons pecking. Flow of people in and out. Newspaper said there were crowds but on that rainy day I didn't see a soul. Nor was I sporting the carnation. No one gives a damn for the facts these days. Any second Bonniface will be skidding round the corner on the roller skates.

Mr Smith and Miss Martin, arms laden. Foolish files. All marked go and green. These two figures emerging from a side door of Dynamo House. Into the pleasure of the breeze. Past pigeon feeders with hats propped back on their heads, communicating with the fat birds. Smith taking a flash of fear up the keester. Some unidentifiable ship blasting its hooter. Denoting all tied up ready to debark the living desperate cargo. One of whom is trying to begin a new life without a bean.

So far so good. Unnoticed down the steps. Miss Martin leading. Black high heels bringing one's notice to a rather good leg. Be so nice to be out in the country. Trampling the flowers and shrubs. Between trees and over outcrops of rock. How to explain to Miss Martin the cabin in the woods. With only one bedroom. Albeit a bed either side of the fireplace in the living room. Albeit this. That word steers into my head at the least nervousness. Of course I will give Miss Martin the log cabin while I sleep out on the outcropping of rock. I don't mind the snakes. No, you take the bed Miss Martin, I wouldn't think of it. I always sleep outside in nature. Little poison seeping into a backside never hurt me.

Newspaper kiosk. My face everywhere plastered over it. Terror of having something recognized on you wherever you go. Which you can't take off or change unless to grow a beard which would be utterly objectionable. A friendly face. The chauffeur I've had before.

'How do Mr Smith. See you're getting well known round these parts.'

'I'm afraid so. As fast as you can, Renown Cemetery first stop. O.K. Miss Martin, get in for God's sake.'

'Give me a chance Mr Smith. You're pushing.'

'Sorry. Someone's bound to spot us. This is too easy. I suspect something.'

'Well please don't push, my arms are full.'

Smith stony in the car. Next to Miss Martin. Neglecting to help her pull the rug up over her knees. A slight chill in the air, albeit sunny. Albeit this. My nerves. The vehicle pulling away with speed. Cruising up to the first traffic lights. Through the fish market. The dark shadows in there, the poor boxes of flounder, the big dead eyes under the ice. Don't worry I've lurked around there witnessing the whole-sale death. Being also fond of the grilled fillet.

Squeal of tyres. Left turn. Crosstown. The square with a statue. Miss Martin silent, won't give me any rug. All right if that's the way you want it Miss Martin. I can be silent and aloof. I may even pick up the phone and call Miss Tomson. Well hi, Sally. Gee. Gee. Mr Smith. Gee Sally. The words I invent under stress. A few hundred cats have popped out of a few thousand bags. Run round wild trying to get them back in again.

'Miss Martin if you'd rather not come. I mean we could drop you at a subway. I mean if you'd really feel easier that way. I'm only suggesting.'

'Well maybe you'd better, Mr Smith.'

Smith reaching for the microphone. How does one get out of this. Dear God don't let any subway entrances suddenly appear. Never bear being in the country utterly alone. No one to hole up with. Lock out the naughty world. Act as a buffer to the flying acorns, grapes, eggs. Miss Martin and I have been through a lot together recently. One mingle among the mops.

'You're sure Miss Martin. It's only that I feel you might not like it. Way out in the woods overlooking a river down deep in the valley. Lovely sound of the water rapids. New green buds on the trees. Dew on the fields. Nature in all her glory. It might make you unnecessarily nervous, beauty can, you know.'

'Mr Smith if I back out now, my mother will suspect something.'

'I'm glad you brought up that point. I can see we're committed to our plan. Heavens. The river already.'

Wind down there bending newly planted trees. Flood tide beating up foam on ships anchored midstream. Sun glinting copper on the tall buildings standing over the park. Great silver threads strung holding up the bridge ahead. And nearby here there's an institution with people playing bridge and poker showing each other their cards. No need any longer to conceal. Face other citizens with smiles, laughter, and jelly beans bouncing round in the palm of the hand. What relief to be crazy.

Black vehicle through the green golf course. Specks of players swatting their little white spheres into the green distance. The cobbled road ahead. Trolley on the tracks. Roaring north. Always wanted to ride it. And ahead the gates. And my God, a gathering. Of the press. Cameras. There has been a security leak.

'Miss Martin, Christ.'

'Mr Smith, O dear.'

'Let me under the rug. On the floor. All we have to do is get in the gate.'

'Mr Smith what's my mother going to say if this gets in the papers.'

Interesting that in times of terror, when the boom is to be lowered, people you hire to save you trouble and trembling, think instantly of their own skins. As things come out of the void to get you. Bullets, buses, trucks, germs. And now a group of gazeteers.

'Miss Martin behave as if you're on your way to see your dead husband. While I lie rather low under this rug.'

'Mr. Smith, the cameras. They're blocking the gates.'

'Driver, drive on. Beep, beep, if necessary.'

The bubbling bow tied voices outside the window of the car. Come on, Mr Smith, we know you're under that blanket, give us a flash of face. Who's the doll. Hey Mr Smith, what do you do for a living. Come on, one picture.

Smith crouched in the woolly darkness of dust and smells. Revving of engine, trembling eight cylinders, each one doing its little job to propel this black vehicle forward. Worms and gears under the floor, meshing, spinning, pistons pumping. How's your piston. Say some women like it long and slow. Other like it short and fast. And those like Shirl who just like it. Any way at all.

Clang of gates. Smith nipping head up. Five security guards forcing the great black spokes and curlicues on the whining hinges back against the group of gazeteers. Flash bulbs popping. Shouts of outrage. Freedom of the press. Who does that guy think he is. Somebody.

Miss Martin scared. Biting her lips. Looking to George Smith crawling back to the seat on hands and knees. One green file of papers spilling out. This whole manoeuvre is a disgrace.

'Mr Smith if my mother sees my picture.'

'Be quiet.'

'I will not, why didn't you let me get on the floor too.'

'Can't have an empty car go through.'

'They knew it was you all the time, what does it matter.'

'I don't want my replica in the papers.'

'You bastard.'

'I beg your pardon Miss Martin. What did you say.'

'You heard me.'

All I need. For Miss Martin to go agley on me. Pout, stamp and generally upstage my authority. When they learn about your inner life, wham they take liberties with the outer. Until one is driven to putting on the stone face with creases downturned around the eyes and mouth. Scowl. Miss Martin's calf. Had no idea that little muscle was so nicely turned. Nicely contrasted against the car seat.

Momentarily the black car stopping at the Renown Cemetery office. A gentleman darkly clothed coming down the steps and climbing into Smith's car. Which pulls away leaving behind the big gate and the pushers on either side, as it stands shut, tall and iron between them. Thanks be to metal.

'Miss Martin this is Mr Noble. My secretary Miss Martin. Now Mr Noble.'

'It's beyond my comprehension how this has happened Mr Smith. Every precaution has been taken since work began. As you know we have so many contracts but we made every effort to avoid anything unseemly.'

'We can only but pick up the pieces now, Mr Noble. It's put me in rather an embarrassing position. But silence is the only answer at this stage.'

'There's been this woman in black, Mr Smith.'

'I've heard.'

'We just don't know if there's any connexion. I mean to say Mr Smith the cemetery management want to extend every apology and assure you that no one except our Mr Browning knew the situation. And he, of course, is above suspicion. Will you have a cigar.'

'Thank you Mr Noble.'

'May I use your telephone, Mr Smith.'

'By all means do.'

'I'll get in touch with the North Gate and make sure the way is clear. Anyway Mr Smith we've screened in the site. Like to cruise by.'

Under the budding trees. The lilting tips of green. The little shrubberies. Marble steps, pillars, stones, Stained glass in spring sunlight. Wheels humming on the pebbled drives. Smith giving signals through to the driver. A gauze screen standing high and white shaking in the breeze.

'I'm glad you've done that, Mr Noble.'

'We thought it would take care of any more snoopers Mr Smith.'

Along the main avenue of Renown Cemetery and down a winding hill. An iron fence on top of a high stone wall. And beyond, the train tracks, a park and small river. Tall old elm trees. Magnolia all ready for the blossom and bud. Car slowing and stopping just past a building set in the side of a hill with two long canopies extending out to the road. Uniformed guards saluting Mr Noble stepping out of the car. Bending over to say parting words to George Smith.

'And just for the record, Mr Smith, on behalf of the corporation, management and myself, I extend our most sincere apologies for what has happened. You go off now Mr Smith and forget about any more trouble with this.'

'Thank you Mr Noble. I appreciate it.'

'The way is clear. Reporters think you're leaving by the West Gate Mr Smith.'

'Ah God.'

'Never mind Mr Smith everything's going to be all right.'

'One parting word, Mr Noble, hardly know how to put this, but if someone should come along, I know this sounds crazy, but should someone take up position near my site playing music on a piece of paper pressed against a comb, just ignore them.'

'I'll pass that on, Mr Smith. Anything at all. Like that cigar, did you.'

'Marvellous, Mr Noble. Bye bye, now.'

'Best of good luck to you, Mr Smith.'

Gasoline station. Smith's car stopping to get filled. The windows wiped and polished. Smith sitting, one hand resting flat on the seat. And in the silence. On top of that hand, came the hand of Miss Martin. Pressing down on Smith's own flesh. Stirring his mind. Closing up the ears. Choking up the heart. For somehow one wants to cry. Salty flow to wash all the terrible misunderstanding away.

Smith's car creeping by a coal siding for freight trains. Out on to a dark road along a river and train tracks. Clicked along here in the club car, the evening with Miss Tomson. Parents dead. Miss Needles of the post office fighting a losing battle against chisellers, twisters and louts. Miss Martin trembles. Poor kid. She wants warmth and friendship. Instead of the elbow jostling everywhere. Wrap my arms around her. God give me nerve. Rest on one of her breasts. White soft comfort. All hangs on a thread. Putting her hand on mine. Chilly cold thing comes up in the mind, you think how can anyone really feel heartfelt for me. There I am in the newspaper. Had a dignified mother and father carrying their backs straight. Never hurt a soul where a lonely sea beat waves up on a shore. And two trains a day went by. Hooting. Miss Martin a little hesitant secretary. On her first day she wore a filmy scarf, so shy stumbling over her words. Now says, you bastard.

Northward through low hills and tidy white clapboard towns, neat, stark and full of dreams. Countryside growing green. Long narrow lanes now, between woods and then crossroads with a white church and steeple. Wide shady porches of houses tucked in under the trees. Smith telling out the turns in a low voice into the little microphone, driver raising a finger quietly shaking head as he gets the message.

The road dips down, cross a bridge over the rapids of a river far below. Over another little bridge and up between dark tall shadowy pines. Light shut out from the sky. Left turn past a farm and red barns. And two little houses sitting like children's toys on a lawn. More woods. An old clapboard house, seven kids standing on the porch and two on a swing under a big tree. The road narrowing.

'Mr Smith, is there a hotel way out here. The road's ending. What's it called.'

'Miss Martin, ahem.'

'It's got a name.'

'No.'

'Hotel with no name. But we're at the end of the road.'

'Everything's going to be all right Miss Martin. Now don't worry about a thing. Driver, take the right turning. Through the pines. It's perfectly safe, just a little bumpy. Right, here.'

Miss Martin sitting straight up in her seat, staring ahead and left and right, thick pine needles on either side. Blanket of brown years of needles underneath, dark and snake forbidding. Over a little hill in the road.

'Mr Smith, no car's been down here for months it's nearly grown over. Where are we going.'

'Miss Martin. This is not exactly a hotel.'

'What is it.'

'A moment Miss Martin, little trouble ahead with these branches. Driver, just proceed – I'm responsible for any scratches on the car.'

Car squeezing between the low branches and new green leaves of maple trees. Down a little hill and ahead a clearing and the brown faint shingled roof of a log cabin. Stone chimney peeking out of the greenery. Driver turning round smiling through emerald tinted glass. In sight of shore.

'I'm not getting out Mr Smith.'

'We're here Miss Martin.'

'I'm not getting out.'

'Don't be silly. The driver is waiting.'

'I'm not getting out.'

'Why.'

'I'm not getting out.'

'Miss Martin, that's the northern office I've spoken about.'

'You've never said a word to me about a northern office. This is utter desolation.'

'There's a telephone in there Miss Martin. A bathroom, kitchen, fireplace, fifty wave radio, which sends, receives and even dances when no one's looking.'

'Don't try to be funny.'

Smith with one hand on the handle of the door. Driver out. So discreet. Sensing the fly in the recent ointment. Don't try to be funny. Never been so distant from a laugh. Or hearing this kind of common chat. Such a big world with different kinds of personalities everywhere. A slaughter house.

'Very well Miss Martin, suit yourself. I'll get this stuff out. And the driver will take you home. Hand me that file please. And my gloves. My stick. I'm sorry there's been this misunderstanding between us. I know this outpost seems unused to you.'

'You said a hotel Mr Smith. I thought it was The Goose Goes Inn, you had some notepaper from there, that's what I thought. You never said anything about this place. It's all so uninhabited. I'm scared to be way out here.'

'Chauffeur's walking around enjoying it. Hear the rapids down there, the Worrisome River.'

Miss Martin primly sitting. Hands on her knees. Keep an

eye on the fingers to see what they're doing. Don't let the golden moment go. Show her the long door back to town at the mercy of the chauffeur. He might look back through the green tinted glass, grinning. How would you like that Miss Martin. Here, you just retire to your little bedroom and I lie out in the big drawing room with the embers of the fire on my face. And sweet dreams. In your little beddy bo you will be comfy save for the giant spiders. Harmless creatures though huge. And when you scream running into me in your nightgown. Of course I'll save and protect you.

'Mr Smith what are you thinking.'

'I was thinking, Miss Martin, such a pity for you to go back to town. You do need a rest so. Few days in the fresh air. Away from the grime, dust and dirt of the city. You look tired. But I don't want to distress you. If you feel being out here will in some way make you unhappy. I wouldn't want that.'

'God.'

'What Miss Martin.'

'My mother will kill me. She'll ask me the name of the people. Then she'll look them up in the phone book. Then she'll telephone them and ask if I maybe left my gloves there or something. Mr Smith, I'm scared.'

'Now now.'

'I am.'

'Vouchsafe.'

'What do you mean.'

'I don't know myself Miss Martin. I'm just saying the first thing that comes into my head. What can one say.'

'I don't know I feel you're an operator.'

'I beg your pardon.'

'That there's been a whole string of girls up here, or something like that.'

'What are you saying, Miss Martin. You've seen the entrance. Overgrown. Besides I think that's a little uncalled for.'

'Don't send me back with this chauffeur.'

Miss Martin sitting. A frozen silence. Her eyelids go up.

And I think I just catch her teeth pressing secretly into the lower lip. But by God I am dying to protect her. Save her from harm and loneliness. From fear of the future. That she should ever want or need. Or go without shoes. Butter or wholesome bread. Lies often have beauty.

'Miss Martin give me your hand.'

Smith patting the sad metacarpals. Giving them back, gathered as they are in their white softness of flesh, a tender blue vein to keep them all alive. Smile. Help her out of the car. Herbert popping back from the woods to carry items to the cabin. Can't beat Herbert.

Under the low leaves. Smith struggling with the stiff lock on the door. Finally putting shoulder to it and smashing it open. Herbert and Miss Martin amazed at this casual display of forcefulness from the slender Smith.

All shifted. All unpacked. Herbert saluting. One smile followed with a little bow. Car roaring, then purring quietly. Disappearing out under the awning of new maple leaves, crackling tiny dead branches on the road. Sun high up. Dancing on top of the green.

In the log cabin. On the brown mat on the entrance floor. Next to the little pantry full of dishes, and tin cans of food. Lay a white envelope. Smith putting his armful of files on the stove. Miss Martin pushing past, stepping over it. Smith picking it up with the tweezering fingers. Ripping it open. One look. Ah Jesus, it was a sad day some fuckpig picked up a twig and made a sign in the sand.

>   We reiterate that
>   a sufficiency
>   is enough under
> George Smith   this heading.
> The Cabin (Log)
> The Open Woods.
> Dear Sir,
>   We know you are dying to know how we know you are here.
>   Yours truly,
>   J.J.J. (Rural)
> P.S. Just wait till the full history is told.

131

'Mr Smith, you mustn't get upset.'

'Miss Martin. Ah Jesus.'

'Come sit on the chair.'

'Get your pencil poised. Miss Martin. Got to rattle something back. Attach it to a tortoise and send it on its way. Ready.'

'Yes Mr Smith.'

'Dear Sir and rural Junior. Your fly is open. Yours sincerely George Smith. Urban. P.S. Is your real name Wang.'

Miss Martin pressing her pencil on the white porcelain kitchen stove. Writing with her upsidedown left hand. Looks up. A smile at the deflated Smith legs akimbo on the kitchen chair. Head lolling on chest.

'Mr Smith.'

'I'm all right, Miss Martin. Just assuming this attitude for a few moments. I'll rear up once again I assure you. For a minute it's just nice to sit here, slain in battle, as the heart beats its last, pluck one final arrow out of whatever they keep them in, and twang, let it loose to find its way to the heart of the enemy.'

'You speak so beautifully at times, Mr Smith.'

Smith smiles. And stood up. Says this way Miss Martin. This way. Come, let me show you. And by the elbow, steering this left hander into the drawing room. The boulder fireplace. A big round stove. Screens on the windows. Beams across the ceiling. The monstrous radio. A bathroom, small but working. Twist the faucet and rusty water pours forth. Black telephone in the corner. Which bounces when it rings. And I know from experience you can pick it up and talk to the most strange people all dotted on the map in the miles and miles of these woods.

'And, Miss Martin, last but, ahem, not least. Your bedroom.'

'O Mr Smith it's lovely.'

Smith providing one surprise after another. And the maple table for the repast. A bookcase. As Smith opens up the binding and displays the long line of distilled spirits. And wines. Not to mention some unheard of aperitifs.

'A drink, Miss Martin.'

'I don't know.'

'Have one.'

'I really shouldn't.'

'Bust out.'

'Gee.'

'Full bodied sherry. A round madeira. Iced muscatel.'

Smith at the bottles. The long necks, the little, the fat. Green, brown, two red and twenty deep dark green. All gently cared for through the cold winter, sealed off safely in their temperate darkness.

'I'd like a whisky and soda, Mr Smith.'

'Fine and we'll make a little fire.'

'I had no idea, Mr Smith. What a place. That where you sleep there.'

'And the embers at night, Miss Martin. Glow. The firelight licks across the ceiling. Like being ushered somewhere precious to sleep.'

'I like the way you speak now Mr Smith. Gee it's nice.'

Smith ladling out the whisky. Into glasses filled with ice. Armloads of logs fetched. Miss Martin opening the can of pressed ham. Corn. Peas. Pans bouncing on the red hot rings of the electric stove. Sun lowering in the sky. Shifting in under the newly born leaves. Miss Martin pausing at the front open screen door. Saw a deer. She sneezed. And it ran.

Little flowered mats on the table. Steel eating instruments. A vase on the window sill full of wax spring flowers. Which poor Smith would never dare pick from the snake lurking shadows. But Miss Martin went out with nary a thought for the rural dangers. There were daisies. Pick them and wet the bed at night. The afternoon is dying. Sun nearly set. Leaves flutter. Smell of corn. Woodchucks out there. And hear a black snake moving over the leaves.

Smith doing his little bit. Polishing the glass. Rinsing the dusty plates. Miss Martin opens and closes her mouth as she cooks. Raising her eyebrows. Seams of her stockings dividing each leg neatly in half. Somehow in the skidding about in deals, one never lets the mind rest enough to catch sight of the neat shape of Miss Martin's calf. Out here in the country peace. My God it looks good.

'Miss Martin this is a nice little morsel you have dished up.'

Smith across the maple from Miss Martin. Thank God he made that tree. Her hands so delicate. A marvel. She twists a spoon so certainly. Puts out the peas steaming on this ornate clay plate. Only need now fresh butter, fresh lemon. Goodness me, there is beastly craving again. Never satisfied. Always want more.

'Miss Martin you have excelled yourself. You really have.'

'I like cooking. Salt, Mr Smith.'

'Ah, please. I have always fancied peas. Defenceless little green spheres somehow they don't stand a chance between the choppers. So sad.'

'You seem a different person in the country, Mr Smith.'

'Shall we have music Miss Martin. Tune in to some wavelength.'

'That would be nice.'

'Do you fancy light, jazz or the serious kind.'

'I like serious, Mr Smith.'

'Splendid. Fits the sadness of the peas.'

'I never knew you felt that way about peas Mr Smith. I'd bring some to Dynamo House, could cook them on the burner.'

Violins came out of the big radio. With some other instruments. A flute. A horn. Smith sat. Looking across the table. Smiled. Behind Miss Martin the screen front door. Two steps down to the ground, and the gathering green darkness down the steep hill to the bubbling, roaring of Worrisome River.

'Mr Smith. I'd like to ask you something.'

'Yes.'

'You won't mind.'

'Not at all.'

'What do you want to be. I mean not that you're not something, you know what I mean. Sounds as if I don't think you're important but I do. But is there something you would like to be.'

'A great criminal.'

'Ha ha, Mr Smith. Really what would you like to be.'

'That's it Miss Martin.'

'But you're crooked already.'

Smith's steely Asian eyes. Muscles dropping on his face. General rigidity. Bleak silence.

'I don't mean that. Now I've ruined everything. I put words into my mouth I don't mean. You're not crooked. No. Mr Smith I swear you're not crooked.'

'Thanks.'

'You're not.'

'I'm glad you think that.'

'Gee, I don't know why I said it.'

'Pass me the corn Miss Martin. When one proceeds straight in life there is always an obstruction.'

'You're an honest and good person, Mr Smith.'

'This is great corn.'

'Mr Smith pass me the peas.'

'Certainly.'

'I didn't mean what I first said.'

'It's all right, Miss Martin.'

'Gee you're so different in the country.'

Smith ladling up the yellow kernels. Outside a breeze in the leaves. Yellow light flooding out the door. Music featuring a variety of horns. Lifts the spirit. Suddenly one can look at Miss Martin and see her in all her glory as a cook. Out here with all this good loneliness. Wafts away that feeling of the haunted hunted dog. Until the telephone rings. That black thing. Bouncing in the corner. Of this primeval forest.

'Let it ring, Miss Martin.'

Little jangling bell. Phone tilts to the side. Bounces. Trembling to the edge of the shelf rigged to the corner of the wall. And falls on the floor. Taking handle sliding across the maple.

'Ah Jesus.'

'Mr Smith.'

'Shush Miss Martin. We're trapped. Put your hand over the speaker.'

Miss Martin picking up the phone. Putting the part to the ear. Frowning.

'Mr Smith. It's someone saying what the hell is the matter with you George.'

'Nothing is the matter with me.'

'Shall I hang up Mr Smith.'

Smith rotating his hands. Looking across the room at Miss Martin as she stands both hands gripped over the talking instrument. Times in one's life when you think there is good news. And you listen.

'Mr Smith. He says he's catching the train. That he has little or no money. And is presently trying to sell his shoes to pay for the ticket. And four embroidered handkerchiefs which he sold this morning for the price of a glass of ersatz orange juice. He says he just wants to talk. And why, O dear, he said an awful word, the hell are you behaving in this extraordinary manner. Why are you trying to hide. Is there something the matter, I must say something, Mr Smith.'

'Tell him I've shifted further north.'

'I can't do that, Mr Smith. He's a cultivated gentleman on the phone.'

'Do as I say.'

'I will not. He's saying, why are you listening and saying nothing. I've got to say something. Mr Smith, he says he is in an unbelievable nightmare. That all he wants is just a few hours away from it all.'

'All right. Miss Martin. Tell him I'll meet him tomorrow morning. An eleven o'clock train comes from the coast. Tell him alight at Cinder Village.'

'Hello. Yes. Yes. Mr Smith says he will meet you on the eleven o'clock train tomorrow morning at Cinder Village. Yes. Mr Smith is all right. He's here. It's only that he's not available at the moment. I'm sorry you've had to sell your shoes. Yes. Certainly. God's goodly wishes to you too. Goodbye.'

'God.'

'Mr Smith he sounds like a real gentleman.'

Smith with sad reflective eyes. Outside the bark of a fox in the wood. Miss Martin picking up the dishes. Brings them to the sink in the kitchen. Runs the water. Breaks her long fingernails. Peace. Dark. An evening chill. Another log on the fire. Smell the orange glow and woody fume.

'Miss Martin, let me help with the dishes.'

'No Mr Smith. Just sit and be comfortable.'

Smith reclining. Placing the wicker chair near the fire. Reaching behind the bottles. Taking a long cigar from the humidor. Lighting up. Blow a cloud of whiteness out. Flick off the electric light. Moths from everywhere. Bumping the screens. Light is hope. And everyone is after hope. And away from the sad desperation. To become grasping hearts after emoluments. Riches, trusting nothing else. Bonniface sold his shoes.

Bedtime hour. In the woods. Miss Martin came shyly out of the kitchen. Paused looking over the reflective Smith puffing on his cigar. Smith rising.

'Miss Martin, do sit.'

'It's late, Mr Smith, isn't it. Perhaps I'd better make up the beds. Are there sheets.'

'In the bathroom cupboard. But you shouldn't. I'll do that.'

'No Mr Smith I'll do it. I'd like to.'

Smith took a little smoke down into the lungs. Let it pause there a few seconds. Purifies the blood. The trembletude and strain sleeping alone. Need something to hold on to. A life preserver in this big sea. Two white breasts. Miss Tomson, I thought of you yesterday. That you were stepping from one nightspot to another. In giant strides. With a group of friends.

At George Smith's shoulder. The bent figure of Miss Martin making the bed. Tucking in the sheets tightly. Popping on the clean pillow cases. When she bends over. Calm these hairy hands. Please glow little light of hope. Everyone is trying to blow you out. Save Miss Martin. Might blow you out myself. Walking down the street smoking a cigar of dynamite.

Smith looking over his shoulder at the backside of Miss Martin. Puffs out a cloud of smoke, descending in a ring round her bottom. Target of two globes. Wave the smoke away. Miss Martin straightening and turning around. Looks at Mr Smith. Mr Smith nods. Smiles.

'Don't want to smell you up with smoke Miss Martin.'

Miss Martin standing still in the shadows. Fire light across her face. Lashes close once over her eyes. God gave her good lips. Upper resting quietly on the lower. Freckles. Friendly one on the tip of the nose. Fox bark. Little tremor of Miss Martin's.

'Can I get you anything, Mr Smith.'

'No thank you Miss Martin. I'll just sit by the fire here and finish my smoke.'

'Well I guess I better –'

'Miss Martin.'

'Yes.'

'Miss Martin I don't want you to feel uncomfortable.'

'I'm really fine Mr Smith. I have to get used to the silence. And sound of I guess animals out in the dark.'

'Thank you for washing the dishes.'

'Goodnight, Mr Smith.'

'Goodnight, Miss Martin. Sleep tight.'

Smith crossing legs. Taking in a deep breath of air. Quietly stirring up to the book cabinet. Ladling out a glass of brandy. Back to the chair. Cross the legs. Taste the tobacco leaves and the sweet stinging grape. Miss Martin's door closes. Hear her light switch on. Bonniface tomorrow on the train. Some terrible tale. Disaster on the high seas. Blows on the back of the neck suffered abroad. Escape to the land of opportunity. I met Bonniface. First one night in a suburb of the university town. Where he resided with his pregnant wife with large beautiful teeth in a big beautiful mouth. We had spinach and poached egg. Toast and tea. His landlords were gentle people who showered their tenant with turf fires, much hot water for baths and first use of the daily newspaper. Bonniface was a stickler for justice and fair play. And he raised his rent accordingly as the landlords heaped presents and services upon him. I tripped down the front stairs that first evening and was laid out on the couch in the landlords' parlour. Coming to, I viewed the strange smiling face of Bonniface looking down. God forgive those incorrigibly strange of spirit.

George Smith. Chin on chest. Eyes sad. Night chilly. Low moon making shadows in the trees. Hoot of owls. Out here the black snakes. And the tan and red and poisonous kind. Ready to slide over the pillow and wrap round the neck. Come up from under the house. Miss Martin to bed without a qualm. In that licking lashing fire flame. Miss Tomson. That great lollypop of a girl. Bite her, wherever she is, with a friendly pair of steak hardened jaws.

Smith locking latches on doors and windows. Turning off the faint music on the vast radio. The light out under Miss Martin's door. Sitting on the edge of the bunk, unlace the shoes, tug off the black socks. Miss Martin won't mind if I sleep without a garment. Be up before her in the morning. Thrill her with the smell of coffee. Tomorrow newborn. Leave today behind. And my footprints in blood. From Owl Street to this cabin far away.

> Running
> Without underwear
> Hiding without
> Shame.

Rich
Without reason
Rotten without
Rhyme.

The country darkness. The quiet azure peace. Smith putting his head on the pillow of lavender scented linen. Shutting the eyes. An elbow up over the ears. Digging the ankle and toes down slowly to the bottom to feel it free of animals. Miss Martin knows now in her own bed I only wanted company. Longer lived than shenanigans. Although when the smoke ring settled over that part of her it became a desperate moment. The look in her eyes when she looked, so silent and still. All the cash registers of the world ringing at once.

Eyelids down. Heart gently ticking over. Night marauders moving over leaves. Dream of a snowy tundra. Over which a man approaches speaking one hundred and five languages. He said the last five were nearly impossible to master. Then a nun skated by. Shirl. Taken up the religious life. Miss Tomson stood, a big stately bitch. And said as she held out each ripe breast, you want a nice delicious peach buster. And laughed, her great white teeth breaking out just like sun after rain. I said hush they'll hear. She said when will we ever be on farting terms together Smith. My name echoed all over the valley. Turning into screams. A bang of a door. The pound of bare feet across the floor.

'Mr Smith, O God, Mr Smith.'

Smith rearing up out of a dream of many hands of personal oppressors pulling on the hair as one attempted to dig up stakes to take off for the tundra. Miss Martin centre cabin floor, wrapped and twisting in the trailing bedspread, shoulders atremble staring down round her in the dimness.

'Mr Smith it dropped off the ceiling. Right on me. I felt it. A spider. It's stuck to the bedspread. O God get it away. Big horrible thing.'

Fieldmarshal Smith up out of the covers. Naked to the rescue. Spider a great hairy thick legged thing on the floor. Big as a hand. Rearing back on the hind legs. Two front claws held up.

'Kill it for God's sake Mr Smith kill it.'

'I'll get a shovel.'

'Don't leave me here with it.'

'Easy now, Miss Martin.'

'O God God.'

'Throw the bedspread over it.'

'I've nothing on.'

'You must. It's our only hope.'

Spider retreating back into a dappled ray of moonlight as George approached holding up the bedspread. Miss Martin huddled bending, arms over breasts and pubes in the shadows. Smith, private parts jangling, in this present rodeo. Rolling up the spider in the cloth. Sneaking a gentlemanly look at the figure of Miss Martin. Taking this insectivore to the door. Throwing the lot out into the night. Miss Martin shyly trembling by the telephone. Smith locking the screen.

'This is most awkward Miss Martin.'

'Mr Smith I'm terrified to go back into that bedroom.'

George advancing upon Miss Martin. As she stood naked and alone. In need of comfort. Shook out of her wits by the hairy ten legged crawling creature. Feet bottoms dusty. If the phone rings now, one rip and its out of the house altogether. Bump bump bump, hearts thumping. Droplet of sweat on the brow. Comes dripping off the tip of the nose. Lick it in between the lips. Touch of a hand on Miss Martin's shoulder. This is no mop closet.

Tears in Miss Martin's eyes. Better than terror. Flap of wings somewhere out in the trees. And she puts her arms around George Smith. And her head and hair on his chest. His arms around her shoulders.

'I don't know what to do George.'

Smith mumchance, picking up Miss Martin. Carrying

her across the room to the bunk. Lay her there. Unless one strains irrevocably with this display of strength. Long tiring day. One short circuit after another in Dynamo House. Provide for that spider and its heirs in my will. Her spine. Mouth. Teeth. Her hair. Which while in Golf Street she rinsed in blonde tint. To cloak the mouse brown. After all the months of repression. Of tight lipped orders. Type this type that. Send this send that. Now take this. Tickle. And taste. As you said you cried. When I stood on top of the hill and the white river flowed by.

'George.'

Smith, one ear on Miss Martin's breast. Her lips and mouth on the back of his neck. She raised her legs in the air, curling up her toes like fists. Shook them. Display of abandoned agility. Thank you spider.

'George.'

Soft pressure on the face. Miss Martin I have something to tell you. It's brief. Just to say. Hello. Soft between your legs. Narrow niceness round your waist. Little belly over your crinkling hairs. You'll never forgive me because I can't remember your name. Got crushed out of my mind in the excitement. Get my mouth on yours and shut us both up. Among the molars. All the internal beauty. Nature gives love without warning. As well as this ass. O my God as I put it in you Miss Martin, the battle of control over. The upper lip curling, trembling, doing anything. Arms squeezing feeling tearing. Locked round it. You so graciously are. Strange to hear you groan, twist and gyrate, can hardly hold you on the bunk. You morsel. I might say so long tempting. Sniff under this arm. Honest sweat of fear. Green lawns. Where tennis is played. Remarkable backhanded volleys. After the match the losers' jamboree. For one tight minute I felt it would not fit. I pushed. Miss Martin pushed. We pushed together. In. With one long chested groan. All so friendly. Hold her by the wrists. She says a lovely pain. O my God Miss Martin any minute now. Give me back that breast that elusive nipple. Give me that ear. Tart taste. And your hair, you wore it up and

down. And folded round. Stuck with bobby pins. Came to
Golf Street, in grey, in green, across the plenty trouble-
some months. A godsend. Up out of the subway, through
the narrow financial gloomy streets. As the other thousands
sit down to desks, light lights, shuffle the papers, fill the
files, take the particulars and it was all so much easier
years ago to take the fish out of the sea and sell it so much
a fresh pound. Till a hundred college graduates stepped
between. To freeze the poor fish while they mark up a
profit for the boss. And in the door you came of 604 while
I got up draughty off the wretched couch. Must ask you to
hold my legs sometime out the air shaft window to peek
at the sky. I'm going to explode. Miss Martin. Right into
you. Tremble and clutch with more behind me in life now
than there is in front. Dear God do you have any old
friends who sing operas. Or who travel the seas bandjaxed.
Or go to their head doctor on Wednesdays, Herr Shrinker I
was smashed off the tit at ten. Presto, bravo, Herr Patient.
You mean Herr Shrinker I have had an insight. You said
it, Herr Patient. Why do you laugh and chuckle so, Herr
Shrinker. Ha ha, Herr Patient, you are too inquisitive, but
perhaps I am amused by your little stories. Miss Martin
you rear up so, dying ember light on your torso. How could
I have ever realized what you were each long office day,
tired over deals, trembling over contracts, cowering from
letters. World like a lot of falling steps. Everything going
into you, great cascade of white river while you stood that
day the bottom of the hill and nasty old gossip women
wailing and wracked. These two breasts your secrets.
Pinker than I ever thought. Sharper and tilted. Lily white.
Sixty miles back to town. Four thousand to the north pole.
Shirl will sue me. Bonniface will make me skip in fear.
And you will tell me to do my own typing. Mr Stone will
lurk to catch me sneaking out the service entrance of
Merry Mansions. All too unlovely for words. I charged at
you Miss Martin, weapon raised. I was amazed. Having
measured it recently. Now bigger than ever recorded. A
fountain for a white river. Sprinkled like stars. Vanishing

143

away when the morning comes. Leaving the little light
left.

> To glow.
> And grow
> Inside
> You
> Thank
> You
> Spider.

9

Distant hilltops spreading a canopy of new green across the rolling land. A spiral of smoke from George Smith's cabin in the woods. The white twisting Worrisome River singing on this Saturday morning. And the long lonesome wail of the steam engine coming up from the coast carrying a passenger for deposit at Cinder Village.

Breakfast cooking in the cabin. Smith stretched stark on the bunk, hands folded under head, elbows sticking up. Birds achirp. Miss Martin wearing one of Smith's sweaters and her pair of black high heels as she clicked in and out of the kitchen cooking for the lonesome tiger lightly napping.

Canned ham grilled brown. Matzos. Big mugs of tea. Miss Martin smiling down at the lengthwise Smith and with a light finger flicking up his gentle pecker. No hebrew he. She sat chewing. Smith renewing. This quiet morning in the country. Her brown hair down. Long thighs and remarkable muscles around the knees.

Minutes by full of peace. Of all the fresh untired sounds out of the woods. Open up the ears wide. The eyes. Even dare think. That Miss Martin is forever part of me. Sits there eating. Watch the swallowing down her throat. She said one or two strange things while she lay sleeping. About a mysterious phone call to a place of worship. A cultured voice which suggested it would place sufficient explosive on the premises to blow it sky high next Tuesday midnight. The prelate to go with it. And Miss Martin sat up and I gently pushed her back down. Must have worries on her mind. Then she slept quietly snoring in my arms.

Smith finishing breakfast. Stood up and pounded his

chest. Coughed. Padded to the bathroom. Standing in the tub under the chilling shower. Marching back to the living room. Pulling the towel zigzag over the back. One display of vitality after another. Miss Martin shyly peeking from the kitchen. Comes in. Smith lifting her sweater. Nuzzling face between two white pears. Give Miss Martin a friendly morning embrace. Happy in the cabin. Great to be alive. Till the wail of the steam train on the other side of the Worrisome River headed for Cinder town.

Brief moments of unfettered solitude left. Smith and Miss Martin entwined. Opening up her mouth to say there's the train. And Smith whispered last night you said sleeping the prelate would be blown. Sky high.

'Did I.'

'You did.'

Smith flexing the knees. Picking up Miss Martin carrying her to the bunk. Train pounding up the valley. Ten minutes more to town. Ten years between Miss Martin and me. Takes one back to high school. Fastened to her young body. Jesuits walked around. All the other kids were there. One tall faced thin ecclesiastic cleric said what is your name. Where do you live. I felt located. He was the prefect of discipline, hatchet faced and feared. Coming out of nowhere to grab you defenceless by the collar. Twisting. I wanted to say, hey watch the garotte. But he had a system of torture called jug. To walk round and round in circles for hours. Miss Martin pressing against your belly would have been forbidden. Lectures on sex. Every Friday. Boys today we discuss the process of generation. White haired and ancient this prelate was easily given to tears. As he said there is a fleshy shaft from which two spongy balls hang. There were terrible whispers. You old clot. Marriage was the holy joining together of two people. Without use of the rubber covering of the organ. Boys as you sit there now before me. In the sight of God. Don't dare use rubbers. I'm not. The shaft is sacred this prelate shouted. Standing here before you today boys, remember that thought. These young beautiful innocent girls who come each year on the school boat ride. Are of the purest and whitest. Dare you look or feel up their innocent dresses. Dare you. Or think impurely. The wretchedness the writhing the Lord God will smash down on your heads. Everyone in the class looked around at me. As the prelate shouted evil companions. They are the ones dear boys. Miss Martin. Wish you did not dream of dynamiting the prelate. As this one shook his fist right at me over the heads of my class mates, screaming shaft. Fleshy shaft. The smart alec behind me whispering between my shoulder blades, that he was on his way home to pull his right out of its socket and didn't give a sacred fart what the Lord God smashed down. While he was pulling. All that seventeen years ago Miss Martin. We had class nights with apple pie and soda pop. And swam in the swimming pool. The bushy sight of our language instructor for months in black and now in nothing. I was voted having the biggest one at the secret ballot on the lengths of shafts. A disgraceful little group of boys. Amused by my member. Which God help me I wanted to roll up that day so it wouldn't show at all. Never take it sadly out again. Till the darkness of last spidery night Miss Martin fooling with it said you have such a beautiful one. Held in her fingers. Said her father died. Building the bridge. She rides the train across to work. Her mother never had the money to move away from the bitter memory. Miss Martin you must have been a funny little girl father protected till you were six. Wham. A big girder. Best time of day to do it now, fresh as daisies. Just shut down the brain. Let instinct take over. And first thing this morning, Miss Martin out dusting crumbs off the table. Speeding to and fro in her high heels. Were my fellow prepsters and presiding prelates to see me now they would say he has turned out, that Smith, just as we thought he would, bringing the school name constantly into disrepute. With that shaft of his. And Shirl was impressed by such a splendid school. Till she married me and said the kids took so much out of her. Slaving to their little wretched wants. Greedy little heads spinning on a nipple as she said I want to live the way the rich live, go through life and hold my head up in the air being noticed and liked by everybody. This month of May. As age comes slowly and hardly notice it at all. Miss Martin makes such a fuss. Rolling her head. Brought breakfast. Time to meet the train. Bonniface. Will wait in the shade of the platform. And get a shock as I arrive. We'll stand there under cedar shingles. Just three. Miss Martin in black shining high heels. Grey dress, soft wool that clings. Bonniface perhaps without shoes. The train will pull out again. I will introduce Miss Martin to Bonniface. He will bow. And click. A thump perhaps without footwear. Miss Martin I am collapsing like a pack of cards. Filling you with white river. What do you see in me. Other than miraculous humility. You walked across this cabin floor this morning, bare arse wagging. I jumped up and held it two handed tightly just as you were slipping into the kitchen. And turned your face around again. Kissed you on the mouth. And kiss you now. And smell your sweet sweat and gamey breath. Under your hair around your arms. Lick your eyes. Tell the lids all these tales. How when I wanted to step out bravely into the world dressed in the best suit I had, speaking with the best voice I could and the school head master said he caught me in a lie. That I told all my fellow prepsters to lay the girls on the boat ride. To lift their dresses. To plug them as he claimed I had put it. You clerical lout. We sailed up the river. Between the steep cliffs my dear Miss Martin, God you are soft and full of warmth. How can it be such gay and painful summertime. The boat whistle blew. We strolled the decks. Sun glimmering on the water. Prefect of discipline head back to view indiscretion lightly this favoured day. The boat ride. Up the river to a park in the trees. Dance band. And all the proper little boys in sport jackets and flannels. And we swam and played ball, and jumped and ran and raced. I tried to star. For I met a girl that day. I had, true, told the school, who listened to me spellbound. To indeed plug these convent girls. None of whom could be plugged. I knew. Blessed creatures they were. Full of the Lord. And the mother of God. And the dream of hubby nine to five for forty years till dead in his tracks with a handsome policy. We passed a prison. Sitting on the shore. Grey and tight. Stone. And the prefect, Miss Martin, came by and said ha ha Smith, ha ha, that would be a place to keep you in line, ha ha. And I silently stiffly passed that remark by. Come to my funeral Miss Martin, be there. Please. And when they say wretched things about me, how I was fake, liar, and grew up out of all proportion to my prospects, shout back, say I was good o humble and gentle. While they carry me away, music playing across my laundered lawn barbered round the sepulchre. They said why did I do it. Build a monstrous monument. Because I had no friends. No respect. Yet never went bald from worry. Nor bleached white codes. Hashed up a few of the dark. And one or two white with my secretary. The ground I walk on she'll never worship. Born to know to whom to bow to whom to scrape. Much dumb demeanour everywhere. In that town full of faces erasing all the traces of what they feel. Just as well. Leads to a lot of embarrassment. A crackle of a twig. Lain here an hour. Miss the train. Bonniface.

'Can I call you George now, George.'

'No.'

Miss Martin stiffened in Smith's arms. As she tried to get up. Her eyes opening wide. Pressing her elbows between the two bodies. Forcing Smith back.

'Don't touch me.'

'Why.'

'I'm as good as you are.'

'No you're not Miss Martin.'

'I want to get out of here.'

'There's the door.'

Miss Martin standing. Looking down at Smith lying there prostrate looking up. Teeth clenched inside her mouth. Fists held out from her sides white and tight. Raises them up. Shakes them down. Breasts trembling. Tide of tan round them and her thighs from last summertime. Eyes blazing.

'You deliberately got me up here.'

'Sit down Miss Martin.'

'Don't Miss Martin me. You bastard.'

Smith cool faced. But wincing in the heart. Tell a fact and they fling back epithets. Give warmth and they wrap you in a chain. Behind her on the twin bunk, the file marked go. Which I thought in all my acute innocence would speed us into the solar system. Instead of being grateful they turn on you. Wretched left out world it is. Miss Martin troubled by how good she is. Of course you're not, Miss Martin. As good as me. I tell you for your own sake. To save you airs. The whole world will tear off you. With insults. Come now, no churlishness. Women lie and cheat, twist and steal. Can't help it. Nature gave them these little habits. To use when hubby takes off for the tundra or is drunk in bed. I need you Miss Martin. Please don't go. Stay. I want you to cover me up with your soft self. Keep me warm and safe. Another crackle of a twig. A sound. Of music strange out under the trees. She stands still. Staring back. If you can stare I can stare Miss Martin. As long as you like. Stay here forever. Unwavering eyes. Stony globes. I'm as honest as you can get. That's why Miss Martin I ask for all this respect. And why I confound all those who stood faithfully waiting for my every little failure. While I sidestepped slowly away down the various little alleys of success. Brown eyes. You stare. I'll stare. You out Miss Martin. Be sure of that. Don't you feel chilly or at least foolish without a stitch. Nipples clutched up with cold. We can't keep this up forever. You must have won contests at this in high school. To find some chink in my spirit. That's it, you got to straighten up. Caught you staring bent over. O it won't be long now before you must avert the eyes. You morsel. All this wasted time I could be looking at the rest of you. Breasts geared to giving. Bush beneath the belly. So late now to meet Bonniface. Have Miss Martin call the Funeral Director of Cinder Village for the hire of a car. Or ha ha hearse. She's breaking. Saw that flicker of the lid. Nervous moment there with the lip. Jesus Christ. Miss Martin. Catching her breath. Turning clutching her arms around her. Splickety lick for the bedroom.

George Smith turning. There featured in the window. Dimly beyond the copper screen. The thin face. The smile. Little black comb with a piece of paper held. To take the blowing of musical air. Rumpled green shirt. Loose brown jacket. Slender green tie. Cedric Calvin Bonniface Clementine. The awful. Bonniface.

'My gawd.'

Smith rubbing his eyes. Pulling up the sheet somewhat over the naked parts. As the grin on Bonniface widened behind the comb. And the music continued. Smith rose. Smiling, crossing the floor to greet and say hello and how could you find the hidden cabin. How did you get from Cinder Village. I trust you are not utterly banjaxed. Cast up on the shore. God forgive dreadful things that happen aboard those steamers.

Smith stepping near the window. Stopping at the screen. All that is here. Just some greenery of leaves. And bushes. And no Bonniface at all. At all. And I've insulted Miss Martin. And who was at that window. Who. Miss Martin saw something too. And I heard.

Smith opening and leaning out the door. Looking this way and that. All ending in green. Something spooky out here. Some man roams mad. Stands about. Mooning. Making gestures. Carving things on trees. I swear I saw that face. That smile. I'm shivering. Cold sweat. There's something out in the woods. I must quickly make friends again with Miss Martin. Before I lose every vestige of nerve. And that thing comes in and gets me.

Smith in the sheet. Grasped up round the shoulders. Crossing to the bedroom door. First peeking in the bathroom. And the empty space under the tub. In the cupboard. On the shelves. Where. That unblessed visage. The Bonniface. Or is the loneliness here too much. Or the staring contest with Miss Martin. The general feeling spreads that the world is rampant with mischief.

Knocking on Miss Martin's door. Once. Twice. O Gawd.

Not a sound in there. Please Miss Martin I beg of you show some sign of life. Zip up. Make a noise. Even bust wind if you must. Make it mystical.

'Miss Martin.'

George Smith stood rigid. Ready and frozen. For some hand to be placed without warning on the back. Reaching out of the silence. Hair stands up wiggling on the neck. Miss Martin believe me when I say you are worth ten of me. Or eight anyway. I'm lowdown. Without references. No business heading. No title under my name. Just a vague fixed address which is beginning to move. Gawd. Standing here. Three miles to the first civilization. The house by the road with seven kids and one thin mommie.

Smith in the white toga. First in fear. Now in fever. Heart jumping all over the chest. Turning to the black defenceless telephone. Must have transport. Wrap up files and get out fast. Take the deer track. Dare not look in on Miss Martin in case she's transubstantiated. Get on this talking machine.

'Operator.'

'Number please.'

'Brandy.'

'Number please.'

'Brandy, funeral director, Cinder Village, please operator.'

'Why didn't you say so.'

'I've just said so.'

'Has there been a death.'

'None of your damn business.'

'O.'

Smith decidedly executive. Toga drawn tightly. Leaning back against the wall. The soothing voice of Mr Brandy any second now. Unless he's out busy. Ah. George Smith here, Mr Brandy, I'm fine, nice day, how are you. Good, nice day, that's splendid. No. Haven't seen the new sign yet. Could you send a car. Instantly. That's splendid. O you read that. Don't believe all you read, Mr Brandy. And could you have your driver get here as fast as he can. And send another man with him. Fine. Yes, nice day. Bye. Bye.

Times in one's life requiring unprecedented action. And

on this rural sun dappled Saturday morning, take a few steps back. Raise each knee to test the suppleness. Bend to touch the toes. Eye the door. I will go through that thin pathetic pine. Like a steam train. Splinters flying. Panels asunder. Ere that ghost out there flitting between the trees. Will get a goodly taste of poison ivy.

Smith charged. Leading with the left shoulder. Hooking with the right. Brave bull. Feet nicely grasping all traction from the maple floor. Lightly flying with a thunderous crash through the door. Which shattered, fell to the floor. Hinges ripped. Screws flying. Smith on top. Miss Martin lying stretched on the bunk head buried beneath pillow. Oblivious to this stalwart. Sometime stallion.

Miss Martin, please understand the meaning of Bonniface. Proud culprit. Unconvicted world traveller sporting the canvas boots. Collector of second hand gravestones and urinals in quantity. Foot stamper, shouter and singer of the threnody. As one hears things strangely on the air. A voice out there in the woods. Faint. High pitched. Echoing far away from the other side of Worrisome River.

> Jews and jailbirds
> Bad news
> Urinals and gravestones
> Thrice used.

10

George Smith telling Miss Martin to get dressed. To stand up and face life like a woman. Forget keeping a face on things. Put on your grey dress. Buy you a beer in Cinder Village. Here, have a little tender hug. Mr Brandy is sending a car. We will meet Bonniface. This nice day.

Smith stepping out of the cabin. Sweet warm green smells. As the car ordered from Brandy, merchant of death, drove into the clearing of trees. Staring dumbfounded. Approaching the two dark figures in black top hats. Consternation.

'Look here, is this the car from Mr Brandy.'

'Yes sir.'

'I did not order a hearse.'

'Look Mister Smith, here, here's the card the kid brought over to the garage. See for yourself. What it says.'

One Hearse, George Smith,
The Cabin,
take left fork on the trail at the end of Layabout Lane,
Worrisome River Rapids.

'I'm meeting a guest. This is most awkward. I'm late already.'

'We're sorry Mr Smith. But that's the message.'

Smith leading Miss Martin out under the trees. To take the seat next to the driver. Smith sitting behind on one side of the casket rest, extra man on the other. Immobility of face. Disposal of the dead. Fear of ghouls. Bound for Cinder Town. Gazeteers, Shirl, Mr Stone, Miss Tomson, Goldminers, Prepsters. Line the road. Bless the one horse saloons. The roar of trains. Iron wheels thundering on the rails. Women when they lay down for love get a present forever. Thank you spider.

Long gleaming hearse. Passing out of Layabout Lane. Dragging a few stray branches. With the unmerry mumchance passengers. Down the hardtop road. Between the softly rolling hills. Through a shady village past a general store and rambling houses of old inhabitants. Grey women on the porches. Tickling flowers on the edges of lawns. Smith's features an uncomplicated cast. Traffic never stops even when you're dead.

Cinder Village. Past the establishment of Mr Brandy occupying a grassy fork in the road with a new neon sign. Further in the town, a square of old trees. The library. Drugstore. Houses of prominent citizens. Open high doors of the volunteer fire station. Rocking chairs on the porches. Hearse stopping for gas and oil. Down the little hill. To the cedar canopy over the tracks. A waiting room. Meeting a casket arriving on the train. One awful ghost.

'O.K., driver, wait here. Come Miss Martin.'

Smith climbing down from hearse amid stares. Saloon across the road. Sun hot and shining. And no Bonniface. Ask the station attendant. Nope. Can't say I did. Wait a minute now you mention, saw a guy with a brown cardboard suitcase, all busted. About half hour ago. He took out a comb, leaning against that post playing some kind of music with a piece of paper. Thought he was taking a breather from the state institution. The song he was singing. Wearing a pair of crazy canvas boots, open down the front. Some song.

> I was
> Tested for the
> Institution
> And was crazy
> Enough
> To pass.

We thought the guy was nuts. A friend of yours? We were going to call the cops but he was gone all of a sudden. Left an envelope. On the window sill of the office. Are you from the institution.

'No.'

'Letter addressed to George Smith.'

'That's me.'

'You George Smith.'

'Yes.'

'I'll get your letter.'

Smith standing in the shade of the platform. Miss Martin next to a cart. Mr Brandy's consorts whispering, leaning against the engine of the car. And through a loop hole in a green iron pillar, men lined up in the saloon across the street peering out the window. Silent hostile looks. From between the cardboard bathing beauty slugging beer. Hot shiny tracks down there on top of the pee sprinkled stones. Wintertime little boys stick tongues on the rails and they get stuck and the train comes and lops off their heads.

'Here's the letter. Ain't being nosey. But you the Smith. The George Smith. Paper's been full of.'

'Lots of Smiths. Great many Georges.'

'You sure look familiar.'

'Bye bye.'

Smith taking Miss Martin by the arm. By a soft touch inside her softer elbow. Moving her down the platform. All eyes. On a bench cross the tracks. Two workmen. Glaring. With short legs, short arms. All one did was to arrive in a hearse. To meet an ancient friend. Who came to my college room for tea. And munched hard boiled eggs at various embassies during those golden years abroad. Full of happy research into the future troubles trembling we knew were brewing. We married young beautiful wives. Stepped into the exciting garden for croquet. And got promptly slammed about the head and ears.

11.30
Platform
Cinder Village

My dear George,

I am most terribly sorry not to have waited for you longer. But I am in an acute state of distress. However, on the train I met a most friendly person who has helped me. And has kindly

156

availed me of his house so that I may at least rest up for a few days before proceeding further. God knows where.

He asks me to enclose this letter to you. I can be reached through him. I hope I have not inconvenienced you in any way. And that the things I hear about you are totally untrue. I would be grateful for a loan. Nudum pactum.

> Godly blessings
> Upon you
> In your fear.
> BONNIFACE

P.S. I have one woeful case of hayfever with which I can hardly breathe and can hardly see at all. Also a slight case of shingles as well as blistered feet.

> C.C.B.C.

Smith opening the next letter. A hooked finger ripping open the flap. As uncontrollable phrases pass through the mind. Dear Sir, we will be interested in viewing your residue what's left of you.

> Pomfret Manor
> Cinder Village

Dear Mr Smith,

May I make so bold as to address you? I feel I know you as an old acquaintance through your friend Mr Cedric Calvin Bonniface Clementine who told me much of you on our enjoyable ride together on the train. It seems we too live in your neck of the woods, although this may be news to you. But briefly let me come to the point. My wife and I would most assuredly be proud to have you among our guests this weekend, tonight 6:30 onwards. It would be a real privilege. No jamboree but we hope it'll be fun. Any of your friends are welcome too.

> Cordially,
> John Jiffy Jr.

P.S. Since writing this on the train. Mr Clementine informs me he has missed you, and I have taken the liberty of inviting him over. Perhaps you will join us for a few drinks.

> J.J.J.

Stare at these three capital letters. Consecutive and cold. Cast off this casual coincidence. One J for junior. Or jolt. The last and third for jamboree.

The afternoon. Blew up. In sky high beauty. Smith in the face of friendless village eyes. Commandeered the hearse from station to the self service store. Traffic made way. Miss Martin in the acreage of foodstuffs, filling a wire gocart with frankfurters, peanut butter, jars of olives, sauerkraut, vitamin reinforced bread and one little glass of pineapple cheese spread. Mr Brandy's cohorts lifting the provisions out to the hearse. Together with forty five bottles of wine and spirits. Not to mention the ice cold beer and four avocadoes. People whispering on the sidewalk under the old elm trees. Smith wagging a finger at an old lady. Naughty. Whole kit and kaboodle in the death wagon. Trundling off to a picnic ground seven miles north of Cinder Village.

Smith and Miss Martin sitting away by themselves in the deeper grass. Cohorts at a rustic table downing canisters of beer. Little babbling brook. Flowing down between two steep wooded hills. Green peace. On this afternoon. A swish of snake cruising through the grass. Black long reptile disappearing in an array of picnic garbage. Pulling the zip down on the back of Miss Martin's grey dress. Feel the side of her lonely tit. You're like a little dog. Wagging and nuzzling. The many miles of trees and trees. Cool wind. Old music. Years of love cooped up in the heart. To spill several drops today. On Miss Martin's throat. Under her brown hair. In the deserted picnic ground. She little knows. All I think. Fuzz of hair over her back. Of all the times I tried with fist thumping, brain spinning to wind some cocoon. Safe from hands reaching to take the precious away. She said would you ever marry me. Be mine. And she broke and wept. With the married man. Little girl, hello. Gift of trust you wear in your eyes. While it shines I'll take care of you.

> Sun darkening
> Red
> Sinking faster
> Than usual
> Over the trees.

11

Seven fifteen in the evening countryside. After the picnic, more beer. Smith taking Miss Martin and cohorts to a road house, called Casual Cabin near the little airport. Travellers in shirt sleeves without ties not admitted.

The long bar. Tinkling fairy lights. Gleaming dance floor. One round of beer after another. Smith throwing up an arm.

'Ha ha, drink up death deliverers.'

'Mr Smith maybe I think we ought to be getting back or something. Brandy will be wondering what happened, maybe needs the truck.'

Smith abloom. In one curious smile. Pointing to the door. To the highway. Along by the lake. By back dirt roads. To one inn and din. And then another. Your smile Miss Martin. Your breast. Watch me pick elderberry blossom. Sure cure when stricken on a cross country tour with ague.

Smith climbing aboard the hearse. Stretch full length on the casket rest. A clutch of elderberry blossoms upon his folded hands. Shout to the cohorts.

'Pomfret Manor. Haste. To the Bonniface. Middle eyed king. Of the slippery of spirit.'

Hearse containing George Smith and party, turning off the road into a sweeping blue pebbled drive. Flanked by roses and low freestone wall. Lawns and shrubberies. A field of dairy cows. Led in a line to milking. Walled enclosure of pines. Faint white gravestones of a little burial ground. Drive curving through a thickening of trees and opening to circle round a great mound of lawn. Rambling ivy clad grey stone mansion. Hearse gently pulling to stop before a dark porch, and balcony above. Grey haired, blue silk gowned woman stepping out, a pince nez to her nose to look down. Upon this hearse with the stretched figure behind the chiselled glass. George Cadaver Smith under the elderberry. Her scream full of a tired agony floating out across this richly tended place. A thump. As her fat person fainted out of sight.

Chunky figure emerging from glass open doors to the lawn at the side of the house. Laughter, merriment and black bow ties. Round face, round cummerbund belly approaching. Bald pate ringed in grey hair. Tufts of ribbon on the gleaming tiny feet. Miss Martin biting her lip on the pebbled drive. Two cohorts silent by the open hearse doors. Whispering in to the prostrate figure.

'Mr Smith, Mr Smith.'

Rotund person, displeasured brow acrinkle and faintly crossed with white fear. Walking up to the cohorts, standing rooted, black toppers in hands. In a manner taught by Mr Brandy for the graveside presence.

'What is the meaning of this. What are you doing.'

Smith slowly to a sitting position. Rotund man rearing back.

'My God, what. Vas.'

Crowd collecting on the lawn. Tinkling thin membranes of glass. House lights flooding out in the evening gloom. Somewhere in this great spreading dark mansion dallies Bonniface.

'I'm Mr Jiffy. What is the meaning.'

'I'm Smith.'

'Well you're George Smith. Well. Ha ha.'

'Sorry if I gave you a fright.'

'Well welcome, Mr Smith, sir. Ha ha, your arrival. Well.'

'Miss Martin. Mr Jiffy, Mr Jiffy, meet my drivers.'

'Hi there. Come on in.'

Little gathering moving into the big gathering. Under the massive stone porch. Pink scattered way up in the distant skies. Jiffy's hands on Smith's elbow, sir you must meet my wife. Alas Jiffy out of a slit of eye I saw her keel over unconscious above us.

Great entrance hall. Flanked by spears, daggers, armour.

Sandstone steps hung with a balustrade of crimson rope. Sign my guest book, Mr Smith, while I find my wife. Miss Martin scratching her left handed signature. Mr Jiffy in search of spouse. Martin sneaked in an X. Good sign this night.

Miss Martin clinging. Mr Smith I feel so out of place, with all these people in evening clothes. Smith nudging a feel with an elbow. Miss Martin digging her fingernails into his arm. George's knees gave with the pain. Jesus Christ Miss Martin watch the nails, will you. As they passed now along a hall. Tall portraits of ships and horses. And down steps. To a sunken room. A balcony high up round the walls. Gigantic table and transparent clock. Clutches of people. Whispers and turnings around as George Smith with one brave hand filled two pewter tankards with champagne. A word of mausoleum. Of market. Of money. And one loud voice out of a thin reed of woman. Love to expose my body, marvellous lunacy.

Further over the heads. Down more halls. A peek passing the dining room. White table cloth covered with silver coffee machines. Black uniformed maids waiting in white lace aprons. And the library. Whoops, behind each book a bottle. Gloomy tall windows flanked with brown tomes. A ladder on wheels. And further the sign of a canvas boot high up, searching in the vellum among the manuscripts. Visions everywhere. Do not look further up that leg. Come Miss Martin to the conservatory I spy at the end of the hall. Full of palm, Monkey tree. Hydrangea.

Under a dripping vine by a strange flower. Two lurking unblinking eyes. Between the heating pipes. Smith bending near to get a better look. Snap. Wham. The jaws of a goodly sized definitely loose alligator, hissing. Jiffy is distinctly outdoor. Smith draining the tankard. Miss Martin tugging. Mr Smith I want to meet people. Sign of betrayal. Not to lurk quietly here with the alligator, Miss Martin. You want to saunter in the high life. Greet and meet nobs. Well then, come.

Smith taking Miss Martin down the hall. Nearly dragging her along. No one these days wants to sit and talk with just you. Mr Smith it's only that I've never seen people like this before or been in a place like this. You only have a little cabin in the woods. With a spider, Miss Martin. But this is a palace or something, full of important people. I see, Miss Martin. You think because I hold out in the mere and barren room of 604. Because my suits are repaired. Underwear ripped. That I cannot shiver all these ears.

Pomfret Manor's lonely evening grandeur. One side the sloping lawns. The other sheer rock cliff with a dining terrace. And back road. Looking down on tree tops and further into a deep valley. Moon up. The lake lit far below. Smith tucking into another tankard. Stray folk making curious ways to shake his hand. I want to say someday I met you. You made the big boys cringe. To these dreadful flatterings. Smith quietly smiled. Looking for a sign of Bonniface. Miss Martin coyly across the room with a tall gentleman, grey hair well greased back with distinction. Four medals on his chest. I recognize as military. And I am left alone.

Mosquitoes. Crickets bantering under dead leaves all out through the woods. Two gigantic wolf hounds strolling licking faces among the gathering. Footmen and flit guns spraying the night. Murdering insects. Trays and trays from the pantries. Bonniface is in this house. For whom I search, from whom I run. In the kitchens sneaking a fist into the cookie jars. I could kill Miss Martin. Use me the way she has. My seed. Not one word of thank you.

'Ah sir you look lonely now, would you like to fill up your tankard.'

A maid. Stiff cowl of lace across her dark hair. Smiling.

'Thank you. What's your name.'

'Ah sir, you wouldn't have any interest in knowing my name.'

'You're beautiful.'

'Sir, flattery will get you somewhere. You're the gentleman as arrived in the funeral car. I had to laugh. Himself had a fright he won't forget. Ah my God it's been some day. Since the gentleman with the cultivated ways arrived. I wouldn't want to tell you. The house is no longer safe. We're in fear of our lives. It's exciting.'

'What's your name.'

'Now. Enough's said. Who are you pretending you would have anything familiar with the poor likes of me. You're a friend of Mr Clementine, now isn't that so. Ah it's so. I can tell by the green glint in your eye.'

'What's your name.'

'You'll be trying your hand on me next. Like your gentleman friend. I'm Maureen. Ah Jesus I love men. They're great. Jesus, that Mr Clementine. O God that man.'

'Where is that man. Maureen.'

'That man if you ask me is God himself and he can strike me dead for saying it. He'll be in the closets.'

'I beg your pardon.'

'That's where. It's mesmerizing. Gentleman's hands reach out of the linen. Poor Bertha the cook never had a man near her. Jesus if he didn't chase her right into the ice house, back there under the kitchens. Must get the drinks around. I'll be back.'

Fair skinned. Fresh liquid eyes all blue all cleared and cleaned by rain. Maureen. I'm the saddest creature of all. My gracious. The wolf dogs. Random alligators. And alone here in this spot. No one to talk to. Car doors slamming somewhere out across the lawns. Ice house under the kitchens. If there's a Bonniface at all. That's where he'll be. Blue veined. At dawn in the mornings those university years ago. With an open penny notebook. Scribblings about geology. Studying the long night through in the cattle markets, among the tinkers and renegades. I got rich. He got poor. Both got childer. And not one day in all those college times were there less than smiles. Less than full bows. One wedding of a princeling friend. One morning suit retrieved from the pawn. A white shirt dipped in bleach. His wife picked up the iron to give it a marvellous stiff sparkling collar. With the hot instrument resting on a green painted shelf. One great green smear across the collar. A tear in my eye now. For that day. As we all went. Speeding in from country parts. The bride and groom in their raiment. So handsome it was terrible to behold. She married she said for money. He for beauty. What could be better. Till Clementine. Enraged for the green smeared collar, kicking holes in all the doors of the house. Letting in the fresh air he said till his shoes were of no use at all. Changing to sandals. Stepping out on the road. Hitching a ride to the reception. Stopping the first car he spied. Standing in front of it on the road, hand raised. By God it was carrying the bride and groom. He climbed in and sat between them. Said, how do newlyweds.

George Smith, eyeballs glistening. Alone with tankard. Sallow faced. As the high chandeliers of this drawing room dimmed and went out. With Maureen and two other dark maids taking lighted tapers to candles on mantels, tables and sideboards. Room aflicker. Miss Martin has been led away. By a man of distinction, jangling medals.

Taste of wine. Light white gentle dripping down the throat. Tinkle up the nostril. Jiffy. So round and busy. So bald and bouncing. Grey, wife lies up stairs. Jiffy. John, Junior. Don't try to be too rotund. Hello wolf dog. Nice head you got. Don't bite now. Maybe you know the whereabouts of the Bonniface. Here, fill you a little bowl of champagne. Drink up. My only friend here. All the others have sidled away. Good wolf doggie. Nice mutt. Duties on the estate to chew up any visitor not invited. Doggie, don't think I don't know that.

New guests. More and more. In hunting equipage. A string octet striking up in the distant summer room. Wherever it is. But hear the faint strains of violins. A blue gowned woman. Hair streaks of grey. Undulated up to Smith. Talking down her nose.

'Hello, who are you.'

'Who are you.'

'I asked you first.'

'I am Fang.'

'You like dogs, Mr Fang.'

Tall languid woman. Creamed face. Soft breasts. See through the blue. Diamonds sticking on the ear lobes. Rests on one slipper and then the other. George leaning to peer down her careless cleavage. She put her hand there so he could not see. And grinning weakly she stepped away. Tripping backwards into an empty ice bucket on the floor. Where she fell. Wolf doggies leaping round her. Nipping playfully and growling. Smith prayerfully gazing in the distance, across the crowd. Thicker and bigger. All Bonnifaces. Mind areel. Matilda you black ox. Giant breasted. Giving parties in Merry Mansions while I'm away. Marvellous how one can receive these messages on the ether. That black is busting out. Skin so smooth.

Smith out through the guests. Pardon me. Sorry. Excuse me. Do you mind. I'd like to pass please. What for white. How are you. And into the pantry by the zinc sinks. The sweating footmen. Four of these faces I recognize from Cinder Village. Layabout louts. Side door here. Peer in. The bacon room, hams hanging. Catch Calvin gnawing one of those. Ah kitchen. Hello. Cook. I'm scraping and slaving in here for the stingy likes of Mr Jiffy. You know Maureen. An upstart of a girl. Gentleman such as yourself would not want to be friendly with the likes of her. Into bed with any pair of pants. Mr Clementine. O my God sir, that one. I mean with all respect. O what a merry kettle of fish. Do you know his whereabouts. And sure I do not. And the quicker the likes of him are last seen in Pomfret the better. Ah now, cook. Don't call me cook. Madam then. How do I get to the ice house. Don't mention that place to me. Under our feet.

Smith bowing at the kitchen door to the cook. Across a hall. Peeking into the servants' drawing room. An ironing board. Peering out on a porch. An ice cream churn. Down the stairs. Musty, damp and cold. Cobwebs in all the corners. Peeling paint. Deep passage way. Cinder smells. And hay. Damp. And rot. In these cellars in the direction under the kitchens. Ah. A gigantic door. Of stout massive timbers.

Great bar of iron. Squeezing it shut. Hinges size of thighs. In here the ice. Cut in winter down on the lake. Hounds will find me here full of guilt and chew me up.

Smith reaching grasping the great iron bar. Pushing it up. Pulling the giant door open. Plenty of knowledge about doors. Open up to darkness. To the cold air in there.

A cackle. A quiver. In the dim light. The blocks of ice. Six feet down. In the far corner. On a cold throne. Cedric Calvin Bonniface Clementine. Encircled with brown bottles marked export. And X. A piece of cheese. One ham. A giggle. Of a dark uniformed maid making for the door to the outside world.

'My dear George, come in, join me. Cooling off down here. Think I'm mad. Think I'm going to ask you for money. Terrified. True I'm going to ask you for money. George. So good to see you. The trip here, goes without saying, was shameful. I do not mind a ship pitching. And rolling. But when there is the pitch, the roll and the lurch. Then by God.'

'Hello.'

'You build a tomb. Make mountain of marble for moment of last chill. Mean you have money. Me big temporary chief.'

'You're drunk.'

'O me chief. You build tomb. Much money. Me have none. Me want money. Me want big suitcase full of. I will tell Mumchance to come get you. The MacGillicuddy. He come too on big boat. We all come on big boat. After you. You desert your wife and children in the sticks. Shame. Naughty. You have black help in your home. Naughty. You ride with two way telephone in black auto. Naughty. I am old friend. We go college together. We depart. I go down. You go up, Evil. I walk hot pavements. You hide out in cool country. I fry egg on street corner. Nearly get hit by taxi. Ask man directions. He runs. I phone you. You run. Make escape. Me meet Jiffy. Jiffy is big joke. Me mount his wife. She say who on me summit. Me say me on summit. She old. She like it. Me like it. Ah George. Good to see you.

Pale face. Her Majesty wept when you sailed away. She knew you in your celluloid penis stage. She said.'

'Good bye Bonniface.'

Smith hands and feet on the rungs of the iron ladder up out of the ice house. Musty chill. Bonniface enthroned in the corner with the leather cushion on the ice blocks. Deep down in Pomfret Manor.

'George don't go. Listen to a little song on comb and paper.'

> Chase out
> Cheats
> Rid the world
> Of suffering.
>
> Jump on
> Twisters
> Rid the world
> Of harm.

'Good bye, Bonniface.'

'Why don't you talk about your children George. And about Shirl. Don't you love them. They frighten you too. Look for money from you. I scare you. Make you want to run. As the years go by George, there is less of life to spend and the risks are cheaper. Stay.'

Backstairs maid shyly sitting with Bonniface on the ice. Smith stepping back from this dark chilly scene. The many months. Of bantering. Dear Sir, we will get you. The phone-calls and doorknocks. Smith climbing the ladder. Bonniface. One last shout. George. Turning round. Calvin trembling in the hand. The drink shaking out over the glass. Brown liquid lurking on the lips. Bonniface's eyes quivering in their tears. Said George. Don't go. Don't hide. From me. Bear with me. I suffer.

Smith climbing the ladder. Stepping out into the endless cellar hall. Pressing the great ice house door closed. Smell of cinders along the corridor. In a door the vast machinery of boilers. Giant asbestos covered tanks. Whoosh of great spurts of oil, billowing into flame and roaring. Need all my money for myself. Bonniface married a debutante. Lost his glasses on a delayed honeymoon with the first six month old daughter. Who in the hot afternoon of a cheap city hotel slept on Bonniface's chest as he lay snatching a few moments rest between the narrow streets. It was after lunch. The baby crapped. Late in the afternoon with heart thumping to a knock on the door Bonniface awoke. He rose. Put the baba aside and brushed feverishly away the thing on his chest. God forbid. With his hair needing to lie back more presentably, he brushed it back with his hands. Smoothing it. O Jesus. In his distracted innocence he went to the door. To greet the debutante friend of his wife. She saw the aristocratic Bonniface. Attempting to bow. She screamed and fainted. George Smith heard the commotion because he was mounting the stairs. Just having arrived in town. And as she swooned he caught her. And then saw the spectre of the Bonniface. The awful. And fell backwards down the stairs, the debutante on top, both entwined, rolling to the bottom. Where they looked back up. Spectre on the landing. The Bonniface. Covered surely in shit. And this debutante head in hands in tears sobbing. The awful. The awful. She had been presented.

Tonight George Smith climbing up the servants' stairs of Pomfret Manor. Back sadly through the kitchen, giant pig ears sticking out of the pot simmering on the stove. Through the pantry, the workers, with rolled up sleeves washing glasses. And through the swing door to the dining room. A commotion of barks. Growls and lashing of teeth and savagery. Screams. Furniture breaking. Three gigantic animals shooting by. Round the tables and chairs. Flying blood and hair. A monstrous animal locked in mortal combat with the Jiffy wolf hounds. Claws scratching up the rugs and floors as they ripped into each sharp turn. Out of the room. Into other rooms. Back again. Random voices. In the melee.

'Ouch.'

'Someone has fingered my wife.'

'Give me ass or give me death.'

'Sure.'

'Gee. Thanks.'

'I didn't want to see you die.'

Smith holding elbows high up to avoid the flashing fangs. An animal bigger than the wolf hounds tearing them to bits. Smith aghast. Attempt to relish this rare marvellous sight of dog eat dog. Gawd. Recognize that one. Goliath. Miss Tomson. It's your animal. And not so many hours ago. Mr Jiffy from person to person, with extended hand, nice to see you, glad you're here. Now gone. Fleeing in all directions.

Gently slowly down the staircase in the great hall. One hand on the banister. Breasts large and blue, turned for a moment east and west. With high hips, legs starting at the shoulder blades. Like all the tall buildings in town. She said herself like some guy was sixty miles up. Wearing one gold and one silver slipper. Smiling ever so lightly as her dog was winning. Jiffy shouting to stop. Stop. Get that animal out of here. Guests vanishing to the safety of the mosquitoes outdoors. And then the shout of stand back. Stand back everybody. Stand back. Bang.

A smoking gun. Huge Goliath felled. Mouth bared with useless fangs and terrible blood. Legs still running. One twitch. And stopping. The two yelping whimpering wolf hounds dragged away. Alive. Silence in Pomfret Manor. And Smith saw across the yellow flickering candle light the saucer green eyes of Sally Tomson cast down on the gathering. And the dead brown body of Goliath.

All dog.
All dead.

12

Tall blue Miss Tomson lonely and aloof. Descending the stairs and crossing the hall of Pomfret. She stood trembling among the silent guests. Biting her stiffened lips. Eyes moist. White lids thinly holding back the tears. On the dark floor the light blood. Fumes of gunpowder in the air. As she walked up to George Smith and said, take me out of here.

Outside and beyond the stone shadowy porch of Pomfret. Smith standing with Miss Tomson. A wind and purple stormy clouds in a moonlit sky. Along by the cars collected like dark animals crouched on the drive. Her white pearls on her throat she wore months ago on the train. Sad gangling arms from her blue dress. Tears trickling down her face.

Smith driving Miss Tomson's long sleek black vehicle slowly away. Car lights flashing across spruce trees, faint flower beds and a gabled shingled dog house, a figure throwing a glittering dog collar in the window.

'Smith the only thing I ever owned was that dog. And that shit shot him. Thoughtful some bastard giving me the collar back.'

'Your dog was winning.'

'That was no reason to kill him. Men stink. What's left for me.'

'Miss Tomson it's not the end of the world to be dogless. I had a dog when I was a little boy, called Brownie.'

'Was he shot.'

'No. He died a natural death of disease.'

'Well then Smith how do you know. I just saw my dog killed.'

'Which way do I turn.'

'I don't care just get us away. They can push me dead on a cart down a long hall of some hospital.'

'Don't say that Miss Tomson, please.'

'Guys use you. If you love him. Give him everything and they want to get rid of you. You're a chain around his neck. I always had Goliath. Jesus. Any good guy's already married with kids. Already with a padlock and chain. I don't want to be fine. Or beautiful. I want a baby. A rocking chair. A porch in the country undoing my sweater to put it on the nipple. Who wants to be fine. The rats win.'

'That's not always true. Miss Tomson.'

'You just don't know, Smith. What were you doing at that lousy party.'

'A neighbourly invite to a jamboree.'

'Don't shit me Smith. I'm just too depressed. What were you doing there.'

'Tell me about these gears. This right for third.'

'You're doing fine. Just drive. You got a licence.'

'No. But I learned about gear shifting as a child.'

'Jesus.'

Smith motoring north. Past another entrance to Pomfret. Row of granite farm buildings on the road. Down a steep hill through the woods. High wire fence. Locking in Bonniface. Who as I drove Miss Tomson's car out of Pomfret seemed to be a shadow reeling beside the road, arms outstretched, coatless and shouting.

> Stop
> I am Bonniface
> Disposer of dead
> Calvin helper of
> The maimed
> Clementine, the
> Illustrious
> Banjaxed and cuckolded
> And Cedric too.
> Stop.

You bastard
Smith

In these trying times. Of swindles, dog death and utter loneliness, where just another sad body naked next to mine can mean a whole world of peace and tenderness. Miss Tomson who gives money to beggars, violinists, street corner kids jigging with a homemade band, the mute and blind. Any helpless thing she would lift up and love. Like all tall women. When I become a bum drowned in drink. And walk that wasteland street like all the others kicked out of family and home, severed, unshaved, unlaundered and unpressed. Miss Tomson will take my tattered leery self, say O Jesus Smith, you poor poor guy. Feed from the crumbs in the palm of her hand. Lift up my faint face. To hers so fair.

'How many cylinders have we here, Miss Tomson.'

'Eight.'

'My.'

Lonely headlights far away on another road. A red barn. Stone wall above a sunken field. Hides of cows grazing in the night. Use a glass of milk with this cake beside me. Branches bending over the road, grew upturned leaves in the headlights. Monstrous purring engine whispering under this long black hood charging through the dark. Toting this peach, strawberry and cream. My delirious appetite.

'All the best steak I bought him. Perfect report on his three medical checkups. Never even had worms. Could have shown him in the dog show.'

'Mustn't dwell on it Miss Tomson. You look terribly good tonight.'

'You really mean it Smith. Do I look O.K.'

'You do. There's a road house. Let's stop. Get you a drink.'

First few fat drops of rain. Speckling the steps up to a porch under a neon sign. Jerry's Night Spot. Dark interior. Smith tripping over legs, leading Miss Tomson to the dim bar. White coated bar tender, eyes full of I know more than you think. Here come two pupils.

'What'll it be.'

'Scotch for me Smith.'

'Two scotch.'

'Rightio.'

'Smith you look kind of handsome. Wish it wasn't that my dog gets killed just when I see you out of the blue again. You made the papers, even. How are you doing with your enemies.'

'They have vowed to get me. I will escape by submarine.'

'Ha ha.'

'Good to see you laugh again, Miss Tomson.'

Smith surveying her in the faint light. Not so sad now. Lanky arms nearly to her knees. Hair a blonde blowable softness. Cool long fingers of her hand. Must touch so lightly the dashboard of her car, quietly lit panorama of switches, clocks and dials. My little dog I owned had big brown spots on the lids when he closed his eyes. Never cried when he died. Bonniface back in Pomfret. Paralysis in his extremities. Upheaval in the keester. I steal away north and east under the aristocratic weeping rain. With thick wads of fresh treasury bills clutched under the armpits. Looking for homecooked food. While building a little empire. House in the country. Flat in town. Retreats in the woods. Sultry with peace and other things. Thank you spider.

'Smith do you get any letters anymore.'

Smith extracts an envelope. Handing it to Miss Tomson. Who holds it up in the purple tinted light. A yellow paper, address embossed in red.

Eel Street

Easter

(There is no time like the present)

George Smith,

c/o The Game Club

South Park Side

Dear Sir,

It has come to our attention that you would wish to wrestle.

We are not without strength. But rather we would wish you wasn't to insist to a grapple. We hope you will forget you thought you was able to take on anybody.

We remain not kidding,
A.M.D.C.
(For the Committee)

'Very interesting. Have you answered it.'

'No.'

'Tell them Smith you're a mountain girl and not a guy at all. And hope they're gentlemen and supply chaperones. A debutante. And when you wrestle reporters might be watching. These initials be a name like Al Moygrain Diltor Cranzgot. Ask him if he wants to try some thigh trembling. Sign your letter, the knee.'

'Miss Tomson, wish you still were working for me.'

'I know, it's sad.'

'You take the horror away.'

'But now Smith. Your picture and write up in the papers. Made you kind of famous. Take the pressure off. I mean they worry a little more about giving you a pair of cement shoes to walk across the river with. Down there in the mud people would wonder where you are.'

Miss Tomson handing the letter back to Smith. Giving the paper one final flick with her long nail. You know Smith I got something to tell you but not now. Smith sneaking a look at his present shoes. And up again at her face. As she stares into her drink. Twisting it. Cubes of ice spinning around. Rocking and clinking on the tall sides of the glass. Seemed blue shadows round her large eyes. Go back to get Miss Martin. Or Bonniface. Never. Sniff the wheat drifting up through soda bubbles. This Miss Tomson. God was cruel to make just one of her.

'Smith, this true you putting up a memorial to yourself. Isn't that kind of conceited. And expensive. What's the point. What does it matter what happens when you die.'

'It matters all the days you live, Miss Tomson.'

'Looking at you Smith like this you're a strange one.'

'What would make you happy, Miss Tomson.'

'A guy with a large soul. Not the small sneaky rats career-ing around these days. You got some more grey hairs Smith. Why don't you get married before you turn white. Tonight for me is curtains. I'm beginning to understand a guy like you. I could never be faithful to one guy. Even if he was steady and dependable. What is a guy anyway but just a prick and you write your name on it with a wedding. And he goes looking for more names. And no wedding. What is a guy. But just a prick. That's the way it is, Smith.'

'Miss Tomson, I've left Miss Martin and a friend back there.'

'What's she doing up here, Smithy. Sorry. Maybe it's personal or something. They'll be all right. In that skunk's house. Smith, you move on a lot of levels. Can even drive a car. I'm amazed. I like you driving me too, I feel safe. You know I've never really had a chance to talk to you before.'

Miss Tomson standing, this night now, Saturday, north, rain sprinkling tree tops in the wood, a new decision on her face. Miss Tomson, your confidence makes me feel I've turned over a new safe leaf with cars.

'Smith, will you pardon me while I go and powder off my tears.'

Smith down from his stool. A little bow. Her rear. Agony to have it near again. In my own little lonely world. Touch one of those spheres. Have to get drunk to get brave. To descend easily to the cheap antics. Never get my hands on her. Oceans apart. She breezes right into my life and sud-denly I'm standing up to my hips. In mystical shit. She can see and smell. Twisting every little word to make me sound deep, strong, preferably on the brow of the hill, yes, thank you, a little wind through the grey flecked locks, thank you, sunset please, music, some serious variations, low chords please, for Smith's earth shaking meaningful thoughts. And I just know my fly would be open.

'Smith wake up. I'm back. You look like you're in a trance.'

'Sorry, Miss Tomson.'

'Smith, I like you. You cheer me up. Nice tie you're wearing.'

'Thanks.'

Suggesting another scotch each for the road. Before stepping out in the night shuddering with high wind. Lightning zigzagging the black heaven as they left. Miss Tomson taking Smith's arm, running together across the cinder parking lot to her car. Inside warm and dry. She said well Smith. Well Miss Tomson.

'Gee let's just drive. Just anywhere for awhile in all this rain.'

Long black machine pulling away. Across a sidewalk and out on the concrete road. Smith at the gleaming controls. Rain musically on the roof. Flooding down on the windscreen, twin wipers flashing back and forth. She turns sideways, facing me. Her dry sweet smell, light blue.

'Smith do you think I'll ever have a chance. Be like other women. That's what I know, I'm crippled by what I want, because I don't know what it is. Go down that aisle with a bunch of lilies in my arms with some jerk. Where do you find a real man today. I ought to hold interviews.'

Smith's hands gripped to the steering. Eyes searching out through the rain and yellow beam of headlights reaching in the blackness. Miss Tomson's bullets. Land in the heart. After a long day, with all sorts of mystery. And brain throbbing just above the ears. Miss Tomson I'm an applicant begging for an interview. I drive. See. So smoothly down this road cut out of rock. Could help you in the fight for a fair share of human thrills. In the hall of Pomfret you chose me of all the crowd. My composure nearly exploded. Wish I had just once patted Goliath. But in those Golf Street office days I needed all my fingers. My heart is not all cold and black. And if it were. We could make a good mixture and colour scheme.

Hesitate a moment before smashing the hopes of another. Sally. Tiny smudge of purple on your lids. Never say you'll die. Such an expensive car. All this soft black leather. Black angel. You'll have wings. And up on top of my tomb.

You'll stand as a statue. I'll put you there. A sentinel. All sad and Sally.

Dashboard's calm clock ticking after two. Air comes in warm over the engine. Swish sound as Miss Tomson uncrosses her legs. A car approaching on this strange winding road. Which straightens now round this turn through the sheets of rain. And cracking thunder. Fox and toads and woodchucks cowering everywhere. Always find time to think of little animals. Even while guiding all this horsepower.

'Smith aren't you a little on the wrong side of the road.'

'I rather think not.'

'I think you are. There's a car coming.'

'He seems to have more than his share.'

'But you're on the wrong side Smith.'

'Nonsense this vehicle approaching obviously contains a road hog.'

'This is my car. You're on the wrong side of the road.'

'Please Miss Tomson I'm present commander of this tank. Stubborn rascal. If he thinks for one second I'm going to swerve to avoid his oncoming rush he has one vast foolish figment of his imagination to endure.'

'No. George.'

'Get into your own lane you wretch.'

'O no.'

Squeal of tyres. Crumpling of steel fabric. Abrupt meeting of bumpers fenders and headlamps. Lights go out and on again. To illuminate this complicated outing. And eight cylinder concussion.

Small curly headed man ejecting himself on to the road. Falls. Slowly picking himself up, wiping the wet from his person. Raising an outstretched finger pointing as he advances in the glaring head lights and plummeting rain.

'Jesus Christ Miss Tomson, you're quite right I'm on the wrong side of the road. Let me handle this.'

'First it's my dog. Now it's my car.'

'Just leave this to me Miss Tomson.'

George Smith drawing a card from his wallet. Handing it out through an opened inch of window to the curly headed man momentarily stopping his cascade of words bordering on vituperation. The man reading in the cloudburst.

DEAF MUTE — WATCH MY SIGNS

'Come on mister. Hey lady, who's going to pay for the damage to my car. You were right on the wrong side of the road.'

Smith handing out another card. Man holding it up in his wavering headlights.

LADY IS MUTE BUT CAN HEAR

'Jesus Christ Lady. Make him a sign language will you. Who's going to pay for the damage. What's this country coming to, guy's out on the road, can't talk, can't hear. O.K. I know it's a crying shame to be without voice and that kind of affliction but who's paying for the damage.'

HAVE YOU EVER
FOOLED AROUND IN THE HORSE LATITUDES

'Hey lady, read this while I'm getting soaked, see what he's said to me. I'm going to get the cops. Let's see your licence.'

I WILL THRASH YOU FROM COAST TO COAST

'You don't scare me buddy. Where's your licence. Yeah, that's it, how can you have one if you're afflicted. Signal him that lady. Who's going to pay for the damage. I don't want any more of these messages. Who's going to pay. Just let me get your number.'

Smith emitting a long low squeal, body in animal motion, canines showing, hands flashing up stretched in claws. Curly headed man jumping back from the car. Smith switched into gear. Dousing lights. Press down on the pedal. Miss Tomson's car leaping forward. A cry behind them. Roaring off in the dark down the rainy road. In the mirror the rear red glow of lights of the crash victim.

'Smith what are you doing.'

'We must flee.'

'You bastard if he's got my number I'm in prison for life. Police will be looking for us. He'll come after us.'

'If he tries to turn around in that road he'll be in the mud for months.'

'Front of the car must be ruined. I'm scared.'

'Gentle dents, absolutely have them put right for you. I am sorry about this. We'll take this turning. Looks a friendly, empty road. I don't want to alarm you further Miss Tomson but I think we might best get both the car and ourselves in out of the rain.'

Miss Tomson sitting eyes cast down. Hands folded quietly in her lap. Poor sorrowful girl. On a stormy night like this. Back in those days when she sat at her desk in Golf Street. Taking odd items of paper out of her drawers, which she slowly tore up. Then sat thinking hard. Until she would pick up her phone to call the hairdressers or Goliath at the kennels to whom she went woof woof, sweetie. With the marble replica of Miss Tomson on my tomb I will add Goliath on a leash. Have a little elevator to raise me up and down to view them once in a while. Hello Sally, hi ya Goliath. Then get lowered to rest again. All automatic. Never need stir. Now she's next to me a few fabrics away. A good sport about the crash. Didn't even ask to drive. Touch her now and I will light up like electric. All so sweet heart. Pain in my chest of sadness. This car feels like driving a speed boat. I will stop in open sea and have a laugh with a perfect stranger passing in another racy craft.

'Miss Tomson, I think I'm lost.'

'God.'

'Think you better drive and I'll direct the way.'

Smith pulling to the side of the road. Near an apple tree. Stone wall and bushes and pines. Miss Tomson sliding across. Discreet Smith, opening his door, taking one momentary look at one momentary pair of knees. Lightning brightening up the sky.

'I'll survey the damage, Miss Tomson.'

Shielding eyes against the head lamps. Feeling the front bumpers and fenders. Patting them. Kicking the front tyres in an off hand professional manner as one has seen Herbert the Chauffeur do.

'Miss Tomson, glad to say. Not bad fettle. Crack in the head lamp. Few dents. Obviously our adversaries car was of inferior quality.'

Smith climbing back into the long vehicle. Faint dog smell of Goliath. His hairs on the floor carpet. Think of somewhere to go. Behind Miss Tomson's ear. With lips. And travel a nose into her hair. Slight sprinkle of mud on her would be more beauty than ever. To see her feet without shoes, my God. She lights a cigarette. Go down with that smoke into her lungs and lie there. Buried in her blonde chest. Be her baby. Infantile though that be. Her dog shot down in warm blood, her car in collision. And she sits so calm.

'Miss Tomson before we drive off. I want to say I think you're a real sport.'

'Do you.'

'Yes. You could have blamed me. You had every right to do so. To lash out with words.'

'Smith.'

'Yes.'

'You want the truth.'

'Please.'

'I am going to lash out.'

'O.'

'I'm windy about that guy we hit. He might be looking for a small source of income for life. Like dear Sir we would like to bleed you white, taking it in easy stages, so the blood lasts, you know what I mean Smith.'

'I think so, Miss Tomson.'

'Someone gets crosseyed trying to look in your window while you're undressing and they sue you for it.'

Lips widening on Miss Tomson's jaw. A smile like the whole world is going to break down in general laughter. I die to put my mouth on hers. Touch each one of those white teeth.

'You're not bitter Miss Tomson.'

'No Smith.'

'What makes you smile.'

'Just thought of that newspaper report about you. I want to know, did you really fart or something on the steps of Dynamo House. Report it to the Sanitation Department, that was rich. I read it about twenty times. Sweet, a crowd gathering to watch you. Smith you should find some nice girl marry and have kids.'

Miss Tomson starting the immense engine. Any wind she made would be mystical. Not like some of the dust raisers Bonniface has sent up in his time, blowing out window panes, joining a little group known as the Musical Dynamiters. He lies when he says membership is confined to those who can backfire in morse code.

An exquisite driver Miss Tomson. Hands so lightly on the steering. Each cog enslaved by her touch. Ahead a house behind three great pines. White porch. Closed up for night.

'Miss Tomson. I'll find out where we are.'

'Gee we just can't bang on someone's door. You'll get shot this time of night.'

'Nonsense. I know how to handle hicks.'

Smith in the rain. Softening now. Faint flash of moon. Miss Tomson's black vehicle purring under these high evergreens. Tall gate in the iron fence. Hammock tied between two pines. Stone path round the house and another to the wide porch. All the pine cones. Windows from ceiling to floor. Saturday with all Sunday ahead. My throat is dry. Squeak up courage. How can I say it. I want her body next to mine. Hide from all the coming snows. Taste her golden juice. A hidden spring in the nicest little mound of hair in all the world. Go out of my mind thinking like this. Come back realism, big monolithic friend. Miss Tomson says find some nice girl. Have kiddies. Gather little problems, drown in one big one. Rap this door five times. Way to deal with hicks out here, let them know one is a slicker right off. Have a correspondence while waiting.

Dear Sir,

Where are you. So much cash is missing, we would feel better if we knew.

Yours,
Those Who Had Faith in You

P.S. We abided by your regulations, won't you even give us an inkling.

Dear Investors,

It so happens I was reflecting in my mop closet near my office and I regard your greedy communication as a breach of faith. Therefore I am absconding with the funds.

(Up) Yours (If necessary)
GS

Inside this white clapboard mansion, footsteps approaching, down stairs, and along a hall. Help a stranger lost on the road. Tomato garden and great barn down an incline with the woods behind. Flicking hayseed from the hair. Filling their quiet rural moments with bushwacking and wang pulling. In Cinder Village there's a hick called puller Pete, whispered with one so long, took ten minutes to unfurl. Just see the glow of Miss Tomson's cigarette in the car as it brightens. Nor will she ever know how I kept one of her long golden hairs she left behind in Golf Street as a bookmark.

'Who is it, out there.'

'I'm lost on the road can you tell me where I am.'

'You're right here, stranger. You got me out of bed. Clear off before I sprinkle your ass with buckshot.'

'I beg your pardon.'

'You heard me.'

Smith retreating backwards a step. Not going to be easy to gain a foothold of rapport here.

'It's a dire emergency.'

'Don't try to be a smart cookee stranger.'

Smith shifting weight. Turning briefly to survey the rear for running. It would finish me forever with Miss Tomson to be caught coward. This double grey door. Through which the buckshot will come. This is no moor of college days setting forth with Bonniface arsebone in heather, gamekeeper toting the decanter of sherry. All kinds of crazy game raining out of the sky. Please mister behind that door. You've got me wracked with fear, and I've got Miss Tomson the most exquisite human of them all sitting out there in the car.

'All I want is the general geographic location of this spot.'

'Clear off. How do I know that's all you want.'

'I'd like to make a phone call, too.'

Lace on the window. This hick won't see the reason of the slicker. Kind who wears a shirt with the detached collar. Life seems to be out of doors these days. This critter inside might really let go with a barrel, if I whisper lilly livered in the keyhole. Or slip a mute card under the door.

DON'T BE A SHID AS WELL AS A HICK

A hand laid itself upon George Smith's shoulder. Stiffening without letting out a squeal. Turning. Miss Tomson nodding her head back to the car. Smith enough's happened already without you getting shot. Reaching the iron fence gate. A voice from the house.

'O.K. Stranger, you can use the telephone.'

Tomson and Smith stopping under the pines.

'Ah see Miss Tomson.'

'Guess you're just a sweet guy Smith.'

'Miss Tomson, I may as well ask you right here. Will you come with me to a port in this storm.'

She stood still and tall and strange under the pines, lips apart. Eyes crinkling. Looking into the eyes of George Smith. At his lips. Nose and into the left eye and then the right. Hers with flecks of so many colours, yellow with green making a magic blue. Dripping rain drops spotting her dress. One silver slipper, one gold. How do I say now, forget it. I was kidding. Just one of those things you suddenly blurt out. Just wanted a port to be safe. And it sounds so stark and maybe even sneaky. Speak. I take it back. Right into my mouth again, down my throat and into my heart where it came from near the bottom. Let me go Miss Tomson. Let me run.

'You poor guy, Smith. You really want me to come to a port with you don't you. I like that.'

Night. Rain and her black car sitting on the road, glistening with a few bumps and scratches too. A carpet of brown needles and pine cones. Two of us. Besides the hick with the shot gun. Her eyes light up because every single part of her lives there. I swallow mouth juices. Head full of tears. Pressing on my eyes. Hardly speak ever again. But must because if I don't the world will go rushing on without us.

'Yesh.'

All so quiet now. Famished and lonely adrift at sea. And land on a shore. She says yesh and I can't believe my luck, or ears. This blonde flower circled by so many bees. And your long strand of hair I've kept all these months. Each time I took it from the book I would let it gently curl in my hand and feel it between my lips. And some voice breaks this stillness.

'Hey you out there, you want this telephone or don't you.'

Smith with a large leap took the four grey stairs landing on the porch at speed. A commotion inside. Hick levelling the blunderbuss at this sudden assaulting shadow. One thing to be squeezed out in a population explosion and distinctly another to be blasted for sprightliness.

The double grey doors on the porch opening. A squat man with strands of grey in the hair. Under a blue woolly dressing gown his shirt showing with the detached collar missing. Shuffling ahead of Smith, heels of his slippers clacking. Telephone hanging on the wall. Next to a coloured white bowl with a great green flower. Wow, little spine shiver, seen one other flower like that. Just one second before the alligator tried to clamp its jaws on my arm in the Jiffy conservatory. And how does one work this antique telephone.

'Just wind her up mister.'

'I see.'

'Operator's usually asleep this time of night. Sorry I kinda levelled my gun at you. You came up them steps kinda fast.'

'Where are we here.'

'This is called Green Flower Corners. After the flower.'

'O.'

'Down the dirt road three miles, is the main route. Past the cemetery. Turn left follow the dirt road. You'll see signs.'

'Thank you. Hello. Operator.'

'Hello.'

'Operator, I want the Hotel Boar.'

'Sir, don't you know the number.'

'I think it's Bug 2–7222. But there's a life at stake. Do please look it up.'

'Please spell that, caller.'

'B for bugger, U for unseemly, G for goose.'

'Pardon but gee I like your voice, it's really cultured. I'll connect you.'

'Thank you, operator.'

Little clicks, strange small sounds of voices on these wires over fields and through deserted woods.

'Here's your party, sir.'

'Hello, this is George Smith, I want to speak to the maitre de hotel.'

'He's asleep, this is Norbert can I help you, Mr Smith.'

'Hello Norbert, this is an emergency. I require a suite within the hour.'

'O sure, like the last time you needed it fast.'

'I beg your pardon.'

'Sorry Mr Smith. I was meaning maybe the same suite. Saw your picture in the papers. Gee, just like to ask a question, what's your recipe for success Mr Smith.'

'Keep your mind free of emotional ingredients when looking for profits.'

'Gosh. Simple as that.'

'Yes. I'm in rather a hurry, if you wouldn't mind organizing.'

'O sure. Good to talk to someone who knows what he's talking about.'

'I'd like the key left in the lock of the suite.'

'Now this emotional ingredient, that how you function, Mr Smith, I mean pardon me for asking this time of night.'

'Morning.'

'Yeah morning.'

'And I'm imposing upon the graciousness of a country citizen. This is an emergency.'

'O sure. Just remembering that. Free the mind of emotional ingredients when looking for profits. I need investment advice. My wife wants to know why you want to spend all that good money getting buried.'

'If you don't mind Norbert, the suite. Flowers and hot punch if you will.'

'Sure Mr Smith. Good to hear from you again. Just goes to show, my whole life I've been getting all emotional looking for a profit. The key will be in the tunnel entrance.'

'In the door of the suite, please.'

'Sure Mr Smith, anything you want, you know me, boy I'll bet you've got some doll tonight –'

Smith lightly hanging the little ear piece on the fragile hook. Hick turning from the door where he was peering out in the night. At what must be Miss Tomson. That gun makes me nervous. Don't suppose he's ever seen her likes before in tight blue satin, slippered in gold and silver twiddling a pine cone in this vague neck of the woods. He may make bombs in his attic. George Smith tendering a crisp treasury bill.

'Nope stranger.'

Smith taking leave gently on the grey porch. With a thanks a million. Once is enough stranger. And stepping down three steps to the hard path underneath the three great trees at the fork of this road. Turning to look back. The shadow standing in the light of the hall, gun at port arms. People who live in the country like strangers to call out of the blue.

The dirt road goes down winding, twisting and turning. Lights flooding the passing woods enclosed in an endless wire fence. A small pond. Up on a hill again faint grave stones of a cemetery. Apples must grow there and drop on the dead in summertime full of flavour. Handfuls of hair round Miss Tomson's head. Turn right at this turn, Miss Tomson, left at the next. Silent cruising through the night. South. Catching up with the storm splashing down the heavy rain. A rabbit popping on the road, Smith isn't that sweet that rabbit.

'Miss Tomson what were you going to tell me, back there in the bar.'

'It was nothing.'

'Come on tell me.'

'It embarrasses me now.'

'Please tell me.'

'Well. You know when I was working for you. Saw you get all those letters, and the pathetic little set up you had and all, in Golf Street. I can't tell you. Seems too silly. Might make you sore.'

'O.'

'You'll get sore if I don't tell you.'

'No I won't.'

'I just used to add money to the petty cash box because I thought you were really having it rough. You'd come out and when you thought I wasn't looking you'd take it back into your office and count it and come back looking so pleased because it was more instead of less.'

'I never did.'

'You're getting sore. Real sweet, the way you used to look with that cash box. Even cried one night over my pay cheque but next morning I thought what the hell, this is a jungle, and paid it into my account. Which way do I turn.'

'Go straight.'

Smith slumped back on the leather. The tiny sound of windscreen wipers fanning across the glass. And down into a valley. A swollen river. Raindrops flickering through the light beams. Across a stone bridge and train tracks into a sleeping town. Spread across a hillside, a hotel, terraces built out on the jutting rock. Car mounting an incline towards a great brown door.

'Smith, where we going can't you see the door's closed.'

'Drive on, it'll open. Watch.'

'Gee.'

Hollow bubbling sound of Sally Tomson's long black car sliding in out of the dark rain. Three moss green armoured bullion trucks. Vast concrete wasteland. Miss Tomson turning and looking at George Smith. Her hand slowly sliding across the black leather to his. Entwining his fingers. Her face a little flower. As the lids lift up on the eyes. Her voice so soft and low. Saying O and O and O.

In the vast underground garage. Their voices echoing. Smith with a finger raised. Beckoning. Come Miss Tomson. Cross this chill interior. Your legs. Watch you walk ahead of me through life. To open doors, buy my lamb chops and pay the milkman.

'Where are we, Smith. This is crazy. I feel they move dead bodies in and out this door.'

'For God's sake, Miss Tomson.'

'I just was thinking this place is built for death.'

'This way.'

'This elevator is like a little church, Smith.'

In Miss Tomson's eyes, down the steps, at the bottom, is her soul. When she was a little girl she had a little boy friend who looked up her dress every Friday after school to see if anything had changed. Easy joys of childhood.

'Smith.'

'What.'

'I know I said yesh. About a port. In the storm and all.'

'Miss Tomson, what's the matter.'

'Please take me back down. I'm going to try to get back to town.'

'Miss Tomson I can't let you go out in the stormy night again. Might be trees down across the roads.'

'This the down button.'

'I wish more than anything you wouldn't press it. Wanted to bring you somewhere dry.'

'Smith. I just wish it wasn't you. I just wish that tonight wasn't tonight. Don't be sad. Come on, don't be.'

'I'm all right.'

'I know it's silly but the tunnel. I'm nervous, a little scared. Smith I've been thinking I've got you figured. I haven't got you figured at all. Face to face like this. I'm a coward. I've been bluffing. Like I'm some sort of careless society girl. I'm a hick.'

'Please Miss Tomson.'

'And I'm just scared.'

Panelled door sliding back. The tunnel. The steps to the underground garage. Miss Tomson's beige medallion on her tan figure. Wet tyre tracks of her car. Worship the cement she walks on. Across this entrance of death. Night time nearly over. Smacked up her car. Stood by while her dog got killed. Mustn't cry. Just watch her drive away through clear, cool eyes. Got to be hard. Let her go alone. Never see her again. Milk truck bumping, grinding by outside. Her door clicks, engine roars and spins the wheel. Backing and turning around. Don't go. Look back at me. Please. Standing here. With the nice tie you said I was wearing. Two little corners of a hanky I pulled up to show from my breast pocket. To look natty for you. Wave.

Good-bye. Into the faint light of morning. Goes Sally Tomson's car.

> Sad
> Starts
> Under the eyes
> As age begins
> With lies
> Laughing hardly at all
> The way to
> The grave.

13

Smith back up these steps. Two minutes ago she left. Train thundering through the station in the town. No anger. Gave her fear. I mind so much. To keep her, must let her go. My hands folded under elderberry blossoms today. All marked with dying. Start off in the carnation smell of Brandy's death wagon to meet Bonniface on the train. Find him enthroned on an ice block. We all get left.

Smith rose in the elevator. To a room full of flowers. Low table with a bucket of ice and thermos of wine. Across soft green carpets, a bedroom. Fat white marble lamps. The window looking down at the train tracks. Shingled roof of the station. The road under the bridge and up round the war memorial in front of the hospital, curving down again to the river and the highway that has taken Miss Tomson away.

Lock the door. Draw the curtains tightly. Sit. Take a sip of punch. Close eyes. What you want so much you lose. Die and carry me away. Once at college, I thought I'm dying. And tried to run. From the terrible loneliness. Bereft in those university rooms, cold and tall ceilinged, late at night. I fell to my bed. Looked from the top of my head down to my toes. Said I'll never make enough money to live. And too young to die. I thought at least I would make a stagger for it while ticking my last. Go down from a standing position. And out I went from my college rooms hobbling down the old stone stairs, clutching wall and bannister. Yelling to two students busy peeing against the college granite. Said help me I'm having a heart attack. They looked at each other and tried to smile. I said through my faint breath, I'm not kidding, I'm George

Smith of number 38 College and I'm dying. They carried me out across nightly lit cobble squares of college. A moist dark wind blowing. And slumped in their students' arms, they finally carried me by the feet as well. At the porter's gate I squeaked tell my tutor to please see to my affairs. Porters made a space and let the red glow of embers shine on me. My china, cut glass, plain glass, and collection of Georgian decanters are bequeathed to college. My tapestries too. To help remember me. Dead so young. My head fell back against the lodge wall. The porters' scary eyes. Which were tickled at first for the college was famous for jokes. I said call a taxi, and one pulled in under the archway. I was loaded in. An ambulance too white for my last moments. All said good bye. Waved. Like I did to Sally tonight. A hope to bring you back again. In front of the hospital I crept for the door feeling I must not make any movements, said taxi man I'll pay you later. And he nearly had a seizure, gasping he wanted it now. I dug into my pocket. Only that it was necessary to give all my energies to my own heart attack I would have hit him several times. I limped inside. Three medicos I knew by sight from the university having tea. They made a merry word. Not to be cheered I asked them, listen before it ticks its last. Out came the stethoscopes. They said together, my God, what a heart. Will pump for years. Are you sure. We are certain. Are you absolutely. We are and will write it on a piece of paper for you. And sign it. And Sally it was dawn that night too when I went back to my college rooms sheepish and took up this little note which has lain in my wallet since and read it now, worn and old round the edges.

YOUR HEART IS ALL RIGHT

D. Romney

M. Bradfield

And tonight these many traumas since. Smith sliding the slip of paper back in the wallet between all the thin treasury bills. Shine gone from shoes. Death certificate all filled out. See Mr Stone in the lobby of Merry Mansions. A fair minded man. He'll say to Hugo Mr Smith's only a documentation now. Stretched on the feather filled cushions here. Chase Tomson down the roads. And into the hereafter. I let her go. When you must take women. Open their lips with fingers. Speak to the flower. Each petal then will curl back as you tell it with your voice. Big stately bitch you are.

Smith put his tired softness on the bed. Arms spread out, head across elbow. Where to go. Where to be. Sting of her slap on my face would have been better than nothing at all. Could have led her by the hand to bed. Untwisted any wire or garment on her large blonde frame. Unlatched the straps behind her back. Dive in, a soft mountain water full of her cool long fingers. Will ask God something while I sleep.

> Please
> Wish you would
> Give everyone
> A pot
> To piss in
> So they would not
> Ask for mine.

Pots are ringing. Like strange bells pinging. Hear it all in my ear. The phone. I fell asleep. Who knows I'm here. Who is that ringing. Like a hand reaching out of a closet door. Ding a ling. Let it ring. Ding a ling. Someone knows I'm here. Smith picking up the talking instrument.

'Hello.'

'Mr Smith, night porter here, Norbert. Gee, look there's a party down here, I had to disturb you. Says they want to speak to you, said they knew you were here. I said I'd ring and find out but that I had no knowledge you were in the building. You know I wouldn't want you raided.'

'What are you trying to sell.'

'Nothing, this particular party sir, didn't occur to me, I was pretty shook up, you might say it was a dish.'

'What do you mean dish.'

'Well, you know what I mean, dish, someone if I was you I'd be seeing I tell you, only I know you're busy. But maybe interested in an hour or two.'

'Look here, who is this. What do you mean by this extraordinary conversation.'

'It's Norbert, plain old Norbert. Just telling you what I know. Hey by the way, been thinking over your investment advice. I told the chef what you said, he wants to come in on the advice as well. Says he'll send you up a souffle.'

'It's five twenty by my watch. In the morning.'

'I know. I know. That's what I told this dish.'

'And don't call me again. Good night.'

'Gee. Good night.'

Smith derobing. Flicking off the lights. Leave a feeble glow of lamp in the sitting room. That son of a bitch Norbert. Thought I was on the job. And add a thrill with a phone call. A dish in the lobby asking for you. The whole world tries to get in touch and have some sort of ring side seat. Even at toilet of a morning. Ring the village bell. George Smith, gentleman, has made a motion. Without incident. The bell echoing down the valley. Thankful the town folk paused and clapped.

> A motion
> This side of the ocean
> Producing a tidal variation
> Upon the opposite shore
> One could not ignore.

Ding a ling. Smith sitting on the edge of bed. Trousers down. World wants to know time of tomorrow's movement. Pick up this phone for the last desperate time.

'Gee Mr Smith I'm really sorry, this is Norbert, night porter, on duty the Boar Hotel, again. There's some misunderstanding down here. And boy this party, the dish is on the way up by the private elevator. Told me to mind my own damn business and slapped me. Christ. Said get lost, buster. I'm not tussling with any more of these parties who want audience with you Mr Smith. If she wasn't so beautiful I'd let her have one on the jaw, sure she's no friend of yours. Even the papers say you have assets they don't even know about. That's what I've been saying to the property owners around here. I say, so what, you own property, I tell them get a gun, this long, about a foot, go down your cellar and start blasting. They're crying about their taxes, sure I tell them, sure you got taxes, sure, you go down your cellar and start blasting.'

'All right, Norbert.'

'Sure I say, you got your taxes, all these property owners, sure, go down your cellar and start blasting.'

'Thanks for informing me.'

'Start blasting, that's what the property owners –'

George gently put down the phone. Norbert's got some kind of affliction. A gentle knock on the door. Opening it. Sally Tomson standing there. Stepping across the threshold.

'Kiss me. I'm so desperately sad.'

'You poor kid, come to me.'

The drink of a refreshing fountain. Her long tall frame. The perfume of her neck. In under the tresses of hair. Find the ear. Say something but can't think of a thing. Except how your open mouth has such tender softness. So much younger than I think. More afraid than I knew. You didn't want to drive away in the rainy world. Who would help or keep you safe. All cold. Come in. Put this door shut with a nudge of toe. The hours before we touch and then touch and everything is all right. Skins together. Melt the chill conversation to tiny groans. You tremble. Peek out of my eyes close up to yours. Arms around my neck. Underneath your closed lids come dropping big tears. Down the side of your nose they go, around the nostril. And sneak between our lips. We have no future. All the sad spoils we spend. You thought me some cheap operator, waltzing from one soiled little deal to another, extending a hand here and there with a nice to sue you. I'm kind to those who love me. Soft and tender to the helpless. You kick off your slippers to make you smaller. Stand in your stockings. Dress unzips down the back. Caught me without trousers at all. A leaf you are, go all golden, full of autumnal beauty. Reach up, Miss Tomson, I am your buffalo.

'Jesus, Smith, what old fashioned underwear.'

'Christ, Miss T.'

'I've never reached into a man's pants before.'

'Feel free.'

'Think I'm lewd.'

'You're no wall flower.'

'Shouldn't have come up here the way I did. I was mortified in the lobby. Made a scene. You just let me go out of the garage. Why didn't you stop me.'

'Because I wanted you to come back.'

'Take me into the bedroom. Carry me.'

'You're a big girl. I might rupture.'

'Gee you look handsome. Smith, I'll carry you.'

'Mustn't let you. Miss Tomson.'

'Come on, I'm strong.'

'You'll strain yourself.'

'I want to.'

'Let's walk.'

'Smithy, hold hands.'

On the green carpet with a swing of linked arms. Her blue dress open down her spine. All those bones are pearls. Jasmine flowers on the curtains. Deep throated train trundling through the station, whistle wailing. Below this unholy hotel. Full of the strange spirits lain here before.

'You're strange Smith. It's sad.'

'Why do you say it's sad.'

'Wasted all this time. I never thought you liked me.'

'O God.'

'You do. Smithy.'

'Yes.'

'I like you. I think. I do. Yesh. Let's get off our clothes.'

Untie the tie. Unbutton the shirt. Minute ago so light with loneliness, nearly blew away. When her clothes are gone. One by one on the floor. Leave your pearls. Makes me gulp. Such an impertinence sticking out like that. Cast iron. Apologize. Nurses can sting it with a rap of the finger on the end and make it go down. Mine's flying. Zeplin, biggest it's ever been. On its mooring. Look. No time to be shy. Got to turn away. A gasp.

'O God Smith.'

'What.'

'I saw it.'

'O.'

'It's big.'

'It's normal.'

'Honest to God it's not. I never would of thought it was as big. It smiles. That's why I gasped. That is really something.'

'Thank you.'

'It's beautiful. You're an endless surprise.'

Smith waving his flag. Black ones are even bigger. Matilda tells. Miss Tomson I'm pleased you like it. Maybe it's all the months its wanted to rear for you. Compass needle. True north. Corrected pole. Room to write Sally Tomson. It chuckles too. All yours till coffin time.

'You've got a fine body Miss Tomson.'

'Yeah I know. You're trembling Smith.'

'You have the most beautiful body I've ever seen.'

'Isn't it something.'

'Yes.'

'Gee you're trembling.'

'I know.'

'Let me hold it, this crazy thing.'

'Wow.'

'There for the grabbing all the time in Golf Street.'

'Sally your hair.'

'Such a beautiful prick. Got to look at it. Kiss it. Makes me feel weak behind the knees.'

'Golf Street.'

'Thirty three. Why some nice girl hasn't got her name tattooed. Right here on the side.'

'Miss Tomson.'

'Could choke to death on it. Gee I'm shaking a little too. Grab me.'

'Yes.'

'Like my pent house shakes sometimes. You're slender Smithy. Wonderful sneaky guy. It's just like you never kissed anyone before. I want to tell you things. Feed you. Damn you with that, not telling me.'

Smith closing arms around the lanky soul. Just in a string of pearls. Now you know. Your breasts shine. Twin beams from a lighthouse on a lonely coast. Lift them a little to put a kiss. Hair on my hand. Warm. Kneel between your legs to pray. And in deference to the jungles disappearing the world over, growl.

'Smithy what a marvellous sound.'

'Grrrrrr.'

'You're so close you could give me a heart beat.'

'Bump.'

'Was that it.'

'Yes.'

'Thanks. Bump. There's one for you.'

'Thanks.'

'Christ I can't wait. Give me that. Give it to me.'

'You're laughing.'

'I know.'

'And crying. Tears.'

'Of course I am. Get it in. Before I die. Of all the simple things. Jesus. Bump. Have a heart beat.'

'Thank you.'

'Feels like an oak. Don't move.'

'Don't cry.'

'I've got to cry. O Jesus. Shake the hay seed out of my hair.'

Tomson smiling. Months of dreaming of this sunflower. Opened now. Head rolling, a little ship back and forth on the sea, delicate white nose a sail. Long hands sliding down Smith's back. Clutching over his simple arse. Warble of a bird. Crossed tonight, the wide rambling lobby. Red carpets spreading warm under a black piano, gleaming. Played with sad hands. On your breasts across your chest. Under me here. Inside you. Singing out your groans. Never knew you were so musical. Lungs dragging in air. Flattery. So soothed my nervewracked mind. Pleases you. Apple end you said. To eat. Down your mouth like all of me you tried to lift in your arms. Treetop out the window. Knockings in the radiator. Tiniest lines of age round your eyes. Where sadness starts. Feel I'm crashing. Into a country dance at a cross roads, as nearly I did once rushing towards the West with Bonniface for a toothbrush holiday at his unsteady country seat. Give you this gold ghost like the one I was driving. Taking an instant detour. Through a white cottage at the side of the road. In an explosion of stones and dust and within a hand's breadth of a gentle old soul having a cup of tea. Miss Tomson, she spilled not a drop. In you. Zounds, as we went through a hedge and field and back on the road, Bonniface screamed. First and only time ever had him scared. But I left every dancer unscathed and right as rain. Smithy, I've got a ruler in my handbag. Make you embarrassed to measure it. Widen my field of interest. The size. No one will believe me. God you helpless little guy. I am. Two women in one day. Both my secretaries. Ports in storm. Smithy I'm breaking in two. Hold me together. Don't let me go. Or leave me. Even when it's coffin time. Smithy, not so loud, you poor poor guy. Let it go. Under the waves. Got you wrapped. Tickling me under the heart. It is. You rascal. Tell me a story. Were you ever honest. Sally. You see. Bonniface said at the University, realism was our friend. Both of us cheated. And they caught the poor Bonniface. Who threw you Goliath's collar in the dark. But the college officials were mesmerized by his brilliance and candour on other issues. As the father of a child, waiting tensely for another. Smithy I feel pregnant already. Shush Bonniface was grim that day crossing the cobble stones glistening in a recent rain, tutor at his side. To appear before an august body and great clanging bell that rings your future. Your balls Smithy, they're slippery. Listen. I stole to watch in the window of the great hall. Bonniface's tutor, a man of love brilliance and sorrow. Who stood brushing grey hair aside, said gentle-

men I stand here before you to plead to put facts, sad and
uncomfortable. Mr Clementine need not have sat his
examination to get his year but elected to do so because
he felt he could excel. Four days prior to sitting his paper
he was notified by his landlady to quit his premises. Sally,
he peed all over them. At the same time, gentlemen, he
found that his wife was pregnant again. Gentlemen, most
of us have known the onslaught of fatherhood as it woe-
fully pounded upon Mr Clementine. Smithy, these little
balls are antiques. Sally, of a priceless period. But outside
the window that day, Sally, chilly and cold. Bonniface's
tutor had tears in his eyes, and a left fist raised gently. I
could bear to hear no more, tears in my eyes too. Smithy,
love to see you cry. And suddenly a shaft of sunlight struck
down. Across the features of Bonniface as he smiled. The
august body rose. Alone Bonniface shook his tutor's hand.
And that night walking forth from those university walls,
Bonniface said, Smith, my dear George, my name is cleared.
I must have drink. And out we went on the granite streets.
Gently torturing and tormenting the town. Untold human
horsepower in reserve. Bars aswamp till the pubs were closed.
Bonniface said get married George. Say yes to love. See little
babies grow.

> Through trial
> And misfortune
> Through misery
> And pain
> Maybe later
> Vaulting fences
> Like their
> Daddy.

Smithy, I feel so good full of you. Want to kiss it up again.
Does it need a rest. Did you get drunk with your friend
Bonniface. Yes, near the canal. He said he desired malt,
must find malt. And ripped a divining rod from a nearby
innocent fence. Held it high in his hand, said, ho. Ho what
gives. Ho. We crossed the bridge. As the divining instrument

led. Yours Smithy. It's up now so small and sweet. We went under the trees. By the little gardens. Up a path to a green door through flower beds. Ho. The door of this house ajar. And we walked in. Bonniface behind divining rod, through the blackness. Up stairs. I was holding to the back of his coat. I said vouchsafe. He said me leader. Follow. Down a hall. Another door ajar. Bonniface fiddled with a switch and lo, there was light. Jesus saves and satisfies. Smithy, do you ever think he's been laid. Sally there were a hundred bottles marked X and Watling Street on a table in a room. Which we grasped and consumed foolishly in the dark. Bonniface said will the world ever be this way again. And if not, why not. Good things are now. Not hereafter. Smithy you've often been silent. Did the world do something to you. To make you such a quiet man. Because it's so good to hear you talk. I must pee. That's what happened that night. Bonniface said, Smith I do not trust this divining rod to steer you to a suitable bowl. Therefore suggest you use the window this dark night. I said I wouldn't. Jesus don't pee out this window Smithy. But Bonniface said, my dear George, let me show you how. A manner and method in everything, thus, you raise the window, quietly. Handling the part carefully out through the opening made thereby. A mechanism I don't quite fully understand in the skull sends a message to the apparatus, pee, it says. And whee, signal received, a stream now emits arclike over the window sill. Cascading down upon the old fashioned flowers spied walking up the path to the free repast. Just as Bonniface lectured, tasting each beautiful vowel. I heard unbecoming stirrings in the room below. A trembling of voices. Lights had been switched on to watch the demonstration. But with the murmurings below, Bonniface requested smartly a dousing of illumination and pronto return to stoicism. We sat stony in the dark, each with a refreshing thick brown beverage to hand. Steps up the stairs now, following upon the slamming of a door below. And click click along the hall. Another click. The switching on of the lights by an unknown hand. Bonniface yelling out the window, O my God

I will roll mothballs in your direction soon. The door which was green swung open, the lights blazing, just as they were when the world was born. A brutal busty madam of fulminating nature stood framed in the door, shouting, what are you doing in my house, who's responsible for that disgusting downpour. Bonniface looked up from peaceful reverie. My good madam, how dare you address my friend and I in such a fashion. How dare you. And interrupt this gentle and kindly celebration following upon the heartfelt pleadings of my tutor. Mr Smith, here, was a field officer in the last conflict. Many footsoldiers gave willingly of their lives under his command, as he busily figured new strategy. Furthermore I envisioned for him a nice mercantile future, with marriage, children and ponies for them to ride. She said, get out of my house I'm calling the police, you bastards pissed right in my bedroom window on to my husband and me in bed. Smithy go and do yours and come back, and tell me. You're shy, aren't you. Yes Miss Tomson. Go to make a tinkle. Tinkle. Now tell me Smithy, push in close, let me hold them again, gee too small for tennis, if I phoned you, said I was full of a baby what would you say. Delighted. Would you. And what did Bonniface say to Madam. He said Madam I find it impossible to forgive you your manner in which you suggest such foulness. Who wants to waste piss on you anyway when it's needed for the benefit of roots and stems of flowers. Smithy you've never talked like this to me before, such a sweet story. Did this madam belt him one. Well madam was not lightly to be dismissed by the logical hauteur of Bonniface. She shook and trembled rather violently in the flesh. Made a rash charge at the Bonniface, who catlike was up, entwining wiry arms around her, her bosoms unflatteringly bursting forth from one of those modern manufactured fabrics. She screamed manhandling, fingering. As one heard a couple of hours ago in the Pomfret. Frequent fingering universal. And a figment, Bonniface said, of her imagination. Then gripping her person, as madam shouted loudly take your dirty hands off my tits, if my husband wasn't a cripple down there he'd come up and kill the both of you. Bonniface chucked her back out into her hall. Dare you madam, interfere with my social life. Nor should my lily hands toy with your mortal appendages. Vouchsafe they are huge. Wait till I get my stethoscope. Me mental and moral scientist madam. Bonniface then turned, said, my dear George, do pardon that unwholesome mar upon the evening, drink up, while I finish my pee. Smithy I really thought you were going to do yours out the window. Get us raided. Cops streaming in. We're on private property, Miss Tomson. You have it all figured, you scare me Smith. Guess we're both of us operators, without clothes, let me try a punch, watch this now, this left hook below the belt, all them hours you spent at The Game Club. Christ Miss Tomson, got a nice little punch there. Smithy you see, I could really take you, I could. Want to fight. No, please Miss Tomson. Come on Smithy. Anyway, even though you're getting yellow, I like your stories. Little incident was rich. Whole big world behind you, I knew nothing about. You're a lion, you're loving what I'm saying, you bastard. I'm such an open hearted girl, do you think it will come up again. I'll make it. With a kiss. O poor Smithy I ask for too much. You got grey hairs here, and now I know why they make lolly pops. It stirred, ah ha, you don't know how exciting to make it stand up. Sort of sentimental, can I think it's all for me, it does. Yes. Sweet, I wouldn't play tennis with them, fun to tell you everything I think. Hold my breasts. Was going to tear up the newspaper a moment before I saw your ad with the slave pay, the funny sequence of words got me. Miss Tomson, I'm going to advertise more if it finds the likes of you. Smithy how did you escape madam. She rushed out her front door, turned and shouted up remonstration and got caught in the undertow as the Bonniface unleashed the urine once more. Gee he really needed a pee, Smith, like to meet him, in a raincoat, if we add up both our ages what would it be, length of it in feet, it's beautiful, to sit on. Miss Tomson. Open up my eyes at you, sitting so pleased, and all you had to do was look and ask and up it went again, when I nearly think it can't, it won't, you said make it, you'll kill me, I'm dying, slipping right down, can't hold on, fingers slipping, shade pulled quietly over the brain, good-bye, don't go yet Smithy, I'm coming. Glued together. Sally, I'm only going just as I'm coming too. Sally. God. Don't mention him Smithy, they'll hear screaming in the lobby. Sally, you blanket over the desperate cold cares and mailmen lugging all the undelivered dread. Wait now till Monday. Till perhaps the Bonniface will come again rapping on the empty door of 604. Or enroll in The School Of Higher Graduation across the hall. My former friends will turn my funeral into rout. With some vulgar word drifting over the quiet peace. Four simple threadbare letters brought together. Scattering my acquaintances into the landscape. All listening cowering behind the gravestones and edifices to a meek Bonniface song.

> In twilight
> Too true
> The enemy farts.
> Get ready.

Miss Tomson throws back her long fishing rod arms. Two mouse blonde powdery puffs of hair. Steamy incense of her sweat. Kiss all down the inside of the arms. And ask her now.

'Miss Tomson.'

'Yesh.'

'Will you come to my funeral when I die.'

'Jesus Christ, Smithy. You poor kid. Sure I will. But you're not going to die. You've got a long way to go. Sure I'll come to your funeral. But you're going to live for years and years. Tell me who was the first woman you ever slept with. So I'll have plenty to think up when I write your epitaph. I'll come to the cemetery with it written on a sign. You know you were the sweetest employer I ever had. When I hold this. It's going to be a great shame when you die.'

Miss Tomson's eyes gone grey because they do at dawn she said. Marble canopy over my last remains. Few miles south of here. And she'll walk that day on her tall blonde legs through the gate of the garden of deads. In her hand a little bunch of violets. Crossing the pebbled paths, a wind blowing and bending the branches of trees and some leaves will fall and float to the first step of my tomb. Near the grass verge with its little sign. Perpetually Endowed. And Sally it was that latter word the first woman I ever slept with said to me. She was a queen with hair like sugar cane and her face and lips like soft sweet putty. She saw it and said you're well endowed. The night it happened I had been tempted away from my college rooms. Had a crazy man who visited me every Friday afternoon and smoked a cigar in front of my mirror. Would laugh loudly at his image uttering dramatic remarks, and said he was an actor. I left him and went to a tavern by the quays where the college bucks were drinking and singing hymns. There was Giles who invited old men back to his college apartments for games. Members of the rowing club riposted, for God's sake, man, clean up your life. Outside this pub ships were wheeling in the river, winches trembling, cables stiffening across the dark waters as they pulled bows towards the sea. And under a table there was her leg. She was blonde like you as well as a queen.

'Don't leave me Smithy not for a few hours anyway. Promise.'

'Promise.'

'I'll drive you back to town. You know. I went by Golf Street once. Taking Goliath for a walk. It was so sad. Looked up at your office and all of it empty and I nearly cried. Cigar guy, out viewing his big time display window comes across the street. Wants to know if he can help. Told him to mind his own business. You know what he said, sister if you got any connexion with that guy, they caught up with him, so you better beat it. I said sic him Goliath. Did that guy skidaddle. I was gloomy. I thought God, here I am making all this money, and my poor friend Smith had to beat it. Felt like leaving you money in my will. Even talked to my lawyer about it. You know they made a plaster model of me, it's everywhere all over town. Gave me the willies thinking what some guy might do to the cast. They had to tame down my lines. I don't know, you don't think they're too big. Why do you smile. You know Smith I don't even love you. I'm going to look at you as a curiosity in my life. You never even took me out. Or even bought me a soda. All the while I'm thinking you're broke. Till I see your apartment then I think you're the biggest tightwad who ever lived. I still do. And here you are in my arms. You haven't even offered to pay for smacking up my fenders.'

'These are fine fenders.'

'Just fit your hands. Wish I didn't have troubles. I'm supporting my brother. He's out of work, trying to start a corporation. I said why don't you operate like a friend I know which was you. I said he just has four walls and a pencil and cleans up. My brother wants his own building with his name on top. Said it's necessary with the kind of people he knows. God Smith you're so beautiful just lying there. You even have shoulders, not much, but impressive. If I tickled it like this it will grow big again. You better realize I'm just an innocent girl. Saying it to such an innocent guy. Sure I'll come to your funeral. This will need a little box all by itself.'

Sunday morning down on the station with big stacks of newspapers lifted off the train. Cars come slowly by and take one home. The Boar Hotel, four windows curtained, closed to the light. Rain cleaned sky, with white puffs of new clouds coming from the west. Miss Tomson's black long car parked with five others on the circular drive. She pranced up two steps and waltzed in between the shrubberies. Perhaps took a right swing towards Norbert's jaw. God will never keep her out of heaven. Even when he knows.

Hers
Were large
Without hope
For tiny
Hands.

14

George Smith standing three thirty in the afternoon on the sultry dim lit platform of Battery Station. The day's work done. Express trains speeding by on the central track between the pillars of the rapid transit system. Forty eight days since the Sunday with Miss Tomson. Counted for their lonely, empty deadness without her.

Smith looking at his watch. Three thirty three. Removing a white silk glove to take a square of hanky to wipe sweat off the brow. A slender black briefcase sadly full of onion paper copies of recent correspondence. Miss Martin glum as she types the actionable acrobatic answers in room 604. While I look out at the white lavatory wall of the air shaft mentally writing there antidotes to naughty scrawls elsewhere in the world.

The yellow caution lights go green at the end of the station. As Matilda with her five wedding rings, had white little circles under the gold on her dark finger. Red lipstick on her lips lighting her face. Chopped me little lambs livers for dinner and said Mr Smith you're not ready for redemption. Or burning holy shit. We got tight together on corn liquor. Mr Smith, forget that high class whore Miss Tomson.

Today, like all the afternoons since, I go for a sit in the park zoo. On a bench under a tree hanging with coloured balloons. Mothers munching popcorn pushing new babies by. Forlorn on this Battery Station waiting. To take tea in the hotel with the dull green high bronze roof. And stay to stare down through soft green cocktail light. At my white thick cup floating a tiny bag of leaves. Hunger in stomach and heart.

The disappearing swaying rear dots of a train down the

tunnel. Stale faces. Person there full of rancour. Lurking among a few grabbers at life's banquet taking early trains. Five o'clock my fencing lesson. Hopeless foil lashing in all directions. Can't help smiling behind the mask at my amusing madness. Till yesterday Master Ferendelli wrenched back his head gear, gave me a great show of teeth, said really Mr Smith, it would be so easy to run you through, please don't smile because you think I am a pin cushion.

Hoped so much to show Miss Tomson. My sword play which I took up Tuesday first thing after that Monday morning. Lathering each other in the deep blue tub before we left for town. As she stood in the bathroom doorway ready to wash. Breasts freely flashing. I nearly fainted. Till she covered them with her elbows. Nature gave you everything Miss Tomson. Yesh I guess I'm really something. She sat quietly on the edge of the bed. I pressed it harmlessly against her tit gently nudging her backwards one last time. Timbers shivering. Not bearing or caring to go back into the public world. Or silence as we drove back to town. Said I'd pay for all the bumps and damage, as she popped me out in front of Merry Mansions. Hugo opening the door. I blew a kiss to her from behind his back. And she smiled and waved roaring off down the street.

This leaning lurking shadow near me on the station. Don't dare to look up these days in case Bonniface is staring at me out of those red barrels he calls eyes. His presence has always led me drifting to disaster. The note he sent to Dynamo full of gentle beauty, regretful for the death of Miss Tomson's dog, which he said was buried in Dogdale Cemetery with every dignity. In soft moments admit that Bonniface is the kindest man I know. And after all the unanswered phone calls, I mailed the news to Miss Tomson, said I'd take her there to Goliath's grave, if she drove.

The shadow bumping against Smith's shoulder. Passengers filling the platform. The distant rumble of a train. Sound of spitting. A misdemeanour. Smith looking. Rancid face. Giving one a frosty spine. And a voice growling. At me.

'Why I'm better than you are.'

Smith looking up. Into dark unkind eyes. Glaring. The mean head turning sideways to spit again on the platform. Smith sidestepping into a puddle collecting a drip from the roof. Hoping for the train. Someone throwing a piece of chewing gum at the large rat gambolling down the tracks. A shout said the rat will get electrocuted. Can only see Miss Tomson everywhere, stepping out of the distant ads on the wall across the tracks. Train please come. Before this voice says something again. Clouded in an apple smell of drink.

'Why you fancy pants.'

Smith's cast down eyes. Such random sadness. The world will never rear up green again. And I've had to come out into life to mix on stations, benches, in zoos. To see others living. Walled and curtained off, by the blankness Miss Tomson left. Great dim desert. Coast to coast. Where horses run thirsty and thundering. In our short sleep together I never closed an eye. And she sat up strangely and said help. Help me. I kissed her on the brow and pushed her down again. She fell silent and asleep. Her hand toying between my legs. A touch I feel across all the grey stretch of days. To drown this ugly voice.

'Why I'm going to bust you one.'

Smith stepping back. Naturally. This growling person advancing, putting forth a hand to grab Smith's tailoring and tie held with such a small neat knot. Walked out of a Dynamo house so hushed and still. Checked my watch on the big clock of the Treasury Building. They keep close track of time. My half day rest from letters, phone calls, and the keester harrowing communications by hand. Smell weakness and they close in all at once. Muscles across the stomach in fine fencing trim to take the first blows there before they get lower and lower. Fisticuffs from an utter stranger. Always run into trouble taking a local train. Pee on the live rail you oaf. Electric will jump up the liquid arc and snuff you out. If it's death you're looking for.

Stranger's clenched fist pulling George Smith's face close to his own. For a gaping contrast of class. Smith's left hand with briefcase raised. Right paw tightened hard in its white silken glove. A flash in the air. Smith's fist landing with a thud on this stranger's jaw. Little pearls of teeth shooting out bouncing bonelike in the puddle. A deflating sigh. Stranger spinning slowly to the platform. Brief splash into the puddle. And rolling head first from the platform into the tracks. Now tingling with the thundering of a train.

Two feet thumping over the turnstile. Shirtsleeved man from the change booth. A citizen covering his eyes and peeking through his fingers at the prospective slaughter. Some hands over mouths and a long high pitched scream. Race of more feet. The nose of the black swaying train. Towards the bleeding unconscious figure stretched on the gleaming rail. George Smith lips tight compressed. Brain tabulating all bank accounts, canes, brass pigs and umbrellas. The moments on Miss Tomson, crying out against the nape of her neck. Soft skin of her shoulder. Her hand up over my mouth as I screamed. Hush, O George, it's all right. Yesh. Long fingers pressing in on my back. It's all right. Hold you in this terrible terror. Sleep there gently on my shoulder safely from all harm.

Crowd on the edge of the station platform. Train squealing and screeching. Yards ticking off. Hold my breath one year for each. Staring through the backs of all the heads. Silence. Voice shouting get back, get back. An elbow nudging Smith.

'What happened, suicide, someone jump. They should stop it. Work hard all day and somebody blocks the tracks when you want to go home. And ruin your appetite.'

Smith's lips stiff and dry. Cold tight band of fear around the throat. Human being prostrate in the tracks under a train. A trip up river. To the great pile of rock I saw from the Prep school boat ride. Walk a last mile down the rattling corridor. To the electrodes. Juice must hurt just a little in that terrible instant. Answer the phone Sally, please. Don't leave me any longer with the sound of sirens above in the street. And this manslaughter. Lying down there.

A dark sleeve of uniform. A chocolate coloured face. Looking down into George Smith's own.

'Are you a witness mister.'

'O dear God.'

'Look relax.'

'How dead is he.'

'He's all right. Train missed him.'

'God.'

'O.K. who saw it.'

Hands dragging the body up on the platform. Blood running down over an eye and out the corners of the stranger's mouth, as he wipes a wrist across his face, lips mumbling and stares dumbly at the relieved George Smith.

'O.K. I got hit in the tracks. Maybe I started it. Took me by surprise. I could beat him in a fair fight. Look at him with them white gloves. I can beat him.'

Chocolate policemen stepping in. Firemen arriving. With buckets of sand and little squirting pumps to clean the tracks. Policeman with the stranger and Smith by the arm, nodding back arriving reinforcements. Trains stopped over the whole wide city. Rumours spreading. A guy jumped holding his nose, blessed himself first. Party of police with Smith and stranger climbing up the chewing gum covered steps between the white balls of glass and past a man standing with a sandwich sign. Who was arrested on the spot because it said a large rude word.

Smith all stony and silent with his little briefcase in the police station. The entrance, flanked by green balls of glass. Glass swing doors. Rap of typewriters down long narrow corridors. Little group standing before a desk giving particulars to the sergeant. Doctor examining the victim sitting with a handkerchief up to his face. Chocolate policeman patting Smith quietly on the back.

'Don't worry mister, he started it. I got addresses of the witnesses.'

Smith yessing his head. Flashes of fear over the knees. Silent eyes everywhere. Full of death. Under the lids in the chilled air on this hot afternoon in all the squat funeral parlours dotted here and there on the avenues. Let me go to my little bench in the park. To tea. Back to all the sad memories of my shy big Miss Tomson. Hand under her thatch of hair. On her smooth egg of skull. Miss Tomson's knees bent were round just like the world.

Outside sky grows grey. Leaves of a little tree through bars in a courtyard turning over. Lights flashing. Rain pouring down with sudden white hail. Cooling moist breeze blowing in off the street. Police changing shift. Taking off caps and wiping their brows. The rancid stranger, a boiler watcher in a hospital. Had to talk to his lawyer. Three of his teeth in an envelope. Said he knew how to fall. His father taught him as a kid to be a champion diver. Chocolate policeman said why don't you shut up buddy before you get another bust in the face.

Outside the hailstones are melting in white ribbons along the gutter. Police station's barren windows and faint lights against a sky of mountainous black cloud. Smith with his little briefcase slowly stepping down to the sidewalk. The boiler watcher quickly following behind. Putting a hand to Smith's back and talking to Smith's cold eyes.

'What about my suit, it's all blood and dirty and I'm going to have a plate. Yeah, I need new teeth. What's a matter aren't you talking. I could of pressed charges. Hey, I'm going to sue you. Sure they said I can sue you, see my lawyer. I already got pains in the head. Doctor said it was too early to tell the damage. Wait till I get the specialists at the hospital. Hey, come back. I can sue. Don't worry I got your address.'

Smith walking to Golden Avenue. Stop to look at a ship safely sitting dry in a window. With tiny funnels, lifeboats, and first class cabins on the promenade deck. Sail from one shore to reach another. Across the days till they're all behind. If winter could come charging down this street. Drive all the heat away. Make the people go crouching in the buildings. And leave me to vamoose on a silver sea. With all my money stacked and packed. Guilty hearts lurk in the giant marble merchant halls. Sally you would have been proud how all the eyes of the other successful people on the station took a deep sad interest in me. Prior to the fisticuffs. Those on the hopeful way up in life turned their heads to look as I passed. Think of me. Watch the way I wave down this taxi. Light on my feet and could go into old age like swansdown and float up to heaven. That place Bonniface inquired after when he appeared according to Miss Martin at the information desk at the airport near Pomfret Manor, asking if there was an afterlife and was referred to the meteorological office. They may yet get me in this steamy street. All perforated with paper bullets. Come to my funeral as you promised. Keep what you want of me. A little coffin for it, all of its own.

> Bury it
> In
> Your window
> Box.
>
> A poppy
> Will grow.

15

George Smith in a rented pair of blue tinted eyeglasses, crossing by the fish market and moving down Owl Street past the wide steps of the Treasury Building towards Dynamo House. The middle of the month of August. Reaching out across the weeks to sink clutching fingers into this harmless Wednesday.

Starting at seven o'clock this morning to walk from Merry Mansions. To watch the city awake. Sanitation trucks sprinkling the street. Along the river, breakfast being served in the vast grey hospital. Nights now at their lonely worst. Matilda, an angel fluttering over redemption meetings, home late. While I stand lurking in the train stations, bus terminals. Fly firmly zipped up. Hoping to see some unbelievable golden sign of Miss Tomson's head.

Down in the early morning streets messengers trotting in and out of doors. This instant I feel good. Ships moving out to sea on the high tides. Barges carrying western trains headed north across the narrow waters. Bridges and highways humming with tyres. Smell of coffee across this downtown.

Smith stopping, looking up. Obstructing him in his forward motion, a face coming out of prepsterhood. Quickly steering a detour into the gutter. Nearly getting cut down with machines, and leaping back from the honking horns. Too late, too weak and vulnerable to turn and run this crazy time in my personal history. A smooth jawed figure. Grey natty topcoat, cream shirt and fat striped tie. And eyes that turned on their glow.

'I know you, hey aren't you George Smith. Not so fast like you were at the building site, that time.'

'Beep.'

'Ha you're George Smith all right.'

'Beep.'

'What do you mean, beep for an old friend. We were prepsters together.'

'Beep.'

'Ha ha George. It is you. Greetings. No kidding. Well how are you. I read that nifty write up in the papers. I mean you're a somebody. I mean I'm not doing badly. I'm doing all right. Got myself a little old partnership. But I mean how are you, all right.'

'Beep beep.'

'Now wait a minute. George ha ha. I know this is a funny situation.'

'Beep.'

'But a joke's a joke. O.K.'

'Beep beep.'

'Now hold it. Let's not make a meeting like this in the middle of Owl Street with all the congestion, holding things up. I mean you're located here. What do you say.'

'Beep.'

'Gee George is there something wrong. Are they crowding you. This has kind of gone on too long to be comic. I can take a hint, if that's it. What are you saying this beep to me for. If you don't want to recognize me say so.'

'Beep beep.'

'What is it. Is this a method, something happened and you use this method. I mean they said in the papers you were building a mausoleum, that costs, I know. I mean are you nervous.'

'Beep.'

'It's a method.'

'Beep.'

'I see that's one beep. O now I remember. The rude noise you made to the reporters. O I'm catching on, a voice lapse. It's one beep, maybe, for yes.'

'Beep.'

'And two for no.'

'Beep.'

'I'm sorry, I didn't know anything about this George. Is it permanent.'

'Beep.'

'Gee that's tough, on your wife and kids. I heard you got married. Only guessing you got kids. To Shirl. What a girl. She'd never even give me a tumble. Remember the tea dances. Those white linen suits Shirl used to wear. She was beautiful.'

'Beep.'

'But I just didn't know you had this problem. I guess you're under specialists.'

'Beep.'

'New method like this must tax the mind. You must want to really say something once in awhile. Like an opinion.'

'Beep beep.'

'Is that right. If there's anything you need. I know you have money. But if you're bothered by a problem, spiritual, you know. Why you holding your hand to your ear. You're not deaf too.'

'Beep.'

'O, gee that's tough. You lip read.'

'Beep.'

'You remember Alice. You know I married her.'

'Beep beep.'

'She only mentioned you the other day. How Shirl followed you right across the ocean. The ocean. I'm saying the ocean. My Alice, yes, mentioned you. She mentioned you. This is a really rotten world. Real rotten. It's rotten. Guy's speech and hearing cut off in his prime. I said in your prime. It's a shame. But you can still see. I said see, you can still see. To lip read. From behind the blue glasses.'

'Beep.'

'Thank God for that. Can they do something for you. I said, help you. Can they help you.'

'Beep beep.'

'It makes you sick, doesn't it. A disgrace. I said it was a disgrace.'

'Beep.'

'Believe me I'm really sorry for what's happened to you. I mean that sincerely. I said, I'm sorry. Sincerely.'

'Beep beep beep.'

'That's three. I got it. For thanks.'

'Beep.'

'Only George, I'm sort of in a hurry. Like to hang on, talk over old times. Sure would like to hear what it was like serving in a foreign army. Must feel good to be a colonel. I said full colonel. Must feel good to be one. Get together won't we. I mean sometime, old sport, when you're all right again. You'll be all right. Thing is not to worry. I said don't worry. Looking at my watch. Got to be dead on time, somewhere. An appointment. I wish you all of God's luck that someday you may be well again. Hope your health comes back. I mean that.'

'Beep beep beep.'

'Sorry I got to rush. But if you can read my lips I'm saying the cure may be in prayer George. Pray. So long.'

'Beep beep beep beep.'

'Ha ha, goodbye. Goodbye.'

Smith ducking into the inhuman stream. Entering Dynamo House. So many have wives and little ones. Like the lonely have themselves. I've just the strength to climb these stairs. Ugliness brings taunts and jeers from passers-by. Elegance invites assault from strangers. Old friendships promote beeps.

> As a crap
> Can lead
> To crutches.

16

Miss Martin sitting at her desk in Room 604. Looking up with apprehensive eyes. A tiny smile at the corner of her lips as Smith cleared his throat and said a forceful good morning. In the corner a canvas container stiffly against the wall. Four mornings it's rested there, and while Miss Martin was out purchasing wiener and crumb cake for lunch yesterday I sneaked to take a look and swallowed peering down a narrow bore barrel.

Seems for no reason at all I go beep. But the presence of a lethal instrument makes one tense at any sudden sound in the front office. Miss Martin's been making rapid visits to the water closet feeling sick. Once staying there two hours. Perhaps say a little word before she starts to read her newspaper.

'Miss Martin, the rifle.'

'Yes.'

'I note it has a hair trigger.'

'Yes.'

'I know we're a little informal here nowadays.'

'You left the files in the woods Mr Smith. Not me. Don't start blaming me.'

'Nothing to do with the files. I like to be easy. Informal.'

'If you don't want me around anymore, Mr Smith say so. Don't think I like all this tension too.'

'I'm talking about that gun there.'

'What about it.'

'That's what I want to know. Miss Martin.'

'Well what do you want to know. Mr Smith.'

'Don't be abrupt Miss Martin.'

'Look I'm not going to shoot you with the rifle if that's what you're scared of.'

'I'm not scared.'

'Well what are you asking then.'

'Why you have it.'

'Don't you know. I'm on a rifle team. I told you. Guess you didn't hear me with all the beer cans banging back there.'

Long hard moments. Miss Martin who was putting on fat belligerently, staring into Smith's reasonably honest globes. What harm a few beers. In the office. When one is commander in chief. Big cheese in this two personal outfit. Once ruled a regiment, Miss Martin. Howitzers shelling those positions I figured out in my little wooden shack well behind the lines. A flash focus of the enemy in a field glass. And whamo. But in peace time I take a beer or two while I stare down the clause of a contract and the rebellious beam from my secretary's eye. Morning is no moment for a showdown. Wait till the day wears on. Dim the sparkle in her cheeks. Now apple red. Make a lot of money, gladly lose a lot of friends. Once poor and popular. Now rich and reptile.

'Any letters.'

'One registered I signed for. Two threats. And one bill.'

'What's the bill.'

'Mr Brandy, funeral director, embalmer –'

'What is it.'

'Don't shout. I'm just telling you. What it says here, for the afternoon and evening hire and misuse and additional damages of one hearse.'

'O.K. enough, what's the registered one.'

Miss Martin with her little efficient opener. Pulling out the paper. From here I can see a black letter head. Miss Martin silently reading.

'I think you better read this yourself Mr Smith. Mailman said they've been trying to deliver this for days in Golf Street.'

Smith with a thumping heart. Holding the stiff unrelent-ing paper in such small delicate hands.

Sun Shine & Son
Bicuspid House
Paradise Square
Of This Instrumental.

Mr George Smith
33 Golf Street
And new of Room 604
Dynamo House
Dear Sir,

On a Wednesday of the 19th ultimo, at 3.34 P.M. (approx.) o'clock at Battery Station of the Rapid Transit system of this city you made an unprovoked and savage attack upon our client, Mr Harry Halitoid which resulted in a knockment into the tracks of the said system where there was a sustainment of considerable head and body injury.

Therefore and in view of the heretofore we furthermore establish that our client who is positioned as a master Boiler Watcher at a prominent hospital where many wealthy people have been treated has been unable to preside at work for two weeks, during which the hospital steam has been making unfamiliar pounding noises in the pipes upsetting the inmates and our client himself has been under the care of doctors and night nurses, one of whom is a specialist in soft foods. The upper incisors as well as one canine and one bicuspid are missing from our client's jaw, obliging him to eat slops. Although two teeth were recovered which were knocked from said mandible our client has suffered much mental cruelty and disspirit when he has attempted to smile while having to tour important personages around the boilers.

By way of damages we are asking a sum to offset the physical and mental distress endured by our client as well as making good the suit of clothes which suffered spoilment in the tracks, plus a further stipulated monthly payment as our client is now forced to go through the rest of his life with an unfriendly outlook.

Failing to reach a satisfactory agreement with you regarding restitution and arrangements we advise you that we have been instructed by our client, who has desisted to press charges, to take immediate steps.

Yours truly (very)
Sun Shine & Son.

Smith leaning against the doorjamb. Brood over all the many folk who have skidded on the snake oil. Strange how when passing by the sign across the hall of The Institution Of Higher Graduation, one wanted to crash through the door and land inside begging on one's knees for a scroll.

Smith disappearing into the back room. Returning four minutes later with a paper. Putting it before Miss Martin.

Ward 17
Blockhouse II
Island of the
Criminal Lunatic
Day-light Saving Time

Sun Shine & Son
Bicuspid House
Paradise Square.

Dear Sirs,

I am indifferent to the ultimo. But while here at the institution I have made many good friends, some of whom are often discharged as cured. Upon requiring further communication from me, one of these absolutely cured formerly violent lunatic criminals will deliver my further reprisals by hand.

Yours sincerely,
I. Belt (*Warder*)

Dictated by George Smith and
signed in his absence.

P.S. While dictating, a roving committee of armed warders on show of hands have elected to discharge me as cured, further reoccurring lapses to be dealt with at an out clinic.
P.P.S. Respectfully hoping you are not a cavity in the tooth where you live.

Miss Martin standing. Trembling with Smith's letter in her hand. Her mouth opening, then closing.

'What's the matter, Miss Martin.'

One hand reaching across her brow. Miss Martin slowly back stepped to the shiny horse hair sofa. Sitting bent forward on the edge, hand now dropping across her eyes. Smith in waistcoat, sleeves rolled up. Lifting the left foot on top of the right. Ruin a good shine. Feel stark naked with my battle ribbons and medals pinned to my skin.

'Everything is the matter.'

'Is it the letter.'

Miss Martin shaking her head. Hair swinging out from her ears. Which I felt and kissed and whispered round. These last weeks such a strain. As she comes late to work. In the back room I lurk desperately to find something for her to do. She's changed since the night of Pomfret Manor. Looking so matronly sitting there on the horsehair.

'Can I get you a pill, Miss Martin, Goodness.'

Smith rushing forward as Miss Martin gently keeled over on her side and lay breathing heavily, slightly snorting through the nose. Some terrible instinct comes and you want to jump right on top of her. That in her sorrow and sadness one might take her from behind. Her breasts have got so big. Milk ice cold from a cow. Go through the rest of my life now by mute card or beep. Miss Tomson, who could walk across the town in two tall strides. Tonight I'll go haunting terminals, and lobbies for you. One swat on one jaw on a station platform. And a hook goes fishing in my assets.

Miss Martin's eyes closed. Her breathing heavy. Smith lifting her legs and tucking them in on the sofa. Turning back to his room and standing in front of a round mirror. Lathered on a cloud of shaving cream. Unfold this long razor, and lay it against the flesh. Trip down all these mighty little hairs. High up out of the air shaft planes fly over, buzzing and rattling the window panes.

A dog's bark out in the corridor of Dynamo House. Smith stiffening in the back room of 604. Wiping face with the pink towel, pulling down pink shirt and buttoning cuffs. Throwing arms into jacket and straightening tie. Past Miss Martin still snoring on the couch. Peeking out the door and down the hall. Edging slowly back in again. Out there a man and a brown crippled dog. Who lays down every few feet to rest, panting. And the man leaning over to pat its head kindly while he looked at the numbers of the doors. The aristocratic back, carriage, hair and dishevelled clothes.

Bonniface. Sporting brown attire. Just slip by now and down the opposite stairs. Leave Miss Martin to his mercy. You wretch, Smith. Remember. Clementine, burier of Miss Tomson's dog. In the pet cemetery not far from The Goose Goes Inn. Bonniface preserves nobility while the rest of us have none.

Smith escaping down the side stairs. Across the lobby of Dynamo House and out the wagging doors into a sunny friendly street. Treasury clock bell tolls noon. Raise a hand to shout for a taxi. And another hand comes down to rest gently on a shoulder. And turn to face a warm sad smile.

'Smith. Ah Smith. What about some beer and onions. You think I vault the statues of public peace, safety and justice and land in that little area they call amnesty. You think that. This is my faithful friend here. He is a dog. He is old and tired now, walks only few steps at a time. Then he must lie down and rest till the energy comes back. But I am his friend too, I wait, we both go forward together. Make each other's life worth while. He nice dog. He called Mr Mystery. Nice name. Ah George you go so grey. You worry too much.'

'How do you do, Bonniface.'

'Come George. Flag this taxi here. Come. Pick up Mr Mystery. Mr Mystery, do not growl at George, he had to be mean to make money. But meanness, niceness, it's all the same. Often nice to be mean and mean to be nice. My God George I'm going absolutely demented in this town. I do not know what you do but many rumours fly about you. Mr Jiffy said you were cunning, astute. You escaped with the most beautiful woman. Abandoned your comely secretary. Left me in the ice house.'

'Sorry Bonniface, I can't come. I have an urgent matter to attend.'

'Ah George. Listen to me. Her Majesty is in town. You greet that news with silence. Come now get in this taxi with Mr Mystery and me.'

'No.'

Taxi driver slowly turning round. Honking horns behind in the street.

'Hey look gentlemen. Already I'm taking a crippled dog in my cab, maybe fleas, how do I know.'

'Come George. Don't have a mental struggle. Come. I'll tell you where you can find Her Majesty. I know how badly you would like to know. Don't fight it. And become a sad victim of will power. Melt it down, reharden it later, even harder. Let laxity triumph.'

Smith entering the cab. To speed down Owl Street by the fish market, by the vegetable Pushcart Market under the bridge, to the left, along by a narrow dusty park of benches draped with sprawling men. And further up a cobblestone avenue.

'Smith do you shake hands with yourself in the morning because of loneliness. You desert wife and children. Climb in this cab at the mention of Her Majesty. Never mind reasons. Mr Jiffy has assisted me. Gave me a letter of introduction to a man who owns aeroplanes. Many many aeroplanes. He say, Mr Clementine, you have beautiful manners, let me hire you to run my airport. Ah, George, surprise. Think I touch you for money. Or fill your life with fear. Not me. I just want to talk. Put you on the right track. Give you back your faith in people. They are not out to get you George, you imagine it.'

Cab turning into a tenement street. Of broken houses and steps. Garbage pouring out of cans. Taxi stopping in front of a little green façade of plate glass window and lace curtain. Bonniface slowly clinking change in the driver's hand. Said he was not tipping as it was a holy week in his religion. Two figures entering this establishment. The tallest of them with his arms full of dog.

At a washed maple table. Inside this cool and calm interior. Poinsettias on a shelf. Calendar with a sunset and nude girl ankle deep in surf. Bonniface smilingly toting beer, bread and onion slices over to the sad dark suited Smith. And bending with a special serving to slip between the yellowing jaws of Mr Mystery.

'O.K. George, tell me the truth. What are you up to in Dynamo House. In the Cabin in the woods. In the Merry Mansions. In the Renown Cemetery.'

'Where is Her Majesty.'

'Smith, you pant for Her Majesty, old enough to be your mother. Have a flower for your buttonhole. And for you under there Mr Mystery, another slice of onion. Get yourself a dog, George, ere long. Be a true friend to animals. See how he wags. Eyes sad but full of friendship. Someone pushed him out to die, you realize that George.'

'Where's Her Majesty.'

'Ah now. Patience. Look over there. Those old men play chess. Remember a certain five o'clock on a chilly late autumn day. Across the seas. Turf smoke. Leaves gone from the trees in the square. I came like a moth to a light in the gloomy afternoon, George. Your white coated servant let me in. You gave me a green bowl of tea. I said thank you. How was I to know then that you would deliberately pursue a life of secrecy and possibly shame. All gaiety defunk. Maybe you like men, George. And surround yourself with wife, kiddies, secretaries and girl friends as a blind. You can tell me. I'm frequently having my privates interfered with in this town. Stay off the transit. Stay out of the bed linen market, the outdoor jewellery market.'

Smith standing. Bonniface reaching over with a hand pressing it down on his shoulder. Smith collapsing back on the chair.

'George, don't go. Have some recreation. Then promise to bring you straight to Her Majesty. Look at Mr Mystery down there. Used to like lady dogs in his prime. Bow wow he went. Hello lady doggie. Sniff sniff. Naughty Mystery. Nice lady dog. Lift leg on corner stones and parked motor wheels. I am in command George, walk out on the apron of the airport, hand extended to a celebrity and say, please, this way, with the compliments of Motor Bird Inc. Refreshment is set up. At the flick of a cuff link I am of service.'

Smith looking down upon his cool beer. Foam gently

climbing the edge of the glass. A thick slab of onion. Deeply worn smooth grain of the table. The light eyes of Bonniface. Whose earthly wish he once said was to be taken back into history and there be assigned four porters to fetch him to various breweries on a throne.

'George listen to me. Never let your capability get confounded. I know you've found the mammoth nipple. Have it hidden somewhere in this town. Look out the window and watch the cars. When they stop flowing that's the time to worry. You rich. Me banjaxed. Wait, don't go.'

'Bonniface, I'm going. You and Mr Mystery stay. But I must go. Urgently.'

Bonniface rising, bowing. Mr Mystery flapping his tail on the floor.

'George I will tell you the whereabouts of Her Majesty when you come back.'

Smith entering a delicatessen across the street. After much heated and hilarious argument he bought a paper bag from the proprietor who said they were for customers to carry a purchase. Smith reaching a fast settlement, buying the air rights within the said container. Stepping outside, late lunch stampede on the pavement. Smith into a cab. At a traffic light, driver shouting epithets out the window at another taxi. Why don't you smoke a bomb. Why don't you dig a grave and drop dead. Lights go green. To sadness and deals. And every man's hope.

> To get
> In her
> Without
> A wedding.

17

In front of a tall marble building. Gigantic bronze doors. Smith entering this emporium of finance with his paper bag. Late noonday sun beaming from high barred windows and warming Smith's dark shoulders as he wrote on a little piece of paper. Standing in a line of fidgeting depositors. A breast distinctly shoving him in the back. The mammoth nipple Bonniface mentioned.

Smith's turn. Pushing across his little piece of paper. To a Mister Cheer it said on a little sign, whose face blossomed and nearly flew with friendship. Wide bow tie for a propeller. Who thought for one amazed second it was a stickup.

'One moment, Sir.'

'I can't spare it.'

'O.'

'In rather a hurry.'

'Well you see, I'll have to clarify the situation Mr Smith. I mean is it for the payoff.'

'I beg your pardon. Do I have to sue you and this bank for aspersion.'

'But a cheque this size for cash, well I'm supposed to clarify.'

'How dare you.'

'I could lose my job. This is an awful lot of money.'

'You suggesting that I am attempting to commit fraud.'

'No sir.'

'Then instantly fulfil the sum of that cheque, in brand new notes.'

'Mr Smith I know you must be nervous over being sued. I mean supposing there was some miscalculation in your account, sir.'

'Are you suggesting errors, that the balance forward is a wrong number. And what do you mean by sued and payoff.'

'You're putting words into my mouth. Only want to verify the clarification of balance for your convenience.'

'My convenience is that you answer this cheque in cash instantly or I shall take steps to deal with your first aspersions. Cast irresponsibly on my character.'

'I'll do just as you say. I'm new at this branch. I mean anyone can lose control and attack.'

Mr Cheer like employees everywhere is uttering irrelevancies. Perspiration on his brow now dripping on the banknotes. Fingers peeling up their edges, knuckles banging the marble, making one little neat pile next to another.

'You want to count this yourself, Mr Smith.'

'I measure by eye. Put one more on that pile you'll be right.'

'Better count this again.'

Smith pressed from behind by the mammoth aggressive breasts. Life is too fast to bother to turn and say madam please don't splash those on me. Close this account down with a shattering clang. Nervous being sued. Of course I'm nervous being sued. My mind is hair raising.

'Mr Smith, you've got some eye, you're right, a note short.'

'Just slide them in this bag. Must rush.'

Making sure glass was not in front of his forward motion, George Smith left the bank and turned down the elegant street recently planted with baby trees. Suddenly finding his position blocked by a fat lady, he lowered his head and ran. At the corner hailing a taxi. Giving the driver a designation to go round and round the park. Between my feet a bag of money. For some it grows on trees. Glad I've got such a big forest.

George Smith sat back on the leather, heartily sorry for various sins. One's life now mercantile might suddenly become marine. My sad unfinished tomb. With winter on the way. Still hoisting up the great blocks of marble. They lock together like a puzzle.

Yellow taxi carrying George Smith on its humming tyres

through the park. By bridle paths under bridges. Four young men in lipstick on top of a rock smiling. Little kids rolling a watermelon down a hill. Rowboats and water birds on the sunny lake. Lurking bodies in the bushes. Showing only a sign of a hand, a face and sometimes a more naughty thing. Each elegant back I see strolling, I think of Her Majesty. And it's just another empty face. While my hip bones ache with fear.

'Mister I'm getting nervous driving around this park. You got to give me a destination. I got to go somewhere. Too much responsibility going nowhere.'

'I'll give you an address.'

'Thanks a lot.'

Smith taking a little black book. Peel back the pages, torn, worn and dirty. Decipher a scribble near this great letter T. For Tomson. She reared up in the dark. Shouted, you don't even know where I live. I took the address down. And since. Have been too terrified to go. Pull up my socks now. Steam south and west.

'Driver go to this address.'

'On the paper.'

'Yes.'

'Glad to.'

Down a hill under shady trees. Up to traffic lights and across the avenue. Past entrances that lead to the rapid transit. Something is wrong. I twitch and fear. Would like to have a friend. Just now and have none. At best, Bonniface is a crazy companion. The rest of my life I would stay with Miss Tomson. Near all her chill blue beauty. Threading our way through the throng of opportunists. And hand in hand take one gigantic leap together and wake up in the next world. Wearing red underwear.

'Driver stop.'

At a street corner. Smith reaching through the window for an afternoon newspaper. Slipping out a coin.

'O.K. Driver, on, please.'

Folding open the paper. A glance across the front page. At the bottom a picture and a headline.

A summons was issued today against Mr George Smith formerly of 33 Golf Street and removed to Dynamo House, Owl Street where he was traced. The victim Mr H. Halitoid of Fartbrook claims he was the innocent recipient of a right hook to the jaw in the rapid transit while his attention was distracted with other passengers watching a rat gambol down the tracks. As he and other spectators on the Battery platform (uptown side) waited for the rodent to be electrocuted, Mr Halitoid alleged a fist encased in a knuckle duster thundered out of space and (according to his doctors) landed on his lower mandible scattering biscuspids everywhere.

Interviewed at his bedside this morning, Mr Halitoid declared that terror was rampant in this city and asked this reporter, 'Are our rights to be protected or must we walk in fear outside our homes.'

Mr George Smith whose name at times has vaguely been connected with dealings in the financial district was not available at his business address nor at Merry Mansions where he resides with many other prominent citizens, and show business personalities.

The picture taken by our photographer by telephoto lens (white structure at right centre in trees) is believed to be the only picture in existence of Mr Smith's tomb, still abuilding in Renown Cemetery. The mausoleum when finished will, it is rumoured, be the largest of its kind anywhere and will contain every modern innovation including plumbing.

At the gates of Renown Cemetery, this reporter asked Mr Browning architect in charge of building, 'If he considered Mr Smith's tomb a new note in graveyard antics consistent with the attack asserted by Mr Halitoid.' And he replied to this reporter, 'According to my experience, Mr Smith is a rare gentleman of the old school.'

'Hey mister you all right back there.'

'Yes.'

'Look as if you seen a ghost. You weren't that colour when you got in my cab.'

'It's nothing. An old characteristic of amphibians. Turn colour when they get nervous for camouflage.'

'You don't say. Hey just like that animal maybe they got in the museum right there we're passing, called the Thunder Reptile, brought my kid to see it. Hey that's better, the blue sunglasses give nice contrast to the green.'

'Thank you.'

'Don't mention it.'

Cab heading west, façade of piers in the distance. Windows full of furs. Miss Tomson lives in a rather mixed district. Perhaps she goes to that little diner for coffee and that station for gasoline for her car. What can I say if she sees me. What are you doing in my district Smith. Who told you you could come around here. Just because I let you in bed with me, don't think you got some right to snoop around my life. Miss Tomson you said I mustn't ever leave you or let you go. You poor joker Smith, don't you see I was just making like it was a romantic night. Big deep experience. Don't take words seriously, those things were for the background atmosphere, like a soft piano on a date.

Cab slowing and stopping in front of a tall yellow building. Shooting up out of the tenements. Wrack the mind for opening statements. Miss Tomson I just happened to be passing in a cab when your address fell out of my wallet and blew up into my hand and I looked out the window and found I was there. Pardon my green colour. Don't hesitate to tell me if you're busy. I'm busy. Miss Tomson after all these empty weeks let me kiss your feet. They're clean. Or even if there's a slight odoriferousness.

At the end of a long narrow lobby. An elevator. Little iron chairs with lion paws for feet. Hanging with red tassels. Smith taking off his sunglasses. No names no signs. Pressing a button to ring. Out of a door. Man buttoning up the front of a blue uniform, scratching the sweat from his brow with a white glove.

'Yeah.'

'I'm inquiring after a Miss Tomson, please. I don't know the number of her apartment.'

'Nobody here called Tomson.'

'But this is her address. Sally Tomson.'

'Ain't no Tomson.'

'Are you sure.'

'Look you want me to take an oath.'

'She's a tall girl with gold hair.'

'This is no missing person's bureau.'

'She swings her hips when she walks.'

'What are you, desperate mister.'

'Yes.'

'Well there's nobody here by the name of Tomson. Or I would know.'

'She's beautiful.'

'Don't think I don't sympathize. I see lots of girls, beautiful ones with gold hair. After they're twenty five they're all blonde or red or something.'

'She used to go barefoot in the lobby here.'

'Look I don't know what's bothering you mister. But this could be anybody on a health diet. Everybody's doing it. I'd be doing it, if some of the people in this building didn't think they was big shots and I was reducing the tone.'

'O God.'

'Look, don't be upset. Be the same if I wore sandals. I got ingrown toenails. There are two hundred people in this building. Racketeers, widows, moguls, tarzans, dentists and hat check girls who date customers on the side.'

'Obviously I'm at the wrong address.'

'I mean you want to look for yourself. Here's the whole renting list. Right here.'

'No thanks.'

'O.K.'

Smith turning, tucking the string handle of his paper parcel up on his elbow. In distress open your pockets wide and spend. No reason left for the world to go on. With me in it. Go back and find Bonniface. Find Her Majesty. She had sugar cane hair falling on her shoulders in a cascade. And a snuff box cover with a little boy peeing on a rose.

A chandelier the shape of an anchor, hanging over

Smith's head as he passed out through this vestibule. Walls curlicued with comb marks of some fancy plasterer. And between the two inches left between the door and a clang. A shout from the keeper inside.

'Hey mister, wait a second. Come back.'

Smith peering down the lobby. Keeper pushing his cap back further on his head. Holding a pencil to his renting list.

'Does she have a dog.'

'Yes.'

'Was he a giant.'

'Yes.'

'Goliath his name.'

'Yes.'

'Well you want Dizzy Darling. The model. But if she's who you're looking for she still ain't here.'

'She said yes, yesh.'

'That's her. Lived in the pent house. Sure, that's Dizzy Darling. She roller skated out this lobby one day, but never saw her with her shoes off. Always having to carry presents up, used to get flowers so you'd think there was a funeral. You never saw so many important guys after one girl. I mean excuse me. Are you her father.'

'No.'

'Well she's nearly gone two months. I was just thinking about Goliath a minute ago helping the janitor to put out the ashes. Used to take him for walks down there near the river for Miss Darling. You're a new friend or something. Gave you a bum steer on her name.'

'Yes.'

'That's her all right. Guess it's the only way she can deal with guys. Least she gave you the right address. I was saying to Jake the janitor. Some guy try something with Goliath around. You read this afternoon's paper, that one you got there. Millionaires are on the rampage now slugging innocent people in the subway. Imagine a guy building a place to bury himself and he's trying to kill somebody in the tracks. It don't add up.'

'No.'

'You mind your own business and that isn't even enough these days. We should all have man eating dogs. Just a minute I'll look here and see if I can find a forwarding address. That was the funny thing. She comes back here one afternoon, I remember it plain. I parks her car for her, all smashed up in front and there on the back seat is Goliath's collar. I knew the collar it had gems. But no Goliath. I was going to ask her what happened only I'm not on duty next day and Sam the other doorman tells me a moving van comes and collects and that's it, mister. Nope. Don't see a forwarding address. Wait. Nope. Just to hold stuff. It's all been collected, Hey what's the matter.'

'Hayfever.'

'O.'

'Thank you.'

'Sorry you come on a wild goose chase. Can't help you further than that. Gee she was parading under another name somewhere. But that name Sally Tomson is familiar, now I think of it, anyway it's always been Dizzy Darling to me. Her rent was paid up. Here, have a piece of chewing gum.'

'Thank you.'

'People come and people go but the graft goes on forever. You like that. I entered it for a song contest. It lost. Used to get a big laugh out of Miss Darling. Said I had a good sense of humour. Why not, life's humorous. What do you say.'

'Beep.'

'Ha ha. That's some remark. See that's what I'm saying. Anytime you happen to be passing come in and have a talk.'

'Thank you.'

Warm debris of the street. Smith looking up into the sky at the keeling yellow structure. Right at the top is where she lived. And said cooling in my arms, a Monday two months ago that she was a weak character and didn't want to live in a dump. Look for the highest tower and maybe

I'll find her. In high winds and danger. And two little shrubberies in barrels in front of her address. Run screaming
away through a downpour of lavish toilet waters. Would
have asked her to play tennis. Even though my first service
sends up a smell of burning rubber, immediately requiring
a new ball. And Dizzy Darling would stand there dumbfounded with her racket hanging out, a neat hole through
the centre. Then she'd serve mine. My God, the pain. Under
the hot sun on mossy green. I was just some man to come
to her bed. To drive away the dolour after her dog was
dead.

Smith walking west. A pile of ancient trolley tracks rust-
ing in a lot. A warehouse. And in here they sharpen saws.
Feel each little bump in this street. Somehow I've got to
walk. Towards the trestle there. And the red funnel of a big
ship. And that white little ticket hut. Day excursions. Trip
round the island. Went out into the world from college.
When I should have stayed in those high ceilinged rooms
cold and safe, peeking out across the moonlit square, bare
twigs and night time sky. Head against some hard wall.
Crying for forgiveness. Her Majesty said I looked so innocent, such a young man who minds his business so. I've been
watching you just standing there. Come with me. What
were you thinking about. I gulped. Said yes Ma'am. You
like to be quiet and I'm like that too. And the prospect
of her room out those drab college stairs, gas mantles glowing.

Smith at the little booth bought a ticket. On to a grey
pier and deck of a green and white steamer he slowly
stepped. Holding on to a rail. Dizzy Darling. She could
have told me anything. Least of all her name in the other
life she led. Lips all dust and grime. My false college heart
attack ten days after I married Shirl. And left Her Majesty.
Queen of a kingdom over which she never reigned and said
I had a charming stubble on my upper lip. She stuck her
tongue deep into my ear early in my life till I couldn't hear
or think. By candle light I laid her, under eaves quiet and
peaceful. At the morning dawn she stood before a win-

dow, her kimono open with the sallow colour of her flesh. She was looking across the roof tops and twisted chimney pots at the distant purple mountains. I was young and fearful. She closed shutters over the window, said don't cry.

Excursion steamer pulling out on the grey water. Dirty deep and sad. Sail out now with a beep to watch the city. The top of Miss Tomson's tower. Nothing will light up again tonight. Except that sign which says a casket company. Life's so humorous. As hope blows up in every face. If ever I get to the gates of heaven.

Please God
Let me
Bust in.

18

Retreating lonely by a window in the Epeeist's bar of
The Game Club, Smith sitting bent over a tall glass of beer.
After a swim. Watching down into the twilight, the passers
by collecting on opposite corners and crossing in little waves
as the light went red for cars and green for men. The
sound across the dimly lit interior of back slapping, clinks
of ice and clambake happiness.

The excursion boat this afternoon went under lofty
bridges and grime encrusted girders. By humming highways. Looking out, elbows on the boat's rails, I could spy
some peaceful hideouts in the leafy green on top of hard
rock cliffs. Then the afternoon grew grey. Wisps of steam
and gentle smoke from tops of buildings. Fading little flags.
All waving goodbye.

I tramped here from the river to The Game Club through
the crosstown streets. Stopping to telegraph flowering dogwood to Goliath, cold and dead in Dogdale Cemetery. With a
note to Dizzy Darling she'll see should she ever visit that grave.

> This is George Smith speaking, Miss Tomson.
> Asking you to get in touch. I ebb.

Then I took the relaxing routine of my afternoon swim.
Undressing in a mahogany booth. My little paper parcel
stapled across the top and handed to a man in the steel cage.
Who looked surprised at Smith turned mushroom picker,
sad eyed, staring ahead at what was left of the future. Then
wrapped up in towels, I gazed at the big pointer on the
weighing machine. Registering a reading so sad, to make
me wonder how much it weighed alone. Send the news to
Miss Tomson. And I arched over the green rippling waters

of the swimming pool. On the tiles I thought of all cold things, and dived. Breathed with a nose like a periscope. Used a lazy flap of overhead arm to propel myself back and forth down the pool in a blaze of foam. A few nonchalant laps of backstroke to get an even distribution of exercise. For a finale, I bulleted two lengths like a seal. To break up again through the water surface to hear George Smith paged to the telephone. For an earful of news fearful and fantastic. Club members looking up from their poolside papers. As I hurriedly wrapped up in towels, one draped over the fact. Flapping and dripping, crossed the tiles to the white talking machine under a palm.

'George Smith here.'

'I have a call for you sir. Go ahead please.'

'George. O my God.'

'Bonniface.'

'Yes. I am in woeful trouble. I must escape this town before it's too late.'

'What's the matter.'

'I can't tell you everything on the phone but I'll tell you this much. After you left I bought a paper and read of your tragic misfortune. I should have been warned. Then I thought I would see if you were back at Dynamo House and I foolishly availed myself of the rapid transit for this ill fated journey. One would think it could not happen twice.'

'What.'

'In all true madness I asked another member of the population for directions as to whether we were going uptown or downtown. So help me God he snarled in my face, asking if I could read. I requested the information once again, whereupon he replied the train didn't go anywhere. Upon the third reasonable request as to the direction of the train he asked me if I was a millionaire and wanted to fight. My dear George, I hit him. He toppled into the tracks.'

'Where are you.'

'I don't know. But one thing is for certain. I am about to decamp.'

'Is he dead.'

'Don't say that word. The terrible thing is, some innocent bystander was apprehended for the assault. The crowd closed in on him. Alas it was the presence of Mr Mystery. With the commotion I put my hands out in front of me, stared fixedly at the distant exit and repeated quietly, help me, I may yet see with the help of a secondhand eye. I had a handful of change by the time I got back on the street. My dear George, your good Miss Martin told me how to locate you. May I come there for safety sake.'

'Yes.'

'This is truly too good of you George, I know how much misfortune you yourself have to contend with. But I shall be glad to commiserate with you. Give advice, counsel, in short, steer you right. As well as take you to Her Majesty. By the way, one last request. May I, for the purpose of further respite avail myself of your cabin in the woods.'

'If you do not grope behind my books.'

'George I'm sorry you said that. Be there before this hour is dead. I spoke to Her Majesty only a moment ago and she begged me say where she could find you.'

I hung up the phone. Pulled the towels closely over my fact and barefoot made way along the red rubber carpet and through a glass door to the steam room. Tasting the salty trickles of sweat on the lips in this steamy limbo. Blotting out the eyes as a voice talked about the recent death of his mother which made him worry and become thirty pounds overweight.

Bonniface, your company is cheap as well as fearful. No more days of taking chances with pedestrians. And you're two hours late. Look out here across the park. For God's sake Miss Tomson. See you running there through the trees. If you were a fluttering virgin. And I broke your wings, you couldn't fly away. Summer all over. Winter ready to come knocking. On my hideaways. Find Her Majesty. Her flowered dress she used to wear and a black gleaming leather belt. Search every hotel. Her legs were of lean muscle and small ankle bones, precious gems under her skin. My first year at the university. She put her hands to her eyes and the tears welled up and stole down her cheeks. All the women I know are constantly crying. She said I loathe and fear people. All except you, George Smith. I caught an elevator to rise up through the peerage between us. As we knelt before her icon. I lit the sandalwood. More than the peerage between us. Great gulf of innocence. Until she peeled off her winter woollies.

Smith raising a hand. White coated waiter with his metal alloy tray. Staring down. Belligerence everywhere.

'Large beer. Please.'

'Yeah.'

'Pretzels. Cheese crackers and cheese.'

Watch the people go by. No fun to be neglected. Or wait for Bonniface to come. Last week saw Mr Browning. Who rubs his hands as he sees the car approaching. But this time I walked cross country, between the mausoleums, and evergreens. He was holding a big plan up against a tree and was distinctly startled. Some find nervousness instead of deep peace in the graveyard. He smiled all over his face with relief. To find I wasn't some apparition. We had a jolly talk on the portico. Won't be long now, Mr Smith, till the cantilever is complete. News gave me an exciting shiver. Walked by the cemetery lake, threw a few little stones at the ducks. And chirped to a squirrel. One day little animals, we all will be neighbours.

Smith quaffing another beer. Followed by a whisky. When the sneaky and treacherous have been sent scurrying. Just as Her Majesty said, you'll be rich one day, George, while I owe grocery bills everywhere. The muscles in her arms wearing a wan old fashioned tan. Satin wrists the ends of her limbs. Breast brushed the side of my face. George, the pain I give you offer it up to God. Did any little girl ever love you. As an ugly little boy. Yes. She hid a note in her desk in the classroom. I love George Smith. And the other kids found it and twisted her wrist till it fell out of her hands. They showed it to me while she was crying.

Another beer and whisky from the waiter. Smiling and familiar now. Smith requesting a phone from a green uniformed page. Like Her Majesty's page of the presence. Only three hotels where she could be. Find her without Bonniface. With her race horse body. Smith you're a prude, look at me, hair flowing across my shoulder blades, I smile at you George because you're so hurt, so sweet, so sad and in the eyes of your prep school class they'll think you've come to no good end. Up someone.

'Here you are sir, your telephone.'

Smith busy over these little numbers. Twisting a finger round the dial. To find another voice somewhere and erase this sound of heavy breathing. This table, the last outpost of civilization. Just as Her Majesty said, it's cold come into my arms, I owe my coal merchant and all my children's school fees. Pull the covers up on our faces. Let me teach you how to shut out the world. Tell me what you did at summertime when you were little. Why wouldn't you play with the other boys at the local monument with the fireflies blinking green in the orgasm races shooting sperm over the fence. You tell such tales, so funny, military cadets hanging from the doorjambs letting fly with their lotion shouting no hands. If you entered those contests George you'd be better prepared for this later life. And the profane farts. Albeit carried away by the same provincial wind.

Down the long list. Smith went, telephoning. Hotel after hotel. The residential, the luxury, the least likely and the most. Her Majesty, Queen Evangiline. What is this, mister, a joke, never heard of her. Oaf. The royal nipple. Majestic mounds. Took the pole of this present peasant. Another beer and I'll be a yeoman. No longer nervous looking at you, even with haggard eyes, grey temples, stooped walk. Call you Evangiline the favourite of all your names. I want to escape. Get out. Go back. Into the late summer of the year. When you said, don't muff the first moment of manhood. George, the clean minded community from which you sprang. Elastic and high. And back those years. When a fresh wet breeze swept across the hills outside the city. Milkman clip clopping by to a ballad down below in the streets, all morning and grey. A tram tinkling in the distance.

Smith putting back the telephone on its little cradle. Never trust wires. Get crossed and confused. My heart on one end can never get its warmth to the other. Then all scared I hang up. Must find her. By legs. Ungladly stepping one foot in shit, the other in sublime. Could even pose as the most dangerous human being alive today. After Bonniface. And I'll be afraid to look at her. To see instead the Sally Tomson, that Dizzy Darling, cruising from one pent house to another, with her ruler looking for bigger ones. To measure. And you, Evangiline, undressed so slowly and folded all your clothes. Said no two poles the same, George, yours is a gift of nature. On safari I had four black ones one after another. Anything can be black in the dark. Love your tombstone teeth. I cry because I'm getting old. Nice of you to tell me I'm so terribly beautiful. White in all the corners of your eyes. Taste of honey in the mouth. And George present your pole to posterity. Be remembered long. Rearing up from these sweet short hairs. I hate the priests in this town and all the gossip that goes on about me. Their pulpit stunted organs. She talked her eyes like a frightened horse. Her denture slipped. Whole world moved over a little to the left. I haven't told you all the things how they tried to murder me, cut out my stomach. Jealous green eyed woman because I was so beautiful and a queen. You with such a whopper. Dutch cap now instead of a crown. My eyes go wild, for all that marvellous mouthful. Before I'm bleak dead and buried, part of a field. You plough. Come under my shattered wing, head in my hands, body in a land I cannot love have me as I am if have me you must. With the pip in the core.

> The strange
> Sour
> In the
> Seed.

Smith with paper parcel stepped out of The Game Club and walked east. Past the glittering entrances. Hotels and nightclubs. Doormen saluting to arriving and departing cars. So easy to go in one of these doors. Become a maniac. Buy the whole building out of my little bag of bank notes. Dismiss the doormen, bellboys, tell the customers to go. Clear out. Turn off the lights. Let me be in here. A secluded place to entertain Her Majesty. Supper by candle light. Spinach, egg plant and sour cream. Miss Martin with her gun could stand guard at the door. Shoot intruders. Bonniface as butler. And phantom figures chewing gum seen across in the park under the trees doing strange things with the procreative gifts of God.

Crossing the street to the plaza and the fountain. Smith sat down on the cool stone shelf around the water, with his paper parcel between his feet. Figure which way to go. Put hands up to the cheeks of the face, rest elbows on the knees. A row of jaunting cars and sad horses. On this square foot make another small world. These last few days Miss Martin has been sour and tense. In the recent misery I have not dared to put my hands on her. Could be a restorative for us both. Frisking in the afternoon loneliness of Dynamo House. With the little letters that still arrive.

> Wing of Life Building
>
> Dear Sir,
> At the latest meeting we laughed at your request for mercy. What are your remaining assets. Learning of these we will talk further turkey.
>
> > Yours,
> > Jaws Inc.
>
> P.S. We will squeeze out what is left of your toothpaste.

And for all my worries, I can still broadcast an answer on the ether.

> Arse Square Foot of Plaza
>
> Dear Jaws Inc.
> As George Smith sitting near this fountain utterly alone,

please do not view me as the giblets. For God's sake, would that you behave honourably and vouchsafe the human dignity.

Yours,

Good old George

P.S. There are impurities in the toothpaste.

Two brown shoes stopping in front of Smith. As he looks up in the semi darkness into a stranger's face with rimless glasses. Thigh muscles tightening, ready to run from this possible visitation of more discourtesy. Thank God no transit tracks are near.

'Buddy things could not be that bad. But I know how it feels. Here's a couple of coins. Go have a piece of pie and cup of coffee. Do you good. So long.'

Figure floating away in the crowd. Smith taking the two coins, staring at them in the palm of the hand and slipping them in his waistcoat pocket. A little drop of water landing on the back of his neck and running down inside the collar. Sign of good luck. A pity to meet kindness. Lower one's guard. And wham.

That girl going by looks just like Shirl. I took her along here one summer evening just like this. White coated waiters brought us Scotch and sodas, olives and cheese tidbits. She sat white gloved, an attack of warts on her hands. She always felt she ought to try other men. Because of all she had to give. Months since I've been called Daddy. Thought it was unique to be a father. Get asked for an autograph. And when arrested for momentary unseemliness somewhere, you plead a married man with children. But the world stares back at you, ignoring your troubles, blindly terrified by its own. Shirl has her problems. The starlight shining dimmer and dimmer on her hair. Deep line under her cheek when she smiles. Lying under the coats on the hair sofa of Dynamo House, I counted up all the women I've had. Shirl fifth. I added Miss Tomson, counting in two figures. As Dizzy Darling she's one more. Matilda, that staggering bit of tan. Entwined she was three at once. Said I couldn't lift her. I said you just wait. Tried and dropped her. It was a good game we used to play on all fours.

Smith feeling the chill of stone strike up the bottom. Stood raising parcel to his arm, waving to taxies. Then stopping, turning, to climb into a jaunting car.

Promoting a brief friendly altercation with the driver, who gesticulated with his whip. A brand new bank note sparkling in the air. And they were jaunting up the avenue. Coachman telling Smith what happened to the horseshit. A little old lady comes late evening and collects it for her sky garden.

At each hotel, stopping. Smith dismounting, pulling up a few corners of linen hanky in his dark suiting, another tucked up his sleeve. Foolishly in each lobby. Her Majesty the Queen, please. Eyebrows raised. Twice Smith slipping between the evening cocktail faces. Eyes staring after him as he lowered a brandy for the road. And once next to a dowager encrusted in gems, for one second through the dark light it could have been Her Majesty. Madam, may I trespass upon your buoyant property, God just told me it was mine.

'Why don't you give up mister. We've been to ten hotels. My horse is tired. Street's tough on his hoofs. I'm going to have a lame horse.'

A note flashed crisply. Once more silence. Except for the clip clop. Odd waves from pedestrians. So many fellow men about with vibrant lightheartedness. In the next hotel and bar, I vouch the clientele will merge into one big sigh of happiness.

'Mister this is positively the last. Look where I am. This is a berg.'

'Are you unhappy.'

'Yeah. My horse's feet hurt. I could be held up and robbed in this part of town.'

In front of a grey stone building. A faded canopy out to the curb. A bronze plaque. Dim dark interior. Smith slipping across one more note to the horseman. And another asking him to wait. George reeling quietly through the heavy revolving doors into this elderly place. Little parcel held on his arm. To tip toe across the fat carpet and whisper boo at the reception desk. A balcony round the lobby with little tables, chairs and lamps. Doorman passing by with a miniature dog. Take it out to pee. That tiny canine would have been one mouthful for Goliath.

'Can I help you sir.'

Smith looking out at the eyes. Holding the counter with uncertain hands. Mouth opening and closing. Eyes fixed on all the hanging keys. To open doors. Shirl seems to stand somewhere behind this desk. With her unlit heart. However cold you get, remember me. Gripped in solitude. There can't be a jamboree all the time.

'Excuse me sir, can I help you.'

Smith swaying backwards. Surveying a potted palm. A forecourt, a little fountain. Drapes drawn on windows. Tall grey woman passing, silver sandals poking out under her gown. Marble cornices on the balcony. Across the soft distance of this lobby a green carpet disappearing under closed mirrored doors. Smith delicately separating the strings of his paper bag across his forearm. Focusing eyes once more. To the pigeon holes, brass numbers and red white and blue edges of foreign mail.

'Are you all right, sir.'

Smith a feeble smile and a wave of his hand. Life is made up of a lot of immediate events. Must not sidle across and pee upon that potted palm. Or with the handy screwdriver I happen to have in my pocket go over and unfasten the doorknobs to the ball room. How dare you keep such things there. To think it was only yesterday I distinctly heard a man walking by say he had the whole world under contract. Naturally I stopped and asked if I could buy a piece. Regrettably to find he had only a three month option.

'Look mister, I don't know who you are.'

'I'm drunk.'

'At least you're honest.'

Smith turning to a rustle of dresses for evening. Four pastel coloured girls and three dark suited men. Clean and scented. All so elegant. Please let me come with you. Just to sit quietly by. To watch, listen, laugh. Lift me out of the dark abyss. Take me back into my own foolish life of youth before I wisely made money. A little of it in this parcel. To scatter around this lobby. Can't you see I'm Smith. The big maple, once an acorn. Desperate to be the oak Miss Tomson whispered.

'Perhaps sir, you've got a reservation.'

'Perhaps I haven't.'

'What have you got.'

'I beg your pardon. Are you being forward.'

'Sir, I'm trying to be of assistance.'

'Her Royal Huzzy the Queen.'

'I beg your pardon, sir.'

'I wish to be connected.'

'Have you a prior connexion.'

'I beg your pardon.'

'Sir, I mean are you expected.'

'You're joking, she's not here, bell boy.'

'I'm not joking. I'm not a bell boy. And are you expected sir.'

'I am unexpected.'

'Now please.'

'I am a lamb's kidney. Several people have been now clouted into the tracks. If we keep hitting them there, there will finally be respect, courtesy and kindness for millionaires. Now get me a bottle of brandy and two glasses and we'll have a drink.'

'I can't do that sir. This is not the bar.'

'Do you want me to buy this hotel and reshuffle the staff. Now get that brandy. I'm going to take the heights tonight. Huge deployment of armour on both flanks. Commandeer this reception desk. Gee, I feel champion.'

'Now sir.'

'Then take the balcony. Let the howitzers howl. Adjutant.'

'Look mister, I don't know who you are.'

'I know who you are. Adjutant. At nine you check the mail waiting feverishly for the first coffee break. Then rustle through the few blank papers and sneak away to the washroom for a cigarette.'

'I certainly do not.'

'Adjutant. Silence. Then you make a few personal phone calls before lunch. Get back in time for the afternoon coffee break. Make two erasures before five. Time for pot roast at the automat just round the corner. Then read a questionable book on the night shift which was left in a room by the chambermaid.'

'I never have.'

'Attention. How dare you back chat a commanding officer.'

'I'm not. I'm trying to be of assistance. Is it you want to be accommodated.'

'I want the moral fibre of staffs everywhere to hold up under the strain of trying to seize opportunities for advancement.'

'Sir, you mustn't shout.'

'I want to reverse the decline. Rebound to boom. Land in a field of golden sneezeweed.'

'Sir I don't have the faintest idea what you're talking about. I must hand over now to the manager.'

'I asked for her royal high jinks. This dreadful upcreep of unhappiness. In the bag here I have enough toadstools of the green yellow and red variety with the purple dots to poison this evening's menu.'

'Sir maybe you want an invalid requisite or something. Our manager is coming.'

Smith rearing to attention. Appearance of a dark portly person. Hair sharply parted near the middle. Flat fat fingers, bubbling at the ends, drowning tiny fingernails. Both these hands spread before George Smith on the counter. And a little bow. Smith's visage chill and remote.

'Good evening sir. Good to see you.'

'Hello.'

'Nice to see you again, sir.'

'You've never seen me before.'

'Ah but I have. The brandy is on its way. And you will be

pleased to hear we have not just made it in the back room. Please be my guest.'

'Well. I can see your ancestors did not come from a stock that would make one wonder.'

'You are too kind, Mr Smith. But I always try to feel important, handsome, well dressed. As you are this evening.'

'You too are too kind.'

'What shall we drink to Mr Smith.'

'Havoc.'

'Ha ha. Of course. If you wish. But perhaps, a toast. Her Majesty. She is as you've no doubt heard, a permanent resident with us now. And we are extremely honoured.'

'I'm relapsed. Heigh ho.'

'In that case, Mr Smith my vision is that this hotel will be a refuge. For a safe relapse. Ha ha, nice mix up with words. It's what we're trying to do here with comfort. Every distinction for the distinguished. A client asks for a drink at the reception desk. We have a drink at the reception desk.'

'Good on you Mr.'

'Park.'

'Mr Park. I've been sweating it out too long at my outpost. I'm enveloped by the enemy.'

'A man as measured as you are, is a contribution to the community.'

'Thank you major.'

Four bell boys in their quiet grey uniforms. Gleaming brass buttons on tunics. Smith swaying, smiling. Mr Park clapping hands. Bell boys snapping to attention.

'Take Mr Smith to Her Majesty's suite eighteen B.'

Platoon leading George Smith to the elevator doors. Stepping aside as Smith stepped in. Protocol has not packed up yet. I'll go if her nibs says get out. Shirl said I never offered to get my hands wet in the sink. She'll go into old age without me. Sitting in her empty nest. Small body in apron. Ladling out porridge in the bowls. Here is your daddy kids, shouting for justice and getting his just desserts instead. Your mother says sue. Stretch me out on the altar of the law. When in my heart I chirp.

Meet you
In apple green
July
Hiding
Arm's length
Under the
Uttermost tree
We'll
Play
A pink
Piano.
Become
Each other's
Sadness.

Her Majesty stood at the door. Her arms open. Smith walked between them clutched up tightly to her breasts. Platoon retreating. Grumbling back into the elevator without a tip. Easy money corrupts. Hard to know how long one keeps gripped in greeting. Across the beige room curtains fluttering in an open terrace door.

'George can I make you some scrambled eggs.'

Smith holding Her Majesty away from him. To sight her and see her blueish eyes in soft moist lids. Something unpardonable happening in my trousers. To the sound of her voice. Take her hand and put it there.

'George you rude thing after all.'

'Your Majesty squeeze it tightly. It needs comfort.'

'George you haven't changed. Bold. Grey too. You are, you know. Kiss me.'

Little parcel dropping from Smith's dark arm. Tightening around Her Majesty. One of her soft hands reaching to tug Smith's ear, the other to catch on a lobe of lower haunch and there impart a friendly fingering. North and far away. The Goose Goes Inn.

'Your Majesty you smell so good.'

'Whale sperm.'

'Take off your clothes.'

Her Majesty unfurled her sari. And kindly took her two breasts and put them in George Smith's hands. He said they weighed the same. Lights out. Glow in the sky. All rainbow. Pots of gold everywhere.

'Dear George.'

'It's me.'

A few
Good old
Days
Are left.

19

George Smith taking his personal temperature which was chilly. The thin silver line showing just below the red mark for normal. Last night with Her Majesty. And this cool morning, hungover, mouth dry, head throbbing. A dream. Big fat woman in a green raincoat, really enormous, started beating me with her walking stick. Of all the blasted cheek I said, desist. Miss Tomson stood smiling by on a marble step between pillars and on her blue sweatered chest hung two little golden balls, one below the other, just as it should be and Smith she said, these are yours, I did some alchemy.

Sound of the opening door. A shuffle. Miss Martin wearing low heels. Said men with power were real men. Up against a lot of corporate bodies what was the use of struggling. We're plankton.

'Good morning, Miss Martin is that you.'

'Yes.'

Smith turning on his naked shoulder. Slippery surface of the horsehair sofa, now tucked up tightly to the partition. I fear out of caution for Miss Martin's rifle where a bead could be drawn if still asleep when she came. Also need that added bit of privacy which makes one's lot easier. Plus the convenience of the shelf near the wash basin for the regimen of these mornings. One dark tiny pill of the day's vitamins on one big white plate. Two oranges, oatmeal, cocoa and a bottle of cod liver oil that Miss Martin buys out of the petty cash. Matilda has exhausted me in Merry Mansions.

'Miss Martin, what time.'

'I'm late. They stopped the train and were loading on lumber in the middle of the bridge. For about an hour.'

'I just asked for the time.'

'Twelve thirty.'

'Thank you. Don't come in. I'm indelicate. Utterly frazzled. After being vaguely champion. I think. Last night. O God.'

Nightmare. Somewhere between dreams. Bonniface appeared. Completely regaled in deep sea diving equipment. All the shiny knobs and valves on the waterproof helmet. We met on the sea bed. Bonniface smiling inside the little round window, lugging the great heavy square shoes on his feet. Mr Mystery on a lead. We were having a serious underwater chat. I woke up when the sharks came.

'Mr Smith, there were three men here yesterday. Who wanted to talk to you. They wouldn't say what about. I told them I didn't know where you were.'

'Is there a bag out there, Miss Martin. A paper one with staples in it. Would you look please.'

'I can't see anything.'

'Are you sure.'

'Yes.'

'Look under everything. Is it hanging on the hook. Or the hat tree.'

'It isn't here.'

'O God.'

'What's the matter.'

'Find that bag.'

'Don't shout at me.'

'I'm sorry Miss Martin. Find that bag.'

'I have found something.'

'Where. Let me have it.'

'I'm pregnant.'

'No drolleries this morning please. That bag.'

'Three months.'

Smith spectacular. Throwing coats from the sofa. Knocking over the bathing screen. Miss Martin at the door, eyes blinking at the papers and garments flying.

'Come on Miss Martin, we must find this paper bag.'

Miss Martin silently at the door. Smith on hands and knees looking under sofa and desk, two soiled soles of feet sticking out. Opening the window to peer down the air shaft. Pulling open drawers, scrabbling through files. To turn around wearily and face Miss Martin behind the tiny dark hole of her rifle.

'Miss Martin what are you doing with that gun.'

'Listen to me.'

'I'm listening. Put the gun down.'

'No.'

'Miss Martin. I hope you're aware of what you're doing.'

'I am, you're not going to turn rat on me.'

'I beg your pardon.'

'No you're not.'

'Miss Martin get a grip. For God's sake.'

'My finger's on this trigger, that's all I need.'

'Do you realize you could shoot me.'

'Yes.'

'All right. Put it down then.'

'You think it's a joke.'

'I don't think anything's a joke. Just want to find my paper bag.'

'You didn't even hear what I said. I said I was pregnant. Over three months.'

'This is no time to be hysterical. My eyeballs are rusted in the sockets. I feel terrible, what a hangover. And I can't find my paper bag.'

'I'm not hysterical.'

'Just point the gun a little away.'

'What am I going to do. If my mother finds out.'

'Please, put the gun down. Guns have a way of going off. I know you're an experienced shot. But my army revolver once went off in my holster and split open the toe of my riding boot.'

'Shut up.'

'O.'

'You've ignored me all these weeks.'

'Miss Martin, I've seen you every day. We've talked. Chatted. Short of presuming upon you.'

'You presumed in the log cabin.'

'I rescued you from a venomous insect.'

'It wasn't. I looked it up in a book. You disappeared with that Miss Tomson. Glad her old dog was shot.'

'Just let me put on my trousers, please.'

'No. Stay right where you are.'

'I don't mind being shot but not without trousers.'

'You lousy sneak. You're thinking of beating it. I can tell. Who's going to pay all the doctor's bills.'

'Control yourself Miss Martin.'

'You bastard.'

'I don't mind what you say but don't say it with the gun.'

'I've had nightmares nearly every night.'

'Is it me. The father.'

'It's going to be a satisfaction to see you drop in your tracks.'

'I mean, maybe it's me, all right. Why haven't you told me sooner.'

'Because I only saw the doctor yesterday that's why. You fucker.'

'That's unnecessary.'

'So's your damn burial vault. And the bullet proof car you've ordered.'

'Well. All right. I mean is it any wonder.'

'It's you.'

'O.K. All right. It's me.'

'Yes. You.'

Smith putting one hand on the edge of his desk. Have a little support when the bullet lands. I can take a few low calibre bullets in non vital spots. Terrible to sense she can hit a bee at fifty yards. One has premonitions. Which always come true too soon. Just a few more days and there would have been the armoured vehicle. Thing is keep talking. Leave any time between words and that's where the bullets fit in.

'Miss Martin. I know you're distressed.'

'Shut up.'

'I can't.'

'Shut up.'

'Please you've got to let me keep talking. You might shoot.'

'That's right. Get your hand off that desk.'

'Couldn't you just hand me over my cod liver oil.

'No.'

'Can I have the morning newspaper.'

'I can tell you what's in the morning newspaper. There was another man beaten and knocked into the tracks and an innocent bystander was arrested but the real one got away. That's what's in the paper.'

'Don't look at me.'

'You did it once and you probably did it again. Only now you've learned to run. And here read this filth which came yesterday.'

Miss Martin flinging a white card. Landing against Smith's ankle. Perhaps now is the time to jump her. Through all the war's strategy, map reading, signals to the front, this is the first time I've been held at gun point. Suppose it's better than being lonely. I wish folks' Christmas greetings would come from the heart. Take my time reading this invitation.

Al Moygrain Diltor Cranzgot

AT HOME

12:01 A.M., 7 Eel Street

Explosive Gala Gangbang

To be followed by the mixed racial with serum
available for allergics.

R.S.V.P.   Sports apparel please

'Just a strongly flavoured invitation Miss Martin.'

'You disappear every afternoon.'

'Miss Martin, please, I don't ask you where you go.'

'Because I'm stuck alone in this gloomy dump and you don't care.'

'I do care, very much. I don't want to see you unhappy.'

'You see me underpaid, so how could you care if I'm happy.'

'I'll review your salary. Anytime. Make a memo right now, if you put down the gun. The way I'm dressed, to fall mortally wounded. The papers would be full of it.'

'I'm the one who should worry. You'll be dead.'

'O dear.'

'This gun is pointing at the biggest chamber of your heart.'

'What sort of a raise do you want. Pension. Anything. Mention it.'

'Just keep talking.'

'I'd like to.'

'Make it good.'

'You mustn't get the idea I'm made of money, Miss Martin.'

'You're buying an armoured car.'

'As I've said, considering the present situation. It's reasonable enough. Now please. There are just two of us here. Put the gun down. We'll go out of this wretched room, cross over to the bun and coffee shop. Sit over a nut ring, or doughnuts, whichever you prefer.'

'O boy. I'll bet.'

'It's true. I'm moving office again. Is that what you're thinking. That I was beating it.'

'I'm going to have a baby.'

'If it's me —'

'I'm going to shoot you. Right now.'

'Jesus don't.'

'I knew you'd rat.'

'Hold it.'

'You're a rat.'

'Behind you Miss Martin. Is an apparition. I can see it. Hold fire. Just let me enjoy this vision before you shoot. Full of all the colours of the rainbow. And a mist, a light gentle rain. Like tiny tears that maybe an insect might cry. Just another ten seconds. Then shoot. After this, I want to go. Pray for me. I haven't got much religion but I believe. I'll just get down on my knees here for a moment.'

'Why don't you die like a man.'

'I will but please just look the other way. I would like this few seconds to be private. Don't want you to remember me as if I were begging. Please, don't watch me praying like this. As a final wish. Burn all the files. Sue my estate so you won't be without. Be blood for a blood test. Any reasonable judge will award enough for you and the little one. Now turn away. Cough before you shoot, I need an advance signal before I meet my maker. He lives on a hill for miles around with buttercups sprinkled in the green. According to a recent remark in this apparition.'

George Smith slowly bowing his unkempt head. Pink tails of his shirt lightly touching the greyish sycamore floor. Which I only notice now is from my second favourite tree. Not even time to put on a tie. It's going to be wild in Renown. Simply wild. Bonniface and Mr Mystery will be there, one leading the other. A dog always looks good at a funeral. Wagging his tail, sorry to see me go. As I'm lowered into the crypt. I've got to lunge for her. At least get the charge reduced to manslaughter. He tried to kill me when I told him I was pregnant, your honour. So amusing I should still want everything to look good, even in court. I'm proud Miss Martin should want to shoot me like this. Shows she cares. I would turn rat. I have excuses. Can't go into them now, but always good things to have. What did I do with my bag of dough. Brace my toes, just find a little purchase for them. The Game Club at least has kept me in trim. I won't look bad laid out on the slab. Music now would help. Going over the top into the big circus on the other side. Shake hands in heaven. With the biggest wheeler dealer of them all. In Miss Martin's belly the tiniest heart is ticking. Later little legs will kick. George Junior. Miss Martin if only you could have looked upon it as a present. Which you give back to me. Instead of this firearms. Ready now. To hop into eternity flexing at least two joints. As I dive the bullet will go into the back of my head. Goodbye, world, not all that nice knowing but you taught me a few lessons I won't forget in the next.

Smith sprang. Low level. Uncoiling from the crouch. Shirt tails flying. Sharp, brief, crack of gun. Miss Martin falling backwards. Gun smoking, pointing at the ceiling. George Smith alive. And well on top.

'O.K. Miss Martin. It's all right. Just lie still. Just let's get rid of this gun.'

Smith pinning her arms gently to the boards. Taking a deep sigh. Miss Martin's eyes closed. Little bubbles of tears rolling down her temple sides. Amazing how well she looks. So pink. And blossoming. White all these weeks. Attempted murder brought all her colour back.

'I haven't hurt you, have I Miss Martin.'

Little hard blue artery the side of her neck. Only thing that moves. Dear Miss Martin. If the bullet hit me I might be popped into a plain pine coffin. Unclaimed. Lifted on a barge. With hundreds of others. A number and body photographed on a slab. Don't want to go down that way dead. Like an amputated arm or leg. On an island in the river estuaries. With muskrats big as dogs.

'Hello there, Miss Martin.'

Her head turning. Breathing up dust. All your rectitude. Milky breasts. Label on your coat that keeps you snug to carry the little life home each evening on the train ride across the flat lands and water. Then down your street. Look out across the beach. Liners burning brightly on the dark horizon. Headed out of turmoil. A cold way on a deep sea to an old world.

'Please. Let me help you up on the sofa.'

On the horsehair Miss Martin lay quietly shivering. Smith emptying the bullets. Rolling them one by one out the air shaft window. Two of them firing at the bottom. Windows opening. They'll look up. Stick my head out and look upwards too.

Smith sticking legs into trousers. Wiping feet bottoms on Miss Martin's coat on the floor. Pulling on socks and shoes.

Collecting up the edged and pointed instruments. All letter openers and nail files hereafter locked in the drawer.

Crossing to Miss Martin. Head down close to hers. Buy her a bottle of inexpensive perfume. Kiss her on the cheek. Incredible but I want more than anything to take off her clothes. Fill her up with love. Just ease it in. Like the deed already done. We could have walked cold and hungry into a little automat somewhere, bought coffee buns and goodies.

Smith gently closing his door. Picking up Miss Martin's telephone. Finger in the dial. A wail from the back room. Door opening. Miss Martin full of distress and cascading tears.

'Please Mr Smith don't call the police. O dear God I swear I'll do anything if you don't call them. Don't have me arrested.'

Smith phone in hand. Miss Martin, her hunched quivering shoulders in the doorway. High on the wall behind her a shattered glass and hole in Smith's prep school diploma. Standing in her stockinged feet. Looking down on her wet twisted handkerchief stretched between her hands.

'I'm sorry, Miss Martin.'

'O no no. Let me go. Please let me go. I'll have my baby. I won't bother you. I swear.'

'I'm sorry. Miss Martin.'

'O Mr Smith, please forget everything I said. I'll be a good girl. I'll die in prison. My baby. I'm just a working girl. Please. Please. I'll put on my shoes now. Where are they. There. And I'll go out the door and you'll never see me again.'

She has nice little feet. All parts of her put together won't flash in beauty. But each is shaped with grace. So sweet cruelty. Love every one of her sad crying words. Fighting for the baby I gave her. Hello spider.

'All right, Miss Martin. Go back to the couch. I still must make a phone call but it's not to the police. Shut the door.'

Soon one is driven to take the blood blot test. It reads a red hand ready to grab at the coat collar. Remember some whispers from Her Majesty. Why don't you get out while you're ahead. But suddenly I'm not ahead. She said Cedric Clementine had invited her to the airport. Where he treated her like a queen. Rushing back and forth in his dark suit, keeping Mr Mystery in a little tent with water, gruel and a sign do not disturb. Ah, a voice, clear and heartless.

'Excelsior, may I help you.'

'Yes. Suite eighteen B. Please.'

'Thank you sir.'

'Hello.'

'Your Majesty, did I leave the bag of toadstools at your digs last night.'

'This is not Her Majesty.'

'Is this suite eighteen B.'

'Her Majesty's secretary speaking. Who is this please.'

'Get Her Majesty.'

'Who may I say is speaking.'

'You may say I am speaking.'

'What name shall I give.'

'I just don't feel like saying my name this morning. Please, do you mind. Her Majesty. Please.'

'I'm sorry, but I must have a name.'

'Are you trying to make life unbelievably painful. What's your name.'

'I don't see how that matters.'

'Is it Hilda.'

'No.'

'Olga.'

'I'm afraid I shall have to hang up on you.'

'I'll kill you.'

'I beg your pardon.'

'I'm sorry. I have a terrible hangover. But I just cannot bear to have to say my name this morning. I've just been through a rather distressing fifteen minutes here. Not that this could possibly matter to you, however, there's something rather important I must ask Her Majesty.'

'About a bag of toadstools.'

'Yes. Collector's items. Botanical rarities.'

'I see.'

'I may have left them there. You do have a kindly voice. Now if you would just ask Her Majesty about these foolish fungi for me.'

'Very well.'

'Wait. I know it's rather reversing the situation somewhat but I would like to know your name.'

'Lettia.'

'Strange. I knew it ended in a.'

'Ha ha.'

'Ha ha. Lettia.'

If only I hadn't made such an entrance that night. I might use Her Majesty's as a retreat to hide. Vague memories. In suite eighteen B. Vouchsafe decorum devoid. Was a Bonniface motto. I feel close to life again. After nearly being out of it. And in the round darkness of last night. I remember getting up to wee wee. A decanter of brandy gripped in the fist. Walking out through an open door to a roof garden. Wisteria. A little wooden door, balcony with vines shrubberies and trees. Must have disgraced myself. A sundial and paved red brick chevrons. Remember sitting on a cold stone bench staring at them, thinking I once had a suit, put together just like the floor. Please. I did not pee off the balcony eighteen floors down into the street. Laughing as the wind turned it to spray. Feeling I was doing a favour for window boxes everywhere.

'George Smith.'

'Your Majesty.'

'I have several rather unfortunate things to convey to you, my dear boy. Which cannot be said on a telephone.'

'Your Majesty. I was terribly drunk last night.'

'Obviously.'

'Still am. But is my bag of toadstools there.'

'Don't you remember.'

'Remember what.'

'Dear boy. What a pickle.'

'O God.'

'Just take a peek in the papers. Even now the police are trying to control the traffic and crowds.'

'This is a nightmare. I thought I dreamt it.'

'No dream dear boy. I would say one thing, however, at your age you ought to have more sense. If it's your idea of fun, I find it in extremely bad taste to say the least. I will of course see you. Provided, one, you're sober and two, you ask to be shown to the water closet in future. Good-bye.'

George Smith stood over Miss Martin. Touched her on the hair. And lifting up some old newspapers, covered her. She sleeps. There may not be rain today but one feels the need of an umbrella. And lip mask.

The hall empty outside 604. A shadow moving across the glass of The Institution Of Higher Graduation. Must be a candidate. First sign of life I've seen in that establishment. Ironic when my neighbours on this floor begin to prosper I languish.

Opening an umbrella down the hall. Passing the mop closet. Miss Martin will make a good mother. In that pail behind that door began our first feeble indelicacy. Hounded by the gazeteers. Shut Her Majesty out of my heart all together if that's the way she wants it to be. Very best people use basins, parapets, balconies and alas, Bonniface says, when there is no bone china, there is only the open honest window left. Ask to be shown to the water closet, what crass presumption.

On the first floor landing a messenger running blindly up and nearly into George Smith gave a squeal of fear at this somnambulant slowly stepping down. Few little accessories and one easily spreads the fear of God. Presently possessed in abundance. After all the solid months I sat entrenched in Golf Street. Each morning prancing purposely out of Merry Mansions. Man of decision. Delegating authority. Striding in all weathers along the river. Nearly running when Miss Tomson worked for me. The sweaters she wore. Blue vision of blondeness. The pearls. If Miss Tomson has a little one too. Be a whole bunch of babies born together. Later in some side street by the river, could all play in a garden. Start their own band.

At the kiosk Smith buying an afternoon newspaper. Tucking it under the arm. Umbrella miraculously parting the crowd ahead. Walking east, threading through the noon day rush. Further north to disappear in an entrance marked, Supplies Of Ecclesiastical Pyrotechnic Fireworks. And emerging, a large box under his arm, umbrella blossoming black in the mid day sun. Ambling south along the river past the Watch Museum, where so often one means to visit but never finds time. And a chauffeured car flashing by nearly running Smith down, containing a face one knew but could not place. Life is spooky.

Facing the river piers, a little coffee house in which Smith sat with a cool glass of lime juice and a confection of chopped walnut flavoured with goat's milk butter and drenched in honey. Spread out the newspaper on the little table. Looking up and down the columns. A headline.

IT RAINS DOUGH AT DAWN

While most of the city slept an eerie scene of groping bent scurrying people started what later led to a full scale riot extending from Breevort to Constola Streets along Golden Avenue which fully lived up to its name just before dawn this morning.

Witnesses to the early spectacle said that out of nowhere money began floating down in the semi darkness and accompanied by a fresh wind, was blowing in all directions over the Avenue. At first, the bills, which were of a high denomination, were happily being collected by only a few pedestrians.

It was claimed trouble first began with the arrival of the Department of Sanitation's cleaning vehicle whose three occupants jumped to the roadway and declared that the money was technically litter, which as servants of the city they were empowered to collect. Fighting quickly broke out.

As word rapidly spread the crowd grew. Office cleaners, watchmen and night shift workers were joined by stevedores and porters from the nearby fish and produce markets. By eight o'clock, motorists were abandoning their cars in side streets, blocking traffic and hampering police and ambulances hurrying to the district. Captain Tigerson whose mounted patrol men threaded their way in, said he hadn't seen such inhumanity between persons in his twenty seven years on the force and that the street could have been a beachhead.

One man retreating to a doorway to slip money into his shoes was pounced upon before he could lace them up. To be seen a few minutes later in his bare feet being helped to an ambulance bleeding from wounds in the head. He was treated on the spot for abrasions, four sprained toes and mild shock.

An elderly gentleman stood weeping against a cigar store window, with eyeglasses shattered, nose bleeding and coat ripped, still clutching a torn bill in his hand. He said, 'Look at me, I'm a grandfather, and look what they do.'

More severe injuries were sustained by a young man who received two stab wounds in the chest from a woman's umbrella. He was removed, as were the many other victims, to the Mercy Hospital two blocks away where the nuns described his condition as critical.

One of the lighter moments was related by an unidentified witness whose glass eye fell or was torn out in the hostilities. As he later searched the gutter for his hand made optic, a woman approached and handed it back to him none the worse, saying it had found its way down her cleavage in the shindy.

For nearly three hours the bitter bedlam raged up and down Golden Avenue before mounted police finally quelled and dispersed the mob. At its peak there were estimated to be between four and five thousand people involved. Two fire companies stood by throughout ready to use fire hoses if necessary.

Police are now conducting an investigation to trace the source of the money. Because of the large sum and fresh condition, the notes were first thought to be forged. However, Captain Tigerson said there was no question but that the money was real and was dropped, swept or thrown from a building somewhere below Breevort Street and blown north by the wind. He also said it was a crying shame to see the human teeth marks on some victims and a sad comment on people's greed that hardly a note survived intact, and the only ones to gain were the pickpockets who swarmed the neighbourhood and had a field day. Three income tax inspectors were also in evidence in the area but refused comment.

'Waiter.'

'Yeah, mister.'

'Another lime juice and one more baclawa.'

Big trucks rumbling up and down the avenue. Passing shadows of public people by the half curtained window. High up over the entrances to the piers, ship's funnels poking. Bottles of soda pop and cardboard images of frolicsome girls, mouths full of teeth ready to be refreshed. Shoulders just like Sally Tomson's. As they were in my arms, so neat and smooth under her hair. Please see me in my recent romantic antic. Generously scattering a drop of my fortune on an early morning sea breeze. Should have jumped after it. Grabber at life's banquet follows a fortune to doom. As folk fleece and fisticuff in street.

'Waiter. Check.'

George Smith at the counter. Reaching and digging in his pockets. Back ones, front, the waist coat. Empty wallet. I am without funds. Just two coins the person gave me at the fountain. My God. And these are not enough. When I could have bought the whole street last night.

'Look.'

'Yeah, mister.'

'I'm sorry, but it seems I'm a little short.'

'Yeah.'

'I can pay for one baclawa, and one lime juice.'

'You had two baclawas, and two lime juice.'

'I can only pay for one.'

'Cash. Guys been coming in here all day trying to pass torn bills.'

'I understand.'

'Hey, Lucifer, come out here a second.'

Two swarthy persons viewing Smith with his little box tucked under the arm. A couple of whispers. Lips dry under the lip mask. Umbrella flapping at his side.

'O.K. bud. We have fifteen cans of garbage back there, need to go on street.'

Lucifer lifting up the flap of the counter. Smith following with umbrella, parcel, into a back steamy interior. On chopping boards, mounds of sliced onions, carrots split in four, and potatoes ready for hot fat. Don't fight it. Go with it. Till there's a chance to go elsewhere.

Through the door into an alley. Smith apostate, darkly noble, nostrils flared to the sweet reek. Lucifer jerking thumb towards a green shed. Up the dim narrow alley the light of the street. Distantly above, a square patch of sky. Under which I work for the first time. In foot poundals. To lift with a hand. The satisfaction deep. The rewards are small. The smell overpowering. Taste brandy in the sweat dripping down my nose.

Lucifer standing watching. George Smith staring stiffly back. Driving him into the kitchen door with aloof chill distaste. Adjusting his lip mask. Kneeling to retie tightly each shoe. To look like one is making ready to work, instead of run.

Smith wafting his hanky, taking a scent of attar of roses up the nostrils. Wheeling out a barrel of banana skins. Raising a foot up. A push. Leave a little skating rink behind.

Smith spun around the corner. Briefly looking over a shoulder at the two hefty proprietors standing shirt sleeved in the street. After a struggle up a slippery alley. Sorry gentlemen, must rush to a board meeting. With my gavel, crystal pitcher of water and newly sharpened pencils. To announce a regrettable deficit. And avoid a woeful winding up.

Smith sitting heart thumping on a bench in the wide open space of the park. A little boy with a jumping toy on a string. Mother rocking a baby carriage ten feet away. To take him by the hand. Too near the strange man. True madam.

Room to look out. Across the harbour. Grey water chopped up by ferry and barge. Over there stands a little round fort I could use. After free refreshment. Lose one's self for a moment in fancy figments and land arse first in reality. Miss Martin mounting a machine gun in Dynamo. In the cabin in the woods, nature tells you go ahead put it in. Rest it there in softness. Off it went like a cannon. Didn't mean to pull the trigger. Bonniface in the morning paper, me in the afternoon. Both of us in a noose. Miss Martin please don't tell your mother.

Here on this little bench. You left me wretched, Sally Tomson. You left me sad. Last night on Her Majesty's balcony couldn't you see me wave. In the light breeze weeping. Her Majesty sleeping. Laughed lightly letting treasury notes slip out from fingers. Down over the city, separating away in the dark. Fell so silently. Without pomp in the crazy circumstance. I thought let urine be followed by gold.

Just
For
A
Change.

20

On the corner of Eagle Street near the river, this chilly autumnal evening, Smith leaning back against a dead wall, head tilted towards a tiny luminosity decorating the night. A personal little star. Siren sounding in the distance. Tiny puffs of steam from a sewer cover in the middle of the road.

Barges and tugs melting green and red colours in the darkness. A doorman along the curb with two doggies. One manoeuvring on hind legs to disgrace the gutter. Avocado green letter box lonely stuck on a pole. Where Hugo strolls from Merry Mansion to pop in the mail. Tonight he stood in the lobby fingering his nose in front of the long glass doors. Rumours rampant that Mr and Mrs Goldminer had turned to religion. Filling their flat for days with hammering under the supervision of Mr Stone to erect an altar in their drawing room. Where they knelt naked, holding hands and praying. Matilda said she could smell incense in the delivery shoot.

Up the avenue. Bathed suddenly in the flood light of an apartment entrance. She comes right on the dot of eight o'clock with a smile on her face in the crisp of evening. Raising her eye brows amused. In seal skin. Alligator shoes. Where have all the animals gone.

'Hello, Miss Tomson.'

'When are you going to call me Sally.'

'Or Dizzy.'

'That's a crazy story I'll tell you about when you're older.'

'How are you Sally.'

'That's better. I'm fine, Smithy. And you. You look like the international gentleman. That collar's the best sable, Smithy.'

'That's the best seal.'

'What's the matter, we're meeting on this corner like two clothes racks.'

'You look so splendid.'

'Just my image. The inner Tomson is in a sand storm, the outer one is skiing down the sunny mountain, smiling.'

'Shall we bring the inner Tomson somewhere for a cocktail.'

'Let's.'

'What would you like, a place, dark or dazzling.'

'Tell you the honest truth Smithy, for the inner Tomson I'd just like a glass of beer in some cozy joint with a booth. What have you got in that paper bag.'

'Difficult to explain, Miss Tomson. I'm trying an experiment. That the human organism won't do the same daft thing twice.'

'Looks like you've been mushroom picking.'

Smith raising his arm. A long dark squat gleaming vehicle pulling out from the kerb and coming down towards them on the avenue. With a whirring groan on its fat tyres. Chauffeur stepping round, a white gloved hand opening the door. A salute for Smith.

'Wow, what's this, Smithy.'

'Miss Tomson, have you met Herbert.'

'Don't think so, hi.'

'Please to meet you, Miss Tomson. I see your picture a lot.'

'No kidding.'

'I'd know you anywhere.'

'I can't recognize myself. But thanks.'

Dark deep capeskin interior. Smith stepping past Miss Tomson. Leaning back in the softness, hunching shoulders up in the sable collar, a left black gloved hand wrapped tightly round an apple walking stick. Tie with the three legged golden stars. Black shoes, black silk socks. Black briefcase of unfathomable facts, twice as foolish as fiction. And the onion paper copies of correspondence under the file heading, Discourteous.

269

'Smithy, I don't get it. Real lighthearted socks you're wearing.'

'Get what, Miss Tomson.'

'This car. The richness is crippling. You rob a bank. These blue tinted windows.'

'Can see out but can't see in.'

Miss Tomson rapping a knuckle. Turning to Smith, bun of blonde hair softly folded at her neck. Eyeballs still so white and laughing.

'Are you a perve, Smithy.'

'I beg you pardon Miss Tomson.'

'The windows are solid. This car's bullet proof.'

'Absolutely ordinary vehicle. Little extra thickness here and there. The bumpers are perhaps of the heavy duty quality.'

'Someone's trying to rub you out, Smithy. You need a friend. It's sad. Even a microphone.'

'Must tell Herbert where to go. Hello. Herbert.'

'Yes, Mr Smith.'

'Go crosstown two blocks. Then left down the avenue. I'll tell you when to stop.'

'Smithy, come on, why would they want to air condition a sweet guy like you.'

'Bullets are the least of it, Miss Tomson. One can always deal with those. It's the insinuation and discourtesy I find weighs heavy on my spirit. I've missed you.'

Miss Tomson looks out at a lighted marquee, a lobby filling with people before a performance begins. The car turns left downtown on the wide avenue. And her lips purse and open slowly.

'Surprise you I was only living a block away from Merry Mansions. Under the name of Tomson too.'

'You never tried to get in touch.'

'Smithy, you know, things happen. It was one thing after another.'

Smith slowly pulling off gloves looking at them in his hand.

'You don't believe that. All right I'll tell you. You got a

wife and four kids. A certain log cabin, in a certain woods, and a certain secretary, you want me to go on. You see Smith, what you don't know about me is. I got principles. What shit, sorry about the language. This vein of talk is a sure way of ruining an evening.'

'Tell me.'

'If I phoned you up and said hello George, I'm expecting a baby. What do you say, Sally, that's great, but I got four already. I know you got to be a tightwad with your commitments. Don't get scared, I'm not pregnant. See what I mean, you had a real look of fear.'

'Just concern.'

Miss Tomson's big eyes slowly sheltered by her lids.

'Smithy. It was great strolling out in the fresh air tonight to meet you. Walking down the block. To see you there standing against the building. Just like we were kids or something meeting for a date. You've never taken me out on a date, a real date.'

'I'll take you tonight.'

'I can't. I'm giving a party. One of those after midnight things. So suicides out the window don't kill someone innocent in the street. Maybe you'd like to come. Some interesting people.'

'I'd be out of place.'

'Smithy, you're fishing for compliments.'

Tomson leaning her hand across to take Smith's. Locking her fingers with his on the capeskin. Tender world spreads. Looking down at her ungloved hand. And a sparkling gigantic diamond.

'Don't ask about that, Smithy.'

Limousine pulling to a stop in front of yellow lighted steamy windows. Herbert giving his hand to Miss Tomson's elbow and an eye to her knees. She stands. Awaits Smith's emerging. Smiling her loveliest of smiles. Up on her lissome legs.

'Smithy I got to laugh at you. That get up. The paper bag. The cane.'

'It's a stick.'

'A stick. I mean you been taking some kind of advice maybe. You know, you're so out of date that it doesn't matter.'

'Thank you.'

A long mahogany bar. White aproned waiter whisking shoulder high trays to booths. Schooners of beer. Heads turning as Miss Tomson pushes in the door. An unseemly whistle. And lowly mumbled remarks at this apparition of the international gentleman.

'Miss Tomson, perhaps this place is unsuitable.'

'It's fine. They just want a harmless laugh. Someone appears stepping out of some drama a century ago, why not a chuckle. That's why you're so sweet Smith with all these old fashioned ideas. Take no notice, it's just a beer joint.'

Waiter flourishing menus. Looking like an emperor some ridiculous century ago, with eyes staring down on Miss Tomson who lays back the glistening seal skin from her shoulders. All the blonde rest of her in black silk. Waiter rubbing nose with a knuckle. Tomson flicking menu with a fingernail. Smith measuring out his best voice.

'What's for you Sally.'

'Just a beer.'

'Mind if I have some wiener and sauerkraut.'

'Feel free, Smithy.'

'Beer for madam, beer, wiener and sauerkraut for me.'

'If that's what you want.'

'That's what we want.'

Raucous laughter from along the bar. Thumps of back slapping. Little raps of whisky glasses. A curtain of smoke. Man pulling up a trouser leg to show a scar. Another opening coat to count out notches on his belt. Flashes of merriment erupting from the calm misery.

'Smith it was sweet of you. The dogwood. Thanks. I was in Dogdale Cemetery all by myself. Got a little white stone up. With a quotation. You know I began to see the point of your pyramid in Renown. I nearly didn't see the card, got covered in blots of mud, ink almost faded away. I saw those two last words. I broke up. I was saying hey Sally, you can't be like this over two little words. And the, this is George Smith speaking. I clutched. I could really hear you.'

Miss Tomson's smile of friendly sadness. Peel a grape for her to crush twixt those teeth. She stands and the whole world turns to look. And applaud. My hand on her breast. Nipple between my teeth. A hundred telephone calls away.

'But Smithy you're not ebbing. Just need a little more fat on the face. I phoned you a couple of times last few days at Merry and at that new office. I ask for George Smith and after a few seconds a pipe and drum band fades in and some crazy song away in the highlands or something. Your wires must be crossed. Operator said she couldn't explain it. You rascal.'

'Little phone difficulties recently.'

'Ha well tonight just had an instinct. I was going to wash my hair in the shower. I was all undressed. I pick up the bathroom phone and dial you at Merry Mansions. And I hear, this is the tabernacle of the dark complexioned redeemer. Was that Matilda. I was about to hang up until I heard you. Black bitch. Shit. Sorry about the language. I was promising myself I wouldn't be uncharitable. Smith you busted a guy into the tracks. I couldn't believe it was you till I read about the cemetery and that last line. I laughed. Gent of the old brigade.'

'School.'

'That got me. My brother is getting jealous of your publicity. Wallflower Smith, the small backroom operator. Marvellous how you come out in the paper as if you were something important with your ritzy bone house. Even I was saying to somebody, I know that guy. They said you're a mystery, till I told them.'

'What, Miss Tomson.'

'That you're real. Guy my brother knows, Ralph, a big mouth, as if he knew you, that it was interesting how you sold out your closest friends first, double crossing distant acquaintances last. I socked him right on the jaw. He thought it was funny because he didn't feel it. So I grabbed him by the hair. Boy he started screaming. Think I had him by the balls or something. If he has any. Just a jerk in show biz said he could do something for my brother, who isn't too well recently. Too many dames and cotillions.'

Waiter with steamy tray. A plate of copper coloured glistening futters in a light grey sea of sauerkraut. Setting a beer before Miss Tomson and a beer and white plate before Smith, who smiling sat, socks pulled up. An arm's length away from the blue wisely lit eyes of Sally Tomson, full of sparks and narrowing strangely, full of woman. Her finger glittering with an overture to a complicated contract. Like one I agreed with Shirl. Tied together with four kids. That come tripping you up during the waltz. Go sleigh riding down the other side of life in the sixty foot winter shadows. Hoping to land in May and wallow among the daisies of July. Instead of pushing them up.

'Smithy what do you think about when your eyes go away like that. Like you belong to the committee figuring the solution to the prevention of do it yourself whipping in isolated convents.'

'Ha ha.'

'Give me a wiener. Please.'

Smith spearing the defenceless cylinder. Lifting it dripping with sauerkraut juice to Miss Tomson's open lips. As she softly sucks it in. A flash of white teeth. For which I searched waiting in train stations, lonely seven, eight and nine o'clock at dark. Left me all these many weeks tarnished and vulnerable till the phone rang tonight. And my heart nearly exploded. Letting the seconds tick in silence listening to her voice like one two three freckles under her right eye where there used to be four. My God Miss Tomson please. Come walking back as Sally into my life. Wearing nothing but your pearls.

'Come on, what do you think of.'

'Just pleased you're here chewing a wiener.'

'We're kind of like old friends now. I said I'd go to your funeral. So if I ask you to my wedding will you come.'

'Miss Tomson, this is a terrible conversation.'

'I know. I better go.'

'Don't go.'

'Got to get back. Could only spare an hour anyway.'

'Please.'

'Why keep up a pretence. I'm going to try the wedlock. Hands in the soap suds, squeeze out the socks, wax the furniture. Gee I make a terrible liar. Only thing my hand will go into is a glove, holding a cheque book. The guy's a dynasty. If I want an ocean liner, I whistle. Those are the facts. I keep amassing them. End up with one gigantic fiction. It's in his grandfather's will that when we march down the aisle, we got to have the guy's ashes thrown over us. I don't want some dead guy's ashes on me.'

'Miss Tomson, what will you do for love.'

'That's nice, the way you said that.'

'What will you.'

'I don't know. What I always do, cry. I'll be crying and whistling. I'll make a stinking wife and I know it. I'm taking him for his money. I told him so. Sweet thing about him is he said he was marrying me for my brains. I thought that was so rich I accepted on the spot. After he'd been begging me for six months.'

'You do have brains, Miss Tomson.'

'Thanks.'

'You have.'

'A head full of pigeons. Sometimes I tie a message on one and send it out. Like the letters you get. Dear Sir, I'll casserole you. Hardboil your jewels and use them for billiards. See. The pigeons get out, just like that last remark. Gee I don't love this guy. What good is my body to him. Or what's more important, to me. When I worked for you, it was my first honest job. And what lousy pay. Sorry I said that. But boy it was low. Even so I used to go home happy at night. No kidding. Woke up laughing. Because I had you so scared.'

'I wasn't.'

'You were. You used to lurk behind your door for hours thinking up something to say to me, so it would look like you were running some big enterprise and your next move was going to have consequences everywhere. But I thought you were nice too. I really felt a few times, why don't I tell this guy the truth. But if you knew I was a big time celebrity, it would have made it awkward. Only my dog was shot that night I would have fainted seeing you at Jiffy's.'

'I was there by accident.'

'Gee Smithy.'

'What.'

'I don't know. I think about you a lot. While the rest of us are skidding around, there you are in your own little world. It's so sweet. I got to go.'

'Don't.'

'Why do you look so funny at me, Smithy.'

'I don't want to lose you.'

'Smithy, gee, you've got moistening in the eyes.'

'Yes.'

'You're the most surprising guy.'

'I feel I'm never going to be alone with you again.'

'Sure you are. I mean I'll see you tonight, Smithy.'

'In a room of crowded people.'

'But we'll see each other. Let's not turn this into a funeral. Here's a hanky. You give me yours. Maybe I feel like a tear. This is just great. Sitting bawling into the sauerkraut.'

'Sorry to behave like this, Miss Tomson.'

'I like it. Feel free. Don't mind crying, it's the guys who pray. I don't like. Nice to see you break down.'

'Thanks.'

'Don't mention it.'

'Kiss you on the nose, Miss Tomson.'

'Sure. Anywhere you want.'

'Covers a lot of ground.'

'Good, I want it to. Why don't you buy horses, Smithy, and sport around the resorts. We might meet up. Spend an evening on a verandah watching the fireflies. Was my favourite as a kid. Wait for a shooting star, holding hands on a porch swing. Ask you to come back to my place now, but my fiancé is going to be there, the poor bastard, got in a rut inheriting millions. That makes you smile. That's better. Say you'll see me later. Come on.'

'I'll see you later.'

'That's it. Black tie, but you come as you like. Building opposite corner where we met tonight. I'm at the top, 1A. Floors are numbered, the highest first.'

'Let me get Herbert for you to take you back.'

'No thanks, I'll catch a cab Smithy. No one's trying to rub me out.'

Miss Tomson leaning across the table. Gathering her seal skin up round her black silk and kissing George Smith on the brow. Her tingling perfume. Ache to reach up and hold her breast. A last shred of feeling.

Good bye.

21

Across a black bridge, web of trestles over the river cold. Past the tops of warehouses and factories and down into dingy intersecting streets. Further to faintly lurking people along a rialto lined with stores blaring neon lighted bargains of socks, camping equipment, batteries and used parts of cars. Sad rows of houses east and west.

Herbert steering the dreadnought limousine through the night, black cap on his black head. Dusty dark sky hanging over the upturned teeth of a cemetery. Sign of a can company rearing up, laying a carpet of orange light on the headstones. George Smith hands enlaced in lap. Lines darkening down the face. Leaving deep chasms of care.

One hour ago Miss Tomson left me. World gets gloom again. Red light stops the car. Old bearded gentleman crossing the street. Towards a glowing star over a temple entrance. If ever there was a place to hide. Out on these dismal flat lands. Feel all my blood is up for sale. Offered to medical science. Body steeped in bottles.

A highway lit with snakelike haunting lanterns. Blocks of buildings. Plastered box living rooms. Evening aprons and shirt sleeves. Where the men are sick and brides are brave returning from their honeymoons. While I was busy in another land. Poised with Shirl over a canapé. Instead of in these cardboard sprawls of charm and beauty. Where wives lean just gently over the coffee table. Taken from behind. Whisper what's your role in our relation.

Herbert raising his hand at a sign. Car pulling off the highway past a dark little park in a blanket of leaves. Under a bridge, the highway above streaming with the lights of cars. Herbert pointing. A forlorn brick apartment above a window display of medicines. Another window of a bar full of darkness with coloured lights blinking far inside.

From the sidewalk Smith looks up. A few yellow lighted windows. Glass double doors into a dim tiled hall. Line of brass mail boxes on the wall. Running a gloved finger on the mottled metal. White square envelope sticking out. Between two names an engraved card from another world. C. C. B. Clementine, Apartment 6C.

Smith pressing the button for the bell. Waiting in the hollow emptiness. Door slamming inside. Sound of feet down the sairs. Someone talking to a child. Woman opening the door. Gasps, recovers and takes a little girl by the hand.

'You want in.'

'Please.'

'Sylvia hold the door for the man.'

'Thank you.'

Smith with barren steps climbing the stairs around empty landings to a brown metal door on the sixth floor. Knocking. Evening newspapers and empty milk bottles on mats by other doors. Roar of cars floating up from the highway down below. A dead squeak, the door opening a brief inch. Peer of a red eye. Part of a pink arm.

'My God. George. Come in. Thank heavens my message got through. Tell your Miss Martin I'm deeply and forever grateful. Welcome. Forgive me while I crawl. Just this length of the hall. And my attire. Only thing I have left is my hunting pink. My iron has burned holes in my airport uniform.'

Smith walking slowly behind Bonniface crawling with an odd bark towards a sitting room. Through an open green curtain, a stove bubbling a pot of spaghetti.

'George I'm trying to teach Mr Mystery to walk and bark again. I crawl to encourage him. Sit there, on the box. Which used to have oranges only I ate them all. Full of sunshine.'

Bonniface pouring out a jar of wine. Handing it to Smith, who crossed his knees and tilted his head to listen.

'Smith it can't go on. Woeful things have befallen Mr Mystery and me. We're nearly prisoners in here. We have spaghetti, we have each other. Woof woof.'

Bonniface with white silk cravat stuck with a pin of pearl. Smelling into the spaghetti steam. Popping a handful of shattered black olives in the pot.

'George, I have not deserved what has happened to me. Have a plateful of this.'

'I've just had frankfutters and sauerkraut.'

'Combine it with this mixture. Blast off to heaven.'

Bonniface ladling out the squirming starch. A trembling face throbbing with the veins around the brow. A little bowl. As he opened French curtained doors a mite, to slip through from the sitting room. To return and smile.

'An entrée for Mr Mystery.'

'What's your trouble Clementine.'

'Smith you're nervous and anxious. You tremble to go.'

'It's a long way here.'

'You rushed away from the beer and onions. Smith I do not want to give you distress. See you unhappy. As your great mausoleum rises a beacon to your cunning. Your astute mind and grave habits. I am your friend. I know the sorrow you suffer with your lonely austere richness. Have more wine. I don't question what goes between you and Her Majesty. I have Mr Mystery. We go bow wow together into the future. The cold blank heart you have Smith. Come with me out to the airport. See the multi motored birds spread their throbbing wings and go away into the sky. Watch me in action as I check their tickets. I am a clerk. At the bottom of the ladder. You hear that, Smith. I give service to the best of my ability. But now I fade. I must get out.'

Bonniface digging into the spaghetti pot. Forking out more wiggling whiteness. Looking sadly down and shaking his head. With a trembling hand to the neck of a great wicker wrapped bottle. Pouring out the red sublime. Looking across a musty carpet at Smith wiping lips with his square of linen.

'Before moving here, I took up lodging with a person who could not read nor write. She steamed open my letters and took them to a relative to translate the contents. A little group was formed, other relatives were invited. Letters which I had written and torn up were pasted back together again. My little incident in the transit tracks came to light. They are blackmailing me. Tracked me here.'

Clementine, standing lifting a piece of spaghetti from his cravat. A glass to his lips. Years ago he was thirsty. Took his own bride under the marriage bells and crossed swords of his regiment. Raised his little kiddies to the tune of finer things. Strutting through his rented castle marvelling at the damp contortion of each antique. Took George Smith by the hand to lead him to wedded bliss with Shirl. From the vintage arms of Her Majesty.

'George, it's not funny. No longer amusing to be poor. I came here to catch my breath and reorganize. Promised a future at the airport. They demoted me. The winter comes. I lost my eye glasses on the subway on the way to Golden Avenue all the way from the airport when a departing passenger came through with the news. The train was so crowded at Breevort Street no one could get off or on. Mr Mystery was being trampled. You threw that money off the roof. Why in God's name did you do it. Answer me. All right. I don't ask for much. Just a life preserver in the present tribulation and trial. I don't want to add to your troubles. But I need instant help. If not hard currency. Then spiritual peace. Unless I get out of here I'm doomed. Three minutes on the street brings me some misfortune. Without my glasses, I ask for directions, unable to see. I meet with unspeakable ignorance and implacable stupidity. Then on a bus I met a woman. We were sitting together. Travelling in some God forsaken direction. We looked out the window our knees pressing. We struck up a conversation. She asked me home. She lived miles and miles away in an attic. An area regrettably called Fartbrook. Took three hours, changing trains and buses. When we got there we climbed a fire escape in the back of the house. A window opened downstairs. A man and woman started shouting out wretched and unseemly words at her. I should have been warned. But I climbed on. In the kitchen she made me coffee and gave me a bun. I listened to her over the table. She had married a policeman. He made her commit variations at gun point. Unwholesome suggestions as to how his organ should be played. And even where it might be put. She had no breasts. The doctors took them away. Cost her all her money. The gas company squeezed off the gas. Electric company switched off the juice. Strong men took the furniture. Loansharks cruised outside, jaws snapping.'

Smith jumping to his feet. Glass of wine splashing on the floor. Closing his coat and tucking his shoulders into the sable collar. Pulling on a glove quickly, gripping his walking stick. The Clementine eyes, wild and red. Burning with specks of glittering fire. A curtain fluttering at the open window. And the waves of light spreading across the concrete upturned palms of highway. For the rubber wheels humming east and west.

'What's the matter George. Sit down. You'll want to know about this. How she bought a set of encyclopedias, signed her name to a form at the door. Man told her a whole new world would open up of knowledge leading to extra earnings. She read till she was so tired she lost her job at the bakery. They tried to take the books back. But she clung to her treasure trove of learning. Put down that stick George, take off those gloves. Give them to me. Me Bonniface. Her name, Euphemia. She tried to dry her underwear on a string hooked to the attic ceiling. Which leaked. I blessed her. The clothes line collapsed. I nearly strangled. It was cold. Rainy. We got under the covers in the bed. We read the encyclopedia under the letter S, for sued, staggered, screwed, soul, swine, syringe. Then a crash as the kitchen door came right off its hinges. In the doorway was her husband behind his service revolver. I turned to D. To read under death and deliverance. I looked him right in the eye and introduced myself. Said I could not help finding his wife attractive. He stood there boggle eyed. We went out to a saloon. All three. We got drunk. I was only sorry I had not looked up flatfoot in the encyclopedia. As well as flog, frenzy, fondue and fandango not to mention fulminate and fustigate.'

Smith looking at the round light reflecting on the tip of his black gleaming shoe, bouncing quietly with each heart beat. Bonniface's eyes flooding with a warm regard. Tiny smile tugging the edges of noble lips. Leads the whole world to the brink, holds up a hand as he peers down into the darkness and says let's have a drink before we jump.

'Smith, I know you came here in a long somewhat strange car. I watched out the window. I want you to take me to the airport four miles south. I'm late for duty. We will take Mr Mystery. He understands. Bow, wow. Woof woof. He knows. Wags his tail when he is near the big runways and hears the metal birds roar up into the cloud banks. Smith let me try on your garments.'

Bonniface pulling on Smith's gloves. Putting arms into the sleeves of the fur lined coat. Looking down the long line of his person.

'Smith in a moment of wretched hopelessness I took my hunting horn to the airport, just to bring back memories. And sounded it while seated in the crapper. After a few sentimental blasts the police descended answering a summons to bugle blowing in the gents. Comes a time when one is forced to take matters out of God's hands. Across these lands it throbs and thunders. They are happy in their fat. I must go look in my bedroom mirror at this fine garment.'

Bonniface opening the curtained French doors. Shattering crash. Smith stiffening, standing, A yelp and bark from the bedroom. Sound of scrabbling.

'George help me, they've got me.'

Smith parting the doors. A huge bed lay like a hillside against the wall, propped crazily on books and magazines. Bonniface flattened beneath an ironing board, his fist gripped round the neck of a gigantic wine bottle. Photographs strewn on the floor. Of children, meadows and ponies. Bereft outpost, like room 604 Dynamo. Personal trinkets scattered between barren plaster walls. Sad enough to laugh. Just as he wandered without warning into Fartbrook. And I, two weeks ago installed a bath in 604 Dynamo, desperately needing to wallow in the warmth of water. Secret plumbers came. They fiddled with the pipes. While one of them put his foot through the ceiling. A poor lone guilty operator in the office below saw the emerging leg and got down on his knees and started to pray. And just as he felt relief as the leg retreated, and the guilt was swept away the other one came crashing through.

'Smith help me get out from under this. I thought it was them. The white coats. Lurking and jumping on me from behind.'

Entanglement of wires, a wake up coffee machine, an ironing board stained with burns. Floor strewn with cigarette stubs. And in the corner a gable roofed doghouse, the face of Mr Mystery peering out upon the holocaust. As Bonniface crawled away to the bathroom. Legs jutting out the door. Head encased in shower curtain. Man of desperate strength, magically fading through walls, haunting the flatland boulevards. Ushering travellers out across the tarmac to the waiting big birds. Waves them bye bye. Leads the blind, taps out code to the deaf. Walks stiffly, quickly. Knowing every pause invites a punch out of nowhere.

Smith retreating to the living room. Twisted with spectacular death. Come tonight all the way here. With Bonniface twitching his elegant heels. Striking sparks with each click. Now sporting my coat and gloves. As night outside groans away with wheels. Bonniface swan dives from his ironing board. Till the bed hangs down from the wall. As my reputation waves in tatters. Overrun by a horde of low voltage hearts. The hot sunny day when the salesman took me, his prospect, through the marvellous leafy avenues of Renown. Told me of the beauty and permanency. Mr Smith you rest in peace completely free of any rodent threat. In this little temple. Airtight behind that slab. Cleaned and polished daily. Fresh flowers on the mantel. And as we left stepping down from that mausoleum on the hot sunny day. It blew up. Salesman ran for cover. Found him lurking in the shrubbery weeping over his lost sale. But I bought. One day I will scatter up the birds with a blast out under the trees. All salesmen, battle fatigued, are sent away for rehabilitation.

Bonniface combing his wet hair. Please let me wear your coat George. Just tonight. To have the fine feel of fur next by underwear. I'm not going to last, tuck up my cravat between the dark sable hairs. You have a car. I need a coat.

Bonniface leading Smith into the cold dark hall. Finger to his lips for silence as you go. A shivering Smith tip toeing down the stairs. Behind cool Calvin who said the janitor tried unseemly approaches for rent. Leaving a child's squeaking toy on the stairs. To make a squeal. Things they do to the near blind.

Bonniface's little key opening his letter box. Bringing forth a white square expensive envelope. Smith spies familiar handwriting Bonniface nervously ripping it open. White jodhpur legs showing from beneath the black coat, and pair of grey socks nearly meeting the lower band of underwear.

Bonniface smiles over a purple bordered white card. Holding it to the light. Reflecting the engraved gold into Smith's sad eyes.

George Smith
requests the pleasure of
your company at the opening
of his memorial
at Thistle Plot, Buttercup Drive
The Renown Cemetery
on Thursday, 17th November
at 3:30 P.M.

Flat 14
Merry Mansions
2 Eagle Street

R.S.V.P
Decorations will not
be worn.

'Smith very yeasty. Your pretensions are exceeded only by your outrageous nerve.'

Together standing on the step outside the apartment house. Where nary a moth will ever come to smash its little dust on a Bonniface window pane. Who stood a strange cold gentleman on the brick steps. In summer there were flowers and ivy grew. Smith waving an arm. Upwards four faint stars. A dry biting wind. The empty stretches of street bubbling with lonely cars. And the odd scurrying figures disappearing in the beeswax buildings.

'Smith forgive me if I don't reply formally to your invitation. Which I should like to accept. It's the hurried times. How about a slab for me. Tomb of the unknown failure. You walk sideways Smith to present a smaller target, and hunched so the high bullets go harmlessly over. Have your horoscope cast. Know the truth of what lies ahead. Do I look properly shaved. One more weary effort getting nearly electrocuted to lop down the bristles. Hold that bottle tightly. My God Smith, what an extraordinary machine.'

Herbert backing Smith's car into the curb. Stepping out and smiling sheepishly at the two figures, strange in the surroundings, and the stiff trembling far eastern Bonniface.

'Herbert I'd like you to meet Mr Clementine. We are taking him to the airport. As quickly as possible.'

'Howdy, Mr Clementine. Chilly night.'

'How do you do. Indeed, a witch's tit.'

Door closing on the two passengers. A deep throated click. Big cat of an engine. Purring. Exhaust tubes leaving white little wisps of cloud. Car rolls under barren branches. Away from this outpost. Pink brick by day. To a red light the end of the road. Along the edge of a cemetery. Up a narrow lane to merge with the fleet of cars beetling by.

Smith tucking up his parcel close under an elbow. Buildings flashing, big empty faces looking down on the traffic stream. Smith's dreadnaught threading a way through the cars ahead. Warm sweet country freshened air floating up under the legs.

'George let me telephone the airport.'

Smith putting the nervous Clementine through on the line handing over the instrument. Bonniface's hand clutching it tightly, knuckles white. Eyebrows at half mast.

'Hello. Air Traffic. Fritz. Who is this. Get off this line, imbecile. Fritz, do you hear, I want Fritz. This is Gessunt, air traffic manager. Fritz. Gessunt here. Cedric Bonniface will be late. He was involved in a collision on the highway. Pile up of forty six cars. No. His was thirty eight. He's all right. Just a little shaky. Insists upon reporting for duty. He asks that his makeshift garment be overlooked. I suggest he be given a free chit for the Monarch lounge. Yes. Pity. Quite. He's utterly devoted to duty. However. Goodbye.'

High wire fence. Flat lands and beyond, the wide marshes, meadows and creeks. Over railway tracks. How are you Shirl. Bonniface unsmiling. Be an asset in my business. Personal all round secretary. Assistant ever ready with a ruse. Or fandango. Miss Tomson lays out her canapés this night. Big ring glittering on her finger. Amusing friends, maybe flicking mayonnaise in their eyes. Said men with big ones should wear long ties. Have her cool blonde hand between my legs. Light it up like a torch to shine in any darkness ahead. Her marriage. Her party. To which I will tremble as I did to my first. When I wore a lavender suit. Went with just my innocent heart without presents or invitation. Hoping to get the jello, ice cream and pop. Instead of the two sad words I was served. Feeling aglow and different, little white lace trim around my broad collar. All washed and neatly ironed. Skinny legged down the street under the summer trees. Turn right between the green low hedges. Into the concrete back yard where they kept horses. I petted the blue furry dog on the head. Up the cement steps to knock on the screen door. Could see dimly inside across the gleaming tiles feet moving around a table murmuring with goodies. My idea was friendly. And they came to the door. Opened it, looked at me. And said go home. I waited all the way out to the street again. Tight throat holding down my lungs which pushed out my tears as I walked away. Back up the street. And home.

'Smith you nervously clutch that paper bag. You convert foolish riches in your heart and beautiful dreams in your mind, into worldly cash. Shame. Me think take pneumatic drill to get into this car without a key. Only simple pleasures left. My black liquorice toothpaste. My apartment mates think it strange. Steal some from me. And think I do not know. Yesterday I sold two pints of blood. To buy chop meat for Mr Mystery. Smith. I took him to the park to meet other doggies of his own retirement age. We also can barely sniff or lift a leg. But Mr Mystery turned up his nose at friendship. Like you do Smith. Don't hold the world in distrust. It's nice out here. Provided you have padding for the ribs and protection for the groin. Good of you to take me to the airport. Talk George. Why don't you talk.'

Smith eructing delicately.

'As you wish. Have you switched off the flow of gold to Shirl. Cruel man. Made her work. Wrapped her lawyer up in statutes till he screamed with the lethal legality. The habeas corpus haberdasher. The Otter clause. But me Smith. I don't mind. Others think you hard. But me. I have one request. Just one. I should like to wear decorations to the opening of your memorial. To offset forever the cremation ashes my father in law threw over us at our wedding. Of a mixture from the family's bankrupts. You like that aspersion. You smile. See. We approach the lights now. Beacons wave round the sky. There. A thunderbird goes up, full of folk flying to get there. And when they do, fly to get back. Enables more time to fit in misery at destination, than by rail or sea. Fandango. One good heap of heartbreak. Here we are.'

'Herbert, stop at the entrance there.'

'George give this little slip of paper to Herbert, he can refresh himself at the bar and restaurant without stint.'

'I must go back, Bonniface. I have a call to make upon a friend.'

'George I want you to see this port in action. Just for a

288

few minutes. Watch me do my duty. Surely the passing of papers, scribblings, figures, dockets, stampings, trampings must be of interest to you. Go wait at the central pillar in the skyways hall. Please. I ask you to do this. Just to have for a few random minutes, one human being close by who can see me in perspective. Smith. I'm truly sorry you are evil.'

Throngs of people. Down causeways, ramps. Roar of engines. Smith in his dark suit. Spying after Bonniface Clementine, walking with Smith's black gloves, black sable coat, stick rapping the floor, blinking unseeing into the crowd, the white underwear covered shanks sticking into a pair of black shoes as they hurried him wayward and trouserless. Other eyebrows raised and faces turned as he passed. And approached the whispering clerks behind the long black counter. Two were pleasant looking women to whom he bowed. And they giggled.

Customers lined up to fly. Smith standing behind the pillar, in the centre of skyway hall. Bonniface, the crustacean, back and forth, a white carnation stuck in the sable.

Smith silent. A lonely life watching from this post. Women with baskets. Trailing little children. Wild eyes in sallow faces. An odd executive in the swarm looking at his watch with confidence. Try that significant gesture, and my timepiece halts. There's a corporation president staring ahead into the next deal, chin jutting, hand ready to grip some other fish like appendage appearing at a profit. There goes Bonniface, penniless and amusing. On a mountain of cash one looks down with sad but wide open eyes. At the wailing below. Drop it down to them from the sky, promptly it lands, the eye gouging begins.

This dark journey across the flat lands to see the Bonniface. Share some of his misunderstandings. Least one does for a college friend. Like nights so many years ago. Standing under lamp posts, bottles bouncing in the dark. Find a ragged girl to lay up against some cellar wall. In a smell of rats and dead cats. Dream to be a merchant prince. Marble houses round the world. Run through the streets to

Her Majesty's high brick house, shutters closed over the windows. Past stone masons chiselling by candle light with the great deal of dying. Rollick royal. Buds in the all-together. All comes to this. Bonniface scurrying by. Lower legs in underwear. Little sheaf of papers clutched in the hand. Makes a sign language to a customer under the blaring loudspeaker. Promptly retreats the whole length of the counter. Stooping under at the end and into the gents. For the fifth time. Wants me to witness his kidney control in these jammed conditions. Goodness. He's back again. Some bladder.

Must get my coat back. Or appear at Miss Tomson's without outer accoutrement. Protection from her smart friend's elbows. Merry big Miss Tomson. I put it. All measured and mild. And upon it you slipped a painful ring of teeth. Feel them wherever I go. Even here, faint and foolish by this pillar. Your silken folds of wondrous little beads of caviare. A step into heaven. Hide me. Passengers swarm. Rest in there. Away from switches and wires ringing and binging. Bound to be a mistake. There goes Bonniface again. Under the flap, across the corridor. Into the gents. In view of your peeing history Bonniface, sprinkle the counter, and be done. Give air company little spray of heartbreak. While Herbert tanks up in the bar. Asks me home to eat with him and wife. Has tropical fish who rush to the surface as they hear him walk across the floor. Mrs does my darning to save Matilda trouble putting my socks down the incinerator. To go essence of feet. Up the chimney.

A record established. Bonniface working for two whole minutes behind the counter. Pulling open a drawer. Another one, rustling in the paper. Just like Miss Martin does to show she's on the job. Whoops. There he goes again. Ah. He stops. Smiles at me. Gives my invitation a wave, as he streaks to the end of the counter. Under. Across the corridor. Into the gents. Must tell him, I go. Hither. Away from wind socks, control towers, loudspeakers, and beams scanning skies. And madness on the tarmac.

Smith leaving the pillar. Threading a way through the

advancing ceaseless mob. Side stepping a business tycoon standing in his tracks making an assured decision formulating future profits. Makes one homesick for Dynamo. Relive the thrill of that deportment. When they make the counter offer, smile thanks and regret one must repair to the country where it will receive constant thought till one's return to town when the price will be double, sorry gentlemen. Why you. And next week, triple.

Smith blowing nose. Frighten away nervousness. Push through the black swing door of this gents. A narrow long corridor. Neat row of piss basins at the end. No gentleman would take water from a conduit pipe. Please, a porcelain pitcher poured into a wide basin of same on the marble washstand. Joy of rinse, of towel. As Her Majesty washed, nose a symphony of flared nostril held haughtily with a delightful bone to a soft tip she often pressed upon my eager ear.

And here wash bowls, towels automatic out of machines. Do not pull twice in one minute. I beg your pardon. To such impertinence in the gents. And this square tall room where Bonniface does not seem to be standing. With his usual luminosity. By the hairoil squirter. Press. Personal pomade. Two squirts for the more particular. Prevent hair raising at the next business conference. Never to call a board meeting again. Or sadly sit in the chairman's chair. Faces of destiny flanking down the mahogany. Odd cough and sneeze. Gentlemen please don't be too scared to make a suggestion. I'm listening. Pass the water. Has no one something to say. A scribble or gesture at least. Just so Miss Martin can shorthand some minutes. I want contribution from your minds. To cheer the single shareholder in his loneliness in carting all the profits away to his bereft, unloved vault, without bravos or handclap. Gentlemen, sorry, directors' fees this year will be in the form of free tuition at the School of Higher Graduation, for the diploma of Satisfaction On Lower Income. Bonniface has already graduated, ghosty and gone. To other confusions. Worry kills quickly in a sober crystal mind.

Smith looking at the small holes in the ventilators along the ceiling of the lavatory. Two oblong windows of a variety of glass impossible to float through. As well as bars on the outside. Over there. Nine booths. Three in use. What a pass to be viewing legs engaged in a function which clashes with my spiritual mood of the moment. No shanks of white legged underwear. In one of these he sounded the horn. Lone call back over yester year. As he sat, master, pink white and black amid the horsey cavalcade. Baying chiming hounds, high fat tails wagging. Who blames him for sounding loud and clear in some distant cubicle. To call back the splendid country grass down the vale. Garlic lightly in the air. Bonniface leading the mounted contingent. Her Majesty laughing, as he got them, hounds and all, regrettably lost in gorse. All however right later that night at the randy roundup. The memorable farmyard antics at the hunt ball.

Smith standing dumbfounded in this latrine. Two gentlemen giving him the suspicious eye. A squat person winking and leaving his fly unmentionably open. Stay here and be detained maybe for attempted tinkering. Some sneaky reaching for my particulars. This is what I get when I answer a summons of a last twitching. Bonniface, the mirage at the log cabin window, rendering song on comb and paper. Been haunted enough. Saw you come in here. Wearing my warm coat. Miss Tomson will think I rented it just long enough to go with the car to meet her on the street corner. Instead of its disappearing on a spook.

Smith taking one last bewildered look. Feel thin, cold and banshee out this long hall. Eyes deceived. Too many months of irregular correspondence. Tripping into walls. Down open sewers. Last only a few seconds with the rats. Should never have come. Could be near Miss Tomson instead of lurking coatless in a latrine. With youth replaced with cunning. Age replaced by worms. Worms replaced with birds. And they go shitting out of a tree on my white linen suit in the summertime.

At the end of the hall. Set in the grey wall a door. Just

inside the entrance of the latrine. Says private. Who knows. For mops. For first feels. Like I got from Miss Martin. Open it. In memory of a foot in past pails. Turn the nice smooth round knob. It will click open if not locked. Tug. My Gawd.

Squeezed and crouched. Former master of hunt, hounds and urinary horror. Bonniface. With coat open, two hands held high above his head. Gripping the gallon basket of wine. Turning with a gasp to Smith letting in the light of the outer world. Wine cascading from the bottle aloft. Shower over his head. Unstoppered by his mouth. Pouring upon his person. Unholy red down the white underwear. Drip drop from the sable. Bonniface attempts to bark. Choking under the flow. Hair flattened, full of wine. Struggling to get the bottle down. But blocked by the long handle of a waxing machine.

Cedric Clementine. One afternoon in autumn proud. Pink upon his pale horse. Boots and saddle gleaming. Waiting for the fox to be roused. No hound shall fault in sheep. One capital day of sport through bottoms and spinney. Across frost, furze and fog. From the gravel apron of Laughington Castle. Instead of here, deluged in wine. Employed and mortified. Full grown foundling. Unpromoted and sad.

> Hello
> Little someone
> Anywhere
> Dark and cold.

22

The dreadnaught approaching the web of cables holding the bridge across the water with great black girders and trestles. Ropes of steel all tight and cold. Smith slumped asleep, waking to see the lights ahead. Burning little brains in the buildings. Get to the grave with as many comforts as possible.

'Is there something wrong, Mr Smith.'

'I'm all right Herbert.'

'Don't mind me, Mr Smith, I just couldn't help noticing through the mirror. If you don't want to talk or anything it's all right.'

'I was thinking Herbert, all the engine birds and wheels. Roll roll.'

'You look tired, Mr Smith. Maybe if you're not doing nothing, you might kinda like to come home with me and have a meal. Plenty for everybody. You know, if you're not doing anything.'

'Thank you.'

'Wife's always glad to see you. Says she gets a real kick out of some of your remarks. Steak and kidney, I know it's your favourite.'

Smith slunk deeply in the kindly leather. World goes by so grey on these streets. Man stumbling against a wall in tatters. Grey smile, and silver hair. Newspaper wrapped around a shin. Luckier than poor old Bonniface drenched red in his underwear. Bought him a dozen hankies with a blue letter C from the gift counter to mop up. I offered him cash and he asked for understanding. And a long loan of the sable.

Granite pillars above the wide steps. In there they ad-

minister justice. Only takes a minute to attach the electrodes. Just pop one here on the top of the head, couple
little straps around the arms and legs. Dynamo House sadly
named.

'Where to, Mr Smith.'

'Left around the park. And down Golden Avenue.'

'This is where the money was flying round.'

'I remember.'

'Human nature had an outlet that day, huh, Mr Smith.
Offer about the meal stands. No trouble.'

'Thanks Herbert. Miss Tomson's holding a party later.'

'O sure. You want a rain check.'

'A rain check.'

'Don't mind me saying, Mr Smith, but she's some girl.
And funny, a real nice person. Real nice. You know.'

'Yes.'

'Where you want me to stop.'

'The big building, Hotel on the right. That'll be all for
tonight.'

'This is the Excelsior.'

'Yes.'

'Sure you're all right, Mr Smith. You know you look very
very tired.'

'I'm fine, Herbert. Fine. Airport was a little hectic. Mr
Clementine rather takes life lightly. I suppose I'm of the
dour outlook.'

'You're not dour. Hey look, what about your coat. You
want the bag, paper bag. The cane.'

'Mr Clementine was a little short on garments this
evening.'

'You take this, now Mr Smith.'

'No, no, Herbert. I couldn't possibly.'

'I insist. I really do. I don't like the way you look
at all. So you're going to take this, whether you like it or
not.'

'O.K. Take my stick too never know when it comes in
handy.'

'Might be a little big around the shoulders that's all.'

'Herbert will you keep this paper bag in the trunk and lock it.'

'Sure.'

Smith stood on the kerb. In Herbert's dark overcoat. Coming to attention with a smile and wave to Herbert taking the dreadnaught to its deathy garage. Go back then to his wife and nice little home. Full of kitchen smells, of spice and pretty woman. Ah God. Any more of this and I'll fold up and dissolve on this pavement. Lean on the apple branch. Guess I just want someone to come out of somewhere, reach my ear. Whisper in. George. O George. You're good looking, trustworthy and kind. And mysteriously exciting. Here's my life, love. Let's waltz the rest of the road together, to get wrinkled and grey. May our distinction and flamboyance be mature.

The lobby of The Excelsior. Faint smiles upon some faces. Mr Park at the ball room door. A wave. A grin. Like some little hometown coming. Need a haircut. Cheap quick trip into the Barber College. Get trimmed by an undergraduate. The evening bristles mowed down. Otherwise I feel terrible. Brave Bonniface of the strange strength. They drag him down by the heels. He makes a pulley arrangement on the other side to go whizzing up again. Footpoundals ablaze. Hang on by fingertips George. Hang on. Shore up. Company Sixty Two. Deploy left flank. Howitzer the fuckers. Command gone to pieces. Under six months constant shelling. And candied parsnips for chow. Must make it to the elevator as if nothing is the matter with me.

Elevator boy sizing up Smith. That's true sonny, the coat doesn't fit me. Her Majesty's door, grey gleaming gun metal. Printed right across my eyes. See a mirage. Dear Sir, we invite you to dance with joy, before we make you hobble with affliction. Yours very truly. The Hoods. Gentlemen, vouchsafe a dance to the tune of the fandango. Open up, Your Majesty. Let me fall in.

'O. Is it.'

'George Smith.'

'We've met. On the phone. I'm Lettia Calvin. Do please

come in. Her Highness is dressing. May I get you a drink.'

'I would cherish a glass of beer.'

'Of course.'

Miss Calvin. I cannot imagine a connexion with a certain Cedric. Lady in waiting, blue lilacs in her hair. Where have all the kings gone. I would be their friend. Her Majesty is such a pleasant queen. Made a country out of this room. I'm her footpig. Reach for this beer with a trembling hand. Forty thousand people agreed to get together to whip out the carpet where I stand. My golden invitation. On the mantel. Must arrange the menu for Thistle Pot. Tureens of giblets supreme. The fried egg miraculous little sinking suns on the sideboard. And the speciality of chopped livers for the Bonniface. The end is near, when you want it far away. Kids kick all premonitions out of one's head. And then, silence. Death rears. Who dat ahead. What dat up dere. Matilda said God was nervous. Because he's black. And so much white trash elbowing into heaven.

'George, my God.'

'How do.'

'You're white.'

'Of course.'

'But terribly white, George.'

'I'm fine.'

'Let me feel.'

'O God.'

'Don't crack George. No fever. You're going to be all right.'

'I'm not. Your Majesty, the airport is too harsh for Bonniface. Employment too much. But what can I do.'

'Give him a private income.'

'Your Majesty let me water your plants before they die at this altitude.'

'Don't you dare pee on my terrace.'

Smith deeply reclining in the feather crimson softness. Her Majesty standing room centre. Light glinting on her hair. Laugh lingering around her eyes. Each deft line little magic wings to make her face a wreath to lay upon my mind when I die. Slip down under the waves. Why all the ash flinging. Bonniface at his wedding. Miss Tomson at hers. Never imagine her wagging up the aisle in white. Terrible moments asleep coming back from airport, dreamt she married in black amid black lilies on the altar of the church. In a musky summertime. Her blue eyed face, her blonde hair tied up. She threw the black flowers to me. In the third row. Said catch Smith, hold them for me while I'm busy dying with this guy. From this summer wedding.

> Dark cloud
> Came
> And fell
> Black snow.

'Shall we go, George. Shall I call down for a car.'
'Take you by horse cab. Where is the Baron Mumchance.'
'He's become a bartender who occasionally mixes me free drinks.'
'O my God the decline.'
Two strange specimens passing out the lobby of The Excelsior. Her Majesty wrapped in a python stole. Two little glittering eyes in the fur at her neck and twined round to a tail trailing from her own. An attic heirloom she felt like bringing to life again. So easy to worship her. Eyes full of all her escapes from tragedy. A heart sad, worn, and splendid. Whispered to George he was incorrigible as he slipped the doorman a valueless foreign coin. An inspiration to begin a collection.
A taxi to the horse cab rank. Where the man said it's you again. Memory for faces. Snap of the whip. Away. Through the cars. Lake edged with ice. And a skating rink flooded with light. All the windows up there where they trim the toenails, lacquer the lips and look down to the terrible doings in the park. In my dream Miss Tomson asked me to the summer place of the man she married. To make music with my trembling organ. Said Smith Smith, soon soon, I'll dump this guy. Then all the black lilies I threw you at the wedding. Bring them, I'll wear them over

me and take them off one by one. And I asked her meanwhile. To come to the sale of damaged hearts. Such good value. Buy me.

Clop clop. Smith's face at the window of the horsecab. Watching the evening marauders trouncing deviate victims. A little group there. Seven. They turn to jeer. Get a space of distance between us. Give them this gesture. Little insulting shits. Jesus Christ they're running to catch us up. Me and the Queen.

'What's the matter, George.'

'The kids, they're chasing us.'

'George, if this is some more of your mayhem.'

Smith looking out through the glass. A nimble double jointed midget ahead of the others, catching up. Whoa. One foot nearly up on the step. Incredible. Just a tiny gesture. And they're after you. Good o driver, hit him with the whip.

Kid ducking. Horses nervously meandering. Part of the gang branching off, taking a short cut through the woods. May stop to beat up some people on the way. This little incident is growing by leaps and bounds.

Smith holding the door closed. Kid tugging to pull it open. Smith suddenly letting go. Door flying wide. George's hand snaking out closing on the kid's collar whipping him right into the carriage just as his knees were bouncing on the road.

'Sonny, one peep and you're dead.'

'Don't kill me Mister.'

'Get on the floor.'

'Anything you say, Mister.'

'The point in your back is the business end of a small blunderbuss also known as a musketoon from an early century with which you may not be acquainted but it will blow your fucking backbone out if you so much as sneeze.'

'I didn't do nothing mister. I got a sister studying to be a nun and you're cursing in front of a lady.'

'George, please, he's only a child.'

'Shut up, while I'm in command, this kid's got to learn a lesson.'

'Mister you want to do a deal.'

'Shut up, I'll tell you when to talk.'

Remaining horde losing ground. Four of them wearing that look of we'll get even. A traffic light red ahead. Gang getting a new impetus. Increasing their efforts. While we stand stopped. Such darkness in the trees on all sides. Drag you in there to deliver the stilettos. This walking stick has come in for a lot of little uses. Throughout one's carefree cafuffles. Her Majesty ashen faced, tight lipped in an aloof huff. They're gaining, bobbing heads passing under the street lamp. Driver, onward.

Horse cabbie in a paroxysm of sweaty fear. Gang of six within ten yards. Light turns yellow. My God caution. Green, thank God, go. Five yards. We're moving. This kid's got some white eyeballs looking up from the floor.

'Kid, if you want to save your life, do as I say. Your gang is trying to cut us off. If they succeed you probably will not live. But there's one chance. When I give you a poke in the back with this blunderbuss like this.'

'Ouch.'

'You scream at the top of your lungs that unless they lay off, you get your backbone sent through the bottom of this horse buggy.'

'Mister give me a chance, I promise just to do like you say.'

'I say there George I will not tolerate this any longer.'

'Your Majesty do you want to have your brains beaten out.'

'Mere over spirited boys.'

'Each with a homemade cannon. These kids could play havoc with a platoon with tactical pieces of armour.'

'You exaggerate, George.'

'No he doesn't lady that's right we could clean up an army outfit.'

'Shut up, you.'

'Mister I was only telling her.'

'Save your breath. Or it may be your last.'

'Mister you're talking like some kind of cowboy.'

'Never mind my western experience.'

'George such a mountain out of a molehill.'

'Under which, Your Majesty, I have no intention to lie. Dead in this park.'

'Hey mister, please don't hit me but is the lady some kind of Majesty.'

'She's Her Royal Highness, Queen Evangiline.'

'No kidding mister, a real Queen. Queen can I just touch you, the guys in the gang would be glad you was a Queen.'

'Of course sonny. You can touch me.'

'Move one finger kid and I'll kill you.'

'George I've had enough. Let this poor boy out. What's he done to you. Let him touch me.'

'In a minute his friends will be out blocking the road ahead of us. This driver trying to string out the distance, is taking us around the long leg of a triangle.'

'You're such a cheapskate George. I saw you slip the doorman that questionable coin. You're rich.'

'You'll have these kids asking for ransom.'

'Hey mister what kind of people are you I never even seen people like you in the movies.'

'You impertinent little pup, for the last time keep, I said —'

'Ouch mister.'

'Keep your mouth shut. I knew it. There's the gang ahead on the road. Driver, you up there, pull up at the group of boys.'

'I will like hell, mister you think I want my cab wrecked, what do you take me for.'

'They'll panic the horses you thick idiot. I've got this kid as a hostage. Pull up.'

Driver laying the lash of the whip on the horses' backsides. Two of the kids with flying leaps catching the reins and hanging on. Horses rearing, nearly plunging back in their traces. Honk of horns. Traffic swerving. George with blunderbuss pressed hard against the backbone of the kid.

Hoof sparks on the road. Driver shouting regrettable language. Lashing out with his whip. Taking a more moderate look at the situation when they announce.

'We just want that guy and the member of the gang inside.'

'O my God George, they mean business.'

'I told you Queenie. O.K. kid, tell them what the score is. For them to stand back or else you get a blast in the backbone. Go ahead.'

'Guys, he's got a gun in my back don't do nothing.'

'Now tell them to stand back off the road.'

'Hey guys there's a real Queen in here, a real Queen, leave her alone. But get the guy it's no gun he's got but just an ordinary cane, I saw it.'

Smith with a swift motion catching the kid by the hair and raising him to the window. Encircling his neck with an arm and compressing it to a sudden strand of shoe string, mouth open, tongue out, eyes popping.

'The first one of you to touch this carriage and I break his neck.'

Across the spidery tree tops the sound of a siren. Gang gesturing to the half strangled speechless kid. George Smith's calm hard eyes. The driver relaxing waiting for his male passenger to be dragged out and kicked to death in the short bushes. A small gurgling noise coming out of the hostage's throat. The gang wide eyed, yelling at the steamy glass window.

'Hey mister you're killing him, he's choking can't you see.'

'Step back or I snap his head off. Back further.'

'You better let him go mister, we'll get you.'

'Driver move on. One of you takes a step after this cab and I throw him out dead.'

Gang leader holding up a staying hand. Faces peering out of the quickly passing cars to view the parkland spectacle. While running up their windows and locking their doors. A population to which you could appeal for help. If you wanted to share your money.

Clip clop. Forging on. Smith releasing the kid's neck. Her Majesty leaning over him as he collapsed gasping in a heap. A flash of lamplight striking his face. A choir boy. For a moment. Law of averages have failed to prevent one disaster following another. Smart kid, with the right idea. Call the bluff always, because if the other guy's got the gun you won't live anyway. Her Majesty silent. Constricted in her fur. George out the window to the driver.

'Slow down. I'm dumping this kid out.'

'Bring him to the police.'

'Slow down. Wretch.'

'Hey mister what's wrong with you bring the kid to the police.'

'I said slow down.'

'It's my cab mister, dump the kid at the precinct.'

'See this stick, you want it wrapped around your neck.'

'Look mister, don't get hot under the collar, I'm slowing down.'

'O.K. kid, I'm kicking you out. But I'll be in this park every night till I track you and the gang down and strangle each one of you, so enjoy life till then.'

'Mister ain't you got no mercy.'

'Just for myself sonny.'

'This is a jungle, just what I told my sister who wants to be a nun, kind of people around like you don't understand human decency.'

Smith's foot pushing. Boy leaping. Landing on a bridle path. Standing up to make a rude gesture at Smith as he waved good-bye. Clip clop. Strings of light and flashing beams across the trunks of trees. Along by a lawn and the vacant back of the museum.

Smith paying off the horsecab. No safe way to travel. Cross this road to that coffee shop. Full of fluffy haired debutante girls. Buy Her Majesty a box of cheeroots. And get into this phone booth. Little clicks, tiny beeps. A bell.

'Herbert rescue me.'

'Why sure, Mr Smith. Where are you.'

'By the entrance to the Art Museum in the park. I've just

had a rather unfortunate canter in a buggy through The Ramble, should be renamed.'

'I'll be right there. Maybe take me nine minutes. I'll use the siren.'

Her Majesty so white and diminutive. Chilled, wrapping her arms round herself. Bonniface cruelly said of our relationship. She was robbing the cradle as I was robbing the grave. Look up under the great portico of the museum. Pigeons huddling in there, cooing in the shadows. One couldn't help finding the little rough neck charming. And ideal business partner.

'George, can't we wait in the coffee shop instead of the cold.'

'Evangiline. Your pomp and my circumstance, why don't we live together far from mayhem, up there in the contemporary sky.'

'Are you proposing.'

'Yes. Bonniface best man. Baron Mumchance usher. The Excelsior a refuge.'

'I'll tell you later.'

'Yes Ma'am.'

Siren up the avenue. Approaching. Smith smiling. Gives one the inner sense of running everything. Boss. Big wheel. Sitting back in safety. Glad to see you Herbert. With the vehicle. Seems only a minute ago I stood in front of Miss Martin's one man firing squad. Sure enough she shot me. My Prep School diploma reframed. Everything coming together. Old friends. Reception at Renown. Will bring a new letter from Shirl's lawyer. Tie him in one more legal knot. Help Her Majesty into the car. She's gone all silent. Maybe Mr Park has tried something funny. Off duty.

'Stop at Merry Mansions, Herbert. I've got to change.'

'Siren, Mr Smith.'

'Please.'

Dreadnaught singing out its wailing tune. Pedestrians turn heads. Cars stop. Guilt spreads everywhere. Had I run Bonniface to the airport with it blaring he would have refused forever to leave that hilarious safety.

'George.'

'Your Majesty, you think I'm overdoing it.'

'You're a dreamer.'

'You'll forgive me for peeing off your terrace.'

Crosstown streets. Between darkened stone houses, brown, grey, the tops lit like skulls. Dreadnaught's tiny green light glowing on the black roof above the windscreen. Stands at the moment for go. And disturbing the peace. Police always salute. Think I'm the chief. Chief thinks I'm the commissioner. Commissioner thinks I'm the Mayor. Mayor thinks I'm the governor. That's how God was made. Head of heaven.

'George, will you have a butterscotch. Will Herbert.'

'Thanks Ma'am.'

'Herbert, butterscotch.'

'No thanks, Mr Smith.'

We are so pleasant sucking the sweet. Twice escaped near certain death. Miss Tomson. That's why must ask you. A little message. Can't we lie quietly in each other's arms. My pole against your arse. Whispering against the back of your ear. No. Not The Goose Goes Inn. Or. Like to get you right there. No. Just Miss Tomson, Sally. Together. What can be more than that. Until I die. For if a whisper means anything. If it means you'll hear it. Believe it. Be like my first little girl friend when they twisted her arm. Made her tiny note drop to the floor. Followed by her tears. When they made fun of her. And I loved her ever since.

> Guess now
> Comes
> All winter sky
> Purple pink and sad
> Crossed
> By tree twigs
> Waving mad.

23

'Gee Smithy, glad you came. Take your coat.'

'Nearly didn't get. Got attacked by kids in the park.'

'You're kidding.'

'Sally Tomson. Evangiline Voninnocent.'

'Hi.'

'How do you do.'

'Evangiline will vouch.'

'That's O.K. Smithy. I believe, little kids are always trying to beat you up.'

'Alas.'

'Now come meet everybody. My fiancé. There he is. Gee I'm glad you came. I was just thinking the second before the door slid open, where's the missing link. And you look so smart. You rent that.'

'Sally, not so loud.'

'Claude here he is. The one and only. I'll miss out the first eight initials. Claude H D N. And it's Van in, gee.'

'Voninnocent, Sally. Evangiline.'

'Gee, see. Well I know you're George Smith. Sorry Evangiline.'

'Not at all.'

'How do you do.'

'Hello.'

'Glad you could come Mr Smith. Sally talks about you. Quite a lot.'

'Gee this is tense, isn't it. Let's break up. Claude you take Evangiline and introduce her. I'll take this cookee.'

'Sally you're drinking.'

'Smithy, I am not. Hey I am. Here, you too, best bubbling wine. How do you like it. The place.'

'Little breathtaking.'

'It's something isn't it.'

'Where does the staircase go.'

'Up. Two more crazy floors on top of this. And there's one room you're going to like. I always think of you when I'm in it. Don't get any ideas I'm not paying my way. I mean at least part. This is my place. I want you to like it, I really mean it. Come on. Take a drink. You don't want to meet people.'

'O.K.'

'Isn't this nice, this staircase. Goes round. All the way up. I drop golf balls from the top. Like a crazy roulette. See which one of the stairs it bounces back up on. O Smithy.'

'Sally.'

'Smithy.'

'Gee let's run up the stairs. Hold my hand. Bedroom's this floor. Another little library. And a crapper there too. What I always wanted. Books and a crapper side by side. Isn't that a crazy little table. There. I polish it every day. Put the fresh dog flower there. Still got yours. Pressed it in a book, how to succeed in business or something like that, so it would sort of help you along. Now. In here. How do you like it.'

'Miss Tomson.'

'Isn't it something.'

'An altar.'

'Yesh.'

'I don't know what to say, Miss Tomson.'

'I play organ music. Burn incense. And I sit in there. Have the delicatessen bring me around smoked salmon, potato salad, olives and maybe ham. On rye bread.'

Smith standing in the gloam. On the last step down into this high ceilinged room. An altar set with tabernacle. Candles flickering. Reflecting on Smith's shimmering lapels. Miss Tomson's dress floating out from her hips and narrow waist. An emerald set in silver above her milky white breasts. Her long slightly helpless arms.

307

'Come down, Smithy. Here. You light one. I'll light one. Put them here together.'

Smith lighting his candle. And lighting Miss Tomson's. Pressing the white wax on the brass spike. Oriental carpet. Tapestries under the high window. Strange blue black glass on the sky. Miss Tomson's sedan chair of glistening hide. Where she sits listening and chewing. Two new flames. Goldminers naked holding hands in front of theirs. Ask Sally. Can we kneel. Clothingless. But all the people, her friends, a distant swell of voices.

'We're going to be married in here. Sort of special ceremony after the church. O gee. I didn't want to be like this. You like me, don't you.'

'I do.'

'Gosh, I know. I like you. Smithy it's your eyes. I don't know. I don't want to cut you out of my life. The part you were playing was swell.'

'And small.'

'Come on. It's important. But a guy, when you love him and you're his. Well like a rag doll. You get thrown in the corner when they're finished with you.'

'I wouldn't throw you in the corner.'

'Smithy, Jesus. That's what I'm thinking. O shit, that's what I'm thinking. Sorry about the language.'

'That's all right.'

'Just to avoid getting shunted by guys. I got a career. Wanted my freedom. I only got these looks for so long, I guess, to drive guys crazy. Aren't our flames nice there. Wish my body was big enough I could spread it around and you could have it too. Like could send it over to you when you needed it. You look sweet. Right now. Funny, you're always hanging around in my mind, in your crazy old clothes. With your quaint little problems. Glad you brought your mother with you.'

'That's cruel.'

'Who is she.'

'A very old friend.'

'She's pretty impressive, I'm only kidding about the age,

she's pretty beautiful too. I'm jealous. Never seen you in evening clothes before. It's a revelation.'

'Why do you sigh like that.'

'I don't know Smithy. I throw guys over because they try to own me. I never threw you over. And gee, your invitation. There it is, resting here on the altar. It's great. Ha ha, I'm dying to get there.'

'You're shivering. Miss Tomson.'

'Yesh. Funniest thing. Keep thinking I'm carrying black lilies up the aisle.'

Miss Tomson raising one eye brow. One smiling eye in her head. The other so sad. Looking slowly down Smith's elegance. Stopping at his fly and smiling. Smith laying a modest hand across.

'Miss Tomson, really.'

'Gee Smithy, it's right there. Wow, I better turn on some music.'

Tomson turning knobs. A control panel under a shelf of books. Faint drums and horns. She's so beautiful. Lights up the darkness of the room. Can I tell her. Save her. Say, Sally let me spill my blood. A bit. For you. So scared all those weeks you weren't there. That I was too small time. Too much of nothing and you were everything. With all the people you knew. My mangy little office. Horsehair sofa. A bath running rusty water. You lived so high up, it was a long way to reach you. Each time I phoned it rang in the distance. And I'd hear a ship's horn trumpeting in the river. Boop. Boop. I thought of the deep deep water and maybe you had gone away altogether. Then I got hard. Wished I was famous, wished I was the centre of attraction with friends calling, going in and out of my life. And I said, and shouted, you were cheap and sham. Worth nothing, just a climbing bitch, sticking heels in faces. You are. Because you must. Do what you're doing. I'm married in all my chains. That in a big world, where we touched hands. Whispered. Told each other tiny sorrows. It's all there is. Can't ask for more. Because there is no more. Only a moment of feeling skin, your heart under your breasts, and screaming

in your car as you grabbed me by the simple arse. That was
it.

'Sally, I don't want to lose you.'

'O.'

'I don't.'

'Gee.'

'I don't want to lose you.'

'I know.'

'You won't let me lose you.'

'Smithy.'

'I want to tell you.'

'O.K.'

'That if I lose you I have nothing left.'

'You do.'

'I don't.'

'You do.'

'I could buy you.'

'Could you.'

'Yes.'

'Gee.'

'Can't give you a contract. But could give you laughs.'

'Smithy, ha ha, yesh, you give me a chuckle, true.'

'And it wouldn't be enough, would it.'

'You're the most surprising guy. You don't know how
close I'm to saying, yesh it's enough. Maybe I could fit you
in in the afternoons.'

'Would you.'

'I don't want to lose you Smithy. I don't. I can't two time,
I just can't. I'm funny people. I don't love this guy. But if
I'm honest I'm not really taking him for his money either.
Gee. Hear that. Boat in the river. Funny time to blow such
a sad tune. Left all my guests. I don't care. For a minute
anyway. Don't ebb. Jesus don't ebb.'

'I will.'

'I grew the hair under my arms. Just for you, because I
knew you liked it. Not much I guess to do, to show affection.
It nearly ruined my career.'

'How did you know I liked that.'

'I'm not telling you.'

'You never told me there is a real Al Maygrain Diltor something.'

'Gee, didn't I say he was a real guy.'

'No.'

'O. I know him.'

'He sent me an invitation, Sally.'

'I know. Don't ask me, it's a laugh.'

Smith's head upon Tomson's soft bosom, ear against her breast, hard corner of a jewel. Her hand reaching in his hair. The beautiful danger of letting her nails near my eyes. As they touch, could claw. Lay the fingertips gently. Gently they lay.

'I want you, Smithy to stay in my life. I do. We're like two little kids standing here.'

Swaying softly held together. Strains of a highland march. Buy her. Get what. But if you don't fight. If you don't go smashing in upon her heart and grab it in both hands, hold it tightly, make it squirm under the crushing fingers. Got to do that.

'I'll buy you.'

'Smith what can you offer me. You'd give me money.'

'Miss Tomson we're two wretched folk.'

'You see Smithy, the price is so high. I want a father on tap for my kids. To play with them on the rug with trains. If you were giving me money. I mean, gee it would be miserable for you having to part with all the cash I would need. This is terrible talk. Between us. Because suddenly I'm not kidding. Maybe it's all because you haven't got brown eyes.'

'I have the lonely green variety.'

'O Smithy. Gee.'

'Miss T.'

'Mr S.'

'Can you hear that sound, Miss T.'

'No.'

'It's me. Tip toeing.'

'Where you going, you tip toeing.'

'Out of your life.'

'O no. Gee I sort of yelled didn't I.'

'You did.'

'We better go down.'

Tomson holding Smith's hand tightly. Stepping up the steps out of this temple room. To put an arm around, squeeze you ever so gently. I know that when I tip toe and go. You wanted me to stay. And so, when I go, it won't be as cold. A warmth I can wear. Your fingernails leave. Last thing of all. My steel heart snaps shut. Never open again. Painful asking what are you doing tomorrow. Sally, where are you today. Tyrant tide. Comes up to cover us. And you're tall. Golden gypsy. Running way up into the sky. Laughing and dry.

> The sweet heart
> In the lily
> All black
> Or white
> Like snow.

24

The square high vast room. Two a.m. More arrivals. Throats
of pearl. Wrists of diamonds. Hearts of. Who knows. I'm
throwing no pebbles. With vaults of bullion. And followed
Miss Tomson down her spiral staircase back into the
crowded voices. Hands reach out for Sally.

Slip away now behind her back because I feel a stranger.
To hide. From people together like this. They see me. My
myth gets shaken and shattered. Lift a morsel from this
passing tray. Thank you. No spiders anywhere. My God
Her Majesty is popular. No one coming to my little corner
to ask me who I am. Who are you. I yam der yingle
humperdink. Vas ist das. Nooding.

Winter air in the door from the terrace. Blazing logs
under the head high marble mantel. And a portrait of
Sally. Holding Goliath on lead, top a windswept bluff. Milk-
weed and stormy bright spring flowers. Poor Merry Mansions just hasn't got what it takes. Too late to buy the top
tip of a building. Rent some cheap space under the water
tank.

Smith near a doorway. Dark serving girl taking and
hanging coats. Miss T took mine. Never even asked where
the sable went. Or come back to talk to me. Don't go down.
And as I went into Merry tonight, with Her Majesty. Hugo.
Came snapping to attention. Saluting Queen Evangiline.
Bowing, kissing her hand. As I nearly fell through the glass
door. To find. I had to draw her by the elbow away. Out of
her animated foreign conversation. Unearthing Matilda,
who thank God, thought Her Majesty worthy of an instant
invitation to The Tabernacle Of The Dark Complexioned
Redeemer. And I asked her point blank. What's this with

Hugo. How I stumbled once drunk into Merry. Handing out commands. As one does when fried. In the eye of Hugo as I barked a few parade ground manoeuvres. I saw that burning fleck of obedience. The soldier's eye. Would follow me in revolution. Your Majesty, who is he. George, heavens. A former officer of my household cavalry. When I had a household, when I had a cavalry. I took a handful of the royal backside. To giggles. When she was a girl.

Two black shoe toes appearing beneath Smith's downcast eyes. And standing astride apart, the champagne in my hand just between.

'Who are you a friend of. Friend.'

'I beg your pardon.'

'You ever had a picture in the paper. Maybe a magazine. You're familiar.'

Face leaning in over Smith's sparkling glass. Temperature up one's rear always runs one degree higher. Short hair sticking up on a head out of a blue suit. Rises up on the toes. Down on heels. Legs spread. Rocking back and forth.

'I like to observe when others are not aware. You appear to me a guy who doesn't let a party waste time. By the way, it's Ralph.'

'I see.'

'You.'

'Smith's the name.'

'Hey not George.'

'No perhaps not.'

'Hey, it's George. Sure. Glad I jumped to a conclusion. I mean here, have a canapé. This is indicative. You stand in one spot and don't move. That's what I would have thought you would have done. You want to know by what route I was led here.'

'What route.'

'There she is. I thought she's got class. Right. Right. The mature woman. Of beauty. Hey I witness no rings on your fingers.'

'No.'

'Strange. So O.K. I go up to this personage. Sure. Let's

admit. It figures a personage. Sally doesn't kid around. As who can afford to. So I says, same approach, note, who are you a friend of. Then in the most beautiful voice, like yours maybe, she says. I'm sweet. Hey. I'm telling you. Said I was sweet. I mean she could have said push off, crumb. I mean, right. Right.'

'Yes.'

'Well. I'm smiling. Naturally, I'm thinking wow. This dame. Maybe she's forty but you don't care, eighty, who cares. Standing right there she's thirty one. In any he man's language. Course I told you, my name's Ralph.'

'Yes.'

'Then she just waves her hand. See. Like this. Here's this whole room. But the way she did it, that hand waves right to you. She said, there's my friend. Man, I said, here are real beautiful people. Quality people. Well for Christ's sake, you're George Smith. See. How could I imagine. I mean, just what I would imagine. Well well. Here. Pour you a drink.'

'Thanks.'

'I'm out of words. For a second. And you just staring down at the floor. Come on. Who did you just sell up the river. Let's be frank. I mean I don't mind telling a guy like you the lousy things I did. You know Sally gave me a shot one night, for just what I said to you. Her brother's a friend of mine. It's amazing.'

'What's amazing.'

'You would hit a cripple into the tracks. So who knows two sides to every story. Some of the biggest operators in this town are here. You wonder how they make their money. I mean, that's just a reflection in passing. See the hairy guy, that's Al. He's a no fooling guy. You ever heard of Jiffy. Got a lot of interests, maybe even gravel pits. Another no fooling guy. I mean now, Sally could have got me up to his place. I tell you. Like a real castle. His wife is bald. O you knew that.'

'No.'

'He's insane about Sally. O you knew that too.'

'No.'

'He shot her dog.'

'I know that.'

'Hey prize. You knew that. A canapé. Caviare. You don't mind I call you George. I mean someone with your accent might not like it, first names just like that. You see I know.'

'George is all right.'

'OK George, here's the caviare. You know this is a great moment in my life to meet you. No kidding. And boy I'm impressed, everybody throws dough around to make themselves look good living. So what refreshment, a guy. Who wants to look good dead. Right.'

'Perhaps.'

'I've seen it. Your mortuary. Went up there night after I read the mention. It's swell. Now what do you do.'

'What do you mean.'

'Why you send me an invitation to the bust out.'

'I beg your pardon.'

'Hey. The memorial opening. Like decorations won't be worn. Some touch that is. Decorations. So I don't have any.'

'Pity.'

'Shake. I feel you're a real friend of Sally's. She hates my guts. Thinks I ruined her brother's career. I sweated my ass for him. I nearly had to come in the service entrance to-night, that girl's ruthless. I mean I don't mean she's not nice. She's just God damn ruthless. Do you know, in the garage of this building, three hand made cars, the kind you get a flat and have to send it back to the factory. Hey, just off the record. You packing anything.'

'I beg your pardon.'

'A rod. You know. Bang bang. Rumours around, you travel under armour. Just thought I saw a bulge under the jacket. I mean, none of my business.'

'Perhaps not.'

'A sharp eye. You know, I really admire you. It's engraved ivory. The handle. You shouldn't lean over like that. Doesn't it make you sad.'

'What.'

'Guys blasting. When they could argue insults. So what's words, if maybe you said the wrong thing the first time. I mean look at me. I'm nervous now, you got me nervous. I said things. Look forget what I said. You're a swell guy. I mean. Just wish I didn't see the gun. That's all.'

'You didn't see it.'

'You're right. So right. I'm blind.'

'What's your earning power.'

'Mr Smith I'm glad you asked me that question. Really, I am. It's just I don't want to damage our friendship by mentioning it with a figure right now. I could give you my job history.'

'Shoot.'

'Don't say that word. But listen. You're ruthless.'

'I yam der yingle humperdink.'

'What's that lingo. Why don't you talk. Could we do a deal. I mean you could have the upper hand.'

'No.'

'You think I'm the human condition at its lowest.'

'Yes.'

'Can I pick up the telephone and call you sometime.'

'No.'

Sally Tomson across the room. Lifting her chin. A flat final line of her lips as she stepped from group to group. Four cars below. Handmade. Nudge me under the tennis balls, Sally. Kiss your flowering parts. World's so big. All in one room. High above the streets over a staggering stack of humanity sound asleep.

Ralph with his hair plastered down. Cruising elsewhere. Smith letting the great thoughts of the century float by. And Miss Martin shoots them down with her rifle. To let strange horrors come to mind. Standing here. Sally's brother shouting he screwed my sister. I'd take a bow. In front of all these spongy hearts. Time to leave. Step down into the rapid transit system forever. Get Herbert's coat. Collect Her Majesty.

'Smithy, you're not leaving.'

'Yes.'

Miss Tomson standing in front of Smith. Taking his elbow. Leading him backwards. Across the foyer. Staring in his eyes. As if a slap had landed on her face and she slumped, hanging to my lapels, looking up. Blue. Like the flag raised to the mainmast. Five minutes before sailing. As we float into a bedroom. All pink, couched and satiny. Deep silled window. Stars out there in the long night. Cold in heaven. And motor birds crossing the sky with a pencil ray of light pointing towards Bonniface cooped up with his trusty bottle in the mop closet. Alone with his secrets.

Behind a wall of sliding doors. Sally Tomson's clothes. Glass case of little gleaming square boxes just like the automat and in each, a pair of shoes, gleaming, precious, slippers, gold and silver. A table, two lotions, three waters, four perfumes. Fewer than I thought. Her face when it lay cupped in my hands. Her mouth open over her teeth in the tiniest most exquisite of smiles.

'Hey what is this Smithy you're going.'

'Yes.'

'O.'

'It was marvellous.'

'That isn't a word you'd ever use Smithy if you meant it.'

'I do. I enjoyed myself.'

'Stay.'

'It's good to look at you, Sally. I like you.'

'Smithy you're easily pleased by beautiful things. And we never even scratched each other like monkeys.'

'When can I see you again.'

'Come on, Smithy. You talk like you're never going to see me again.'

'Can I see you again.'

'Shit. Yesh.'

'What's the matter.'

'I don't know. But. Yesh. You can see me.'

Miss Tomson, slender satin straps, holding lightly the fabric over her bosom. Soft swelling lines, the gentle nipples. Smiling and doubling up her fist, leaning back with a wink and slow motion and clipping Smith lightly on the jaw as he rolled with the punch.

'Nice moving, Smithy.'

'Guess I'll get my coat.'

'You could have been a fighter.'

'I've taken instead to foil, epee, sabre.'

'There's so much I want to say, Smithy.'

'Say it.'

'There really is but no time.'

'You won't miss my funeral. When the bullets blot me out.'

'No, no. You give them hell Smithy. Make your bark more scary than your bite. Then you avoid using the teeth too much. They won't get you.'

'You're on my side.'

'Yesh.'

'Should we shake hands.'

'Yesh.'

'I like your bedroom.'

'I stretch and yawn here every morning for three hours.'

'Wish I were here.'

'Smithy I know. I know.'

'I do.'

'Be patient. You line up with a woman don't you. And you never leave her. You might add more women. You never leave any of them.'

'Save a page.'

'Of what.'

'Your appointment diary. It's there, by the phone. Put me in.'

'Sure. What day do you want.'

'Any day.'

'Afternoons on Thursdays. I'm not kidding.'

'I'm not either.'

'Smithy, let's have the now. Although the past is nice to have around as well. I want to grab it right now.'

'Grab it.'

'Wow. I yam der yingle. Ralph said you said.'

'Shake it good bye. You humperdink.'

'O gee. It's saying hello. It's shaking my hand.'

'Sally, my God we're being watched.'

'Whoops. Beat it Ralph.'

'O yeah, sure.'

Ralph, his back hiding a frown all over his face clicking the door closed behind these two lovers.

'Tell me, Smithy, is it true.'

'What.'

'About the machine you have installed. That claps and roars. Out of a loud speaker.'

'Who told you that.'

'I'm not telling. Does it really roar and cheer.'

'Yes. At the end of a sentence.'

'Why do you need it.'

'When I'm lonely, sometimes, and feel powerless.'

'O come on.'

'Just nice to stand in my room in Dynamo. Switch it on, on a bereft Saturday afternoon. Has a seeing eye. Shake a fist. Thirty five thousand voices roaring. It says on the label.'

'And if you let this out. And waved it. Flashed it to the machine.'

'Yes. Roars and claps.'

'I'll join that, Smithy, you know when I tried to phone you the last day or two. I had dreams about you. You were wearing pyjamas and spectacles and you stood at a window after opening these heavy metal shutters. And you know what you were holding. A pneumatic drill.'

'I beg your pardon.'

'I was a street girl walking in front of an opera house. You came out with the drill. I came up to you talking another language and wagging my ass. Followed you right by your shoulder, you didn't even look. Then I just stopped and watched a bunch of guys dressed in blue with big thick leather boots coming up out of a sewer in the road. They were saying hi to each other, like long lost friends. Some dream. A bellybuster. Don't go, now. Stay.'

'I must.'

'I keep leaving all my guests for you. Claude had to run out for a minute.'

Smith's hand on Tomson's backside. Quiet light of her bedroom. A servants elevator up to this labyrinthine house of hers, touching the clouds. You sleep with a lot of men, said it was too much trouble to fight. Easier to let them in. Nearly kept me out. On an island surrounded by milk white water. See through the crack in your bathroom door, rozy marble and steps to a sunken bath. Feel poor. With a flick of your fingernail your world is so full of blue and gold. My bath stands on makeshift cast iron lion paws. And you step down into yours, like a beach with two tides a day. And all I have is a little rubber pillow to rest my head while I wallow. I need cheering, roars of crowds. Once the machine went wrong, something slipped. Just as I was shouting I'll win. And thirty five thousand voices went hee hee.

'Smithy will you ever put on diapers and babies bonnet and go through the street blasting a trombone.'

'Most certainly not.'

'I like that. Say it again.'

'Most certainly not.'

'Come and stay for breakfast. Watch the sun come up. Right up over there it comes, red as anything.'

Tomson leaning back against her bedroom wall, raises her slipper, scratches the back of her leg. Voice out there among her friends, says where's Sally. And toot toot down there on the river. Her back is shivering. Trembling. After our little nuzzling. All without warning. She breaks in two. Precious. This flesh. One drop. A tear. Falls on my own black slipper, neatly between the bow. And what she is. As I held her head in darkness between my hands. Put my fingers around her throat. She didn't take them away. As Shirl always gently did. But left them there for me to kill her if I liked. To trust. Calms the nerves. Her death under my hands, a strange beauty.

'Smithy I'll never get up the aisle. I know it.'

'You will.'

'I should have seen you in all those missing weeks. I

wondered how you were holding out against the dear Sir, do not be a zurd. P.S. You know the letter we mean for Z. Smithy. I want to hand you one of my kidneys.'

'You're tremendously nice.'

'I'm sorry, behaving like this. You think, travel light and you'll get far. Should have given me over to you as a bargain, without labels or locks in some kind of phoney closing down sale. Like I was a temperamental bankrupt.'

'I'd say thank you very much.'

'My hand's reaching right in for it. Guess a girl should say, I've never done this before.'

'Shades are up.'

'Sort of sad no one can look in my window, except from an airplane. They keep building the buildings. Higher. Everyone thinks it's progress and all it is are a few friendly cockroaches infesting at the bottom, sneaking up to the top. They have to pull it all down to get rid of them. If I threw my life away on you. Sort of wasted it. Would you appreciate it. Don't laugh at me. I'm not kidding.'

'Here, my noseblower. It's clean.'

'I can use my sheet.'

'Use this, please, I'll cherish it.'

'Smithy, would you do one thing for me.'

'Sure.'

'I know it doesn't sound sane.'

'Tell me.'

'Send me one of your dirty shirts.'

'Sally.'

'I mean it.'

'What for.'

'Please. Do it.'

'All right.'

'I'll wash and iron it.'

'Miss T.'

'Would you do that. Really, For me.'

'Yesh, I will. Sally.'

'Thanks. But please don't kid me. Smithy.'

Against the window panes, a wind. Cigarette smoke

turned blue. Leavetaking. Swish of silk. Last tinkle of glass. Little laughters. I'll see you. At the races. In the tops of other high towers.

George Smith, dark strange shoulders in Herbert's coat. Children open their eyes in the dark. Little souls. Teddy bears and puppets. All their own. What you do for love. Take her hands put them on my shirt, shaking it in the suds. Iron it smooth. Send me out into the world. Fresh and neat. With just a wave. To her saying good bye over the heads. Old fashioned Sally. Another ship. Toot. On the river. Bewildered by betrayals. Frozen your blue blue eyes. Each five little pressures of your hand. Blood pink nails. Kissed you, smack. On each cheek of your ass. Easily pleased you say by beautiful things. And said yesh to you.

> That my
> Bitter root
> Were a big horn
> For you to
> Blow
>
> The tunes
> Of the wide world
> Were there
> Such melody
>
> For bitter root
> Or horn.

25

Afternoon city covered with dark western clouds. Light dry snow flakes falling. Street lamps light up. Smith stepping out from the dreadnaught under the green canopy of Merry Mansions. Which in a wind a week ago floated right away up into the sky and landed, a big green grasshopper in a roof garden. Now anchored safely from jumping once more.

Herbert waving out the window as the dreadnaught glided away. Two days ago, the warning from Mr Browning. Completion day delayed by the hurricane. Revised invitations sent out for the last Thursday of November. Her Majesty declined to attend. Said the night of Miss Tomson's party, my nerve knew no bounds.

Look down at this blue carpet up these steps. Times numbered that I will walk into flat fourteen. I hear a hymn. Matilda. Right through the steel door. Singing. Strange how we've stuck together. In her heart cooks all the grief and sporty hysterical games, in one big pot.

A key in this door. Whirring little gyroscope, steady as it opens. Matilda's bare foot prints across the film of dust on the hardwood floor. Table with my wax dogwood flower. Stack of letters under a free sample can of baked beans.

Flick on the light. Evening coming, afternoon going. Out the window, the snow thickens. Sent two shirts to Miss T. One pink, one light blue. Goldminers upstairs left three weeks ago on a long cruise. I asked if I could visit their altar for a little prayer I wanted to say. They looked at me. As if I had made an exposure. Said it was blessed and sacred. I put my nose as high as I could. Two wretched hypocrites.

And on the way to the pier I watched as Hugo helped them into their car. They were crying like babies.

'Mr Smith. What are you doing here.'

'I live here, Matilda.'

'O sure. But I thought you was at the world championship rodeo.'

'No.'

'O Mr Smith, what are they doing to you. Let me get you a whisky. Never you mind, those guys will come to a smelly standstill.'

'Have a whisky with me, Matilda.'

'Thanks, I was going to do that.'

Matilda in her green silk. Slit up the side. Her big bosoms. Two vast dark waterfalls. Stand under an umbrella. And still get soaking wet. Glasses look clean. Two soda bottles.

'Thanks Matilda.'

'Mr Smith I've been looking all over and don't blame me. I swear I didn't burn them.'

'What.'

'Two shirts. I swear they were right on the top of the hamper. I know because it's the tabernacle colours. Pink and blue.'

'They may be at Dynamo.'

'But they were dirty.'

'Only a couple of shirts Matilda, forget it.'

'Say that when the next pair of socks are missing.'

'Matilda, sit down. I want to talk about something.'

'Who dat white sinner dere, want to talk.'

'This isn't a joke, Matilda. I'm deadly serious.'

'Mr Smith, you want to tell me I'm fired.'

'No.'

'What else is deadly serious.'

'I may be going away.'

'Beating it.'

'No. Just going away.'

'So you have no need for my further services.'

'I'd like you to stay in my employ.'

'That what you call this.'

'Shit. Matilda.'

'What you said, Mr Smith.'

'I just want you to come, at the same salary, dust and clean. Put the mail in the safe. Just stop the place from rotting away.'

'Think I need a little sting more in this glass, Mr Smith.'

'I'll have a sting more in my glass too if I may.'

Snow drifting on the window sill. Light across the street. Where has the grey headed father gone, holding head in hands. Over his eight curly headed mistakes. Another Christmas coming. Last week strolling by the river I stepped in and stood in the waiting room of the hospital. Gazing down the long halls. Guards toting guns. Wooden benches. Beds and carts. The dirty sheets piled on the dead.

'I'll do that, Mr Smith, dust and clean.'

'Thanks Matilda.'

'Mr Smith, something bothering you. Staring out that window like you got no friends.'

'I'm all right.'

'A cultured gentleman, a Mr Clementine, phoned yesterday. He said you were expected as guest of honour at the Funeral Director's Exhibition. Said you weren't at Dynamo. I told him to try The Game Club.'

'I was there.'

'He phoned back said you wasn't.'

'I was. In the library.'

'Reading the papers.'

'Yes.'

'Society columns.'

'Yes, as a matter of fact.'

'It's that Miss Tomson. Getting married.'

Smith turning to the window. Kitchen lights on across the street. Watched that little girl sitting at the table get bigger and bigger. Her boyfriend waits for her on the stoop, smoking a cigarette nervously looking up and down the street. Perhaps she dreams of growing up. A Dizzy Darling. Gay, wild, willing. Up on her high terrace just around the corner, could spit or pee right down on the roof of Merry.

'And Mr Smith, it's bad. That you should be carrying that gun again.'

'Matilda, find my sandals. My foot's hurting in my shoe. Herbert will be back here, in half an hour to pick me up.'

'When does my service here abruptly discontinue, Mr Smith, sir.'

'Cut it out Matilda.'

'Scared I'll have parties, drink the wine, smoke the cigars.'

'No.'

'Why don't you admit it.'

'All right.'

'You admit it.'

'Four cases of whisky. Have vanished.'

'Two.'

'You admit it.'

'Who dat pagan sittin' dere.'

'Me dat pagan sittin' here.'

'When the flock is thirsty the dark complexioned redeemer leads them to drink. Mr Smith.'

'I'd prefer the redeemer to lead them to his own whisky.'

'No hard feelings. What's whisky, Mr Smith.'

'Expensive.'

Matilda's glistening eyes. If the days would unravel. When my guests stand over the polished plates, tureens in Renown. Matilda in her black china silk. Bonniface in hunting pink. Her Majesty could have handed him out The Order Of The Underwear, instead of being insufferable. Send her some smoked eel. Could cross the carpet and kiss Matilda. Hold her close. The terrifying strength. Of her arms. Massive legs. Could put up some fight.

'Mr Smith, what are you thinking.'

'I was thinking of kissing you.'

'Come on.'

'Herbert's coming.'

'We got twenty minutes.'

'Not much time.'

'Let's break a record.'

'We better not.'

'Come on. Pull the curtains.'

'You were singing a hymn when I came in. Sing to me now.'

Matilda in her high and in her low haunted voice. Tiptoeing from octave to octave.

> How
> Much of her
> Was muscle
> How much of her
> Was sad.
> Which of her
> Was fat
> Which of her
> Was glad.

Solemn darkness. Autumn leaves gone. Lie on her dark breasts. Fallen on her black steely hair. The tired evening. The city on the way home. Cold chill lurks in all the bones.

'Matilda.'

'Mr Smith. I'm hungry.'

'You smell good, Matilda.'

Fluttering eyelids on the neck. Crushed butterfly wings lifted from a summer flower. Mr Smith I'm not hungry, I'm horny. Miss Martin's round white ripeness. Matilda's bulge of tan. Close up Merry Mansions to desertion and dust. Move to The Game Club. Live high up. Each afternoon after a swim and steam bath. Sit staring in my lap amid the silence, the glass book cases, the tinkling kindly chimes of the library's old clock. Chess players murmuring down the vaulted hall. Steam whispering in the radiators. And down below in the streets. The sirens and gongs. To fires and murder everywhere.

'Mr Smith, why don't you sleep here at Merry anymore.'

'Woof woof.'

'Down Fido.'

'Woof woof.'

Smith lightheartedly lowering to all fours, crawling on

the rug. Between Matilda's legs. And snapping at a few imaginary flies. Sandals flapping. Bonniface is right. So nice to bow wow. Be someone's little dog. Faithful and true to the last. With a master all of one's own. Little gable roof. Bed of straw. Little roughness on Matilda's ass. Where she sits so much. Silken smooth all the elsewhere. Me Fido. Man's best friend. Woof woof. The buzzer.

'Matilda, that's Herbert.'

'Don't go.'

'Got to.'

'You don't got to go.'

'I must, a ticklish task ahead.'

'Ticklish task here. Fool around some more. You old Fido. Yummy.'

'Bow wow.'

'Nice Fido. Good dog.'

'Call down, Matilda. Tell Herbert I'll be five minutes. I'll be back later.'

'I got a tabernacle meeting, at nine.'

'Where.'

'Here. Where else. You wasn't expected. It's the Second Communion of the Brown Angels.'

'I see. That'll be another two cases of whisky.'

'Don't be mean. Feel me. Right across here.'

'Fantastic stomach muscles, Matilda. How do you keep them like that.'

'By laughing. And laying.'

'Tell Herbert to come back in an hour.'

'You sweetie pie, Fido.'

'I yam das yingle humperdink woof woof.'

Matilda wagging to the foyer. Big dark feet flapping on the floor. Voice mellow and low.

'Herbie, Mr Smith is deliberately delayed by the unavoidable, you know the circumstances unforseeable and all that commotion. An hour. And fifteen minutes. Good-bye.'

'Come here you, you brown angel.'

'Herbie says he don't know how far he can go in this snow if you wait. Baby baby.'

'You have gorgeous eyes Matilda. And the most smooth skin.'

'Hee hee, you don't have to flatter this unhandsome Matilda. What beauty I ain't got is enough to go round the world.'

Strewn garments. Brown steam engine, puffing away. Delighted to be pulling out of the station. Moving once more. Loaded with a heap of hustlement. Of all the Hildas and Matildas. See you in the black and white hereafter. Without lashes without eyes. Crease gone from all my trousers. Choo choo down the rails. Where you going on that train. Where you pounding on that track. Waving out the window. When the world was waving back.

'Whoo hoo, Mr Smith.'

'Choo choo, Matilda.'

'Say that little thing again.'

'Vas.'

'Like dat sumpersink das dinkity rink.'

'Mean dat yingle humperdidink. Das woof. Dee bow wow.'

'Nice doggie.'

A lonely birthday party Matilda gave me. Once when I sat unwanted at the window. She came carrying a cake and candles. No one else remembered. Or cared, happy birthday Mr Smith. Lights off. The evening street throwing big shadows of the furniture across the floor. No little children with upturned palms. Here daddy, a present. I paid with my money and bought for you. I kissed Matilda then. All that person warm and kind. On this train clickity clack and blind. Take this turning. Before it bends. Or ask what's your style. Dog. And wham. One day dead. At a board meeting. Slumped over a chair. To the mortuary, change of socks, clean underwear. And evening clothes to sport through the longest night of all. Dear little pussy. Big fantastic cat. Waltzing in an old smile. Ice dancing in a hat.

> Like petal
> Cool
> Like yingle
> Yule.

26

Broad phalanx of cars across the bridge moving slowly through the streaming snow. Towers holding girders wear white crowns and red lights high in the sky. Smith in the back of the dreadnaught, sandalled feet folded one on the other. Wipers fanning two snow frames on the windscreen. To see bolts and metal joists. Rust and grime, covered with the smallest of frozen tears. Wait for rain to wash troubles away. And snow comes and buries.

'Mr Smith, the radio says it's going to be a blizzard. I don't know if we're going to make it out there.'

Out there is a lonely coast. A beach tightly jammed in summer. Bare skins burning and sweating on the sands. Sad drownings, a grey body lifted away. And winter all cold, empty, and chill waves bleakly rolling across the shore. Matilda, let me go. Mr Smith, you can get it up again. Just once more. Kissing one midnight breast. While the other is lonesome. Hers is a big red tongue for games and words.

Herbert's level headed confident look, under his black visor. Man to depend upon in a battle.

'Mr Smith, this is getting pretty bad.'

'Drop me at the first rapid transit, Herbert. I'll forge on, underground.'

Two iron balustrades, two beacon bulbs of light, at the subway entrance. Hosiery sale in that store window. Manufacturer offering direct to the customer at phenomenal saving. Snow melting in puddles at the bottom of these steps. Smith standing on the platform, in the cold gloom, and sandals.

Rapid transit train rocking on its way. Screeching from halt to halt in the forlorn white tiled stations. A fat woman with a dark thick coat. Little slits cut in the bulges of her shoes. Her sneaking eye engrossed by Smith's criss crossed leather on his white socks. Come down here out of the cold high wind, wrapped and shivering, Matilda said, vas dog are you Mr Smith, I yam das yingle frankfutter dog.

And above here on the streets somewhere, lives Bonniface. Vas brand of dog. Ah, Mr Mystery, he bloodhound. You see the sad eyes Smith, and ah, these flaps of skin down over them as they go baying and tracking on the trail, to follow the splashes of blood from leaky wounds and whiffs of fear.

A station. Car doors open. Grey haired and hatted man, melting mantle of snow on shoulders, lurching on the train. Doors close. Man standing, hanging one handed from a strap and other holding a mouth organ between his lips. And clawing out. In one motion his hand coming down savagely on the emergency chain.

Train squealing to a halt. Between the bleak electric bulbs in the dark tunnel. Get on a train. Sit solemn, in honest lonely pursuit of one's destination. Making such good headway. And it happens. The last bugle has not blown yet. This grey figure hissing. Shouting.

'You're all scared. Aren't you. You bunch of bums. Who's going to hit me. Come on.'

And Smith catching a look at the black letters tiled in the white wall. Fartbrook. One should have known. The station ahead, Ozone Plaza. And hanging over George Smith, the wet lipped, weak streaked eyes. And the growling ugly voice.

'Why you bum.'

The frozen dark figure of George Smith. His eyes lifting slowly to stare with death into this unpleasant face. The mouth organ man parting his sour lips. Contest of silent eyes. A twitch in the jaw of the mouth organ man. Tie knot strung down from his shirt. Smell of alcohol. Someone's father. A dim soul dying. Smith's beacons burning into the mouth organ man as he straightens up in fear and withdraws slowly backwards. Fat woman standing up, shoe in hand, bringing it down on this head of the harmonica player. Three male passengers rushing to aid the destruction, felling him with fists, thumbnails and jabs of fountain pens. Mouth organ man's two hands bending back covering his kidneys, groaning on the train floor pink and grey with chewing gum. This wintery night of snow.

Train moving backwards into Fartbrook station. Two police lift away the harmonica man. Doors close. Train on into the tunnel. On the floor, a little smear of blood glistening. A crunched mouth organ. Clucking voices. Bold and fearless. Up there a picture. Miss Rapid Transit. Selected by a Jury. Hobbies are dancing and ice skating. Mine are women, money and religion.

Transit train's sound spreading out on the night. Lifting up out of the dark underground to cross a bridge on the water. Clicking on the track. Driving snow melting down in the light glimmers of sweeping waves. Wind on the windows. That darkness. And beyond are the ships waiting at sea.

Smith hurrying along the cold concrete station, past the bumping posts at the end of the line. Look again at the address. Standing on steps facing a snowy deserted sidewalk. Street of dark wooden houses, large and shuttered. Ocean waves pounding a beach. Out there the lights of a ship, a towering dim glow on the high sea.

Smith high stepping, in his sandals, following former footprints down this street. Man with a newspaper in a lighted window. Sitting in his shirt sleeves with the warmth of his little wife. Slippers under a kitchen table, a plate of two potatoes and sauerkraut. Yas I yam frankfutter. Memorable meal.

A police patrol car cruising gently by. George Smith walking past the looming shadow of a temple in the snow. Police looking Smith up and down from their enclosed darkness. And pulling away again. Bonniface says they stopped him when he was carrying a little bag, asked him what the piece of rope was for. To practise knots. And the piece of cheese. To eat. And George how could one say, for suicide and catching rats. They brought Bonniface under suspicion to the police station. Where he asked for water and a game of chess. And they asked with warm mystery, where does a guy like you come from. And they gave him a cell, and night's rest. Taking up a little collection of money in the morning to see him on his way.

Lonely street lamp on a cold pole in the ground. Telephone wires humming in the sea wind. Slow rhythm of ocean thunder. A number up over the entrance, in faded gold on glass. One six seven two. Mine are the first footprints in the snow to the door. Two little shrubberies. Card in the window. Fink, Bladder and Ball, nature cures. Tired soulless entrance. Butts stubbed out in a sand bucket. Press the button. Elevator doors open. Step in. Press floor five. Up we go. I'm late and sad. Don't know what I'll say. So far away from the glamour of the city.

Colour green, general in the long narrow hall. Smell of old carpeting, newspapers, garlic, and limburger. Door 5C. So hard to present oneself seriously in sandals stepping out of a blizzard, lugging a paper parcel. Hear a voice I know inside, Momma, I'll go. Out of all these doors, streets, miles, through tunnels under the highways. And doors everywhere. Hello. Miss Martin lives here.

'Mr Smith, I thought you were never going to come. What happened. Your feet.'

'I kicked a vending machine to pieces when it failed to produce. Toes too swollen to get into a pair of shoes.'

'O dear.'

'Meant only to give a little kick but the impertinence of the instruction signs, machine fully automatic, I kicked it, I'm afraid, to pieces. And it produced.'

'Come in, we're going to have a few sandwiches. I hope you like tongue.'

Smith shuffling. Shaking snow from shoulders. Stepping into a thin hall. Miss Martin leading him to a lighted room.

'And I want you to meet my mother. Mother this is Mr Smith.'

'I'm so glad to meet you Mr Smith, Ann has told me so much about you.'

'I'm afraid these sandals, Mrs Martin, are the result of an accident. I'm delighted to meet Ann's mother. Ann's been such a splendid help to me through so many unforeseen difficulties.'

'You can see Mr Smith we're very modest here. I've always had to look after Ann since my husband died. Ann take Mr Smith's coat.'

'Sure Mom, I was just waiting till the greetings were over.'

'We just put up the card table, Mr Smith, with some snacks on it. Not much, Ann and I are not big eaters, until well you know, until Ann –'

'I quite understand Mrs Martin.'

'Well may as well be honest.'

'Of course.'

'Ann, you know, was the apple of her father's eye.'

'Mom please, Mr Smith doesn't want to hear all that.'

'Ann is such a spoilsport, Mr Smith. Maybe you'd like a glass of beer.'

'Yes, that would be fine Mrs Martin.'

'Ann get Mr Smith a bottle of beer.'

Mrs Martin sitting on the deep and crimson sofa, with white lace embroidery on each arm. Two thick red glass ashtrays. A piano. A sheet of music on the dark stool.

'Does Ann play, Mrs Martin.'

'We gave her lessons. You know how children are, Mr Smith, they don't appreciate those things until it's too late. You are musical Mr Smith?'

'No, not really, Mrs Martin. Just like to listen.'

'I'm sure you must like classical.'

'I'm fond of several classical pieces.'

'So is Ann. Would you bring in the cream spread Ann.'

'You like cream spread?'

'Yes.'

Ann Martin. She came in carrying a little tray. With the cream spread. Pineapple and pimento. White and brown bread sandwiches. A bottle of cold beer with the little perspiration on it. Ann Martin pouring for George Smith.

Who sat now deeply in the sofa, legs crossed having tucked up the white socks high to avoid showing leg hair. Wind whistling around the windows. A photograph of sand and shore on the wall. Another of a little girl with her father and mother, standing with hot dogs in front of a roller coaster.

'You're looking at the picture, Mr Smith. Taken of us when Ann was just six, always eating frankfutters, never eat anything that would stick to her ribs. Her first ride on the roller coaster. That's her father. He was an engineer. He worked on the bridge across the bay where the train runs. He was killed working on it.'

'I'm sorry.'

'Long time ago now. Ann has been my whole responsibility.'

'I understand Mrs Martin.'

'She means everything to me, Mr Smith. Her happiness is my happiness.'

'I understand Mrs Martin.'

'Please Mom.'

'Don't interrupt me while I'm talking Ann, Mr Smith knows and understands. That's why I've had him come out here. I know you're a gentleman of the world. Well I understand that too. I can be modern in my outlook. But when you see everything you've worked for just go in one night of carelessness, one moment when a girl's defences are down.'

'Mom you promised, you told me you wouldn't –'

'Now Ann Mr Smith understands. He's a man of the world, you're not. You're an innocent young girl, don't pretend to Mr Smith boys flocked after you, because they didn't. But Bobby from downstairs is a boy who has wanted to marry you since you were eight years old, now that's a long time, and Bobby is nicely situated now. He's moving right up. But that chance is gone. How would Bobby explain you off in this dress sticking out a mile as you went up the aisle, why his job wouldn't be worth a cracker.'

'Mom you just promised me you wouldn't.'

'I know what's best, Mr Smith understands, don't you Mr Smith.'

'Yes.'

'What do you expect him to say Mom, when he's out in this berg. Who wants to marry Bobby. I wouldn't let him touch me if I were a corpse.'

'Enough of that smart talk. A lot of girls appreciate his prospects, I'm sure Mr Smith understands. What about your condition. Dr Vartberg doesn't live on charity. You weren't raised on charity.'

'But you've got Mr Smith trapped here, what do you expect him to say.'

'You don't feel trapped Mr Smith do you. You're completely free. To go right now. I'm only explaining Ann's position as I see it as her mother. We have to be adults about this. Ann until she was eighteen was not allowed out past eleven o'clock. I always sat up until she came home. Right in this chair. And made it my business to meet any of Ann's boyfriends. They were all clean cut young boys. From good homes. This neighbourhood wasn't all like it is now. Some of those houses on the shore were owned by prominent people. I organized some bridge games, and met them personally.'

'God Mom, stop. Here's your beer Mr Smith. Shut up, Mom.'

'Don't you speak to me like that.'

'Mom Mr Smith came out here of his own free will.'

'And your free will is responsible for your predicament, my dear girl. I knew when you were staying away those nights there was going to be trouble. I knew it. Don't think I didn't know what was going on, because I did. I suppose Mr Smith you must have a lot of girl friends, don't you.'

'As a matter of fact Mrs Martin I have very few friends of either sex. I'm very fond of Ann. She's been an extremely faithful and dedicated secretary. I don't know what I would have done without her on several occasions.'

'You got her pregnant on one of them.'

'Mom if you don't stop I'm leaving this room.'

'Leave then. Go ahead Mr Smith I want to hear you talk. If there are two sides of this.'

Door slamming shut, Miss Martin retreating. Chill night, cold snowy wind beating against the window. Steam radiator hissing and throbbing. The world stands just outside one's ears. Waiting. Puffing in passion. Cabin in the woods. One grotesque spider. Weak moment. Throw the ashes up in the wind. I'm coming, Miss Martin. Yes yes do. George. Wake up wearing a suit of paternity.

'I see your point Mrs Martin.'

'Of course you do. Easy to see it, isn't it. That poor girl, out like a balloon who's going to marry her now. She could have had Bobby Richards downstairs who's doing well and able to set her up. Now what do you want her to do. You think Bobby's mother doesn't know about this. That the whole building doesn't know that since she began to show she's had to leave an hour early so she wouldn't meet anyone in the elevator. I'll tell you Mr Smith. Ann won't, but I will. You could have prostitutes with your money. And left our Ann alone.'

'I'm sorry Mrs Martin. I understand that you should feel this way but I don't think remarks of that kind help matters.'

'O you don't, well let me tell you a thing or two.'

In tears at the open door, Miss Martin with hands down at her sides, veins standing out on her wrist. Pale pity of her long fingernails. Her arms suddenly so thin and long and gangling from her brown dress. A large curl falling across the light sweat of her forehead. When my eyes were nearly next to her brown ones. Freckles on her smooth face. She tried a bath at Dynamo. When I stood over her big bosoms and peach rotundity.

'Mrs Martin I don't want to be responsible for Ann getting upset.'

'O you don't. You've upset her enough already for the rest of her whole life, she might just as well go out there on the bridge where her father lost his life and jump. You did it to her. You could have found some cheap tramp. Thousands of them. And you have to pick on a respectable girl to do it to. A married man with children. Aren't they enough for you, haven't you got a wife already. And this building you put up to put your dead body in. I'll tell you a thing or two, sure get up, stand up, sure, Ann sure, get him his coat, exactly what I expected from your kind, all educated with fine manners and accents. As if we weren't good enough for you. My daughter comes along and you use her body for your pleasure and throw her in the gutter. Go ahead get your coat and get out but you won't hear the last of this I promise you. And take that bag with you. If you want to know, residents of this apartment wouldn't be seen dead with a broken paper bag and an outfit like that, if you want to know. Good bye good riddance. But you'll hear more don't you worry. Decent people know how to deal with your kind, let him go Ann, he's not doing any fast talking. Not now with me he isn't. Next time he won't be so fast with an innocent girl from a good background and respectable people.'

Little creaks and groans as the elevator went down. Miss Martin stood at the door. Reached out her hand and put it on my arm. Slight pressure of her fingers. Face streaked with tears. Strange for the first time. With breathing so loud. Look in her eyes. And see friendship. And her strange distant dignity.

Snow deeper. Night darker. On this icy strip of land of ramshackle wastes and marshland stretches of Far Bollock. Throat dry. Ears red and burning. They get cold again. Ghostly waves. Big ocean has a tongue. To lick so many shores. And again this year no one will send me a heartfelt Christmas card.

> Or remember
> I was
> A prepster
> Once.

27

Fingers spread on the window sill. Staring at the afternoon Saturday sky. Up the airshaft, through a mirror installed two days ago in the forlorn room, 604 Dynamo House. White fluffy clouds on blue and tinged in pink from a setting sun.

Saturday where there are no footsteps out in the hall. Mail no longer arriving. Save for one letter from Miss Martin. Postmarked Far Bollock.

Dear Mr Smith,
    I am very sorry for what happened on Monday night.
So long.
Ann Martin

All week, each morning, wait for her to come to work. And lay in my tub looking up in the steam. Suicides high after the snow. When the city was hushed and still.

Standing here. Three o'clock. Wearing shoes again. Five days till the reception at Renown. Purple bordered menu. Providing a feast of baby beets and onions. Succotash. Triumph of shelled prawns. Choice of three wines and two pickles. And tureens of smoked eel. Like I gave Her Majesty. She sat stiffly when I handed over the box. She though it was some stunt instead of the eel it was. Raised her eyebrows and said I suppose George you've heard. What. About poor Bonniface. Who was reading a book, something about bodies were the external essence of the mind. While standing on a platform at three a.m. in the rapid transit system. And he walked off the platform and was picked up unconscious from the centre of the tracks.

And Thursday near the botanical gardens and zoo I

visited the hospital. Sat by the Bonniface bed. His hands seemed white and strange. And all round his face a look of lighthearted resign. I heard a rustle under the sheets. He put his finger up to his lips. Then he leaned over, whispered, woof woof, Mr Mystery. Is here.

I waved good bye to Bonniface. And his white bandaged head. Nurses smiled. Herbert left the oranges and liquorice by the bed and I said we would come and fetch him to the reception at Renown. Bonniface rubbing his hands together said it was in earnest anticipation he waited. And would brush his teeth specially in view of the menu. Her Majesty had brought him pussy willow out of season. And he was finishing the book about the body essence, interrupted by his plunge into the tracks. Things at the airport, without him, he said, were reptilian.

Sky all the darkest blue now. Whole day long and hungry in this forlorn room. Slowly tearing up letters, sheets and sheets of paper and documents. Legal loops, summons and twists and twirls from Shirl. Rip them up. One's hands so glad to tear them all to little pieces. Because yesterday. I walked away alone from Dynamo House. Nothing to protect me from the outside world. No appointments. No plans. I took a taxi to the Grand Central Station to make believe I was catching a train. Stood there in the emptiness looking up at the balcony where once I saw that head moving, tall, blonde and collected above the rail. Christ, Miss T, why don't you come running for a train right now. And miss it. And meet me.

Miss T never came running. And from the station yesterday I walked along a marble hall, brass bannisters, up the steps and into the soft lights and carpets of the hotel nearby. Sat on the red leather curved seats under the gilded clock. Hands in lap. Must have looked the quietest man who ever lived. And two feet came up and stood in front of me. Small faint brown high heels. Exquisite, expensive. And before I reached the ankle bone. I knew who it was. Could hardly look up. No braveness. No courage. Until she said.

'You can look up George. I'm not going to be unfriendly.'

'Hello, Shirl.'

She sat down beside me. This dark meeting place under the clock. Put the back of my hands up to my eyes because I was going to cry. And I said, my dear chap. You can't. You better not. Because people will be looking. Caught like this, by Shirl. Just as I was. Without friends. Laughter. Conversation. What was I doing here. Aren't you waiting for somebody. No one. And before it could happen. Anything at all. Shirl looked at me with her brown eyes. And said you look so tired George. Her hand reached up to touch me. Even though it never left her lap or the inside of her beautiful soft leather gloves. She never said, why don't you come home, George. Back to us. But she said, as she sat, with her shoulders and hair, and even the crossing of her legs. She said come back. I know, George, you can't come back. But I'm saying come back. In this little moment, while only two of us are in the world. George, you never give in, do you. Sit even in your worst terrible sorrow, all alone. George, what I want to say to you, even though I'm not saying it, that I don't care, I won't mind, I'll forgive even as I ought to be as cruel as you, I won't be, lay your head on my mother's bosom, I'll kiss it there, you foolish thing, you ran from me, and built up your hard stone castle to shut us out because I know there were just some simple little words I said in fury and hurt just to put a whip lash around your heart which had been flailing mine. And I said that. You foolish thing, because now I know. You do. You want so much for traffic to stop for you. When you're dead. I know you do.

In that hotel lobby. Dimly lit counters, blue soft carpets. Husbands, lovers and wives. Trains deeply below. Worming their way under us. The deepest deepest brown. Shirl's eyes. All the women one loves. And between the hearts, time seeps. To leave us strangest of strangers as she spoke.

'How have you been George. Really tell me. I want to

tell you something. The law is not going to come between us. Do you hear what I'm saying. The law is not going to come between us. Even though I have to starve with the kids. Do you hear what I'm saying.'

'Yes.'

'And do you think I mean it.'

'Yes.'

All as simple as that. And we went for a drink. Then took her to her train. Bought her a newspaper. She stood on the train platform, looking out the glass door, her eyes glistening.

Faintest tick of the big desk watch hanging from a nail in the wall of 604. George Smith turning from the airshaft window. Silence of this Saturday. Takes a minute to tear up a year of litigation. An hour to burn a century of it. What is that tapping. Four minutes past four. Stomach aches. Emptiness. A funny whisper. Tapping. Seems so real. Someone at the door. A knock. Is that someone in Miss Martin's room. Felt that whisper. Words breathed on the back of my neck. Is that Miss Tomson. Here. Yesh. Come back to work. Look and see. Smithy, I'm here, outside. Thought you'd like to hear from me. Where. Here. I know you've got no one now, so I just thought I'd come back, wasn't doing anything this afternoon just four past four. Just some ice skating but I can do that anytime. So here I am. With a whole lot of change for the petty cash. Tapping and ticking. There's no one here. Lift up my hand and put it in front of my face. Thumb and finger on the brows. I was talking to her. As she came back just then. Ice skates slung over her shoulder. Standing right there. In the doorway. I'm sure I said gee. Word I never use. She was wearing a suit. Flat walking shoes. A tweed like winter heather. Thin string of pearls. Soft blue sweater to match her eyes. Could have put my arms around her. My head in the nape of her neck. Slight little shake she gives. My balls. In her hand. Whole world goes golden brown. When I said to her, God forgive, for all the women I made love me. Sure he will Smithy. He'll forgive you. He knows you've got no

343

philosophy, no conscience. And you know, Smithy I don't care that you don't. I sort of like that. Look where my principles got me. I was robbed. What about tea. For two. Just past four.

George Smith turning back to the window. Arms were reaching out around nothing at all. Mirrored sky. Orange blue with evening. Little voice blew whispers was mine. My hands back on the window sill. Lick my lips.

Treasury building clock. Tolling six. Smith walking out the long dark corridor from 604 and down the stairs. Briefcase swinging. Stick tapping. Sound of steps down, all so hollow, all so shut and Saturday. On the apron of Dynamo House. Looking up. Blue crisp sky. Faint new moon just in the crack there between the buildings. White crescent floating on a purple and gold flood of light. Herbert sees me. Waves. Get in the dreadnaught wearing a pair of black gleaming shoes again. My toes back to normal.

'To The Game Club Herbert.'

'Any particular way, Mr Smith.'

'Let's go along the river. Looks a nice night.'

Monstrous black vehicle slowly purring out of the empty street, along by the only sign of life. The Fish Market. Loading trucks. Big jackets of stevedores. Bumping tug boat.

'Like a little music, Mr Smith.'

'All right, Herbert. If you can find something soft.'

In the windows of other cars. Get dead staring glances. A financial hero. No longer looking for worship. Or a splatter of lead bullets on this glass. Piers for ships pushing out on the flat water. Lights blink off across this deep tidal strait. Under the bridge that goes out to Bonniface and Miss Martin. Far Bollock, Fartbrook, points east. Whose mother jumped down my throat. Words say so little unless they're legal. Look at colours. Taste them all as candy. Bonniface likes liquorice so much. Left him that day. Herbert dropped me at the zoo, while he had a haircut. And I stood for a moment thinking beside a great bronze gate. Man ambled

344

up in the crisp cold. Said what a roue you'd be back at the asylum.

'Like this music Mr Smith.'

'Fine.'

Last night I dreamt a dream. Condemned to die in two days. Rushed to the telephone to tell the newspapers to publicise and prevent the unbelievable execution of George Smith. For some piffling item. Shirl said lay your head. Sink my nose in the softness of her mother's bosom. Shirl cried over our first baby clutching it in her arms. Give me my baby. It's mine, that little parcel of life.

Smith in mossy tweed and mustard yellow tie. Dark blue socks above calf leather shoes. On the left there, my favourite building, Steam Corporation Station. Often stood looking at it, walking there afternoons from Golf Street. Selling heat to buildings far away through hot pipes under the street. Sigh with this music. Every fifteen minutes the local news. Over your station of the stars. Drink clip joint raided, customers doped and beaten. Strange this announcer's voice. To go back over the words.

'– And a bulletin just received – Dizzy Darling the model and sometime actress whose wedding was to take place shortly to Claude Grace – heir to the mercantile fortune – was killed late this afternoon on highway twenty two south of Bedford – when her car she was driving hit a tree – Miss Darling was dead before arrival at Bedford Hospital – she was alone at the time and no one else was involved in the accident. The weather man says, clear skies –'

Dreadnaught slowing. Traffic streaming by. Herbert turning to look back at George Smith. Who nodded. Raising a hand. To wave. All right. Drive on. Past the skyport for planes. Under high arches of bridges for masted ships. Trains tunnelled deep in the salt water estuary.

Ahead we turn left. Faint music again. Following the news and weather. Clutch sadness out of a grey evening sky. Bark will be torn off some trees. Bring her baby roses. Fresh green leaves and stems. A distant dust of tiny thorns. To fall. Pink and blue. Wash and iron my shirts.

What is a guy
But a prick
And you write
Your name
On it
With a wedding.

And no wedding
What is a guy
But a prick
She said.

28

Funeral Services
of
Sally (Dizzy Darling) Tomson
November The Twenty First
at one forty five o'clock P.M.
On Board 'Sea Shark'
Pier Seven, Foot of Owl Street
Burial At Sea

A green uniformed page leaning to whisper to George Smith at one fifteen P.M. high up in the silent loneliness of The Game Club.

'Mr Smith, your car is here, front entrance.'

Smith picking up the sable black coat. Lain over a chair. Old clock's tinkle of chimes. Stare out this window to the water tanks on roofs, see other windows dark and empty.

Her picture in all the papers. Her career. Sobbing and broken bodied before she died, her golden hair out across the road. A green sweatered arm on her chest. On a sunny Saturday. Under the biggest bluest sky. A stranger held her clenched fist. If she had the strength to sob. She had the strength to live. Young doctor, hand on her shoulder in the ambulance, said she was dying and she didn't want to die.

Smith taking the elevator down to lobby and street level. Passing by the little light at the reception desk, the message board. A chill wind coming through the revolving door. Sidewalk blowing up a winter dust. Herbert waiting at the end of the canopy.

Dreadnaught gliding away past the lunch time crowds. Crosstown by the bare trees of the park. Awake to a phone call early this morning. Miss Tomson's lawyer. Would I be present at six P.M. this evening at Miss Tomson's apartment to hear something to your advantage. So many new buildings abuilding along the river, to look down on the creeping ships. And a wrecking ball one day will knock down Merry Mansions. Make a nice pile of rock and Hugo will be out of a job.

At the foot of Owl Street. A line of black cars turning into an iron barred gate. Held open by police. Flashbulbs popping. Her casket under a bright flag surrounded by flowers. Barge out in the river carrying trains. Two tugs towing a tramp steamer. On this wooden wharf these gleaming cars one behind the other.

Four blue sailors lowering a chain softened with green felt. Swinging the boom from the tender above the hearse. Great heavy lead container rises up swaying against the sky. Moves over the stern and steadied by hands comes down to rest. Your life was full of celebrities. And once you said, don't ever Smithy, join with those guys who after pulling some ruthless deals, sit back in the warmth of luxury looking everywhere for love.

The flat shores disappearing one hour and a half out across the water. Sea choppy. Sound of vomiting along the rail. Snow flurry sweeping the deck. Get sheltered here against the wind. Claude Grace hatless between two elderly black women when he climbed on board. Rather nice out here. Taste of salt on the lips. All the others gone inside to get hot beef tea. With a shadow left at my side.

'Hi friend. Remember me, Ralph. Did you know the real Sally. It's cold. You never know. Goes out of the house healthy, not knowing her minutes are numbered. Maybe this isn't the time. But there's a rumour. She left you money in her will. Is it some kind of mistake. No insult meant. Beautiful girl like that. The legs alone. Say she slept with a different guy for every year of her age. You want to know how old she is.'

Big white liner passing, passengers look so small at the rail as they wave. On this latitude and longitude of green blue ocean. Of all the surprising things, Miss Tomson has been in the military. Maybe saluting in there on the satin with one of her long tapering arms. And I've got a little simple prayer because you also had religion. From the port stern side of this ship. See the horizon of thin white fingers with a sunlight glint of red and gold. Those were the tip top towers in which you lived. Slip out from under that flag to the fishes dolphins whales, room to yawn and stretch. Command to fire the rifles. One splash in a rolling sea. And bubbles and wreaths are left. But maybe you'd like to know that at night seals sing. They come up out of the water with their big sad eyes.

> Good news
> In the sweet
> By and by.

The Ginger Man

J. P. Donleavy

'In the person of *The Ginger Man*, Sebastian Dangerfield, Donleavy created one of the most outrageous scoundrels in contemporary fiction, a whoring, boozing young wastrel who sponges off his friends and beats his wife and girl friends. Donleavy then turns the moral universe on its head by making the reader love Dangerfield for his killer instinct, flamboyant charm, wit, flashing generosity – and above all for his wild, fierce, two-handed grab for every precious second of life' – *Time Magazine*

'No one who encounters him will forget Sebastian Dangerfield' – *New York Herald Tribune*

The Beastly Beatitudes of Balthazar B

J. P. Donleavy

Balthazar B is the world's last shy elegant young man. Born to riches in Paris and raised in lonely splendour, his life spreads to prep school in England. There he is befriended by the world's most beatific sinner, the noble little Beefy. And in holidays spent in Paris Balthazar B falls upon love and sorrow with his beautiful governess Miss Hortense, to lose her and live out lonely London years, waking finally to the green sunshine of Ireland and Trinity College. Here, reunited with Beefy, he is swept away to the high and low life of Dublin until their university careers are brought to an inglorious end.

'Marvellous, as always, Donleavy's language . . . embellishes incident piled on hilarious, marvellously invented incident. . . . It is Donleavy at his best, eloquent, roguish and at last at one with his world and the terrible sadness it contains' – *Newsweek*.

Also in Penguin

The Saddest Summer of Samuel S

J. P. Donleavy

In this short novel J. P. Donleavy writes of the tiny battle waged
for survival of the spirit in bedrooms and hearts the world
over. Samuel S, hero of lonely principles, holds out in his bereft
lighthouse in Vienna. Abigail, an American college girl on
the prowl in Europe, drawn by the beacon of this strange
outpost, seeks in her own emancipation the seduction of
Samuel S, the last of the world's solemn failures.

'Mr Donleavy manages to be funny about so much that one
would have thought nobody could be funny again – sole
drunkenness, hangovers, American expatriates and tourists, and
cross-talk from the psychiatric couch' – *New Yorker*

First published in the United States in 1966
and now in Penguin

Meet My Maker the Mad Molecule

'In this book of short pieces Donleavy has given us the lyric
poems to go with his epics. They are almost all elegies – sad songs
of decayed hope, bitter little jitterbuggings of an exasperated
soul, with barracuda bites of lacerating humour to bring
blood-red into the grey of fate. These stories and sketches
move between Europe and America, New York and Dublin and
London. America is always the spoiled Paradise, the land of
curdled milk and maggoty honey. The place that used to get you
in the end, but that now does it in the beginning' – *Newsweek*

A collection of short stories and sketches which were published
between 1954 and 1964 in leading English and American
papers and magazines. First published in book form in the
United States in 1964, England 1965.

Plays by J. P. Donleavy

The Ginger Man

Presented at the Fortune Theatre, London, in 1959. Presented at The Orpheum Theatre, New York, in 1963.

Published with an introduction by the author *What They Did in Dublin*, an account of the play's transfer to Dublin where it was made to close. In the United States and in England in 1961.

Fairy Tales of New York

Presented at the Pembroke Theatre, Croydon, England, in December 1960 and then transferred to the Comedy Theatre, London, in January 1961. Winner of the *Evening Standard* 'Most Promising Playwright of the Year' Award in 1960.

Published in the United States and in England in 1961. Available in Penguins.

A Singular Man

Presented at the Cambridge Arts Theatre, Cambridge, England, in October 1964 and at the Comedy Theatre, London, later that month.
Published in England in 1965.

The Saddest Summer of Samuel S